Angel Incarnate: *One Birth*

By CJ Martes

Inspired by a True Story

esa,
u are a gift to
ll who know you!
Learn to see yourself
as the angel do:
patient, kind, generous.
strong, worthy and pure of
heart. We are always
with you.
In Blessings,
Angels

Angel Incarnate-*One Birth*

Official Website: www.angelincarnate.com

Cover Design & Graphics: Beth Moore www.facebook.com/bethmoore

To request use permission for any materials in this book or additional information:

Seraphim Press, Inc.

PO Box 142

Greenwood, MO 64034

800-604-9967

Kindle & E-Reader Version

ISBN: 978-0-9772293-2-1

Paperback Version

ISBN: 978-0-9772293-1-4

Dedications

To Quisalas, my ONE true LOVE...
Without you... I would not have the Sun in my Sky.
Without you... I would not have these Wings to Fly.

Thank you for unconditionally supporting my work and being my partner on this incredible journey through life.

To my Amazing Children
Jordan, Aliena, David and Joshua, thank you for teaching me so much about life throughout the years. I am so proud of each of you!

To Erica
Thank you best friend for playing with me and allowing me to understand that you can have friends that unconditionally love you. Thank you so much for your constant encouragement and for gently pushing me to finish this book!

To My Special Helpers
Huge hugs to my own Earth Angels who have supported and helped me keep the dream of my book alive throughout the past 13 years. There are too many to mention them all, but here's a few: Sheila, Marilyn, Mom, Dad, Cassy, Shannon, Lisa, Liz, Jeanette, Deb, Sunny, Beth, Eva, Teri, Mary, David, and so many more.

To the Incarnate Ones
It's time to awaken my dear brothers and sisters...wake up...

Prologue-*Once Upon a Time*

The Infinite ONE witnessed all that had been created in the UNIVERSE. Ripples of the ONE's sentience had shaped everything that had BECOME. The ONE surveyed all of creation like a silent sentinel. The ONE now observed humanity and that which transpired to the sons and daughters of the Earth.

The Infinite ONE's divine creation resulted from an explosion of knowing that rippled across the fabric of time and space. This knowledge gave birth to the ANGELUS who BECAME from a single thought of the ONE. These new sentient BEINGS were eventually known in the world of HUMANS as the ANGELS.

There were many different BEINGS of the ANGELUS. The entire realm of the ANGELUS became manifest in a variety of Angelic classes or races. Each race of the ANGELUS flowed from the highest frequency of the ONE toward the lowest frequencies of the physical world. They ranged in frequency from The Seraph - who stood at the SOURCE - to the Angelus Primary – assigned to the Earth. All could appear in the physically world to deliver messages.

The Seraphim's frequency was nearest that of the Infinite ONE. The fire of the Seraphim's song echoed throughout the Cosmos, upholding the vibration of the ONE most high. The Seraphim's purpose was to stand witness to everything the ONE held most precious, while radiating in great joy, unconditional love.

As the Angelus frequencies began to beat in unison with the Heart of the ONE, more energies became manifest as Matter, Shape and Form. In an instant a vibrant blue planet unlike any other form of matter in the Cosmos came into existence. The New Planet, Earth, was perfect for the evolution of life. In the beginning, its landscapes teemed with all manner of curious creatures. The ONE filled the sea, the air, and the land with a broad stroke of inspiration. The ANGELUS witnessed the sheer beauty of LIFE. . .

The CREATURES of the EARTH were an infinite splendor of energies that had manifested and individuated over time. The beauty of these wondrous creations pleased the Infinite ONE. After many sun cycles, something wondrous occurred in the Cosmos. A new sentience echoed across the vastness of the Infinite ONE and another miracle emerged into BEING.

HUMANS became the finest creation of the ONE. The Infinite ONE's compassion was a wave that watered and fed the CHILDREN OF THE EARTH. Unlike the creatures that had manifested in the physical world a millennia before them, these special children were given unique gifts.

The Infinite ONE instructed the ANGELUS to watch over the Sons and Daughters of the Earth and to help them remain connected to the pure loving light of their creator, and the Angels began their infinite service to humankind. Thus began the true and Divine Purpose of the ANGELUS throughout the Cosmos.

The original Sons and Daughters of the Earth lived simply, in harmony with nature. They worked collectively as a tribe, existed in rhythm with the cycles of the Sun and Moon, and graciously accepted the gifts of food, warmth, and nourishment from the plants and animals of the physical world.

As HUMANS evolved, a more full awareness of the journey of the individual rather than the tribe. These shifts in perception gave rise to new beliefs about the world and quickly inspired progressive and industrial ideas.

These smart and inquisitive cosmic children of the ONE soon transformed their world into an unending song of progress and praise for the achievements of those individuals who created new possibilities. Populations exploded. People could no longer sustain communal life as their ancestors had.

The Infinite ONE and the ANGELUS soon witnessed many things which became manifest through the inspired hearts of Humans, among them Art, Spirituality, Religious Practices, and Music. Each person possessed a spark of the Infinite ONE's power and this creative force gave rise to modern ideas like Agriculture, Science, Mythology, Philosophy, and Leisure.

The Infinite ONE was eventually called by many names – among them, God, Yahweh, Elohim, Allah, Huwa, The Almighty One, Adonai, Shaddai – each a human reflection about the power of the Infinite ONE.

As HUMANS sought to understand and master both the visible and invisible forces they believed were present in physical world, they developed different awareness of who they were and how they and others fit into the world.

The individual Ego, initially the part of the Human psyche that created an individual's identity, became an aspect that experienced itself as separate from the other sons and daughters and eventually from the Infinite ONE as well. Shadow energies of pride, envy, gluttony, sloth, anger, greed and lust enabled some HUMANS to exercise Power and Control in the mistaken belief that they were exercising Free Will.

Some HUMANS felt they were wiser than their ancestors, many felt they were more important than their neighbors, a few felt compelled to exercise dominion over other people.

When more HUMANS looked to the external world instead of to the powerful Light of the ONE for validation and inspiration, intense suffering began to plague the world. Many mistakenly believed they were flawed at the core and that their precious human life was a harsh punishment, that the Infinite ONE had cast them out of Heaven because of their "sins" or the "sins" of others. Despite the gifts of the ONE and the beings of the ANGELUS to guide them, many HUMANS didn't believe that they could find their way HOME. They became lost in the cycle of Birth, Death and Rebirth that is known as *Samsara* or suffering.

Because of their separateness, prayers for intercession from the ONE became louder from those now lost in utter hopelessness. For centuries urgent prayers poured into Heaven, asking for the Infinite ONE to intercede. The Infinite ONE dispatched Angels to deliver messages of hope, tend to the suffering, and intervene to save those whose light might be extinguished before their purpose was fulfilled.

Despite such compassionate intercession, many HUMANS chose to steer themselves off course, as if they yearned for a life of abuse and suffering, rather than an awakened life filled with joy, happiness and contentment.

The Infinite ONE witnessed ALL that had been given LIFE in the HUMAN world. The HUMAN voices that once had sung triumphantly in collective joy and gratitude were barely audible. Violence had manifested in the HUMAN world. Wars had destroyed millions of precious human lives. The Shadow side of HUMAN life had pitted brother against brother over the trivial matters of wealth, religious beliefs, food resources, philosophy, and geography.

The Infinite ONE then sent the Christed ONE as a gift of hope to the Children of the Earth. The Christed ONE sacrificed ALL to restore the balance between the Shadow and the Light. Through perfect compassion, this lamb reminded HUMANS that the heavens were open to every soul.

Despite this most beautiful gift, the Children of the Earth continued to fight. They saw the Christed ONE differently, some saw him as God's only son, others as a prophet, and others as the Messiah, others mocking or disbelieving HIM, a few following HIS actual examples of compassion and perfect love. This struggle has continued.

The Infinite ONE's will was clear. A new and more direct divine plan to reopen the heavens to all Children of the Earth would now occur during a time that will be called The Great Shift. The HUMAN world had evolved now and would allow for the most direct involvement by divine energies yet.

The Infinite ONE's call to the ANGELUS rang out. It was a plan that would reveal to HUMANS an undistorted consciousness about the Truth of Life and themselves. The first response to this call originated from the heart of the ANGELUS. The choice of this angel was a profound creation that had birthed from deep inside the Sacred Burning Heart of a Warrior Seraph.

"It is time to enter the human world by birth and deliver the message of the ONE."

1- *Revealed*

The fiercely blowing sand stung Brother Francis' face even though it was covered by a cloth for protection. He and the others had been traversing the desert terrain across Jordan for several hours now, following their hired guide Khaled. Brother Francis peered carefully through a small slit. At last he could see the faint outline of the mountains in the distance that were situated near the capital city of Amman.

Francis was accompanied by four younger monks. So far none of them had complained about the arduous journey, but he doubted any of them had ever left Europe before. He could hear their excited voices from time to time as if he were accompanied by school children on an outing.

Of course, Francis knew that he and his companions were not on an ordinary expedition. The others had been told that they were retrieving a holy relic about which Father Mateus had received a vision, and that it was their duty to keep it safeguarded.

The instructions he had received from Father Mateus before they left two days ago had been quite clear: Francis and the other Benedictine monks must travel clandestinely to meet with a contact, purchase the scroll and ferry it safely back to the safety of their home at Göttweig Abbey near the German-Austrian border.

Soon it would be dark. Francis could feel the temperature dropping. He had never traveled so far on foot, and realized too late that his shoes were not the best for their journey. His feet were burning, and they still had a long way to go.

Khaled slowed his pace in order for Francis to catch up. "We'll be at the mountains in two more hours. By then, it will be too dark and treacherous to make our climb, so we must camp for the night. I know a good place."

Francis nodded.

"I am curious, Brother Francis. You and your party are not suited well for such a journey. It would have been less of a strain for you to have flown to Amman and hired your guide there."

Francis had been prepared for questions about why his group of monks were traveling the longest route to their destination, but until now their guide had not asked.

"There are many who wish to stop our holy mission, and if we had done as you suggest, we might be in danger."

Khaled nodded with an understanding that surpassed culture or language. "Of course, Brother. Forgive me."

"There is nothing to forgive. I agree we are hardly well suited for this journey. But we cannot always choose what the Almighty One might call upon us to do, can we?"

2-*Opening*

Horizontal lines of light danced across Catherine Jane Moore as she slept. Normally an early riser, Catherine was still in bed, last night's disjointed dreams haunting her.

Catherine was a young woman of medium build with dark hair and striking crystal-blue eyes. She spent the majority of her waking hours focused on the problems of others. No one would have guessed this formerly starry-eyed child would have become a county social worker.

Young Catherine had plenty of energy for fantasy, spending most of her time daydreaming of a perfect world with gallant gentlemen and genteel princesses. She was always a highly creative child with a keenly sharp intelligence.

Adopted at the age of four months from the Dominican Sisters in Great Bend, Kansas, Catherine was cherished by Doris and William Moore. She knew nothing about her actual birth parents or the circumstances surrounding her adoption or given it much thought. Her new parents had given her everything she could have wanted while raising her in Parsons, a small town in southeast Kansas. Catherine had loved Parsons in all of its small town glory, and had never desired to leave.

When Catherine was seventeen, her life took a tragic turn. On that fateful day, Catherine had abandoned her usual routine and did not attend mass at St. Patrick's with her parents.

On their way home, her parents were killed instantly when a tractor trailer collided head on with their automobile. Catherine's world shattered. Everything in the small town became a constant reminder that she was alone. People looked at her with pity.

For several years she disconnected from the trauma. She managed to go through the motions of life, but couldn't shake the feelings of loss and abandonment. A dark cloud of emotion followed her everywhere.

She tried for nearly four years to remain in her parents' home, keeping herself busy attending community college in the next town. When an Associate's Degree didn't change things, she moved away to start fresh.

Catherine set out for a big city where she could begin again. As she drove away from her old life, she was comforted by her impending anonymity.

She took several odd jobs while finishing her Bachelor's Degree in psychology and graduate school. She started her first grown-up job in 2005 as a case worker with the Jackson County Division of Family Services in Kansas City, Missouri.

Catherine made her home in a one-bedroom loft in the heart of downtown Kansas City, just four blocks from her office. She loved people watching as she walked to work.

After dealing with the intensity of her client's lives every work day, Catherine spent most of her personal time by herself in her apartment or walking around her neighborhood by herself.

She had been much more outgoing before her parents died. People found her open, friendly and trustworthy. Although strangers would tell her their life stories within a few minutes, Catherine struggled to see herself in any stranger's reflection. She had an amazing gift with people but couldn't see herself from another point of view. She couldn't acknowledge the radiance of her deep blue eyes or the comforting softness in her clear and caring voice.

The light on her face caused Catherine to stir. She slowly opened her eyes and looked around the room. Her foggy head began to fill with the intense images of last night's dreams. Her analytical mind struggled to recall every detail and make sense of what she had seen. She remembered the details in sequence, like still-life pictures in a photo album.

I was looking up at a woman with a kind face, yeah, a nun in a black and white habit. I was a baby...so small, she was picking me up. It was warm and safe.

Then I was at home. Mom was cooking me breakfast and dad was reading the paper. I can't remember what mom was saying...then I was at school on the playground.

Memories of grade school made Catherine cringe. She recalled the playground, children laughing at her. She could see in her mind the ugly and distorted faces of the other children. A familiar ache arose in her chest.

I don't know why they were so cruel to me. Why me?

She recalled her parent's funeral, standing among family, friends, and her Aunt Sheila. Everyone tried to comfort her but she couldn't help questioning how God could take them away so suddenly. One moment they were there, the next gone. She had been inconsolable then, feeling robbed of all happiness. A single tear ran down her cheek as she stared at her bedroom ceiling.

Then I was walking down a hallway holding a woman's hand...it was dark at first, then a bright light was in front of us and we stepped out a door... light spread all around us and I could see the whole world. It was breathtaking -- laid out like an Impressionist landscape.

Catherine remembered the woman's features in vivid detail, porcelain white skin, flowing long dark hair and beautiful, clear blue eyes. Their eyes locked. The woman seemed sad. Catherine looked below, transfixed as the landscape shifted and changed. The colors became brilliant, crisp, and clear. As if on fast forward, the dawning sun rose into a morning sky followed by fading light as a full moon appeared in the clear night sky. Happiness, sadness, love, violence, laughter and screams built to a deafening crescendo. When she turned to ask the beautiful woman to end this madness, she found herself completely alone.

Who was that? She was there and then she was gone. Disappeared...What on earth? My heart is pounding. I must be going crazy. Catherine's rational brain engaged. She breathed slowly and deliberately, using a deep-breathing technique from yoga class. She lay there concentrating on her breath.

Relax...

Oh God, its Monday...damn I'll be late!

She jumped up and threw on some clothes. Catherine arrived at the office around 8:05, carrying a large leather soft-sided briefcase full of case files. Catherine frowned as she piled the files on her desk. She hadn't opened her briefcase all weekend. Guilt began to wash over her but was quickly swept away when she saw her co-worker Erica.

"Good morning, Catherine. Happy Monday!" Erica's sunny disposition would brighten any room, but Catherine knew Erica's enthusiasm might not last. Working for the Division of Family Services had a profound effect on everyone that worked there because it was often such a sad place. Erica had started six months ago. Since that time they had grown closer, but for Catherine the process of opening up was a very slow one.

"Hey Erica, how was your weekend?"

"Oh, not too bad. I spent most of it with Mom, ran a few errands. The usual."

"How is your Mother?"

"As well as can be expected." Erica's mood darkened.

"Let me know if there's anything you need."

Catherine had been there longer than anyone else in the department, almost three years. She hadn't accepted a promotion to management because she preferred it in the trenches, hands-on with the families, even though their stories were often heartbreaking. Other people didn't understand her occupational choice or her ability to stick with it. She was well-suited for intervention work and for handling the day-to-day pressures. She had a pressing need to be of service to others.

Catherine collapsed onto her squeaky chair. She reflected on her small space, the window behind her, a single bookcase to her left, and a desk with two chairs. In the corner a small crate full of toys occupied the children who frequented her office.

I am so tired; please let me get through this day.

If she looked out her tall office window, she could see the street below, a couple of office buildings across the street and the front entrance to St. Mary's Cathedral. On occasion Catherine would find herself staring at the stained glass windows.

She looked at the clock. It was almost time for her first appointment, Ms. Olivia Berry, a new case she had inherited last Thursday. Catherine quickly thumbed through Olivia's file.

Olivia had a five year-old daughter named Sarah and was currently separated from her husband. Her daughter was in foster care due to a documented incident of her own violence that was witnessed by neighbors in her front yard. The neighbors had reported the incident to the police and DFS investigated. Olivia was trying to have her daughter returned to her care. This type of case was all too familiar to Catherine.

Erica popped her head in. "Your 8:30 is here."

Here we go…

In one of the waiting room chairs was a fair, petite young woman in blue slacks and a gray pullover sweater. Her dark brown hair was pulled back into a ponytail. Catherine took one look at Olivia and her stomach began to churn. There was something very familiar about her, yet she wasn't sure why.

"Ms. Berry? Hi. I'm Catherine, your new caseworker."

"Hi."

Catherine gestured toward her office door with her right hand. The woman stared at her for a few moments then walked toward the office door. Catherine offered her a seat in one of the heavily worn chairs in front of her desk.

Olivia sat, nervously holding the chair with both hands underneath the seat.

"So," Catherine began, "I'm sorry Elizabeth won't be able to continue with your case, but I will do everything I can to help you."

Olivia looked directly into Catherine's crystal blue eyes, "I want my daughter back. Can you help me do that? She's with complete strangers, people who don't even love her. This is ridiculous. Can I please have my daughter back now?"

Catherine was accustomed to this level of intensity from parents of children placed in the system. There was no way to discuss this delicately.

"Well Olivia, we are required to satisfy certain requirements before we can do that. There are statements from witnesses and a report in your file about what happened the day the police were called. The Division of Family Services cannot recommend that your daughter be returned to you until we are satisfied that she will be safe. That is my job here, to ascertain the safety of your daughter."

Olivia paced nervously. "I love my daughter. Why don't you all understand that?" She shot Catherine a fevered look of desperation and regret. "I didn't mean to hurt Sarah. I really didn't. No one can understand what happened. I have talked over and over to different therapists and the other case worker. No one seems to be listening to me." Olivia stopped, came closer to the desk, and put her hands down. "You have to be straight with me. Is this hopeless? Have I lost my baby girl forever?"

"I can be straight with you, Olivia. I think there's a good chance you'll have Sarah back with you. You just have to keep doing what you are doing, which is going through the steps required by our department. Please continue with the recommended therapy, keep cooperating, and things should go very well. We are doing everything we can to help you and Sarah."

"Oh God, you must think I'm some sort of monster, don't you? I don't know why I did what I did! I would never dream of hurting Sarah, but that day I...I just lost my mind."

Catherine looked carefully at Olivia and knew that she was not an abuser. The case file also contained a documented history of domestic violence Olivia suffered at the hands of her husband. But Olivia had dropped the charge about the last incident a month before she had attacked Sarah.

Suddenly the energy in the whole room became very still. The change was palpable. Olivia's eyes widened as though she had been struck by an intense memory. Her gaze became distant.

Catherine rose from her desk and reached out to support Olivia's arm. A strange sensation ran through her fingertips as she touched Olivia's sleeve. At first the feeling was so slight that she almost didn't notice. Suddenly a tingling sensation moved throughout her body in a wave. Her body tensed and her eyes felt heavy.

Catherine tried to focus but the room around her was dark. She smelled bacon. Suddenly the room flooded with white light which caused Catherine's eyes to close quickly. When she opened them again, she was standing in an unfamiliar kitchen.

Catherine began to panic. She was frozen in place trying to figure out where she was. She could see the bacon she had smelled frying on the stove across the room. Olivia's body, in a pink satin robe, flew past her. A man followed Olivia closely, grabbing for her long hair.

Olivia began screaming and clamoring to get away. The man – Catherine assumed it was Olivia's husband - grabbed her again and threw her to the floor. Catherine looked down at Olivia's frightened, battered face and it was as if she was looking straight into her soul, feeling her terror, pain and sorrow.

Catherine screamed "Stop!" But the two figures in front her didn't react.

What am I doing? I have to get out of here!

The room began to shift and spin, then everything went pitch black. She could hear faint sounds around her like tiny echoes. Catherine's body felt suspended in a wave of nothingness.

Then familiar voices became clear.

"Catherine, Catherine. Are you all right?"

Catherine opened her eyes. She was lying on the floor of her office. Above her were the worried faces of co-workers. The back of her head hurt tremendously, and a wave of nausea moved through her. "I'm fine, I think." She started to get up. Erica reached down to help.

Catherine stumbled towards her chair.

"Erica, call the hospital and let them know we're coming. I want to get Catherine checked out." Her manager Barbara helped her sit down. Barb was amazingly cool under pressure. "Let's all go back to work now. Catherine is going to be fine. We just need to give her some air."

Slowly, one by one, the office crew shuffled out of the door.

Catherine saw Olivia's deep worry lines.

"I'm fine really. I must have gotten dizzy. I'm sorry I frightened everyone. Are you okay, Ms. Berry?"

Olivia struggled for the right words. "I'm...fine. I hope you are okay." A forced smile accompanied the young mother's words.

Barb started to direct the situation once more. "I really believe we should be getting you checked out. It's not like you to faint in the middle of a client intake."

Catherine's only desire was to have a private talk with Olivia about what she had seen.

"Barb, listen, I'm sure it's just because I worked so hard over the weekend. I feel like I'm trying to come down with something. And, well, you know...female issues. I'm sure that's what's going on here. Olivia and I were nearly through. I'd like to complete our session and take the afternoon off, if you don't mind."

"Okay, well, I expect you out of here in thirty minutes and I want Erica or someone to make sure you get home okay. And please, if you don't feel any better later this afternoon, go to the doctor and get checked out." Barb turned to walk out the door. "I can't have my staff falling down on the floor at any given moment."

"Thanks, Barb, I appreciate it." Barb disappeared into the hallway.

Catherine sat back in her chair. She didn't feel all right. She stared out her window, mind racing. Olivia's voice jarred her into the moment.

"Something just happened, didn't it? I mean..." Olivia's voice trailed off. She looked down at her lap. Catherine wasn't sure what to say.

First the crazy dreams and now this. What's next?

"He hurt me so much. I loved him, but he hurt me. Some days were perfect. Everyone told me to leave him, but I didn't. We had Sarah and she was beautiful. I thought she would make our marriage better somehow. Things seemed okay, until that morning when he just went crazy."

Olivia stared at Catherine dead in the eye. "That's what I was thinking about when you touched my arm. Then you said, 'Olivia, no!' and you also said, 'Oh, my God, stop it!' Why? Ms. Moore?"

What Catherine had seen was as real as if she had been in Olivia's kitchen when the fight had occurred. But how could she explain this to Olivia?

Catherine's work mind kicked in. She looked at Olivia.

How sad that so many people stay with abusers. She'd seen it a million times. People just desperately want to be loved. Women will endure all kinds of situations if they feel wanted and needed.

"Olivia, I'm not sure what happened, and I don't remember exactly what I said. It was almost like a dream, but I feel as though I know exactly what happened to you that day."

That came out better than I thought.

"My grandma, she would see things. Go into a trance like we weren't there and come out saying the strangest things. She always seemed to know what was going to happen ahead of time. We just took that for granted," Olivia shared openly. "Your eyes remind me of hers, so clear and blue. You must be like her. God grants some of us gifts. Grandma used to say we all had gifts, but if I did, I bet I would make better choices."

Catherine never acknowledged anything but the obvious. She understood people well, but since her parents had been taken from her, she hadn't given a thought to anything spiritual. Her faith was remote. To her, the world was full of concrete, established facts, a dizzying array of emotions, and life situations worth learning from. She buried herself in her work, trying to make a difference in a very bleak world, a world that, for some reason, she had never felt like she was a part of. It was like she observed life, watching the events around her but not participating in them.

"I don't know about gifts. I've never had anything like this happen to me. I'd appreciate it if you would keep this between you and me Olivia, if that is all right with you?" Catherine rose. She stood at her window, staring at the cathedral across the street. "I used to see things sometimes when I was a child, intense dreams, but that seems like lifetimes ago."

"Anyway," Catherine came back to Olivia. "As I said earlier, I think there's a very good chance that you will get Sarah back. Come and see me in two weeks. We'll schedule another home visit. I'll let you know in advance when it will be."

Olivia took this as her cue to leave. "Okay. Thank you for your help." She walked toward the office door and stopped for a moment. "Don't worry. I won't tell anyone what happened."

Catherine nodded, feigned a smile and began gathering her things to go home.

3- *Danger*

Francis was utterly exhausted. An unexpected sand storm had delayed them significantly. It had taken the group over four hours to reach the base of the mountains instead of two. The others were quickly succumbing to sleep, while Francis pulled out a small flashlight and his small leather-bound journal. He carefully noted the date at the top of his entry before he began:

August 8, 1974

It was a difficult journey but at last we have arrived at the base of the Abarim Mountains. Since we were given the holy task of retrieving the scroll from Father Mateus, I cannot seem to shake a feeling of urgency the further we go. I feel as if I am living in biblical times right now as we travel across this Holy Land.

Tomorrow we will set out for our destination. We are headed for a remote dwelling near the top of the mountain which stands towering over where we will rest for the night. I am told the morning's travel will be fairly inhospitable terrain.

I pray for strength to make the steep climb tomorrow and that we can complete our mission successfully. I offer prayers for our safe return to our home in Austria without injury.

Francis curled up into his garments for warmth against the desert night. Rather than the restful sleep he was yearning for, he soon found himself in a series of restless dreams where he was being pursued by unknown forces.

Francis felt every rock and thorn as he ran barefoot through the moonlit streets of Amman He'd never visited this city before, but was sure of his location as if following an unseen map. He ducked into an empty shack, evading four men who were chasing him. In his hands, he clutched a small silver tube.

"He ran down here, I am sure of it." Francis peered out but the man's face was hidden by moon-cast shadows overhead. "The two of you, go down that way and then circle back around. If we lose him, we'll have Britius to answer to. Marius, you come with me."

Marius fearlessly stepped forward, "Well if the almighty Master Bugiardini were here, I'd tell him to go to Hell."

"Shut your tongue, boy." The leader grabbed Marius by the shirt sleeve. "Let's go!"

The men scattered. Francis looked down at the metal tube in his hands. He tried to remember how he came to be where he was.

Am I dreaming? This feels like no dream...

He unscrewed the tube's lid and a scroll of parchment fell into his hand. Francis whispered, "The scroll. Yes. I must protect the scroll."

Knowing now what was truly at stake, Francis spent what felt like hours evading the men who were after him. Surprising even himself, Francis always seemed to outwit them just in time.

Before dawn, Francis awoke still breathing heavily from the dream. He stirred the others. "We must go now. We don't have a moment to lose."

4- *Contemplation*

Catherine lay nearly motionless in her claw-footed bathtub, a washcloth folded over her eyes.

Am I having a nervous breakdown? God, I'm tense. Calm down. I don't need this right now. I just want to call my parents. God...maybe it's a psychotic episode?

Catherine was always rational. Especially when out of the ordinary things occurred. Her frustration grew as her astute, rational nature failed her.

I touched a woman's arm and was transported to another place in time? I know I was in her kitchen and then I guess, uh, her breakfast gets interrupted because of hubby's violence? I could not have imagined it.

Whether she wanted to or not, she could not deny the experiences, or the fact that the details could be somewhat verified. Even now, Catherine could very clearly recall the smell of bacon, witnessing the horribly violent act, and Olivia's stricken face in front of her.

It's as if I had been there that day...wow, that's some perfect vision. Was that what it was? A vision...?

Catherine knew little about religion or spirituality. Her only experiences to draw from were from Catechism classes in Catholic school as a child.

Did I have a spiritual vision? When I was little I had a very active imagination. Even imaginary friends. This wasn't like what happened today though.

Catherine lifted herself out of the now tepid water.

These experiences left her reminiscing about the past, which she avoided since her parents died. But today she decided to flip through some old photos. She picked up a brown faux leather album and braced herself. She couldn't remember the last time she looked at any family photos.

She turned each page, carefully studying several photos of her parents taken two years before they died. She lovingly thought of her father's favorite place in nature, a special area deep in the Missouri Ozarks near a town called Eminence. The first time they visited the area, when she was 16, her father remarked that he was about to show her the best-kept secret in the entire United States.

She pulled a good photo out of the sleeve. Catherine had been playing with the camera that day, being silly and asked them to pose with the Little Niangua River as the backdrop. Seeing the river again in the photo made Catherine remember vividly the large, expansive river that had flowed past the campground where they stayed. She smiled, recalling the sunburned, inebriated campers that had happily floated by as they headed down the river in large black inner tubes and canoes. Catherine thought it sounded good to be intoxicated without a care in the world, even though she didn't keep alcohol in her apartment.

She put the photo in both hands, closed her eyes and recalled in perfect detail the moment when she and her parents left the campground early one morning. Her dad had a boyish smile on his face as they packed up to go exploring. He truly loved to wander about and discover all the hidden secrets of the forest.

"Isn't the day perfect, Catherine?"

"Yeah, pop. A great day." His excitement was contagious. "It really is pretty here." She loved spending time in the woods with her dad because it brought out his inner child. She studied him as he walked beside her now. He looked like a small child seeing snow for the first time. She loved how the years of sun weathering made his forehead wrinkle when he smiled. "So what's on the list of fun stuff to do today?"

Her dad's eyes lit up. "Oh I have something extra special to show you. I've been saving it for a perfect day like today. You're going to love it, Cat. I promise."

The truck bounced, twisted and turned for nearly 30 minutes down several very narrow roads. "Well, here we go, you're going to love this!" her father said stopping the vehicle just short of a huge rock that acted as a natural divider between the grass and the carelessly strewn gravel parking area.

Catherine hopped out of the truck to see what so excited her dad. Ahead of her was a large swimming area. The forest trees created a fortress around the edge of the water so from even 40 feet anyone might not have known it was there.

Even though it was pretty early in the day, there were already several children splashing in the water. At the far end a large tower of boulders stretched upward creating a steep wall that ended about 30 feet above the water. She watched with wonder as a full stream of water spilled over the rocks. It was a perfect, natural waterfall.

She noticed some children treading water and decided the water would definitely be over her head. Yes, she knew how to swim. It was illogical, but her fear of water over her head made her shaky inside. Plus this was the first time she had attempted to swim in anything other than a pool. Her dad sensed her apprehension, quickly took off his shirt, and plunged in splashing both her and her mom.

"Oh geez, dad, you got me all wet!" Catherine undressed down to her blue swimming suit. She walked to the edge of the water just as her dad came up for air.

"Get in here, girl," her dad said, swimming away from where she was standing. Her mom was already wading into the water as Catherine took her first step

The water was much warmer than she thought it would be. Her Dad and Mom were swimming further away towards the base of the waterfall. Catherine slowly swam out to meet them. Her Dad took her arm as she looked up the rock tower and saw varying shades of tan and gold with sunlight mixed in. The water was breathtaking, a beautiful crystal blue. She swam closer to be near the spray of the falling water, but stopped short.

"Go ahead honey, I'll steady you." Trusting her father, Catherine swam forward despite her increasing fear.

At first, the force of the water took her completely by surprise. As she pushed her hands forward, she gasped. The water rushed over her body and she melted into a feeling of pure innocent joy. The pure emotion leapt out of her as she blissfully laughed out loud. The total surrender washed away every care. The weight of her soul was released in that private moment. She looked at her father and was sure he knew exactly what she was experiencing. He always knew her inside and out.

Catherine leaned into the soft cushion of the couch, releasing a gentle sob. She missed him so much. Still holding the photo, the past loss of her parents came flooding into her heart.

"Oh, why doesn't this get any easier?" she spoke out loud to thin air as if someone would answer her. Catherine wiped the tears with the back of her left hand and placed the picture back in its sleeve.

Why did I do that to myself? Why bring up all this now? Especially today!

Catherine got up to look out the window. Her living room had two large eight-foot high windows that overlooked the street below. She was on the 7th floor of her apartment building, low enough to see the trees that had been planted long ago and high enough for them to block out the constant street noise. She placed both hands on the pane of the window and placing her forehead on the glass. People passed below in business suits and overcoats; it was March and still a bit cold.

As she scanned the passersby, she noticed a familiar face wandering up and down the sidewalk aimlessly. It was a homeless man that she frequently saw at Café Roma on Saturday mornings. Catherine had often wondered what it was like to have no home or destination. She often felt displaced and alone herself.

Her gift of empathy made her a huge asset at work. No matter the case or circumstance, she had the ability to understand the position of those that she met. She was known for creating intuitive solutions to problems that others had not been able to solve. She didn't see it as special gift. She thought everyone could see the world her way. As people often do, she minimized her valuable contributions to the people in her life.

Catherine saw the man asking for "donations" from the passing people on the street. Many ignored him or waved him away. One day she literally ran right into him as she came out of her building. The collision knocked the briefcase out of her hand. She remembered how apologetic he was as he knelt down to help her pick up her belongings. As Catherine reached for her key chain, their eyes met.

He had a wry smile and mischievous eyes that reminded her of Santa Claus in a way, like he knew a joyous secret but wouldn't tell. His eyes were soft, kind and seemed to peer deeply into hers. In that moment, she knew there was more to him than met the eye.

With a breathy voice, he said, "You're simply an angel." He winked at her. "I'm so sorry to have bumped into you like that. I'm pretty clumsy these days," he said, straightening his shirt. She quickly dismissed his compliment, told him not to worry and rushed to work.

Their little accident was about a month ago, and since then she had not seen him around the neighborhood. Her attentive gaze at the street below her was broken by the sound of the telephone ringing. Catherine picked up on the fourth ring.

"Hello?"

"I was worried you wouldn't answer." It was Barb.

"What do you mean?" Catherine asked as if she blocked this morning's event for just a moment.

"After this morning, I felt I should call."

"I'm so sorry, Barb. I must have dozed off." She lied to cover her insensitivity.

"Sorry I woke you. Have you called your doctor yet?" As usual, Barb was direct and to the point about why she was calling.

"I decided it was pointless, Barb. I really feel okay. I doubt it will happen again." There was a long pause on the other end as Catherine imagined Barb pondering what she would say next.

"So what *did* happen to you? I mean, I've really never seen anyone collapsed like that, and, well, you were saying things that didn't seem right to me."

Catherine's face turned sour and lines appeared in her forehead as she realized that Barb witnessed more of the traumatic episode than she had originally thought. "I'm really not sure, but I'm feeling just fine now. Don't worry. I'm going to be okay."

"Well, I want you to take the day off tomorrow to rest. I'll reschedule your appointments. I've seen your calendar and it's not too bad. You work too hard and need to relax for a change. Perhaps that's all you need. If you need more than a day, just let me know."

Catherine almost protested.

"What do you want me to tell everyone? They are all asking, especially Erica."

"Tell them I'm fine. It was just a fluke. I must have gotten up too quickly and gotten dizzy. Please tell Erica I'll call her sometime tomorrow for sure." Catherine had promised Erica to see her mother in the hospital on Sunday.

"Take care of yourself, and see you on Wednesday."

Catherine walked down the narrow hallway to her bedroom. Catherine looked at the clock near her bedside table. It was 5:45 p.m., much earlier than she thought. Her eyes felt incredibly heavy. She lay down and stared at the textured ceiling trying to put the pieces together from last night's dream until now.

I don't understand what is happening to me. How bizarre was that? I only touched her arm. I've done that a million times without collapsing or seeing someone's memory.

Catherine rubbed her temples with both hands as she lay down. In front of her was her walk-in closet door and to the left of that her bathroom door was wide open with the light on. Her desk and computer were to the right near the windows. Farther to her left on the same wall as the bedroom door, books and mementos were scattered across shelves.

Organizing the bookshelf was another project she had yet to finish since she moved into her new apartment over a year ago. Catherine seemed to have tunnel vision sometimes, only noticing things when it occurred to her to pay attention. She remembered as she looked at the half finished shelves, that she had read an article while waiting at the doctor's office which reported that the human nervous system and brain averages everything it sees. This explained the phenomena that people report where they suddenly notice a light fixture in their house that simply wasn't there before that moment, though it had been there the entire time.

The article told a story about early explorers to America. There was a fairly strong eyewitness account referenced in the article from historical documents that said the Indians were puzzled to see a white man. The Indians wanted to know how they had traveled there. The explorers pointed to the large ships anchored in the sea and said that the ships had carried them from far away. The Indians were more puzzled since when *they* looked to the sea, they could not see the ships at all.

The article's theory was that their brains filtered the large ships out as extra information that was unimportant. That article really impacted her at the time. She began to really notice all kinds of things she hadn't before. After a couple days, the newness of her self-imposed experiment dropped to the back of her mind as most things do eventually.

How often is life like that? How much stuff is going on that I don't see? How could I experience Olivia's life in that past moment? It was just a glimpse but I saw it all. No, not just saw it. I felt it, heard it, and even smelled it.

Since childhood, Catherine could not stop searching for answers when confronted with a puzzle or problem. She went over to her desk to sit down. She hadn't even bothered to check her email in the last few weeks, not that she got much anyway.

She settled into her comfy desk chair and reached for her computer mouse. She wanted information on visions or an explanation about what happened to her today. She tried Googling "visions" but thousands of the results were about eyeglasses and things relating to eye sight. She searched for visionaries, then mystics and eventually psychics. For about an hour, she sifted through websites of mystics, mediums and people in similar spiritual professions.

Fortunately, some people had their own stories on their websites. Some talked about how they utilized their abilities to see certain things. There were some stories that were way out of the realm of believability to her.

After much searching, Catherine was frustrated. She wanted to know how a person of her age could simply start having visions out of the blue, for no apparent reason. She hoped she would find a similar story. Many people who acquired their gifts later in life had something traumatic happen when their psychic gifts appeared, such as being in a coma, having near death experiences or getting knocked out. She certainly didn't fall into any of those categories.

Time passed very quickly. It was almost 10. She rubbed her stiff neck and pushed her chair backward, a bit disappointed. Her earlier energy was of a seeker and a detective; now she felt deflated.

Catherine shuddered at the thought of being a person that couldn't touch anyone again due to her visions striking her at any given moment. She imagined pinning her arms by her sides. She laughed aloud at herself, shaking her head slowly, and got up to get ready for bed.

As she brushed her teeth she decided that there was no rational need to try and figure out something that was simply a fluke. There was no way that it would happen again, so why worry about it?

Catherine looked at a tired reflection in the mirror. She smiled at herself, satisfied with her latest point of view about today's ordeal: denial.

5– *Coffee to Chaos*

Catherine awoke to a blinding light in her face, only moments before the shrill sound of her alarm blared at her. She fumbled for the snooze, desperately trying to focus her eyes, but finding she couldn't. The sunlight was too bright. As she tried to hit the alarm, she knocked the clock to the floor. She left it there, as twisted the rods to close the blinds.

She stood there dazed for a few moments, not sure why the blinds were open this morning since she didn't recall opening them. She never did so except on the weekends when she read in bed.

Obviously, it was not a lucid morning for Catherine. She didn't remember any dreams this morning; however she felt as though she hadn't slept at all. The blinding sunlight wakeup call didn't improve her mood. Nevertheless, she decided to shower and go out for while, perhaps to Café Roma to get some coffee. Today was a day when she felt she really needed the caffeine boost. As she showered, she tried to remember opening those blinds yesterday, but couldn't place it.

Well, yesterday was a strange day, so why not today too?

Catherine's thoughts were interrupted with a phone call from Erica.

"How are you feeling this morning? I wanted to check on you before I head out for work, and see if you needed anything."

“I’m okay. I didn’t sleep well last night, but Barb insisted I’m off today, so I can take a nap later.”

“Anything else exciting happen yesterday? I swear the whole office was crazy about you falling down on the floor like that. You know most of them have nothing better to do than concern themselves with other people’s business. I guess they figure that, since we work with everyone’s intimate life details all the time, yours are free game too.” Erica laughed to make light of the gossip, noticing that Catherine was silent on the other end. “Don’t worry,” she added quickly, “It’ll blow over soon.”“Yeah…blow over. No, nothing else happened. It was a hard day. I’d like to talk to you more about it when we have time. You still want me to come with you to see your mom on Sunday?”

“Oh yes, for sure, honey. She’s going to love seeing you again. I know one look at your face will improve her spirits, and that’s so important for her recovery, you know.” Catherine didn’t respond.

“Are you there?”

“Oh yeah, I’m sorry about that. I lost my train of thought. I need some coffee. In fact I was headed to Café Roma when you called.”

“Okay, duty calls. If you need anything, call me at the office.”

“Okay, I will.”

So good to hear from Erica. Now, coffee.

In a few moments she was outside. She stopped for a moment to raise her face toward the sun, inviting it to soak through the pores in her skin, willing it to improve her mood.

Catherine turned the corner walking towards Café Roma, an independent coffee shop opened by an enthusiastic man named Tom. He had one son who helped with the family business. All the shop’s coffee beans were specially imported from Florence, Italy. Catherine discovered Café Roma about a month after she had moved into her apartment. In the spirit of adventure, like her dad loved, she wandered around the neighborhood. One particular dreary Saturday she had wandered into Café Roma and fell in love with the place, not due to the cool atmosphere but because the coffee was some of the best she’d ever tasted. Soon she was hooked

Catherine reached the store’s front door in less than five minutes.

Starbucks, Shmarbucks.

The aroma of coffee beans and sugar hung in the air as she pushed the door open with a deliberate shove. She breathed in deeply, savoring the heavenly smells. The shop was not very big, maybe 600 square feet. It had oversized windows on one wall, with booths placed in front of each one. Scattered around the rest of the place there were three tables, each with four chairs.

Catherine enjoyed uniquely designed spaces. Café Roma was modeled after a true Italian barista shop and the décor was quaintly European. Catherine glanced to the front counter and saw a small line of people there, grabbing coffee to go on the way to work. It was strange to be there on any day other than Saturday. There was a usual crowd on Saturdays, so she often recognized faces. She looked around the room and didn't see anyone she knew.

This made her think of the homeless guy she saw on the street yesterday. Nearly every Saturday, Catherine walked the two blocks to Café Roma to get a huge mug of cappuccino. She would spend at least an hour being fully present in the moment. Some Saturdays she would read a book or simply sit, sipping her coffee and watching people go in and out. People had always fascinated Catherine: their diversity, what made them tick.

I want a great big vanilla cappuccino today. To take home. Or maybe I should wander the park? I can come back on Saturday to hang out like normal. How long have I been coming here? A month after I moved in?

The line thinned out and soon it was her turn. As she walked up to the counter a voice said, "Hey Catherine, what brings you here on a Tuesday? Are you switching days on me?" She looked over to see a very familiar face, Brian, the owner's son. It was comforting to come in and be recognized.

"Good morning, Brian. No, don't worry. I'll be in this weekend too. I just took off an extra day this week."

"Well it is nice to see you, even if it's not the weekend. So...your usual?"

"I want that to go, though."

"You got it."

Brian soon handed her a cup with a drink sleeve.

She paid and dropped a dollar in his tip jar. "See you this weekend. Thanks."

She turned to go, but stopped. "Hey, Brian? You know that one guy from the shelter that hangs out here sometimes on Saturdays? He's real clean, and a nice guy?"

"You mean Joshua? Long gray beard? Mustache? Umm...Joshua is short and a bit overweight. He's an okay guy, very polite."

"Yeah, that's him. So his name's Joshua?"

"Yeah. Joshua Stark. He lives at the City Union Mission a lot of the time. He said he used to live somewhere else but I can't remember where exactly off the top of my head. Why do you ask?"

"Oh, mostly curiosity, I see him a lot and wondered." Actually Catherine wasn't exactly sure why she inquired except it had popped into her head. She saw him often enough to want to have his name.

"Most of those guys don't stick around very long, but he's been around several months now. Actually around the time you moved into the neighborhood, I believe." Another customer came in the door.

"Thanks, Brian. See you soon."

She barely got out of the door when she saw Joshua walking toward her a couple blocks away.

Speak of the devil...

Catherine was uncomfortable facing him all of the sudden and quickly turned to walk back to her apartment building.

I look so stupid running from a homeless man.

Catherine was less than one block away when she turned to look behind her. To her surprise, Joshua was standing there in front of the café looking in her direction.

Oh no. He's staring right at me. And smiling? Why is he doing that?

Catherine quickly turned away, and kept walking until she got around the next corner and out of his line of sight. She wondered at the expression on his face. It was unusual, almost child-like. He seemed delighted to see her. She felt really self-conscious all of the sudden, like getting caught with her hand in the cookie jar.

"Why was he standing staring at me? I don't even know him. Ah, he must have remembered me from the incident when we collided. Duh Catherine."

She pushed the revolving door and made her way to the elevators as she dug for her keys. A few moments later she was getting out on the 7th floor.

Catherine couldn't shake the incredible feeling that something profound was happening in her life, something which should be exciting, but it wasn't. She put her key into the dead bolt lock first. It slid sideways with a thud. She stepped inside.

There was a small oak table in the entry way Catherine purchased at an auction last summer. She liked antique shopping, flea markets and estate sales, peering into other people's lives and history.

She sat her purse on the table and took a sip of her coffee. As she hung up her keys, her gaze dropped to the floor. An envelope was at her feet. She reached down to pick it up.

What's this? Something from building management?

It was a sealed, white letter-sized envelope. There were outside no markings whatsoever. At first she thought it was a resident notice from the building manager but was lacking a pre-printed label. Plus those notices were usually placed in her mailbox, not shoved under the door.

Catherine slipped off her jacket, kicked off her shoes, and tossed the envelope onto the bed spread. She glanced at herself in the mirror.

Catherine, you look like hell!

She poked herself underneath her eyes where she was developing dark circles. As a child she had always loved a good Nancy Drew novel but, in this case, being in the middle of a mystery was not becoming.

So many unanswered questions. If this strangeness continues, I may need to go admit myself to Research Psychiatric.

Catherine picked up the envelope and turned it over in order to use her index finger nail to open it. She fumbled to get the single sheet of folded paper loose from the envelope.

She found five strange characters perfectly centered from top to bottom and left to right on the piece of paper. The characters were large, each about two and a half inches tall. She studied it, puzzled. It seemed to be written using a calligraphy pen. The word appeared to be a code perhaps, or was written in a language she didn't recognize.

The paper had a rough texture, almost like parchment. She ran it between her fingers.

Think, Catherine. Why does this look familiar? Oh I wish the answer would simply come to me from somewhere in the deeper recesses of my brain.

In college she had prided herself in her trivia expertise. No one would dare think they could beat her at Trivial Pursuit™. Her head was filled with extraneous knowledge.

Is it some strange hieroglyph, or a word maybe?

She ran every five letter word she could think of through her mind, realizing that was silly since she'd have no idea if she were right. Plus she wasn't sure it was truly a word. She tried to think of who would give her the note and why, but came up lacking any possibilities other than Erica.

I should call and ask. It's really unlikely but it's a start.

Catherine glanced at the alarm clock on her bedside table as she dialed the phone. It was almost 11 o'clock.

"Division of Family Services, this is Erica speaking. How may I help you?"

"Hey Erica, it's me, Catherine."

"Hey girl, how's your day off so far?" Erica sounded envious.

"Well...umm interesting. I need to ask you a question. Did you leave an envelope under my door this morning?"

"An envelope? No, why?"

"Well I came home from the coffee shop and an envelope had been slipped under my door."

"Really? Well don't leave me hanging, what did it say?"

"That's the strange part. I am not exactly sure."

"What do you mean?"

"There's strange writing on it. I think it may be a word, written in some ancient looking language."

"Ooh, how interesting. I want to see it! Can I come by on lunch break?"

"Sure, come on by. See you in a bit."

Catherine slowly laid the sheet of parchment down on her side table. She decided to take herself into the kitchen and wash a few cups and plates. Being busy was the best way she kept from dwelling on things. She was finishing with her usual cleanup routine when the doorbell rang. Catherine looked up at the sunflower clock that hung above the kitchen sink. It was now 11:45.

Cool. Erica must have slipped out a bit early for lunch.

Erica rang the bell a couple times before Catherine could open the door.

"Hold your horses, Erica, gosh." She was greeted by Erica's big smile.

"Hey there," she said, stepping into the apartment. "So, what's for lunch?"

"Sandwiches? While I'm doing this, go take a look at the writing on that paper and see what you think. It's by the phone in my bedroom."

Catherine started busily taking items out of her refrigerator. She opened a package of sliced turkey and one of cheese, and began to break apart some lettuce.

Erica came into the room shaking her head. "Well, aren't you funny girl." Erica pulled out one of the wooden chairs that were placed around Catherine's two person oak table.

Catherine looked up from her sandwich making. "What do you mean?"

"Well," Erica started in an accusing tone, "you got me really going with the whole mysterious envelope story. Don't you know April fool's Day is still months away? If you wanted company for lunch, you just needed to say so. There's no reason to get this elaborate in order to get me here." Erica grinned.

"I didn't play a joke on you, Erica. I really am curious about whatever the characters on that sheet of paper mean."

"Curious about what exactly?" Erica pulled the sheet from the envelope, opening it with a flip of her wrist. Right in front of Catherine was a single, blank sheet of paper. The color drained from Catherine's face. She grabbed the paper from Erica and turned it over, twice. It was completely blank.

"But... it was... I mean there was writing on it." Catherine spoke slowly but then trailed off. "I swear there was this writing on it."

Catherine felt faint and sat down at her kitchen table, shaking her head. Her mind started racing again.

What the hell is happening to me? How does writing simply disappear? It was there.

"Let me finish these sandwiches." Erica walked to the counter top to pick up where Catherine had left off. Catherine sat slumped in her chair, shocked, and speechless. Erica finished making lunch and joined her at the table. As she placed a plate in front of Catherine, she started the conversation again.

"I read this article the other day while waiting to see the doctor. It had some fascinating information on how stress affects people. You would not believe some of the stories. There was a woman who experienced some type of hallucination. She told people that she saw Jesus appear out of thin air right in front of her."

Oh great. Now my only friend thinks I'm crazy.

Catherine half listened to Erica.

This stuff isn't some sort of stress induced mania. Stress is what I feel now! I sure didn't feel like this before my life started falling apart. I don't know what to believe, but I don't think I see a stress connection.

"Erica, you know me right?"

"Of course, Catherine. Well, as much as I can." They'd had more than one discussion about Catherine's opening up more, letting Erica be there for her.

"Of all the people in your life, do you think I am stressed enough to have some type of psychotic break?"

Erica got a concerned look on her face. "Oh, no honey. I'm sorry. I didn't mean you. I am just trying to figure this out too."

"Do you believe I am telling the truth about what I saw?"

"Catherine." Erica reached out and held Catherine's hand in hers. "You are the most rational person I know. A bit too serious at times, but definitely sane. If you say there was something there, then something was there. I'm on your side."

Catherine breathed a sigh of relief and relaxed her shoulders.

At least I have one ally in this world. Why is it so hard for me to make friends? But Erica had to trust me with her personal life first. Ever since her mom was diagnosed with cancer and she confided in me, I knew we would be friends.

Catherine knew how bad it was to be faced with the unexpected loss of a parent. Even though Erica's mom was still alive, she could relate to Erica's fears about the matter all too well.

"Besides, when have you known me to hallucinate due to stress?"

"Oh never, Catherine never. You never get stressed. You're always cool as a cucumber. Certainly not the hallucinating type," Erica's sarcasm oozed out.

"Yeah, well I don't know about that. I don't presently feel very cool. I'm not sure the article you read, although fascinating, really applies here." Catherine just stared at her sandwich. She'd pretty much lost her appetite.

"I know. I'm sorry. I wasn't sure what to say when I saw the look on your face. I know there was something on that paper. You know how I get when I start nervously rambling. I make a really good effort to say something, anything. Not always the best choice of words on my part."

"I'm rattled too. It's been such a strange couple days and I'm not sure what to make of it. I only know that things are happening to me that make no sense whatsoever."

Erica bravely moved forward, "So, would you like to tell me what really happened in your office yesterday?"

Catherine needed to confide in someone and Erica was her best bet and was more accepting than most people. Catherine began to tell her in great detail about Olivia's interview, the research she did on the Internet, and then the contents of the envelope that she had found this morning. Then she thought to add Joshua to the list.

During her whole explanation, Erica patiently nodded with reassurance. When Catherine finished, Erica sat there for a few moments. Then she spoke rather authoritatively.

"Maybe you have a gift, Catherine. I mean in my family there are a few people over the decades that have had remarkable gifts from God. My family always regarded them with respect and admiration."

"A gift from God? I don't necessarily have an opinion about God at the moment. So why would God give *me* a darn thing?" Catherine took her full plate to the sink. She felt uncomfortable and needed to do something. "I don't go to church anymore. Not since my parents died."

This was news to Erica, but she held her tongue. She didn't want to upset Catherine by asking too many questions.

Catherine pictured her childhood church for a moment, St. Patrick's in Parsons. She tried to remember what it looked like on the inside. She had almost forgotten the church where she spent so much time as a young child yet recalled some of the details very well.

She recalled being five or six, standing in front of one of the stained glass windows, watching the sunlight flicker through it. She could see the towering stained glass windows in her mind so clearly. Remembering that particular moment made her connect with the happiness of her childhood and she closed her eyes.

Oh, I wish I could be that little girl again.

Erica's voice, breaking the silence, brought her back to reality. "What I meant about God was that a vision is a spiritual occurrence. To me such a vision means that all this is somehow connected to God."

"Well if it's a vision, I've never had one before yesterday. Aren't people usually born with such a gift? I haven't heard of anyone simply getting up one day and saying: 'Look at me everyone. I'm having a vision!' " Catherine threw up her arms up in frustration.

Erica tried to soothe her. "Sometimes people do have visions later on in life. Most of the stories I've read are about people that get spiritual gifts after a near death experience or some event like that."

"How do you know so much about this? I mean I have no clue. Last night I searched the web to get some answers. All I got was crap."

"I grew up with this as part of my life. My grandmother could see all kinds of things. People could tell that there was something special about her. She always seemed to know things before they happened. I know she had dreams where she received messages for other people. My mother is also very gifted, but she doesn't use it much. I always wished as a kid that God would give me some special power. If you ask me, you are lucky to have a vision. It's a beautiful gift even if you don't understand it."

"Yeah, well, I don't understand it at all," Catherine responded.

"You know I'll help you any way that I can. How about I email you some better websites after I get home from work?" Erica shot up from her chair. "Oh boy, what time is it?"

They both looked at the clock. It was already 12:55.

"I have to run, Cat. Barb will be all over me if I'm not back there on time. Things were slow so I got Christy to cover the phones early. Barb's in a foul mood today."

Erica hugged her and started for the door. "I'll email those sites to you. Take a look at them and we'll talk more at work tomorrow or Sunday for sure. Call me if you need me." Erica glanced back, apologetic for leaving so abruptly, and disappeared out the door.

6- *Passages*

Khaled was standing in the dark worriedly outfitting his climbing gear. He would be the person who acted as a safety tether for the others. Making the steep journey up was dangerous enough in the daytime. Rock slides and countless other treacherous perils could send one or all of them tumbling to their deaths.

"I do not understand the hurry, Brother. We have 8 more hours. This is too dangerous for inexperienced men without light."

"Yes Khaled, I understand. I cannot fully explain why we must go now. I have a feeling that we are not the only people trying to reach my contact, and it's vital we arrive ahead of them."

"I see, Brother Francis."

"Plus I am certain that we will make it up and back down safely. I believe we are meant to succeed and will be blessed in our endeavor. We must have faith." He placed his hand on Khaled's back. "So do not worry. We shall listen to your instruction, and you will guide us safely to the top."

Khaled shook his head in disbelief but continued his preparations anyway.

Francis' feet were severely swollen after yesterday's trek. It was difficult to remove his boots last night and he was now concerned about being able to put them back on. The swelling had subsided a bit, but when he ran his fingers across the soles of his blistered feet, the pain sent him reeling backwards. Khaled noticed, even in the dim firelight, and tossed him a small tin container.

"That should help your feet. It's and old remedy made from local plants. It will deaden the pain enough for you to reach the top."

Francis was touched by his compassion and could see God's hand in what was happening. He was more anxious than afraid. As he applied the dark salve that smelled like goat urine, he recalled in detail his dream and the men he saw. Knowing they were no match for armed men, he did not want to meet them face to face. After all, he knew God was on their side. The warning in the dream confirmed it.

Francis laced his boots and stood with confidence, wearing outwardly his inner strength. "Much better. Thank you. We must go at once."

7- *Look Mommy*

On her way to grab dinner, Catherine passed many quaint shops that filled her neighborhood. She thoroughly enjoyed the culture represented by the independent shop owners and rarely supported the threatening large chain stores. She'd read many heartbreaking stories about small shop owners being put out of business that way. Catherine always seemed to understand the positions and plights of others very well. Her mother had told her that her empathy was a true gift.

I wish mom was alive. I bet she could figure out what is going on.

As she passed the local bakery, she wondered what would happen if she touched some other random stranger. Would she suddenly see things like she had with Olivia? Catherine looked around nervously. She became a bit paranoid at the idea.

Why haven't I thought of this before? Will it happen again?

She shuddered at the thought.

Quit getting yourself so worked up. It won't, just get to MacGonigle's, grab dinner, and get home. Easy.

Catherine could see the market ahead of her and relaxed. She didn't waste time once inside. She was in the checkout line before 15 minutes had passed. While Catherine was waiting in the checkout line, a mother and young girl about the age of 5 were waiting in front of her. The young girl stared keenly at Catherine, her young, blue eyes opened wide and a happy look spread across her face. Catherine waved to her. The girl giggled and waved back. The mother turned to witness the exchange.

"You must be a very special lady."

Catherine looked at her curiously, "What do you mean?"

"My daughter doesn't like strangers, not ever, but she sure seems to like you." The mother smiled sincerely.

Catherine looked at the little girl who was still smiling at her. "Really? She seems very friendly to me." She waved at her again and the child returned the wave.

"She often hides her face. She's always been that way even with people she's seen many times before."

Just then the little girl spoke softly and her mom leaned down to hear what she was saying. The mother's eyes widened and she half laughed. "My daughter wants to know if you are a fairy princess."

"I don't think I'm a fairy princess, honey, but I know you are." The little girl pouted.

"Sarah! Tell the nice lady thank you."

The little girl did as she was told. In a few more moments, both mother and daughter were on their way out of the store. The girl kept looking back at Catherine with a curious stare.

The checkout clerk Rhonda, who knew Catherine by name, started ringing up her few items.

"I didn't know you were so good with kids, Catherine."

Catherine looked at her, smiled and shrugged, "Neither did I."

Once back home, Catherine busied herself to pass the evening hours. As she was winding down for bed, she went in her bedroom and stopped in her tracks. Her computer was turned on.

What the... why is my computer on? It was not on this afternoon.

She always shut it down before going to bed. The fan was too noisy for her to fall asleep.

Even if I did leave it on by accident, why isn't the screensaver running?

As she got closer to the computer, her face went white. On an otherwise blank document on the screen were the same characters from the piece of paper that morning.

Catherine slowly lowered herself into her desk chair, half expecting the computer to spring to life as if possessed. Her thoughts raced.

How did this get on my computer? Is Erica playing a trick on me? No, that wouldn't be like her. Besides, the paper was blank for her. It's simply impossible. I have no font type that matches this.

Catherine highlighted the text. "Enochian? I don't remember ever having that as a font." Just then the phone rang. It startled her so badly she jumped away from the computer screen and her chair toppled backwards. Catherine and the chair hit the carpet with a loud thump. Her heart was pounding. She struggled to her knees and then carefully steadied herself with her right hand on the bed. Catherine made it to the phone just as the caller hung up. Catherine sat on the bed to catch her breath, frustrated.

After all that, I missed the call. Thank God for Caller ID.

The call came from Erica. Catherine hit her speed dial #4 and called her back.

"Erica. It's Catherine."

"Hey. That was fast. I just wanted to say I'm sorry about running out during our conversation. I just wanted to make sure Barb didn't catch me, but she was gone to lunch when I returned." Catherine was breathing hard into the receiver. "Catherine, you okay?"

"Yes, I think so. It's okay. I know you had to go."

"You sound different Catherine. Are you sure you're okay? Did anything else happen today, since we talked?"

Catherine looked behind her at the computer still displaying the ghost document. "Yes, something did, but I'm tired and would rather talk tomorrow if that's okay."

"Oh sure honey, just give me a call. I only wanted to let you know that I emailed you a few sites to check out when you want to."

Catherine was anxious to get off the phone. "Thanks Erica, I appreciate it. I'll see you tomorrow at work. Talk to you then."

Catherine hung up the phone and wondered what to do about what had appeared on her computer screen. All at once she felt overwhelmed. She remembered that anxious feeling all too well. The last time she felt so shaky inside was when her parents died. Catherine turned to look again at the screen. As she sat down, the writing disappeared before her eyes. It was simply there one moment and gone the next.

Catherine gasped and sat, frozen. She rubbed her eyes.

Am I hallucinating? I feel like I'm going insane.

8- *Climbing for Heaven*

The monks were completely silent during their assent; mainly because they were too busy trying to insure their footing. The jagged rocks provided a decent foothold, but the smooth surface made it was too easy for their feet to slip.

As the group slowly made their way up the mountain face in darkness, pebbles and other rocks tumbled below. So far there had been no causalities among the Benedictine Monks but the progress was extremely slow.

"Keep going Brothers. Pray for strength." Francis' voice of support to the others echoed across the rock face.

It was nearly dawn now and the emerging glow of light made their guide above them start to pick up the pace. Francis strained to keep up with Khaled, who was quite comfortable dangling off the side of a cliff. As Francis reached up to find a finger hold, he thought about his dream.

Who is Britius? He must be an evil man if he's also after the scroll. I cannot allow it to fall into his men's hands. I am certain the dream was a warning. I can feel it all through me.

"Khaled, how far to our meeting coordinates once we reach the top?"

"It's about 2 kilometers through the forest. It will take almost 2 hours. The terrain is not straight up of course, but it's still slow going."

As Francis and his companions continued the arduous climb, he began to pray.

Heavenly Father, please watch over myself and the others. Allow me, your humble servant Francis, to reach the location before those that want evil. Grant me the courage to complete your holy mission. Our Father, who art in heaven, hallowed is thy name...

9- *Broken Windows*

Catherine was determined to try to keep to her usual Saturday routine, despite the upside down mess her life had become recently, and her growing fatigue. She had returned to work on Wednesday and the remainder of the week had been as she hoped, very busy and without incident.

She sat now in her favorite spot in Cafe Roma, a small table in front of the window facing the street so she could look out. Several tall oak trees had been growing out of holes in the concrete sidewalk for decades. It was a nice break from the stress of work.

Today her thoughts were overflowing with everything that had happened since last week. It had been several days since any peculiar metaphysical occurrences, and she was feeling a lot better. It still had her mind working on an explanation but she was feeling much less afraid, at least at the moment.

Today will be a good day if I have anything to say about it. So glad things calmed down.

She held the large, round coffee cup in her hands, slowing raising it to her lips. She took a short sip and then sat the cup back down and continued looking out the window to the street that was pleasantly illuminated by the morning sunshine. Catherine enjoyed these sensory moments, surrounded by people, yet completely alone with her thoughts. These days she was almost always more comfortable with her own company and more sure of her life when isolated from others.

Is preferring to live in solitude so unusual? Erica and I are closer than I've been to anyone in quite a while. I need to try to open up with her more.

"Um, hey there, are you reading that paper?" The man's deep voice startled her abruptly interrupting her internal thoughts.

Catherine looked over her shoulder to see who had disturbed her solitude. *Joshua*. She found herself staring into his blue eyes, even though a part of her didn't want to. Her recent strange encounters made her uneasy, and her face reflected her fear. Joshua reacted to her startled expression and took a step back. He looked away for a moment.

Catherine figured he may be used to uneasiness from other people, and felt shame for her reaction.

"Cause if you aren't reading it, I would like to, um…read it."

Catherine looked away from him and said politely, "That's fine, I'm not reading it. You can have it."

He's probably just trying to make some conversation. So just chill out, Catherine. Calm down.

Joshua looked reluctant to reach over and pick up the paper. Seeing his reticence, Catherine picked it up and handed it to him. "Here you go; I'm sorry how I reacted. I was deep in thought."

Ordinarily she would not have been so suspicious of his intentions, but life had lately become too unpredictable. Catherine turned back to the window, hoping that was their entire conversation. She was expecting to see Joshua's arm holding the paper, disappear from the periphery of her vision.

Come on, Joshua please just take the paper and go.

"Hey, I was wondering, why are you in here alone all the time?"

Catherine started to panic but found the courage to respond. "I don't really know. I just like this spot. It's interesting to sit and watch the people go by." Catherine couldn't bring herself to look up at him. She took another sip of her café latte to have something to do. She repositioned herself in her seat because it felt like Joshua's eyes were boring into her skull.

"Oh, I just thought someone like you would be surrounded by people," Joshua said, as he pointed one short, stubby finger at the window in front of her. "Not in here just watching through that window looking so lonely."

Catherine did not expect the reaction she suddenly felt. His statement had touched a painful childhood memory. She felt very vulnerable and exposed. Her breath quickened as she remembered other kids laughing at her. She thought of the schoolyard and the terrible voices, and her throat tightened. Ever since childhood she had feared being singled out of the crowd.

Catherine rarely spoke without thinking but now she quickly turned to him and said in desperate voice, "What do you mean someone like me?" She had a tearful look in her eyes.

"I mean someone as special as you are. The first day you came in here and I saw your eyes, I knew who you really were." This time Joshua was gazing directly into her enormous blue eyes as he spoke.

"The others didn't notice you but I did." A soft smile came over Joshua's face as if he were proud of this.

What is this crazy man talking about?

Catherine wanted to bolt but instead reacted angrily jumping up from her chair. "Why are you bothering me, Joshua?" Speaking to him firmly and using his name seemed to startle the jovial man. "I don't know what you are you talking about!" Her voice cut off with a high-pitched squeak. Several people, including Brian stared at her. Catherine noticed the attention from the others, and pulled herself together. The last thing she wanted to do, considering her emotional state, was to make a scene.

"I...I...didn't mean to bother you. I mean, at first I thought you were purposely not revealing yourself, like maybe it was your mission to just watch us, and no one could know." Joshua looked desperate for Catherine to understand. He leaned in closer to whisper, "But then I kept seeing you come in here all the time, doing the same thing. So I asked them and they said you were okay. But my crazy brain just started thinking that maybe something was wrong, or maybe you needed some help. That's why I tried to start a conversation with you about the paper."

"Who did you ask about me? Why would I need your help? I don't even know you. You are just a man that I see in the neighborhood. You don't know anything about me. You don't know who I am." Catherine's voice trailed off as she looked around nervously for someone who might help her break this conversation up.

Joshua looked both alarmed and puzzled. He began stumbling over his words, "Listen, I'm so sorry I upset you. I would never do that to you. I just thought maybe you needed something." He started wringing his hands, "I can be so stupid. I'm sorry, Catherine."

Joshua quickly turned and left the shop through the front door. Catherine's eyes followed his short frame as he darted past the window with his hands shoved in the pockets of his tattered coat.

Wait, how did he know my name?

Catherine tried to process their conversation.

How can life be fine and normal one moment and then completely upside down the next?

She felt light headed and a bit shaky as she reached for her cup. Nervously, she lifted it to her lips and finished the rest of it in two large gulps. Then she felt herself running out the door to catch him. Even though she was only moments behind him, once she stepped out the door, Joshua was nowhere in sight.

Damn, where did he go?

10- *Healing*

Catherine was glad Erica was giving her something to do this particular Sunday morning. Seeing Erica's mother wasn't easy: Catherine didn't like hospitals at all. While she waited, she took a mental inventory about her current dilemma.

Yesterday was the strange encounter with Joshua.

As she thought about her experience with Joshua, she realized that there was something oddly familiar about him. The unsettled feeling that welled up inside her felt like foreshadowing. Like all these smaller events were leading up to something, but not knowing what.

Catherine didn't deal well with that *not knowing* feeling either. This was her life, not a play or movie. She thought of Olivia, and knew she was going to have to see her again on Monday or Tuesday next week. That filled her with trepidation. The only thing she felt she could manage right now was to figure out the strange Enochian writing. Catherine planned to spend the evening on that. Catherine wanted answers. She thought if she found out what the letters meant, it might help her discover who left the envelope for her, and why.

Erica arrived at her door shortly before ten to pick Catherine up. Catherine was ready. She stepped outside her apartment into the hallway.

"So how are you doing?" Erica asked, pushing the down button on the hallway elevator.

Catherine hesitated for a moment, and took at deep breath. "Honestly, I'm just in a daze. There's something else that happened last night." Catherine paused, "I saw those strange letters again. And then yesterday, the homeless man I told you about came up to me at Café Roma and he knew my name. It really freaked me out."

"There was another mysterious envelope?"

"No, but my computer magically turned on and the same letters appeared. There was a document open on my screen with the same thing that had been on that sheet of paper."

"Really? Are you sure you didn't turn on your computer earlier in the day? Maybe you copied the letters onto your computer before I got there?"

"No. The computer had been turned off. I hadn't even touched it and the screensaver wasn't running. I was sitting there trying to figure it out. Then you called and nearly scared the crap out of me. I jumped back and I fell out of my chair. Then after we hung up the letters on the screen disappeared."

"Why didn't you say something?"

"I just needed some time to process."

Erica studied her face as they got onto the elevator. "Talk about my usual perfect timing. Well I could tell that something was wrong. I just knew you were not okay."

"At that point I had myself somewhat convinced that I was suffering from hallucinations and should see a psychiatrist."

Catherine put her hand to her right ear as if holding a phone.

"Hey Erica, how are you? Oh by the way, stuff in my apartment is turning itself on and things are appearing out of thin air. Yeah that's right -- it's magic. So, how's your mom? Yes, yes magical letters appearing out of nowhere, yeah, it was the funniest thing for sure." Then Catherine rolled her eyes and hung up her pretend phone. "Click."

Erica started to laugh.

Catherine was relieved. Making a joke of things when they felt too overwhelming was a simple trick she learned early in life.

It was a 10 minute trip to St. Luke's Hospital. As they drove, Erica tried to talk to Catherine about the mysterious incidents. Catherine was only half listening to Erica at the beginning of the conversation then she tuned in.

"So to me, whether or not you are having a vision of these letters or actually seeing them with your eyes doesn't really matter. I believe it must be a message, perhaps a message from God himself. I know you don't go to church anymore, and we haven't ever talked about your religious beliefs, but I think you should consider some spiritual origin here."

Erica paused to see if Catherine would say anything. After a few seconds of silence she continued to speak. "Perhaps it was some type of a message. I know that there are spiritual phenomena that defy any rational explanation. Too many people in the world believe that such things are real."

Catherine silently considered the possibility of the incident at the office, the mysterious characters that she had seen, and the encounter with Joshua to be a part of God's message meant just for her. It seemed ridiculous.

Why would God want to send me a message?

As a small child Catherine had believed in all sorts of mystical, magical things. She felt close to God until her parents were killed. But that connection was only a very faint memory now. Her loss had been so painful that she felt completely cut off from that love. During that experience, she had separated herself from God, blaming him angrily. She didn't know how God could have taken both of her parents away. She felt it was a personal punishment from God. Through the whole experience, her anger had grown steadily. Catherine purposely closed her heart to anything spiritual after that.

Catherine broke the silence when they were nearly at the hospital. "I haven't been able to reconcile my childhood pain with God. I couldn't understand why God would take so much from me, punish me. But I used to believe it was possible to receive grace from God in many ways. If it is a message of some kind, I need to know what it means and why it's happening."

As Erica parked the car, Catherine added, "At least you don't think I'm cuckoo. I'm going to check out those websites you emailed me. Plus I saw the font name in Microsoft Word before the letters disappeared. Doing some research will probably keep me very busy. Maybe I'll find something that makes sense."

Erica turned the car engine off and looked over at her. "Well, that's a start at least. Don't worry about it. I will help you figure this out. We'll get to the bottom of this together." She reached out to hold Catherine's hand to comfort her, and then decided to make her laugh instead.

"Feel anything, anything at all?"

Catherine realized what she was implying and then said, "No! Thank God...well, at least that's something to be thankful to God for."

They both got a chuckle out of it. "Thanks so much, Erica. You don't know what our friendship means to me. I just feel bad to burden you since you have so much already going on with your mom."

"I know how much it means to have a real friend. I really do. You've been a great support for me through all this with mom, it's the very least I could do to listen to your situation and try my best to help you. And believe it or not, you are worth it."

Catherine was suddenly self-conscious that she had selfishly taken up all the drive time. "Oh my God, Erica, I didn't have the chance to ask about how your mom is doing."

Erica's face darkened. "Oh, yes. She's very weak right now. They told us yesterday that she was developing pneumonia. The radiation treatments have depleted her white blood cell count. We had to cancel her most recent treatment to try and get her infection under control. But Mom's still in good spirits. Her faith is the most amazing thing about her. She looks very pale and even weaker to me now. It's hard not to be scared. I try hard not to lose hope." Erica paused. "I know, I know. Mom would kick my butt if she heard me saying that."

Catherine pictured Mrs. Baylor. She was a lovely woman, so kind and full of life. It hadn't taken long to figure out that Erica's mother, Karen, was the eternal optimist.

Catherine couldn't imagine Karen looking sickly at all. She'd been invited to several family functions with Erica after Karen's diagnosis. She was always upbeat and positive. You wouldn't have known she was sick.

"Well your mom's a fighter. Lots of cancer patients get in this situation and come out fine. Now let's get in there and lift her spirits, shall we?"

Erica entered her mother's private hospital room just a few footsteps ahead of Catherine, "Hey mom, look who's here." Erica motioned toward the door with a *Vanna White* impersonation. Karen opened her eyes with a flutter. When she saw Catherine entering the room behind her daughter, her face lit up.

"Catherine! Oh my goodness. I'm so glad to see you." She reached her arms up, pulling on her IV tube, motioning for Catherine to come over and give her a hug. Catherine saw immediately what Erica was talking about and tried hard not to reflect it on her face now.

Karen looked ghastly pale with dark circles underneath both eyes. This was not the person she'd seen a few weeks earlier. Her face was worn and her skin was gaunt. There were monitors measuring various vital signs. There were deeper age creases in her forehead.

"So nice to see you again, Mrs. Baylor." Catherine leaned down to hug her.

"Oh please call me Karen, dear. Aren't we on a first name basis by now?"

Catherine attempted to be upbeat and positive, "Well, Karen, you're looking good today."

"Oh dear, you don't have to lie for my sake. I'm sure I look frightful. I know I must. I don't feel very good."

Karen was always gracious, yet blunt. Catherine had learned that the first time she met her. "Alright Karen, I've seen you looking better, but I'm sure you'll be out of here in no time." Catherine smiled sweetly at Karen.

Karen looked at her daughter and then Catherine. She paused for a moment and then said with a sigh, "I think I have given it my best fight." Then Karen's voice became softer, "When it's your time, it's your time."

Erica immediately grasped her mother's hand. Catherine sat in a chair on the right side of the bed so she could hear Karen but offer support to both of them.

"I've been thinking a lot today, about my life. I've been blessed to do so much. I've been a wife and mother. I have had a full life. With all these things to be happy for, I have continued to pray for God to give me a miracle so that I can stay with my family."

Tears welled in Erica's eyes. "Mom, please don't talk like this. I refuse to give up and so should you."

Catherine's natural empathy made her own eyes get teary. She wished she could take both Erica and Karen's pain away.

"Now Erica, honey, it will be okay. I have not lost all hope for that miracle, you know." Erica fought back the tears, her mom's continued strong spirit comforting her.

Karen saw how upset both her daughter and Catherine were, and started to speak again. "Girls, you need to understand something about life, if you don't already. There are things that simply happen, not because we've lived a bad life or because we deserve it. Some events simply are what they are. When bad things happen to us or others, we must not be afraid. We should not fear that God is trying to punish us either."

Catherine was stunned.

I have always thought that about my parent's death. How could she have known?

Karen continued on with her speech, "We may not always see the larger plan, but I'm certain there is one. If God wants me to stay here, I will. If it's time for me to go, I could choose to be angry or choose to find peace in leaving my very sick body behind me. I choose peace."

Catherine looked at Karen carefully. Given the circumstances it would be normal to see a scared woman talking about her possible death. Catherine saw none of that in Karen's face. She seemed perfectly at peace as she spoke.

How could such a sick woman still have so much hope and love for God?

Catherine could not say the same for herself since losing her parents. She wished she could let it go but had to admit she was still angry. Even so, she knew there was truth in what Karen was saying.

Erica's voice interrupted Catherine's thoughts. "Mom, how could God decide to take you from us? It's not time. You are only 54 years old. That's too young!"

Karen squeezed her daughter's hand with tremendous compassion in her eyes and nodded. "I can feel the cancer spreading now. Only a miracle can reverse this. I now spend all my time praying and making my peace with my life." But then Karen thrust her arm into the air and exclaimed, "Never lose hope ladies, I'm not dead yet!"

Catherine excused herself to get something to drink, perfect timing to leave mother and daughter alone for a minute.

As she returned with Cokes for Erica and herself, Karen launched into questions for Catherine, half answering them herself.

"So what's different Catherine? I must say you look different to me. It hasn't been that long since we've seen each other." Karen eyed her trying to figure it out. "A new hair cut? No, that's not it. Have you lost some weight? You're already too skinny, you know," Karen winked.

Catherine shrugged her shoulders and sat down. "I don't know Karen. Same old stuff happening." Catherine hated to lie.

It's not quite a lie. It's a half-true statement. There have been no physical changes that I know of...

She and Erica exchanged knowing glances. They both knew that sharing Catherine's recent encounters with the unknown might be a burden for Karen.

"Well whatever it is, you look almost radiant to me."

"Radiant?"

"Yes, you are simply glowing."

"Well Karen, you've got me there. Not sure at all why I'd be glowing of all things." She laughed, trying to cover her uneasiness.

"Erica, can you go see what's taking them so long? I hit the call light over ten minutes ago."

"Sure mom, be right back." Erica hurried out of the room.

"Now that we're alone, I want to thank you so much for being such a wonderful friend to Erica." Karen looked deeply into Catherine's blue eyes as she spoke. "I don't believe my daughter would be so strong right now if she didn't have you. Her brother Tom is wonderful as well, but there's nothing like a best friend."

Catherine wanted to tell her that she didn't think she was that helpful, but Karen went on talking before she could. "I see the gifts you have inside you. You may not realize now, but something deep inside you is trying to come out. I have seen it happen before. You are so good with people and so willing to help despite your own pain." Karen paused. "It must be hard for you to be there for my daughter, when you're still struggling with the loss of your own parents."

Catherine looked away, exposed and vulnerable. She was not prepared for Karen to be so direct and candid, and covered her face with her hands. Her feelings hit her so hard and fast that she couldn't hold them back. She started crying into the palms of her hands, while trying to choke back her tears.

"You need to let go of your anger, Catherine. It is a dark poison in your life. I know you miss your folks terribly. I understand that, but I feel I need to tell you that it's not a personal attack from God."

Catherine looked up at Karen with tear stained cheeks.

"Do you really think that your parents would want you to be so unhappy?"

Catherine shook her head. "No. Not at all, they were the best parents in the world. They always wanted me to be happy above all else. How could you tell that I was so unhappy?"

"Sometimes I know things that go beyond what people tell me. I've have had a sense of your deep sorrow since the first time we met. I hope you will consider healing your broken heart and moving on. You deserve to have a wonderful whole life, not the half life you've been living for so long."

Catherine stared deeply into Karen's eyes.

Her eyes are a lot like my mother's, so kind and wise. Mom was so caring and full of love for everyone.

"You remind me of my mother. I'm not sure why it hadn't occurred to me before now."

"Thank you dear. I want to be there for you. You are special to me like my own child. I wanted to offer you that bit of advice and let you know how much I appreciate all you do. Just in case I didn't have the chance again. I have always lived my life without the burden of regrets, Catherine. Never waste a moment dear. Life is too precious to be squandered. It can be much shorter than we like. I should know."

Catherine was grateful for Karen's advice. Something hit home for the first time in many years. "Well Karen, I think it should be me thanking you. It's been too many years since they died. I've been so very sad. You are a very special lady. Erica is lucky to have you."

Erica returned with the nurse and did not notice Catherine's tear-stained cheeks. Catherine slid into the bathroom and shut the door. She, wet a paper towel cleaned underneath her eyes. They were tinged black with mascara.

I look like a raccoon. Yuck.

So much had happened this week, but right now, she felt a little better. Catherine examined her face.

I do have a choice to make now. Karen is right. I need to live my life the way my parents would have wanted.

Karen was a miracle to her. How one person could affect her in that way was amazing. Catherine tossed her paper towel in the trash. The nurse was leaving as she reentered the room.

"You okay?" Erica shot her a concerned look.

At that exact moment, Catherine realized how lucky she was to have a friend at all, considering the brick wall she built around herself. "I'm doing much better, much better now," Catherine smiled at Karen.

Erica was puzzled. "Okay, so what did I miss?" She put her hands on her hips.

"Your mom was helping me see a few things in my life that are very outdated and need to be filed away once and for all. That's all."

After a while Karen's weariness was their sign to leave. "I'm going to take Catherine home and swing by later. How would that be? Anything I can bring you from home?"

"No dear, I think seeing your pretty face will be just fine."

Catherine felt a strange tingling sensation in her fingertips and quickly rubbed her hands together. "Karen, do you mind if I drop by to see you tomorrow?"

"Oh sure, honey, please do." Karen leaned back on her pillow half closing her eyes for a moment. "I'd really like it if you would."

Erica leaned over and gave her mom a huge hug. "I'll see you soon, mom."

I don't want Karen to die. Not now, after feeling so close to her.

Catherine reached over to hug Karen good bye. Her hands became hotter as she embraced Karen. Catherine spoke softly from the heart. "You are a very wonderful woman. I know God will save you, just like you have saved me." As Catherine held Karen, she saw brief, fleeting images of Karen's family. There were lots of faces she didn't recognize flowing through her thoughts. The experience felt like what had happened with Olivia in her office, but much less intense.

She held the embrace with Karen for a long time. As she did, a feeling of warmth spread from Catherine's hands to her whole body. It seemed as though Karen felt it too, because she held Catherine tighter as the warmth spread.

Catherine suddenly felt dizzy and stood up to steady herself. "I will see you tomorrow, Karen. Thank you again." Karen nodded, closed her eyes, and fell asleep instantly.

They silent walked to the car. "So what did you and mom talk about?"

"Your mother wanted me to know a few things, I guess. She thanked me for being such a good friend to you. She wanted to remind me to take good care of myself." Catherine paused for a moment, looking down. Suddenly she felt a wave of emotional pain start to rise up into her chest. A dark sensation pressed in on her and built to her throat. Catherine knew she could not hold it back even if she tried.

A low sob escaped from her throat. "Oh God. The pain I carry is so deep and dark. I was so immersed in my work in order to cope that I didn't realize it. Your mom suggested my parents wouldn't want me to suffer because of their death and that maybe it was time for some healing in my life."

"Yes, mom has a way of doing that for me too." Erica reached her arm around Catherine as best she could. "I always listen to her, especially when she gets that particular look in her eyes. I definitely didn't want to listen when I was younger though. You know how teenagers are. No one could tell me what to do. I knew everything. My friends and I felt we were darn near invincible."

"Yes. That pretty much sums up things before the age of 16."

"I may not have listened at first, but somehow Mom's wisdom would always come back. She has always been the wise one in our family. That's honestly why it's been so hard to face the possibility of losing her." Erica sighed. "I have to trust that whatever happens, it will all be okay, I guess. Mom has taught me to accept all things as meant to happen for whatever reason." Erica was resolute. "I'm glad you feel close to my mom. That means a lot to me."

The two women hugged. Catherine pulled herself away for a moment to look Erica in the eyes. "I want you to know that your friendship really means the world to me. I feel like I haven't fully expressed that to you. I just...well, it's been hard for me. I wanted you to hear it from me."

Erica nodded. "Hey, I have about an hour before I have to be anywhere. Want to go get some lunch?"

Catherine nodded. "How about Figlio's on the Plaza?"

"Figlio's it is," she answered turning the key in the ignition.

During lunch, something changed in Catherine. She felt open to talk about her parents, more than she had the entire time since their death. Things were changing for Catherine, all at once.

11- *Moment of Truth*

"We will not return by going the same route that brought us here. There's a slightly longer path down the mountains to the north. A gentle descent. If anyone saw us traversing the desert, they will not be able to see us again," Khaled explained.

"I appreciate your discretion," replied Brother Francis. "It's best if our transaction today is unknown and unseen."

"Are you being pursued, Brother? It's crucial for you to share with me all details, or I cannot fully guide you."

Francis didn't have anything but a dream to go by, and he knew nothing about his pursuers, except for the name Britius Bugiardini.

"I do not know for certain. This holy object is very important to God, Khaled, and those who wish evil would not want me to succeed today. I had a dream that we were being pursued. I only remember a name: Britius Bugiardini. Do you know of him?"

"I do not know of him, but if this object is important as you say, then I will pray for our safety and courage." He looked at his map and compass. "We are very close to your coordinates."

Francis looked ahead. He could not see much because of the thick tree cover, but in a few moments, they were all standing in a clearing not much bigger than an American football field. At the far end of the clearing was a small domed structure that looked like a house made entirely of branches, twigs and other elements of the forest around them. There were no signs of life, but they were still a hundred yards away. Khaled motioned to allow him to go first. He took a knife from his belt and began walking slowly toward the dwelling. The others followed him without uttering a word.

When they were closer, Francis could tell that the structure was someone's home, but it appeared that no one was present. Khaled approached what appeared to be the door to the place. He called out to alert the owner that company had arrived, but there was no answer. With knife in his hand, Khaled opened the door and stepped inside. Francis and the other Brothers held their breath, but Khaled reappeared quickly. "No one is inside. We have arrived early."

Before Francis could respond, a sound of cracking twigs came echoing from the tree line nearby. Each of them braced themselves as a short, elderly fat man in a long robe came out into the clearing.

"Ah, here you are, as expected. I am sorry I was not yet here to greet you. I was awakened late last night and told you would be early. So once it was light out, I left to retrieve the object."

"Are you Philonious Umbrey, then?" Francis asked him.

"One and the same," Philonious bowed his hands in prayer.

"How did you know that we would arrive early?"

"I already told you, my son! A dream. An angel appeared and told me you were to come ahead of schedule."

"I didn't mean any disrespect Philonious. You'll understand my caution. I too had a dream last night, and this is why we arrived early. We are being pursued," Francis explained. This was the first time that the others had heard this. They looked at each other and Francis with concern. "Brothers, please try to calm your selves. We will be fine."

Francis assured them. "Before we conduct our business, Philonious, please tell me who arranged for us to meet here today?"

Philonious looked at Francis with impatience, "Father Gustav Mateus, of course."

Thank you for understanding Philonious. I trust we can conduct our business now?"

Philonious motioned to Francis to follow him inside the dwelling. Once inside they were alone.

"Here is what you seek, Brother Francis." Philonious opened a leather pouch and produced a silver tube just like the one in his dream.

"Incredible! This is the exact tube that I was holding in my dream last night. I am certain now that the dream was a warning. I wish I understood who was trying to get the scroll and was chasing after me. I only know the man's name from my dream."

"Please, please open the tube before I ask for payment."

Francis did as he was instructed. He carefully opened the tube and then gently slid the scroll out. It bore the mark of the Angels. He quickly slid the scroll back inside. "Yes, this is satisfactory."

"Here is your payment." Francis pulled a heavy pouch out from under his cloak and handed it to Philonious. "Do you wish to count it?"

"No, no, no. I am sure it is all there."

"May we rest here? We will not stay long. We have to keep moving."

"Of course. It was a small curiosity son, if you do not blame an old man for asking. You said you overheard a name? Who is after the scroll if I may inquire?"

"You will not know of him, Philonious. I do not believe he is from around here. The name is Britius Bugiardini."

The old man's eyes widened. "Oh, heaven help us. We must leave now. Go, Go, Go!" Philonious ushered Francis to the others. "I am leaving now and you must do the same. We cannot remain here. It is not safe." Philonious headed straight back into the forest.

Francis caught up to him. "Philonious, stop. Please! Please tell me who this man is." He implored Francis' with pity. "You do not want to know. He's a man who ALWAYS gets whatever he wants. You and your men must run!"

In a moment Philonious was out of sight. In disbelief, Francis turned quickly to the others.

"We must leave at once!"

12- *Moment of Realization*

After her lunch with Erica, Catherine arrived at her own doorstep feeling much lighter inside, newly liberated. For once in her life, at least since her parents had been killed, it seemed things were looking a little brighter. In light of recent events, she was not surprised when she found another envelope in her doorway. It was the same as before, a blank envelope. This time the page inside said a single word, but this time in English.

FAITH

Why would the message say a single word? Why would someone send her the word faith? Is God telling me to have faith?

Catherine stood in the entry way for a while holding the page, and then realized her door was still open. She closed it slowly with her empty hand. She was still standing in the same spot when she felt what was like the sheet of paper in her hand vibrating. Not quite vibrating, but humming. She gripped the paper tightly; afraid it would drop to the floor. She watched in sheer amazement as the ink shifted and moved to create other ancient characters. The ink moved slowly, like water, finding very specific paths and crevices in the paper. Catherine ran her index finger over the letters, expecting them to smear.

These looked wet only a moment ago. Now the letters feel embossed. Pressed into the paper.

This experience felt more like a dream. She was dizzy again, the same feeling she had earlier with Karen. She kept rubbing the surface of the letters as she walked to her bedroom. She took a deep breath to center herself, but continued to feel more and more light-headed. Things around her in the bedroom appeared much brighter and more vivid than usual.

Wow, who turned up the lights!

Catherine felt like a child seeing something beautiful for the very first time as she looked around the room.

What has happened to my eyes?

She rubbed her eyes and blinked them several times, thinking this would change her eyesight back to normal.

Everything is so crystal clear. Wow. And the colors in this room are so vibrant. I don't think I've ever seen colors like this.

As she stared at the pattern on her bedspread, the beauty of it nearly took her breath away. She sat on the edge of her bed and then with a soft gentle recline, she lay on the bed and looked up at the ceiling. The tingling sensation in her body grew. Catherine had a memory of a similar feeling from perhaps long ago, but she could not remember specifically when.

I'm tripping...can you have an LSD flashback a decade later?

As the sensation continued, she felt as if she might float up out of her body and up through the ceiling.

Maybe this is what people feel when they die.

Normally she would have been afraid, but right now she wasn't. There was a subtle unending peace all around her like a blanket. It felt like her mother had her arms around her holding her tight, keeping her safe. She closed her eyes, remembering every detail of her face.

She lay there with her eyes closed and thought about her childhood. As she did so, she felt as if something were pulling her deeper and deeper into a trance of nothingness. She opened her eyes but instead of her room, she saw brilliant balls of light floating all around her, but the light did not hurt her eyes. She felt she could reach out and touch one. The experience was like flying above the entire world.

Then without a transition, she was suddenly standing again, and then walking forward. Catherine looked over to see who was guiding her by the hand. It was the same beautiful, angelic woman she had seen in her dream last week.

When I was a little girl, I thought my mother was the most beautiful woman in the world but she's...

The mysterious woman beside her was wearing a white gown that billowed and flowed all around her, even when she was not moving. Her skin was flawless and pale and she had perfect features. Catherine could not tell for sure but, it seemed that her skin had a sort of luminescent energy. There was light that seemed to appear all around her. Catherine desperately wanted to speak to the lady and tried to open her mouth, but when she did, no sound came out.

What is going on? Why can't I speak? I have a million questions!

She tried again, but her voice was just gone. As they came to a large doorway it opened slowly to reveal a beautiful valley. The woman simply stood there pointing to the door and Catherine didn't know what she wanted her to do.

What does this mean? Do you want me to go out there?

Catherine gave up trying to speak and walked through the open door. She looked out across the valley as she stepped outside onto some type of see-through platform. The landscape was breathtaking below and around her. The colors were like a symphony. The vegetation was so deep and green. Catherine hadn't ever seen anything so captivating.

There are no words...

For Catherine the only place that she could have compared this to was during a vacation trip. She and her dad had gone camping at his favorite place. At that time it had been the most beautiful place she had ever seen. Still it was no real comparison to the deep, rich greens, vibrant reds, deep blues and gold hues she could see below her now.

As she stared at the rich details in the landscape, the entire scene literally came to life. The scene transitioned from that of a still life painting and into a living, breathing work of art. First Catherine noticed the river below her was moving like a force to be reckoned with and as she gazed, she found that she could see deep inside the river too. Thousands of fish were swimming with the ebb and flow of the water.

Catherine then looked up to the sky just in time to witness a variety of birds filling the air overhead. Over time every creature she could think of emerged out of the living landscape. It wasn't like seeing nature or being in the woods. Before her was a living, breathing example of the planet Earth. Catherine stood in awe as if God had opened the doors to heaven just for her.

It's the hum....I feel it...the hum of life itself?

There was a subtle hum, just like the vibration she had felt in the paper. It was a rhythm she could feel move through her entire body. It was like a steady heartbeat that was all encompassing. The other sounds she heard were far too rich to be adequately recorded. She was surrounded by a music that came from the air!

Catherine fell to her knees at the sight and sound. Tears of joy filled her eyes.

I have to know what is going on.

She turned to try to speak to the woman by her side, but she had disappeared. Catherine turned herself around looking everywhere, but found she was now alone on the clear platform.

Panic descended on her and the surface shattered beneath her feet. Catherine was frightened and the fear consumed her. She screamed but no sound came.

Catherine sat straight up in bed with a jolt and looked around wildly. Her heart was pounding. She was breathing rapidly and struggled to catch her breath.

Oh my God I can't breathe. I need to calm down! Was I asleep or awake?

Catherine managed to get up and then became very nauseous. She stumbled quickly into her bathroom. She knew instinctively that lunch wasn't going to stay down.

Ugh, my chest is going to cave in.

After throwing up everything into the toilet, she murmured aloud. "What a waste of a perfectly good grilled chicken salad."

This made her laugh almost hysterically. "Well at least I still have my sense of humor. Dad would love that."

Catherine's body felt so strange. The experience was still with her. The beauty of the scene she had witnessed was now a part of her. Half of her felt drained because of how scared she became and the other half of her was energized by the beauty of what she had been shown. For a moment she felt torn by the two extremes in her head.

Catherine decided to take a shower to try and feel better. She was dirty and clammy after nearly hyperventilating and then tossing her lunch.

Uh huh...that's the best feeling ever.

The warm water felt so good cascading over her. As she was washing off, a light almost eerie breeze swept over her as if someone had abruptly entered the room. Then she couldn't shake the feeling that she was not alone and being watched.

Catherine opened the shower door for a moment to look out, but no one was there.

Who am I looking for? Come on Catherine don't freak out.

Catherine continued to feel uneasy and quickly washed her hair so she could get out.

I didn't bolt or lock the door when I came home.

She put on her fluffy white bathrobe. Still dripping wet, she shuffled back through her bedroom to the front hallway. She locked her front door, turned the dead bolt and latched the chain.

There that's better. It's not like me to forget that. Of course it's not like me to have any of the experiences I've had lately either.

Catherine walked down the hall to her living room and turned on a lamp in the corner. It was just starting to get dark outside. The clock on her wall read 6:45 p.m. which startled her.

Where did the time go? I got home around 1:30 and it's now 5 hours later?

Catherine thought about eating, but didn't feel quite ready to consume anything.

Well at least I know what the Enochian writing said. Faith. Karen has so much faith. I know something of a spiritual nature is happening to me. I just don't know what. I wish I could be like Karen and simply have faith that everything will be okay.

Catherine's own faith was locked away, somewhere inside her childhood memories. She lost all faith when her parents were taken away. Faith was not a relevant part of her life now.

She decided to boil some water. She reached for a large decorative tin in the cupboard. She popped off the top to reveal many different kinds of herbal and flavored teas.

"I'll drink some peppermint tea. That sounds good and may also settle my stomach."

Catherine remembered this fact from something her mother told her when she was little. She opened the bag and dropped it into a clean mug. After making her tea, Catherine sat.

After a moment of silence, her thoughts carried her far away as she tried hard to remember herself as a little girl.

It was hard at first because her parent's sudden death had caused her to lock it all away. Not just the bad had been pushed away though, but the good as well. This block had made most of her childhood disappear.

She did know that she was loved so much by her parents. This lessened the pain of the memories of other children making her the butt of their jokes. Except for one, her neighbor named Jacob. They had been inseparable as children, but strangely grew apart when she left Parsons after her parent's death. She had not thought of him for a very long time.

One memory led in a deluge to all the other memories she had suppressed. As they came back to her, the vibration in her body began and she felt a light breeze. Catherine could now remember clearly the time when she had been so loving and open and yes, vulnerable.

I did have faith once...

Early in her life, a wide-eyed Catherine had faith in everyone and everything. Then she started school. In kindergarten, she started to notice that she was significantly different from other children. Catherine frowned as she remembered that other children often made fun of her, and said cruel things to her.

Her Catholic school upbringing meant that she had attended Mass twice a week and every Sunday with her mom and dad. She had been completely captivated by the ornate statues in the church, especially those of Mary and Jesus.

Wow, I remember now. I wanted to be just like the Virgin Mary or my favorite saint. I forgot all about St. Francis! How could forget? And the song from church...what was it? Oh yeah, Make me a Channel of Your Peace.

A smile came over Catherine's face as she connected in her heart to the church she grew up in, St. Patrick's Catholic Church. The church itself was a sacred place to her and as a little girl she now remembered that she had believed that all the objects inside the church were holy and contained a real kind of magic.

To the younger Catherine, unseen spirits were as real as the physical things we can all see with our eyes. The church building often became her refuge.

Oh, the nuns were so mad at me the first time I snuck away to the church.

One day Catherine left the school building and went next door to the church without telling anyone. After someone noticed she was not accounted for, they looked high and low in the school for her. Just before they were going to contact the police, a nun from administration found her seated in the front pew of the church with her hands folded in prayer. Catherine recalled many times of feeling misunderstood by the nuns even though in her mind they were supposed to be married to God.

Boy, did they punish me for wandering off from school that day, but that didn't stop me from sneaking away to sit and talk with God whenever I wanted.

Her mother never gave her much grief about getting a call from the sisters at St. Patrick's reporting her strange behavior. With her mom, Catherine never felt abandoned or a lack of support.

Mom always knew I was different from other kids. She always made me feel so special.

Catherine's memories now flooded her with an overwhelming sadness. Her mom would be the one she'd want to call and ask for help.

If mom were alive, she'd be here right now and I'd be talking to her about all this. I could use her advice.

Catherine slowly came back from her mental haziness that had been filled by intense memories and thoughts. She was no longer in the living room. Catherine found herself seated at her desk in the bedroom.

It startled Catherine because she wasn't sure how long she'd been sitting there. She did not remember getting up from the couch or even leaving the living room.

How did I end up here? What did I do, sleep walk without being asleep?

This made Catherine's rational mind take over and feel concerned about something being wrong with her physically.

Maybe I should go see the doctor.

She started thinking about a movie that was released few years ago. It was about a man who suddenly had extraordinary mental and psychic abilities. Towards the end of the movie, you find out it was due to a brain tumor and not divine intervention.

Yeah my luck, I'm a goner and don't know it.

She decided to check her email and opened her Outlook.

I'll do some research to see what I can find out. I wonder if I can find that language.

At that moment Catherine thought about her encounter with Joshua.

What did he mean about knowing who I really am? I wish I knew the answer to that question. I must figure out what is happening to me. I'm so glad Karen could help me today. She was right, and healing is what I need to do. Is that what all this craziness is about?

Catherine hit Send and Receive, and 8 messages downloaded. There were several offers she really didn't care about, her encrypted bank statement and then an email from Erica. She read the subject line to Erica's email and smiled, Re: To light your way. She highlighted all the spam and hit delete with satisfaction.

Catherine realized, as she sifted through the information, that the Internet was much larger than she'd imagined. The first website had a number of links to other sites so she decided to follow a few at random. Following the first link in the directory led her to a website about angels.

Then she decided to search Enochian. What she initially found were some biblical references to a man named Enoch who was reportedly taken to heaven and made an angel by God.

"Interesting."

Then there were sites that had more information on angels. Some information explained the hierarchy of the realm of angels in great detail, offering definitions and angelic terms. She found this particular subject fascinating. She also wondered where people got all this specific information to put the website online.

Angels are beautiful, winged creatures who come from heaven. Sure enough.

As she studied more websites, she found a connection between Enoch and Seraphim Angels. Then she saw a link that said: *John Dee's* Enochian script. She clicked it and there were letters that she had seen twice now. She read further and it mentioned the work of John Dee and Edward Kelley and their communication with angels that lead to the Enochian script being created.

Catherine remembered how angels had been special to her as a child. Her mother had a collection of seraphim classic angel statues. She collected them until the year she died. They were beautiful and now Catherine was ashamed they had been packed away for so long.

She couldn't remember any specific angels in her mother's collection but they were hand painted and sculpted out of marble and resin. Her childhood home was filled with all types of angel portraits and statues, all compliments of her mother.

I remember wanting to fly when I was little. My parents and other adults would get a kick out of my determination to fly. I wonder how many times I bounced on that old couch trying to take flight?

Catherine yawned. It was already 9 p.m. She thought of Karen now and wondered how she was doing.

I'll give Erica a call in a few minutes to see how Karen is doing after she returned to see her at the hospital tonight.

She got up from the computer and grimaced.

I hate Mondays.

Catherine went to her kitchen to empty her dishwasher, thinking of the possibility she would have face Olivia again. But she couldn't remember if she was on her calendar for Monday or Tuesday.

Catherine had put away the last of the dishes, when the phone rang. She practically leapt for the phone thinking it might be Erica. No one was there. She put down the receiver and stared at it. Sometimes people try to call but get interrupted or disconnected, so she stood there expecting it to ring again.

After several minutes, she shrugged and walked back to her bedroom.

Must have been a wrong number....

It was about 9:30 p.m. now and she thought she'd slip on her pajamas since she realized that she had cooked and ate dinner, done Internet research and emptied her dishwasher all in her bathrobe.

She picked out her favorite light sweats and a grey tank top from her middle drawer and got dressed for bed. She grabbed her phone from the nightstand and lay down on her bed to give Erica a call at home. Visiting hours were over.

The phone rang nearly five times before her voicemail picked up. Catherine left a short message and hung up. She sat on her bed with a frown on her face. She stretched to put the phone on the hook. It nearly missed, and she fumbled twice before it landed.

Catherine suddenly felt very, very drained. Being practical, she decided that she should get some rest for her long day at work tomorrow. If Erica called her back, of course she'd wake up to talk with her. Catherine got up and walked over to her computer to turn it off. After brushing her teeth, Catherine climbed underneath her covers and fell fast asleep.

13– *Malum Tutela*

A thick dampness hung in the air, mixed with the smoke of the burning candles that illuminated every corner. In the center of the room was a heavy oak oval-shaped table with 12 chairs.

The craftsmanship of the set was spectacular to every minute detail. Ornate ivy spiraled around each table leg. It was clear that this piece of furniture was centuries old, and was worn from heavy use that simply added to its breathtaking beauty.

Scattered around the room were various antiques dating back more than a century. On the far wall stood an enormous stone fireplace that was almost grotesque with massive hand carved stones. It had been quite some time since it was used. The only modern touch to this room was a massive flat screened monitor that took up a major portion of the opposite wall.

Daniel entered the room with a stack of papers in his hand and busily laid information at each of the 12 positions on the table. The boy was dressed in all black, making him blend in with the shadows that were cast along the walls. It was difficult to make out his age in the twilight of the room, but he seemed younger than his formal attire might suggest.

He quickly pulled out each of the chairs as if preparing them for a meeting. Then as quickly as he had entered, he disappeared out of the door.

Shortly after this, a procession of hooded figures in long black cloaks entered the room. As if the seats were assigned, each person slowly took their positions around the table, standing behind their chairs. Last to take his place, at the head of the table was the 35-year-old Razoul Bugiardini.

Razoul was an ominous figure standing over six feet tall with broad shoulders. He surveyed the room, carefully eyeing the other members. His dark eyes burned fiercely as he took inventory of each man standing there with him. He swiftly removed his cloak revealing an expensively tailored black Italian suit. He was always impeccably dressed for any occasion and this meeting was no exception. His gaze and stance was more like a predator, rather that of his outer façade as a businessman.

All 12 men who stood there waiting for Razoul to be seated were rich and powerful in their own right. Their ages ranged from 35 to 75. They each had connections to some of the world's most influential families and had been carefully selected for their position on this council.

The Malum Tutela had survived as a clandestine society for more than two centuries. Their membership and activities had been well guarded since it was founded in 1810 in Venice, Italy by Razoul's great-great grandfather, Armian Bugiardini.

Venice was one of the few sanctuaries available during that time, where the society's members could operate without interference from the Church in Rome or inquisitors who sought to destroy anything pagan, occult or unnatural.

Leadership was handed down from generation to generation to the eldest son who was automatically indoctrinated into the practices of the order when he reached a mature age.

Armian Bugiardini was first of four original family bloodlines that had membership in the Malum Tutela. Armian's first pick for leadership was Antonio Moretti. Antonio had descended from a line of wealthy European merchants who brokered fine art and antiquities all over the globe.

Razoul was the oldest son from the Bugiardini bloodline. His father Britius had been first in command before him. The Moretti bloodline was carried forward by Razoul's second in command Thaddeus. Two other bloodlines, the Giordano and Bianchi families, had recently been lost with no heirs to continue with the work that was being done.

The group studied and kept the practice of occult alive in secrecy. It now possessed an archive of some of the oldest books in the world, second only to the Vatican on a vast range of occult and metaphysical topics. Many of its volumes had come from John Dee's personal library.

These men sought to use the powers of darkness for their own material gain. Their acquired information gave them great power to achieve whatever they wished. All members benefited greatly from the dark magic that was performed routinely in the group rites they performed. The society's true purpose was sworn to absolute secrecy from its inception. Breaking the code of silence was punishable by death, though it had been decades since this had to be enforced.

Razoul sat down with an air of authority and the others removed their cloaks to follow. "Brothers, thank you for coming at such an inconvenient time."

The others nodded their assent, though many reluctantly.

"As you know, the time of the prophecy is at hand. We must act quickly now. All that is currently known regarding the details of who we are looking for is on the sheet of paper right in front of you. I trust you will apply all of your available resources to this little problem."

He paused briefly, waiting for a response from the group. A grim expression spread across Razoul's face. "We shouldn't delay our efforts any longer. With each of us engaged against the enemy, we will prevail swiftly to rid ourselves of the abomination. I want all intelligence channeled directly to me here."

"This is not much to go on Razoul. Perhaps we should wait for more signs before we proceed."

"Surely, Sirius, someone of your standing doesn't mind a little challenge?" Razoul's voice came across far too cordial.

Sirius stiffened, "No. I never mind a challenge. However, I would like to point out that your father would have wished us to be better prepared before pursuing such a lofty endeavor."

Razoul moved fast and was within arm reach of Sirius before he practically spat his words on him. "Had my glorious father, as you just mentioned, not failed at his quest over 30 years ago, you might have more information than this."

There had been some tensions between elder members and Razoul, since he had assumed leadership following his father's mysterious death. Despite these issues, not one of them would ever think of crossing Razoul who was brash and unpredictable.

"My father failed to see the wisdom in taking decisive action. It was his ultimate weakness. This is why I'm alive and he's now dead." Razoul said too casually.

"Of course, Razoul, of course," Sirius placated him.

"Before we adjourn, there's just one little matter we should attend to."

A stench permeated the room only moments before a low, rumbling sound shook the legs of the table where they were seated. A form took shape in the furthest corner of the room. It began first as a shadow and then slowly turned into a hideous creature with long arms and deformed hands that now nearly rested on the floor.

The creature took a deep breath which made a rattling, hissing noise like a dying person inhaling for the very last time. Its long sharp teeth clinched together with a long, grating sound. Its skin was shiny and wet. Oozing superfluous matter dripped slowly to the floor. It stretched backwards and arched its back as if in great pain. The creature let out a half-choking shriek.

Razoul had summoned an ancient demon called a Belphegor who could grant wealth. This demon was well known to in Malem Tutela circles, having been summoned for the first time in 1825. Even with the rituals binding it, such a demon could easily kill them, if not carefully and appropriately appeased. There was always a cost for any transaction with a dark force such as a Belphegor.

"Wha-a-at do you want humans?" the demon hissed at the group.

"You know what we desire. Our current acquisitions in France aren't going to secure themselves. I need some hindrances out of the way right now, and you are going to help us."

The creature's gaze looked contemplative for a moment. It stretched out one of its long, bony fingers, pointing it at Razoul. "Perhaps I should just acquire you instead."

Razoul stood up quickly, his voice booming. "You'll do no such thing! How dare you speak to me that way! I own you and all the others who do my bidding."

The creature eyed Razoul hungrily but did not move. "I'll do as you say; however, you must first honor your part of the contract, pitiful human."

Razoul was visibly satisfied with himself. "Of course, of course." An evil grin spread across his face.

"Daniel!" Razoul clapped his hands to summon him.

Daniel opened the door quickly but kept his head slightly bowed. "Yes, sir?"

"Bring her in now."

Daniel disappeared for a moment and reappeared with a petite 14 year old girl. The girl was wearing a long white dress and her eyes were dazed. She simply stood there as if in a trance.

Razoul turned to the others. "This meeting is over. I trust you all know how to proceed." He looked at the others as they acknowledged his command.

Satisfied, Razoul grabbed his cloak in a sweeping motion and pushed passed the girl like she was of no consequence. He opened the door and disappeared out of the room. The others followed slowly, indifferent to what was about to happen. None ever even looked at the girl as they walked past, leaving her alone with the creature.

The heavy door slammed shut and the lock clicked.

The Belphegor looked at the tribute with predatory eyes, quite satisfied.

14- *Know Thyself*

Catherine was sitting at her desk staring at the plaque on her office wall. It read "Temet Nosce". The phrase was Latin, meaning, Know Thyself. It had been in her family for years after a young Catherine picked it up at a garage sale. She had kept it for herself and not packed it away with all her parents' other personal items.

Isn't it funny? We buy things sometimes and aren't sure why we chose to buy them. Then at some future date, like today, it makes perfect sense. Some would call that divine providence. If only I knew myself better, then maybe I'd be much closer to the truth. Exactly what truth I have no idea, but truth nonetheless.

It was about 7:40 on Monday morning. Catherine felt like a space case. She didn't recall any strange dreams the night before, but felt dazed and unfocused now. She was definitely not in her usual ready-for-work mode.

She got up and walked over to her office window. She studied the cathedral across the street, St. Mary's Church. In the three years since she took her position at DFS, she had not once set foot in St. Mary's for Mass.

While in school, Catherine had several part time jobs. Catherine didn't have to work to pay for college since her parents had left her a sizable trust of money, but she liked to stay busy. It was easier that way.

A family friend name Bob Anderson had offered to watch over the house in Parsons for her. Catherine thought of her parent's house now sitting there full of furniture and old things, just collecting dust.

Catherine's eyes returned to the colorful artwork of the stained glass windows on the church walls across the street.

I think it's about time for me to take a trip home. I should go very soon.

She shuddered at the thought of being in her parent's house all alone. She stepped away from her office window to get ready for her day. Despite the unpleasant experiences in Catholic school, Catherine remembered something that she truly loved, the bells ringing in the cathedral tower. It comforted her somehow.

I wonder what St. Mary's Cathedral looks like on the inside? Perhaps I should go for chapel service some day. I wonder if it's anything like St. Patrick's?

Catherine walked across her office and looked down the hall to see if Erica was at her desk yet. She wasn't. Catherine frowned.

I hope everything is okay. I'm starting to get worried. I didn't hear back from Erica last night. Oh my God, what if there was a change in Karen's condition?

Catherine thought about calling the hospital, but knew HIPAA regulations would keep them from telling her anything. Catherine had to jump through a lot more hoops nowadays to get information on her clients.

"Where is my schedule book?" Catherine got up and went to Barb's office assuming it was still in her office.

"Good Morning, Barb." Catherine came strolling into her office, as she looked up from the computer.

"Oh, it's great to see you, glad you are back."

Barb looked a bit bent out of shape over something.

"Is everything okay? " Catherine asked.

"Not really. It's just a typical Monday morning already and the day hasn't even started. Did you need anything?'

"Have you seen Erica come in the office this morning?"

"No, not yet. You know how she is about being in on time. She's probably parking her car right now and...." Before she could finish her sentence, the phone rang.

"This is Barb Johnson. How may I help you?" She listened intently.

It sounds like someone is calling in sick. Barb just loves that on a Monday.

Barb hung up the phone and said, "Erica is not going to be in today after all. She needed a personal day today for her mom."

Catherine got noticeably concerned when she heard Erica was not coming in.

What on earth is going on at the hospital?

"Are you okay?" Barb was staring at her expectantly when Catherine realized she was waiting for her to say something.

"Oh, yes, I am fine. I really just came in here to see if you had my schedule book."

Barb started to go through a stack of stuff until she produced it and handed it to Catherine.

"Thanks Barb. I'll let you get back to your Monday."

Catherine slowly walked back to her office. She didn't want to intrude on Erica, but felt she must know about Karen.

If she got worse, it is conceivable that Erica could be too busy or upset to call me right away. I don't want to miss an opportunity to see Karen if she's getting worse. I want to thank her again. What should I do?

Catherine quickly opened her schedule book.

Great! I don't have an appointment until 9:30. I don't think I can work or think straight until I find out. The hospital is only a few minutes away. I can run over there really quickly and check on her and then come right back.

Catherine grabbed her purse and keys and left the office. She quickly got to her car and drove to the hospital. It was about 8:15 when she got there. She headed right for the main elevators and went to the 4th floor. Karen was on the 4th floor, Room 445 East.

Catherine got off the elevators and walked briskly up the corridor to the East Wing. As she got closer to the room, she mentally prepared herself for what she might see.

I just need to see Karen, give Erica a big hug, and then I'll go. I will be back before anyone knows I was out of the office.

Nothing could have prepared her for what happened as she entered Room 445. No one was in the room. Karen was not in the bed. In fact the linens were fresh and there were no machines or monitors to be seen.

Standing in the empty room, Catherine's heart sank to the pit of her stomach.

She sat down in the same chair that she'd sat in less than a day before while speaking to Karen privately. When she thought she could hold back her tears, she went outside to the nurse's station, but everyone was rushing around so fast she didn't want to interrupt anyone.

Oh my God. I cannot believe she's gone. This cannot be happening. Not right now. I need Karen. I need her help.

She wandered downstairs and out to her car. Catherine just sat there for the longest time trying to figure out what she should do. She was so frustrated she didn't know whether to scream or cry.

She hit the steering wheel with both fists at the same time. Without meaning to she set off the horn. "What do you want from me? What kind of a God are you? What have I done to deserve such a life? Do I only deserve to be alone and in pain?"

Catherine stopped shouting for a moment, shocked back into reality again by a hard knock on her window. A man was standing outside her car door. For a moment, she didn't recognize him, but then finally realized that it was Tom, Erica's older brother. Catherine met him once at Christmas dinner last year. She quickly pressed the button to drop her window.

"Tom, what are you doing here?"

"Erica forgot a couple of mom's things at the hospital and sent me after them. I saw you sitting in your car looking distressed. I thought you may need some help."

"Oh, Tom, I'm fine." Tears began to fill the rims of her eyes. "I'm so sorry…" her voice trailed off. She became too choked up to speak.

"You don't look fine Catherine" Tom smiled, showing all his teeth.

Catherine looked at him, puzzled. "How did you get here so fast Tom? I thought you were at school?"

"Erica called me late last night and I drove up as fast as I could to get here. When I hit town, Erica asked me to swing by here."

"I am so sorry about your mom. I will miss her so much."

Tom's eyes widened, "Catherine, did someone tell you mom died? "

"No one told me she died. I was worried. Erica didn't come to work today. I hurried over here to check on Karen and the room was empty.

Tom looked at her compassionately, "Mom's not dead, Catherine."

"She's not? Oh, thank goodness." Catherine breathed a sigh of utter relief and wiped her cheeks.

"It's going to sound a bit strange, but Karen is at home with Erica. She was packing her things when Erica came back to the hospital yesterday. She insisted on going home, that she was well. So she's doing very well at the moment. I don't think the doctor's are too happy with her, but they drew her blood to run more tests and let her go."

"The doctors let her go home? How is that possible? When I saw her she looked worse than I'd ever seen her."

"I think Erica argued with her since she didn't think it was a good idea. But since when does mom ever listen?" Tom laughed lightly. "Karen told Erica that she thought her cancer was completely gone. Erica decided to have the nurse call the doctor."

"How could the cancer be gone so quickly? I've heard of remission cases but that's incredible." Catherine had never heard of a 24 hour recovery or remission either.

"Well the doctors still need to run a lot more tests to see if her cancer is completely gone. Mom is already convinced and wanted to leave the hospital last night. Her primary physician ordered quite a few blood tests. He was shocked that all her initial test results were within normal levels."

Tom looked excited. "The amazing part was that many of the tests were also done earlier that day and the results were completely different in the evening."

"I bet Erica is so happy. I can't wait to talk to her and Karen." Catherine was overwhelmed by her happiness. This morning had been intense, switching emotional gears so many times.

"I'll let Erica know I saw you in the parking lot. I know she will want to talk to you soon. Where should she reach you?"

"Tell her I'm at work if she has time to call me. Otherwise I'll call her after work."

"Alright Catherine, I will. Thanks for everything. See you later."

Catherine sat in her car, completely stunned.

Karen is not dead or going to die?

She watched Tom walk all the way across the parking lot and enter the hospital's main door.

I cannot believe that Karen got better within the past 24 hours. It is a real miracle. She said she was praying for one. I can't imagine anyone that deserves one more than her.

Catherine looked at her watch. It was already nine o'clock. She needed to get back to work before someone noticed she wasn't there and her appointment arrived.

Within 10 minutes, Catherine returned to the office without Barb knowing she had left.

Let's see, what pile should I tackle first?

Catherine looked at the various stacks of files and papers on her desk. She had no idea the amount of work that had been created for her while she was off. Her 9:30 appointment had gone smoothly without incident. She remained very busy with her case files and other paperwork for an hour and a half. It helped to pass the time.

Catherine stretched her hands above her head.

Time sure flies when you are having fun. Not.

She got up from her chair and walked across to look out her office window. From this angle, she could see the stairs that lead up to the cathedral entrance. She noticed a pair of large wooden doors that held out the weather. A young couple walked up the stairs as she watched. An elderly woman wearing a blue hat was slowly ascending as well, walking several steps behind them.

Why are people going into the church on a Monday? Oh yeah, a Monday chapel service.

The wheels in Catherine's head started turning. For the first time since all the strange events started happening, she had a solid idea of who could possibly help her.

Maybe a priest would know something or be able to help me? Or think I am plain crazy.

Catherine tapped her index finger on the glass. It had been many years since she had set foot inside a church, but she wanted answers to whatever was happening to her.

15- *The Cathedral*

One, two, three go!

Catherine stood in front of the cathedral and stared up at the large, wooden doors.

One, two, three go! Come on Catherine move your butt.

Catherine slowly started up the 20 or so stairs to the cathedral doors. Her heart started pounding. She tried to make it stop but she couldn't.

What am I going to say? What am I doing? This is just crazy. What could a priest know about the Enochian script, my dreams, or these mysterious notes? Maybe nothing. Maybe everything. I have to try. Get a grip, Catherine! Just walk.

The door was heavier than she had anticipated. It closed behind her with a thud that echoed throughout the high arched eaves of the vaulted ceiling. She stopped in the entryway before going inside. Catherine had learned a bit about the church from a co-worker that she talked to her during lunch one day a couple months before. She tried to recall those details as she studied the interior.

The church was erected in 1870. The building style was transitional Norman which was influenced by cathedral construction practices in Europe. The building architecture was a breathtaking mixture of ornate stonework and heavy, wooden rafters above the dark oak pews.

Wow, it's amazing in here. I wish my heart would stop pounding though.

Her eyes fixated on the main altar which graced the center with a smaller altar to the right that was partially obscured from her vantage point. To the left of the main altar was a baptismal font. That was a shape that was easy to recognize from her childhood memories. Above the main altar's archway was a large piece of wrought iron lattice that stretched across its entire width. They had a soup kitchen that fed area homeless each and every day at noon.

Her racing thoughts were shattered by a voice nearby.

"Welcome to St. Mary's. May I help you?"

Catherine turned to see a middle aged priest with a smile on his face. She composed herself and tried to smile. "I'm here for chapel service, Father."

She felt her throat tighten. She wasn't even sure if she could remember all the Mass anymore, as it had been years since she had attended church. Catherine was really afraid of being embarrassed.

"Ah, well you are just in time. Father Peter will be conducting the chapel service at our side altar in just a few moments. I'm Father John." He reached out to take her hand and shake it, but Catherine avoided it.

"The service isn't conducted right here?" Catherine pointed to the main area of pews.

"Oh, no. Fewer parishioners come for Monday chapel service compared to Sunday, so we have it at our smaller altar." He motioned to the far right of the cathedral.

"Okay, thank you. It's very nice to meet you Father."

Catherine walked into the church. Her fingers instinctively dipped themselves into the vessel of holy water. She touched her forehead quickly, crossed her hand to the left and then the right.

Some things never leave you once you do them enough. I'd like a buck for every time I did the Sign of the Cross while I was in Catholic school.

Catherine walked down the empty aisle between the central area of pews and to the far right side of the cathedral. She made her way to the altar. Her legs felt weak as she noticed that no one else was there waiting.

Oh God, I don't want to participate in Mass all alone. Where are the others?

Catherine turned around trying to find the young couple or the old woman she had seen from her office window.

I should turn around right now and get out of here. What was I thinking? This is no place for me anymore. Since no one's here I can slip out quickly and go back to work.

Catherine turned to walk back the way she came. A voice echoed behind her.

"Hello?"

Catherine stopped in her tracks and turned around. Another priest had seen her leaving. She had turned around just as he had walked out from the Sacristy to get ready for Mass. He was in khaki slacks and looked very young. Catherine stood there motionless. The priest had crystal blue eyes that transmitted kindness. It made her feel more at ease.

"Hello. My name is Catherine."

"I'm Father Peter. Are you here for chapel service?"

Oh great, now I'm stuck. I am a terrible liar. It must be a sin to lie to a priest!

"Yes, but I have never been here before. I guess I'm nervous. I didn't see anyone there so I thought I might be better to come back another time."

Father Peter's smile was infectious. "You don't have to come back another time." He intuitively sensed her fear. "I'm sure others will come shortly. I have a few regular parishioners that attend Monday chapel service like clockwork."

"It's been a long time Father. Something drew me here today."

"I see. Well, Catherine, I'm glad you came to St. Mary's."

Catherine looked around. "It's a beautiful church, Father. Different than the one I grew up with."

"This cathedral has quite a long history. It's also very different from the other churches I've been assigned to. And like you, I am a newcomer to this parish. I was assigned here only a couple of months ago."

Father Peter's eyes seemed to look straight through Catherine, which was startling.

Where have I seen him before? If he's new to the area I'm sure it's impossible that we've met before.

"Well I guess we are both new here." Catherine felt more at ease and smiled. "You look very familiar to me Father."

Father Peter almost looked pleased. He smiled. "Well, it must be a true miracle that brought you here then."

Catherine's eyes widened. "What do you mean?"

He touched her shoulder gently. "Oh, don't worry. That was a joke. I'm afraid that I often fail to get people to follow my sense of humor."

"Oh Father, I'm sorry. I get it now."

"I do hope you'll stay for Mass, Catherine. I must leave you now in order to prepare a few things."

The priest left her standing there collecting her thoughts.

Maybe this will be okay after all. I can't believe how suspicious I am. I think I can handle this now.

Catherine finished walking up the aisle and stepped up to the altar and selected a seat. By instinct she reached down to drop the kneeler in front of her. It was covered in red velvet. She knelt down putting her hands together and bowed her head.

I know it's been a long time, God, and you have probably given up on me by now.

Catherine looked up at the cross of Jesus behind the altar.

I need to ask for your help. I don't know what is happening to me. Help me to understand. I have no one to turn to.

Catherine felt a familiar rush of tingling sensation pass through her entire body. It was the feeling in her body that she commonly experienced as a child whenever she would pray. THAT was the familiar feeling she couldn't place last night.

It was always there when she was celebrating the Mass or talking to God. Catherine had all but forgotten this feeling from childhood. The sensation passed quickly. Tears welled up in her eyes and she let out a long sigh.

I haven't felt that in so long. Maybe God is actually listening.

Father Peter walked out in formal robes. He began arranging items on the altar. He turned to face the large gold crucifix that hung on the wall behind him. He held up his hands.

"In the name of the Father, the Son and the Holy Spirit. Amen."

The Mass was over in about 20 minutes. As the priest finished, Catherine was pleased with herself.

I can't believe I remembered it all. Maybe now I can ask Father Peter if he knows something that can help me.

Catherine sat down and patiently waited for Father Peter to come back out.

About 10 minutes later, Father Peter emerged again, without his robe. He started walking up the aisle.

"Father Peter?"

"I didn't know you were waiting for me Catherine. I'm sorry if I kept you waiting."

"I wondered if you had a moment to talk."

"Sure, I can for about 15 minutes. I have a meeting with a parishioner at that time. There's a bench outside where we can talk more privately. It's looking to be another beautiful day."

Father Peter led her outside to a well-kept garden. The paths were paved with smooth grey stones set in the ground. A variety of wildflowers and small shrubs framed the narrow walkways. Four wooden benches surrounded a large fountain in the center of garden. There was no one sitting on them and they both sat down.

"What can I help you with, Catherine?"

Catherine swallowed hard and looked down at her hands in her lap. "Well Father, I'm not sure where to begin." She paused and then continued, "Do you believe in spiritual gifts?"

"Spiritual gifts?"

"Yes, spiritual gifts like visions, healing powers, intuitions or dreams that come true."

"Well, Catherine, yes. The church believes that God grants some people gifts from the Holy Spirit."

"But do you believe that, Father?"

Father Peter studied her and said, "Of course I do."

Yes, but do they just suddenly appear one day?

"Have you ever known anyone who God had given gifts to?"

Father Peter smiled and nodded. "I have known some people in my life so far. Why do you ask?"

Catherine looked deeply into Father Peter's blue eyes. She was trying to see how to approach the subject or even where to start. For some reason Catherine felt she could trust the priest not to laugh at her. Still, she decided to proceed with some caution.

"Lately I've had some things happening in my life that I cannot explain. There have been some strange dreams." She paused for a moment. "There was also a strange encounter with a case I have at work where it was like I could see into a person's past. There's more than that, too."

"I think God communicates with each of us in different ways. If you have these gifts, Catherine, then there is a purpose. There is purpose in everything. Sometimes it can be difficult to find."

"Then you don't think I'm nuts?"

"No, Catherine. You seem to be a very sincere woman who is obviously searching for something. Why would I doubt you? I believe that God's grace can be given to anyone at anytime."

"I don't know Father. All this has happened so fast and now there's a person I know whose cancer is gone. Poof! It just disappeared. I don't know what to think of it. That's why I came today. I don't know for sure, but I may have done it. It sounds ridiculous even as I say it now. How can I heal cancer in someone? I can't even get my own act together."

"Just remember that God loves us just as we are Catherine. If God chose to give you these gifts then you are definitely worthy."

"Thank you, Father." Catherine felt a bit relieved to have told someone other than Erica. Still she wanted more answers.

"Do you know anything about Enochian script, Father?"

"Enochian script? No, but I know about Enoch. We learned about Enoch at seminary. There are several biblical references to Enoch. I remember him as related to Noah."

"Have you ever heard of a script or alphabet attributed to him?"

"An alphabet?"

"Yes." Catherine looked away from the priest's gaze for a moment. She caught sight of a beautiful stained glass window. It was about 10 feet high. It depicted an angel with wings outstretched. Glowing rays of light cascaded down to the earth below it.

Father Peter's voice broke her gaze from the window "Catherine?"

"I'm sorry, Father. I was just thinking." Catherine ran her hands through her hair.

"I have not heard of an Enochian script, but I do know that Enoch was attributed to a group of writings called the *Keys of Enoch*. These writings are not a part of the Bible though." Father Peter paused for a moment. "I have a friend who is considered a true scholar of various ancient writings who I could ask about it if you'd like me to."

"That would be great, Father. I can give you my office number in case you find out anything. I appreciate your help."

Catherine opened her purse to find one of her business cards. She handed it to him. Father Peter took out his wallet and tucked it inside.

"I see you were admiring the stained glass window over there. It's one of my favorites as well." He smiled.

You don't get much past this priest but I like him.

Catherine starred at the window again. "I don't think I've ever seen one like that. It's incredibly beautiful."

"It's Archangel Raphael shining healing light upon the world. Raphael has always been associated with healing powers. A benefactor of the church during the reconstruction in the 1920's donated it to the church, I believe."

"Do you believe in angels, Father?"

"Of course I do."

"I don't know if I ever had an opinion about it once I was an adult. I used to draw pictures of them as a little girl. I used to want to have wings and fly." Catherine looked down nervously at the stone walkway beneath her feet. "It would be nice to think that we are surrounded by God's messengers and we are not alone. It would be wonderful to know that angels are here helping us."

"There are many things in this world that are here even if we do not see them, Catherine. God's love is all around us if we are open to receive it." Father Peter looked at her with tremendous sincerity.

Catherine looked up at Father Peter unsure what to say next.

"I'm afraid I must go meet with my appointment now, Catherine. I don't feel like we've had much time for me to help you. Would you like to come back sometime this week?"

"No, Father. Just talking to you is helpful. I appreciate your time. Please let me know if you find out anything."

"I will Catherine. Will I be seeing you at chapel service next week?"

"I am not sure, but I'll try."

"Just remember you are welcome here at St. Mary's any time. If you ever need anyone to talk to, just call the rectory number. Anyone who answers the phone can find me at any time."

Father Peter got up from the bench. He looked at Catherine with true concern for her well-being. Catherine saw this and tried her best to smile to convince him she was fine.

"I hope to see you soon. Have a wonderful day." Father Peter started down the path towards the cathedral doors they had walked through to get to the garden.

The Keys of Enoch is a helpful place to start. Father Peter didn't know about the script but maybe this will help.

Catherine sighed and looked at her watch. It was 12:25.

It's time to head back to work. Perhaps I can call Erica to see what is going on with Karen.

Catherine got up from the wooden bench. She had a sudden compulsion to take a closer look at the window.

The stone paths in the church garden were cut geometrically with a square path in the center where she was now standing in front of the bench where she talked to Father Peter. She looked around hoping she wouldn't get in trouble for walking on the grass.

What a magnificent piece of artwork.

Below the window was a scroll with an engraving. "In Memory of Madeline Seraphina."

This must be the family that donated the window and the church patron that Father Peter mentioned.

Catherine studied the images and symbols with wonder. A closer look at the window revealed more individual details of the design. She nearly gasped when she saw what was etched on each side of the window. There were four symbols startlingly similar to those she'd seen on the paper and on her computer screen. It was Enochian, she was sure of it!

It really can't be! What is this doing on the window? Not that I know anything about any languages. Maybe I should write them down to check them once I find out what is going on.

Catherine fumbled in her purse for a pen and paper. She quickly jotted them all down starting with the top side and moving clockwise:

Catherine tucked the notebook and pen back into the side pocket of her purse without even looking down. Instinctively her hands reached out to touch the glass of the huge window. As she made contact with the glass, a jolt of energy quickly heated both of her palms. It felt like there were mild electrical shocks moving through them. She saw what appeared to be a light emanate from her hands and then her world went dark, but her senses were still wide awake.

Catherine felt weightless for several seconds. Her eyes flickered in the darkness and then suddenly she was in a room. The floor beneath her feet was tan stone. She turned 360 degrees around trying to figure out where she was.

Where is the garden? Where is the church?

Catherine tried to calm herself down.

It is happening again. I don't know what I'm going to do. Where is this place?

Catherine looked around the room she was in. There were four tall stone pillars. As she looked across the floor she noticed that there was a very large symbol approximately ten feet in diameter, carved into it. The stonework was very elaborate and Catherine was standing in the center of it.

There was a larger circle of 12 symbols on its outer edge. Inside the circle was complex symbol she didn't recognize. But within the larger symbol she saw a Star of David and a five pointed star.

After a few moments she felt a strange inner knowing. Then an answer unexpectedly popped into her head.

This is the Sigillum Dei Ameth. What? How did I know that?

Catherine stood there stunned.

I swear I've never seen this symbol before.

A noise echoed through the room, sounding like a huge door closing in the distance. Afraid of being discovered, she tried to move to hide herself behind one of the pillars.

Oh my God, I can't move!

She panicked because her feet would not move from the spot in the center of the star no matter how hard she tried. It was as if her feet were cemented to the floor. She could now hear low voices getting closer with each passing moment.

I have to get out of here.

Two robed figures walked into the room through one of two arched doorways. Catherine tried to explain herself, "I don't know where I am."

The two men failed to respond at all. They quietly began the process of lighting 12 tall white pillar candles that were seated on top of standing wrought iron candle holders that were spaced in regular intervals around the *Sigillum Dei Ameth*. A 13th candle was placed in the center circle nearly on top of her.

Catherine's heart was pounding as she watched them.

"Hello?" Catherine said this more like a shout than a simple greeting but nothing happened. Still unable to move, she began to panic. "How do I get out of this room? Someone help me, please."

Darkness closed around her and she fell to the ground.

16- *Emergence*

Michael was the first to discover her. He was taking a walk in the garden to enjoy the pleasant, sunny day. As he walked down the stone path in the direction of the wooden benches, he saw Catherine lying face down on the ground in front of the stained glass window.

Within minutes an ambulance arrived and transported Catherine to nearby St. Luke's Hospital.

The Emergency Room doctor ordered a variety of different medical tests to determine why Catherine had suddenly collapsed. After several hours, her vital signs remained stable. All her blood tests were within normal limits. But Catherine would not revive.

Doctors were simply baffled as to why Catherine had fainted or why she had remained unconscious for nearly twenty-four hours

When Erica tried to call Catherine Monday evening there was no answer. She assumed that Catherine was already in bed for the evening. The news about Catherine's hospitalization came as a complete shock when Erica called the office Tuesday morning to speak to Catherine. Since learning of Catherine's collapse at the cathedral, Erica and Karen had been at the hospital keeping watch over her.

"Thank God she listed Barb as an emergency contact in her wallet. Otherwise we would never have known."

"They said she could awaken at any time dear." Karen touched Erica's shoulder, trying to reassure her.

"Catherine. Catherine. Are you awake? Can you hear me?" Erica's face had several worry lines had appeared in her forehead

Erica stared at Catherine's face for any sign of movement.

Erica turned to hug her mother. "We're the only family she has, mom, and I want to be here for her."

Karen held Erica tight. "I know, dear. I know. We are doing all we can right now. I am sure that Catherine knows we are looking after her." Karen could always keep an optimistic viewpoint no matter what.

Erica broke her mothers' embrace. "I know, mom. It's so hard to play the waiting game. I keep thinking I should have insisted she see the doctor last week. She kept saying she was alright, and now this."

Karen could see that her daughter really needed some air, "Why don't we go get something to eat? We won't be gone long and you need a break dear." Karen urged her daughter to come with her.

"Okay, mom, I'll come. Let's make sure the nurse has my cell phone number in case something happens while we're gone."

Karen understood the stress about leaving Catherine alone. Karen's cancer treatment was stressful enough on her. Now Catherine was in the hospital due to a strange unknown cause.

I hope Catherine curing me doesn't have anything to do with all this. How awful that would be.

17- *Hidden Memory*

Catherine slowly awoke, still feeling pain in her head. She was lying on her stomach and moving her hands on a surface that she didn't recognize. It was soft but the texture was rough too. She spread her fingers wide and then grabbed what almost felt like grass in her fists. She immediately pushed herself to a seated position with her arms outstretched.

The pain began to fade. She looked around.

Where am I? What is this place? Another dream?

She looked around for someone expecting to see the radiant lady standing nearby, but no one was around. Her surroundings kept changing at intervals. It was almost like a virtual reality program that was loading new scenes every few minutes.

Catherine stood up. She was standing on a hill overlooking a small valley. She leaned over to pick a bright pink flower. After she pulled it up, it broke into a thousand individual particles that floated into the air like small butterflies.

What on earth is going on? I remember touching the window, then the strange chamber and then the pain. How did I end up here? How am I going to get out?

"Would you really like to leave already?" a young voice echoed behind her.

Catherine spun around quickly. She was not sure who she expected to see, but she was certainly not prepared for sight of a young girl standing in front of her.

She appeared to be eight or nine years old. The girl had long, dark, curly brown hair and beautiful large blue eyes. She was dressed in white, and she had a wreath of small pink flowers in her hair.

"Who are you?"

"I am a guide of sorts." The girl smiled wide not moving from where she was standing. She seemed excited to see Catherine.

"My guide? Where I am going?"

"I have something to show you."

"Is this a dream?" Catherine questioned.

"This is not a dream. This is the place that lies between. We know you have many questions. That is why I'm here. Some questions I can answer but there will be others I cannot."

"Who is this *we* you speak of?"

"I have many brothers and sisters."

"How did I get here?"

"A hidden memory has created a small opening in the ethers that brought you here. Your physical body didn't take the shock too well, but don't worry, you'll mend soon."

"I remember being in some sort of chamber after I touched the stained glass window. I remember a strange symbol on the floor that I somehow knew the name of." Catherine strained to remember other details, but her mind was blank. Then she continued, "What do you mean about my physical body? I feel a bit dizzy but fine."

The girl pointed into the air and a four paned window materialized 4 foot from the ground. After several seconds, Catherine walked over to it and looked through. When she saw herself she gasped.

"Is that me? I'm in a hospital bed! What is wrong with me? Am I dead? Is this heaven?"

The young girl stepped toward her and a deep breath spread through her whole body calming Catherine.

"No, no, you are not dead, Catherine. Trust me. Your physical body is fine. You are in the hospital because you are in a very deep sleep and cannot awaken yet. When we are finished here, you will return to your body."

"Oh God! I don't understand any of this. One moment I'm checking out a stained glass window, and then I wake up in Fantasia." Catherine looked around at the changing scenery and flippantly said, "Walt Disney would be proud."

"I know this is a lot to take in Catherine. As usual your humor is good." The girl took her hand again and Catherine let her hold it for a moment.

Then Catherine pulled away. "I want to know what is happening to me right now!"

"Please try to understand. I am not here to harm you in any way. In fact, I couldn't even if I wanted to."

Catherine stared at her perplexed. "Well, first I want to know who you are."

The girl giggled. "You should know the answer to that, Catherine. Besides I'm really here to help you. In order to do that, I have to show you something."

"But I don't know the answer, and you should know that!" Catherine was feeling faint and sat down on what appeared to be pink grass.

"I know this is hard, dear one." The girl walked over to Catherine and started rubbing the top of her head like a mother would to a child. "You do know me. But we can talk about that another time."

Catherine looked up gazing directly into the girl's strange blue eyes. She knew instinctively that the girl wasn't there to harm her so she tried to relax.

"Well, what do you need to show me?"

The girl seemed pleased. "OK, then. Please close your eyes."

Catherine closed her eyes.

A humming vibration moved through her body starting from her feet, spreading eventually to the top of her head. She felt light as a feather. It was an exhilarating feeling like she was floating up into the sky.

****

It was Day 2 of Catherine's unconscious state. Karen spent the entire day at Catherine's bedside while Erica was at work. Karen was growing more concerned about Catherine's well-being as she had not seen her move once.

Karen passed the time reading magazine articles aloud. She had heard that people who were in a coma could still hear what was said around them so she tried to talk a lot in hope it would help. Karen fully believed that Catherine was the one responsible for her overnight recovery, but had not told anyone but her daughter. The doctor's called it remission, but Karen called it a miracle.

"Things are fine at work Catherine, so don't you worry. I know everyone misses you a lot. I hope you wake up soon. I haven't had the chance to properly thank you for what you did. I know you have a hard time believing me when I say this, but you are special."

Karen had seen something unique in Catherine's eyes that day when she came to visit her. Karen had a knack of recognizing the spiritual gifts in people. Grandmother Rose had called it *the shine* when God's gifts were given to someone. When Karen was just a child, Grandma Rose taught her many things about the special ability to see deep inside a person's heart and soul. She had told her she was a special girl with amazing gifts from God.

Now Karen recognized the same quality in Catherine from the first time Erica had brought her over to the house for dinner.

Usually those with the gift already knew they had it. Karen was somewhat puzzled about why Catherine didn't seem to know what she was given, especially when she obviously had strong healing ability running through her.

Ah well, she's pretty wounded from her parent's death, that would make you shut off the gift, at least for awhile.

Karen looked up at the clock; it was now 5:45 in the evening. Erica would be around shortly after finishing work. She looked up to the ceiling in joy and gratitude for her own life given back to her. She closed her eyes and prayed.

Heavenly Father, please watch over Catherine and bring her back safely from her sleep. Thank you for the many gifts you've already given me. Please, Lord, hear my prayers.

While saying her prayers, she felt a light breeze circulate in the room. Then it felt like a hand softly touched her left shoulder.

"Catherine?" Karen whispered.

Karen quickly opened her eyes and looked over her left shoulder.

"Is anyone there?"

****

"Open your eyes Catherine." The young girl instructed.

Catherine opened her eyes and looked around. They were about twenty yards from a large two story red brick building that, from where they were standing, looked like an old school or institution.

Long rectangular windows spread across the upper floor and underneath them were several large square windows on the ground floor. Long vines of ivy completely covered one of the outer walls.

They appeared to be standing in a courtyard. The trees and grass looked normal and real. Catherine reached out to touch the branch of an oak tree just to be certain. This in between place did not appear to follow natural rules, but this particular place was normal compared to where they had been.

Before Catherine could ask the girl where they were, a distinct sound pierced the silence.

A baby is crying?

Catherine ran toward the sound, paying no attention to where she was going. She nearly fell when going behind the building but managed to regain her balance. Once she rounded the corner, she spotted a large woven basket on the porch.

Catherine ran toward the porch and the crying baby. As she got closer she saw that the child was wrapped in a pink blanket with teddy bears printed on it. The basket was woven from a rope-like material. It cradled the baby well.

The baby stopped crying when Catherine came into full view her. Catherine was mesmerized. The baby remained quiet and looked directly at Catherine with intense eyes. Catherine questioned the girl who was now standing on the porch beside her.

"Whose child is this? Why did you bring me here?"

"We must step away now, and you'll see. Come on, Catherine, hurry."

The girl guided her to a safe distance away from the doorstep and the baby. The girl pointed toward the porch and whispered.

"Look there."

Catherine watched as the large wooden door opened. A nun in a full black and white habit stepped out of the doorway and discovered the baby. She called for other sisters who were presumably nearby.

Soon the porch was filled with black and white. One sister appeared to be in charge. Catherine recognized her.

I remember her. I know her somehow?

She picked up the basket and carried the baby inside. You could hear excitement and rapid discussion as the others followed her. Then the door closed with a heavy thud.

After the door closed, Catherine realized that the scene she just witnessed was like a brief scene in one of her dreams.

I remember that nun! But if this is the same place in my dream...

"I've seen this. This is from a dream."

"Your dreams tell you a lot about your past Catherine, if you pay close attention."

Catherine very quickly made the connection in her mind. "Was that baby me?"

"Yes."

"Who left me there?"

"We did."

"What do you mean?"

"We brought you to the sisters. So they would take care of you and so you would eventually be adopted by your parents, William and Doris."

"So who are my parents?"

"They are of course."

"That's not what I was asking about."

Catherine's heart pounded. She could feel her cheeks flush.

I cannot take much more of this stuff. I am going crazy. I know I am. How can any of this be real?

"You know you are not crazy, Catherine."

How did you know what I was thinking?

The girl smiled knowingly, "You can hear lots of things if you only listen."

"I was told that I was left at an orphanage when I was just a baby. My parents came and adopted me after I was left there. I have wondered who my birth parents are. But I was too afraid to look for them. I couldn't bear the thought of being rejected by them or finding that they were dead."

"You are starting to wake up Catherine. Everything you need to know will be revealed when the time is right. You will remember and soon see much more. You just need to have faith."

Catherine threw her arms up in the air. "Ah, so there's that word again: faith. How am I supposed to have faith? Besides, what if I don't want to see anything more? I want my life back the way it was before. I was nothing, really. I moved through my day unnoticed, did my job well and that was about it. Can I get off this runaway train? Please?" Catherine shot the girl a desperate look.

The girl returned a compassionate look of understanding. "Oh Catherine, it will be alright. You are much stronger than you realize. I am sorry. I know this is hard for you. Given the circumstances it is normal for you to feel this way. It is hard for anyone born in the human world to see the real truth inside them. Even more so for you! I know this situation is requiring you to put this together very quickly, but this is just how you wanted it. You'll have to trust me on that." The girl hugged her waist.

Catherine felt a huge surge of energy. The in between world that had been fashioned around her began to fade away again and she became aware that the girl's arms were no longer around her waist. She could not see anything and reached her arms out in front of her

"Little girl, are you still there?"

****

It was the 3rd day. Erica was sitting with Catherine before she had to go into work at eight that morning. Erica was contemplating the entire situation. The doctors told her that clinically there was nothing wrong with Catherine. She was frustrated and could tell that the doctors were rattled as well.

Leave it to Catherine to give these guys a hard time. Joke's over though, woman. How about waking up now?

"I wish you would wake up. I miss you so much. You have no idea what you do to help me each day. You are the best friend I've ever had. I know you are in there somewhere. Please come back."

What if she dies right here? My God, life has been so up and down!

Erica reached for Catherine's left hand, squeezed it gently, and started to cry.

A hand touched her on her left shoulder and she turned around, "Oh, hello, Father. It's Father Peter, right?"

"Yes. You must be Erica?"

"Yes, I am."

"I met your mother yesterday. She is a lovely woman. Are you alright? Is there anything I can do for you?"

Erica wiped her eyes with her hands and stood up. "Oh thank you. I am holding up alright I guess. It's been a long few days."

"I'm sure it has. Try to keep hope, Erica. We never know the plan God has for us."

"Well Father, it's difficult to understand the plan, especially when life makes no sense."

"Yes that is true. I guess some things are simply a matter of faith." Father Peter walked over to Catherine's bedside. "Has there been any change since yesterday?"

Erica walked over to the other side of the bed to answer him. "No, nothing. No one has seen her move even one little bit. I think the doctors are frustrated too. You ask them a question and they keep talking, but they aren't really saying anything. I figure they don't have a clue."

Father Peter looked down at Catherine lying there, and then turned back to Erica. "I was with her only a few minutes before she fainted. We were talking on the garden bench for about 20 minutes. I was so shocked when Father Michael discovered her on the ground. She was a bit anxious about a few things she shared with me, but not ill. She didn't even look pale. When I heard she had not awakened yet I was even more concerned about her. Of course, that's why I came out here yesterday."

"I wondered why she was at St. Mary's."

"Catherine and I spoke for the first time just before our Monday chapel mass. Then afterwards she asked to speak to me. She was troubled by a few things going on in her life and needed to talk. I was hoping to see her again."

Erica went to speak but thought she saw, out of the corner of her eye, Catherine move her head. "Did you see that? I think she just moved her head!" Erica grabbed Catherine's hand.

"Catherine?" As Erica said her name, Catherine's eyes opened and looked straight up at the ceiling without appearing to focus on anyone.

"Her eyes are open! Go get the nurse Father. Please!"

Father Peter rushed out of the room.

"Catherine. Oh my goodness you scared the crap out of me."

Catherine's eyes followed the sound of Erica's voice and then looked directly at her.

"Do you know who I am?"

Catherine nodded weakly.

Catherine's nurse Amanda came rushing into Catherine's room to see what was going on.

"Catherine, can you look at me?" The nurse took a pen light from her scrub top pocket and asked Catherine to follow the light with her eyes. Catherine followed her instructions perfectly. "Her pupils are dilating normally, that's a good sign."

Catherine looked confused.

"You are in the hospital. You fainted while at St. Mary's and were brought to St. Luke's Hospital. "You've been here for several days now."

Catherine grimaced, wrinkling her forehead. She looked away from them for a moment as if she was processing the situation.

Am I really here in this hospital bed? The girl said I'd come back so I must really be here.

"Catherine. Catherine. Stay with me, honey."

Catherine focused again on her nurse.

"Can you squeeze my hand?"

Catherine thought about it for a moment. She felt so weak but tried. She was able to squeeze the nurse's hand but only slightly with her index finger and thumb.

"Very good. You may not be able to make large movements right away and that's okay. When you lay in a bed not moving like you have, you lose a bit of muscle coordination. That will come back gradually, so don't you worry."

Erica leaned over her bed, "You gave us all quite a scare Catherine, but you are back now and that's all that matters." Tears started to fill Erica's eyes, and she quickly wiped them away.

"Very good Catherine. I'm going to leave you with your friends here for a bit. I will be right back. I will inform the doctor that you are awake. I need to find out what he'd like us to do. Welcome back to us, dear." The nurse smiled at her and left the room.

Catherine closed her eyes, it was hard for them to adjust to the light in the room, and she felt so dizzy.

Wow, my head hurts. Who was that girl supposed to be? She never answered my question about that.

Catherine spoke so softly that Erica had to lean in to hear her. She was repeating the same thing over and over again.

"Home. Home. I need to go home."

18- *Homeward Bound*

Doctors released Catherine 24 hours after she had emerged from the coma. She told no one about the cathedral window or the mysterious things she had seen while unconscious.

Part of her still felt as though she was now in a waking dream, and that the countless conversations in the past couple days with Karen and Erica seemed a little surreal.

Karen and Erica had both offered for Catherine to come stay with them considering everything that had happened, but she refused, promising to call if she needed anything. Her life felt strange and distant as she turned the key in the lock and walked inside her apartment. She felt like she was stranded in some kind of limbo land.

Catherine dropped her keys on the entryway table without looking down and walked into her bedroom. Beams of sunlight spread across the room through the cracks in her blinds.

Well at least it's sunny outside. Such a beautiful day for a drive...

Catherine opened her closet door and rummaged in the back for her travel bag. In a flurry of activity, she packed it with essentials and left her apartment.

Perhaps a long drive will help. I cannot seem to clear my head.

She kept driving this way for over two hours. Then, it was as if the fog lifted from her head and without completely realizing it, she was headed home.

The journey to Parsons, Kansas was simply inevitable. She couldn't run from her past anymore. There were many things she didn't know about herself. It was hard to remember anything since that day when she had left, never looking back.

It had been years since she had driven down US Route 400 but there were landmarks she recognized right away.

I remember that big farmhouse. Oh, and I remember that giant red barn too. I wonder how much has changed since I left?

She tried not to think about what would happen when she arrived. But as she entered the outskirts, faint memories started to permeate her already taxed mind. C

Catherine had made a list of what she needed to do somewhere between the rest stops she'd made along the way. Organization made her feel in control. She pulled the list out of her pocket.

There were currently 2 items: Contact Bob Anderson to get the house keys and inquire at the convent about her adoption

"Hopefully I can get a hold of Bob as soon as I arrive. I am so stupid for misplacing his number!"

Catherine sighed, "Home sweet home," as she passed the city limits sign.

Now to get a telephone book.

The town didn't look much different, and it surprised Catherine how easy it was to find Al's Hardware to ask for a phone book. She had hung out here with her dad many times but was not sure if Al would even know her now.

She pushed the door open and a loud bell clanged above her. She walked to the counter to ask. Al was no where around.

"May I borrow your phone book please?

The brown haired girl took out her left ear to hear what Catherine had said. "Huh?"

"A phone book? Can I borrow one?"

The girl paused chomping her gum. "Umm. I think there is one around here some place."

Catherine looked at her expectantly but the girl just stood there. Eventually she started digging under the counter and then found it.

"Here you go." The girl lazily let it drop to the counter.

Catherine quickly grabbed the book and started flipping through it. The girl put her other headphone back in.

Teenagers are really hard workers, I see. God I sound like my dad.

"Got it."

She walked away from the counter, flipped her cell phone open and dialed. It rang and a man answered.

"Hello."

"Hey there Bob. It's Catherine."

"Catherine? Is it really you?"

Catherine could hear the disbelief in his voice and felt somewhat guilty. It had been so long since she had spoken to him. She sighed. "Yeah Bob, it's me. I am sure this is a huge surprise for you."

"It's so good to hear your voice. What can I do for you honey? Are you checking on the house?"

"I'm not checking on the house exactly. I'm already here in town, Bob, and need to get the keys from you."

Silence on the other line.

Catherine cleared her throat. "Umm, Bob?"

"Oh sorry, Cat", Bob stammered. "Yes I guess you did surprise me. I'm just so glad you are back that's all. Sure I can get you the keys. Want to meet me there?"

"Are you sure that's no trouble?"

"Oh no. No trouble at all. I wasn't doing anything anyway."

"Okay Bob. See you in five." Catherine hung up her cell phone.

Her childhood home was so close now and the old panic was returning.

I'm shaking all over. I know I can do this. I just know it I have to find out what is going on.

Catherine's childhood home was located on Central Avenue. The home was two stories tall and made of unique grey stonework that had been carefully constructed to last forever. A long porch on the front was adorned with short stone pillars. These looked more like cut stone than the overall stones used for the walls. The porch and stairs were wood and cement and more modern.

In better days the driveway had always been lined with beautiful lilies and irises, plus whatever else her mother wanted to throw in. All the spring color contrasted beautifully with the grey house. It was a wonderful place to live when Catherine was a child.

Enormously tall maple trees towered above. In the back of the house her father had architected an elaborate garden. It had pebble walkways with winding paths that Catherine had spent many hours walking on when she was little.

Inside, the house was filled with oak wood floors and custom trim with little angels carved in it. A hardwood staircase ascended to the upstairs directly from the doorway as you entered the house. To the left was the living room, followed by the dining room, and at last the kitchen. There were four bedrooms, one on the ground floor and three upstairs.

It wasn't long at all before Catherine was pulling in the driveway.

Well here I am. I can't believe I'm here. But I remember the house being much larger.

She pulled down the driveway and found Bob already waiting for her in his old blue pickup. Catherine smiled as she got out of her car.

Well some things never change.

"Hello Bob. I'm so glad to see you."

Catherine walked over to shake his hand.

"Oh honey, we've all missed you so much. And since when have we been so formal? Has the big city taken all the hugs out of you?" Bob hugged her tightly as if willing her to stay there forever.

Catherine let go of her guard and gave Bob a big hug back.

Damn it, Catherine. This is family. Chill out.

"I was beginning to think that you'd never come back, dear, but the wife and I sure prayed you would. This old house being vacant seems a darn shame." Bob looked toward the house. Tears were slowly filling his wrinkled eyes.

Catherine looked around pretending not to notice. "How's Helen doing? It's been too long, I know."

"Ah, she's just as ornery as ever, let me tell you!"

"I am sure she keeps you in line, Bob. You are pretty ornery yourself, old man."

They both laughed as they returned to a familiar banter.

"You've done a great job keeping the place up. Thank you, Bob. It means a lot to me. I know my parents would be appreciative."

Bob composed himself and looked at her more causally. "How long are you staying, Cat?"

Catherine looked down, and then shot a weary glance at Bob. "I guess I have no idea. I'm not sure just yet. I wasn't exactly planning to drive down today."

Bob was never a person to pry so he didn't ask why. Catherine was grateful. "Helen will be so thrilled, you know. She just needs any small excuse to start cooking like a crazy woman. Pretty soon I will be up to my arms in cakes and cookies. You just watch." Bob winked.

"Of course you will have to come to dinner one of these nights? Well don't let me keep, you dear. You look tired."

"Catherine nodded, her mind already wandering to recent events. He handed the keys to her. Sensing she needed some space, he hugged her once more, got back into his truck and drove away.

Catherine walked up the driveway to the front walk, and looked to her left. The neighbor's house looked exactly the same as she remembered it. Then she thought of her childhood friend.

Jacob...

Catherine started to remember details from her childhood in the house and walked hesitantly up the porch stairs still staring at Jacob's house.

It's been so long now. I wonder if Jacob would even know me after all this time.

The key hit the lock and made a hesitant turn, the tumblers clicked and fell. Catherine walked inside. Her steps echoed in the empty entry way. She closed her eyes. Memories came flooding back, like pages in a magazine. Mom was in the kitchen to her left. Dad outside in the garage banging on something or other as he normally did. She opened her eyes now.

Catherine flipped on the light. She was exhausted already. As the sun was setting, it cast a light through the entry way window. She didn't have the strength to tour the house and decided to wait until tomorrow to really look around. She walked up the staircase to her old bedroom. She removed the dust cover from the bed and found some sheets in the hallway closet. Clumsily she fumbled with the sheets trying to make the bed up. She looked around the room.

Just as it was when I left. This is creepy, like going back in time.

Finally she finished making the bed. She laid down fully clothed and fell asleep fast. After an hour Catherine sat up in the bed, waking suddenly out of a dead sleep. Everything was dark but as her eyes focused she saw a light that was shining from the hallway.

Did I leave a light on?

She got up from her bed and walked toward the door. Down the long hallway she saw a bright light. Her feet stumbled forward. The light was coming from her parents' master bedroom. She entered the room with her hand at her forehead blocking the light's intensity. When her eyes adjusted, standing there were both of her parents.

Catherine stood transfixed in disbelief, wondering if she was still asleep. "Mom? Dad? But how are you here? I miss you so much." Catherine tried to run toward them but her feet would not move.

Her mother spoke, "Hello, sweetie. Don't be afraid. We are always here watching over you. You must listen carefully now. We may not be able to see you again. Catherine, you must discover your destiny on your own, but there are several things will need. You must find the one who remembers your arrival...you must...."

As Catherine tried to listen to her mother, her image faded a bit and returned. A growing darkness came into the room, like a cloud of thick smoke. Her mother's voice was drowned out by a loud thunderous roar. The sinister smoke filled the room until she could no longer see either of them.

"Mom! What is happening?"

Her mother was trying to speak to her, but Catherine couldn't understand what she was saying due to the loud noise. Catherine tried to take a breath but the acrid smoke quickly choked off her air supply. She gasped for air, choking. Then she felt as though something heavy was pressing down on her. Catherine collapsed, unconscious.

****

A sharp pain pierced through Catherine's head as her eyes opened. She blinked several times, slowly recognizing the area carpet in her parent's room that she was presently occupying. She was on the floor and it was already morning.

What am I doing? I slept on the floor? What happened?

She pushed herself up on her arms and rubbed her right temple. She was left with many questions. Catherine remembered seeing her mother, but then everything became hazy.

I remember my mom. I saw my mom! She was trying to tell me something. What? Dad was there too. Shit, I can't remember.

Frustrated and still a bit disoriented, she got up and went back to her room to find some clean clothes. Her whole body ached from sleeping on the floor where she had fallen. She was hurting all over, but she knew she would be fine. She struggled to remember what exactly her mother had said before she blacked out.

Nothing.

She rummaged through her suitcase, unwilling to put her clothes away. She still didn't know if she should stay or go. The real world, her life in the city, seemed so far away right now. Coming home was like being on mental overload. Catherine wandered down the hall, pausing for a few moments at her parent's bedroom door, still trying with futility to remember what happened.

She stood in the entryway in a daze which was suddenly interrupted by her ring tone. She opened her phone. "Catherine, Catherine, you there?"

"Yeah, I'm here."

"Where are you? I have already been to your apartment twice, once last night, and then again this morning. Are you okay?"

Catherine really wanted get off the phone, "Yes, I'm fine Erica." A short silence then Erica repeated her initial question. "You don't sound okay, what is going on?"

"I am in Parsons. I went home Erica. I had to figure some things out." There was a long pause as Catherine struggled with what to say. Erica had been Catherine's only real friend over the year she'd been at DFS. Yet, she wasn't exactly certain why she wanted to be her friend, since she didn't often open up. Regardless of how guarded she was, Erica remained as supportive as ever.

"So, how is your mother doing?" Catherine switched the subject which was a very comfortable habit of hers

"She's fine Catherine, really fine, in fact, way better than that. Of course she's not stopped talking about you since the day you visited her in the hospital. Doctors are saying she's in complete remission now, but when they aren't around, she's blessing you and saying that you cured her. Isn't that fantastic? Thank you, Catherine."

"I think your mom has a bit of an imagination. How could I have had anything to do with that?"

"Listen Catherine, we've known each other awhile now and I can't pretend to understand everything you are dealing with, but I know something major is happening. I just want to help you."

"How can you help me Erica? I have no idea what is wrong with me or what I'm even doing right now."

"The important thing is that you know you aren't alone right now, even if I know you'd rather have it that way. Please let me come to Parsons and help you sort this out. Mom will be fine and I've got plenty of leave from work."

Catherine thought for a moment but balked at the thought of involving Erica in what she felt was the longest neurotic split of her mind.

"Nah, Erica. I really am okay here. I just plan to check on my folk's house, see a few old friends and I'll be back on my way home on

Sunday." Catherine nearly convinced herself that the words she was speaking were true as they rolled off her tongue.

"Come on, Cat, this is me you're talking to. Let me get in my car and I'll be there in a few hours. At least I'd feel better." Even though Catherine's personality was the dominant one in the friendship, Erica could easily stand on her own two feet if necessary.

"Erica, this is something I need to do for some reason, by myself. I am not avoiding you or our friendship. I just need time." Catherine knew that Erica wouldn't push it after she said that.

"Alright, just promise me you will check in with me at least once a day so I know you are okay otherwise my mom will probably drive down there herself. Remember you were just in the hospital and I have a reason to be concerned as your best friend."

Catherine couldn't argue with Erica's reasoning, so she opted to agree with her. "Okay, I'll talk to you soon, dear."

"Okay, Catherine. Call me if you need anything."

Catherine closed her phone slowly. The click echoed into the room ahead of her. She scanned the room for any trace of what she thought happened last night and then walked back to her room to get her toiletries to put in the bathroom. She needed to clean up.

Shortly after getting washed up and dressed, Catherine was leaving her parents house. She looked down at the stone pathway her father had put in. She remembered playing hopscotch on the flag stones as a child. When she looked up to her right she saw Mrs. Petersen, Jacob's mom, on her front porch pulling dead leaves out of the stone planters.

Catherine stood there watching for a few moments before Mrs. Petersen looked up and saw her standing there. She squinted as if trying to figure out who was standing on the porch at the old Moore place. Then with a sudden burst of realization, she called out to her.

"Catherine? Catherine? Is that really you?"

Catherine nodded and started walking toward her and they met in the middle of the yard.

"Oh my God, child, I can't believe it's you. I never thought I'd see you here again, after you moved." Then her voice trailed off suddenly as she realized what she was about to say.

"Mrs. Petersen, it's so good to see you," Catherine said politely.

"Well, never mind why you are back. Please come inside for a cup of coffee."

Catherine had to admit a cup of coffee sounded good considering the throbbing sensations flooding both her temples, plus she was curious about Jacob.

"Sure, Mrs. Petersen, that would be great."

Jacob's mother put her arm around Catherine and led her toward the house saying, "Please call me Mary. Mrs. Petersen is far too formal for someone who's known you your whole life."

Catherine hung her jacket on the coat tree in the foyer, eagerly looking around to see the place where she'd spent countless hours as a child playing with Jacob. With the exception of a few newer items of furniture, everything seemed eerily in its usual place.

Catherine's head continued to pound so she sat down in an easy chair. She heard Mary clinking mugs together in the kitchen which was only a few feet away. "Do you take anything in your coffee?"

"No, Mary, thank you."

Mary returned and handed a mug to Catherine before she sat down on the couch across from her. Mary nervously brushed back the hair that was slipping out from where she'd pulled it back with a clip.

Catherine studied Mary's face. She seemed sad even when her face was smiling back at her.

"So, how have you been? I knew you were headed for Kansas City but hadn't really gotten much word since, and Bob over there was no help at all."

"Well, I'm not sure Bob could tell you much about me since I didn't stay in good contact with him. So how's Jacob these days?"

Mary's face saddened, and then with determination in her eyes she said, "I'm very sorry, Catherine, to have to tell that Jacob hasn't been well for years now."

"What do you mean, Mary?" Catherine tried to maintain some composure while speaking.

Mary got up from the couch and walked to the mantle to grab a framed photo of Jacob as a small boy. She touched his face through the glass. "I'm not sure where to begin. What do you remember before you left?"

Catherine thought hard about the time when she was leaving, but it was hard to get past some fuzziness about what happened prior to her departure. "Well, I remember he was going to attend art school, which was something I knew he would do so well with."

Mary nodded. "Do you remember the fight you and he had before you left?"

Catherine suddenly felt self-conscious and overwhelmed. Jacob was her best friend in the whole world back then but even that could not keep her in Parsons. She had told Jacob she had to get away from this place. He wanted to go with her, to be there for her, and she refused him. He was devastated. As she remembered this, tears formed in her eyes and she spoke softly. "He didn't want me to leave."

"Yes, he didn't, which was understandable. You were friends from the time you were toddlers, and inseparable most of your life."

"I know."

"You'd play house and school up in the attic for hours."

"I remember, Mary."

Catherine looked down, suddenly so ashamed for everything.

"When you left that day, he was upset, and he seemed okay at first. After a couple months passed, he started to act strangely. Little things, you know. He wouldn't leave the house for days and days. When he would, he'd leave without saying anything and come back with books of canvas paper and stay in his room for hours. It was just two weeks before he was supposed to leave for school in New York and he just came down to the kitchen like it was no big deal and announced he wasn't going."

Mary's hands were shaking as she took another sip of her coffee. "Frank and I were completely shocked. This was what he had always wanted. We tried to reason with him but he just said no. He wouldn't talk to either of us at all about his choice. We tried to encourage him. We told him he was meant for such big things, but he wasn't himself and wouldn't listen to anything we said."

Catherine reached out to touch Mary's hand for reassurance.

"I asked him to see someone about his problems, but he would only get angry with me and tell me to 'butt out of his life'. Eventually, he wouldn't even come down from his room at all. I tried to get him to eat something but he refused."

Catherine listened in utter shock.

"He even got angry at me when I wanted to see what he'd been drawing in his books but he wouldn't so much as let me peek at any of it. Then one day I found him in his bed, with his drawing tablet and all he would do is blankly stare. It was, like I wasn't even there." Mary got teary eyed and started to cry.

"Mary, I'm so sorry, I had no idea. I feel like all this is my fault somehow."

"No, it's not your fault, honey. It's not anyone's fault. The doctor's say he's got Bipolar Disorder, and you couldn't have caused that."

"Where is Jacob now?"

"He had to be taken to Park Hill Sanctuary, which is where he's been ever since. He lives there. At first the doctors were hopeful that after a rest that he'd come back to us. But so far, there's been no change in his condition at all. He doesn't want to leave that place and come home. He's told me so."

"Jacob has been there for more than eight years?" Catherine questioned her in disbelief.

"Yes," Mary said rubbing tears from her eyes. "I'm sorry Catherine, I didn't mean to get this emotional and upset you. I am so grateful to see you again."

Catherine was shattered by the news. She'd always envisioned Jacob in New York becoming the artist he had always wanted to be. He'd been so excited when he received the letter of acceptance. She had convinced herself that leaving was for the best for her and Jacob too. But now, none of that was real.

"I don't mean to put any pressure on you Catherine, but it would mean a lot to me and to Jacob if you could visit him while you are in town."

Catherine was deep in thought and nodded. "How is Frank?"

The look on Mary's face said it all, and Catherine felt terrible for asking. "He passed away three years ago from a heart attack. You know he was pretty high strung and go, go, go. That was my Frank. It's been so lonely in this big old house since he passed."

"I am so sorry, Mary. I didn't realize."

"It's fine now dear. There are just some things we don't have any control over in this life." Mary sighed heavily.

Catherine wanted to see Jacob's room but was conflicted because she didn't want to trouble or upset Mary anymore than she already had. Finally, she got up the courage to ask. "Is there any way I could see his room? I know it's a weird request."

"No, it's not weird request. I go in there from time to time to feel closer to him, so I understand. I haven't had the heart to change anything. I keep thinking maybe one day he'll be back and want all his things again. It's all still the way he left it."

"I'd like to go up by myself for a bit, if that is okay."

"Yes, honey. Take your time."

Catherine climbed the stairs leading up to the bedrooms with determined steps. She opened the door slowly and took a step in closing it behind her. The window shades were open and a soft warm light was cast around the room making it easy for her to see.

Out of sheer habit Catherine flopped down on his bed like she would have when they were teenagers. The walls were covered in Jacob's favorite artwork, photos, and other memorabilia that he had collected over the years. Her eyes finally rested on an 8 x 10 photo of her and Jacob stuck to the wall with what was now discolored scotch tape.

Catherine rose slowly and examined it more closely. The picture was really torn and faded. She smiled remembering fondly the day when it was taken. They were both 16. It was before she lost her parents.

She reached over to carefully peel it from the wall, using her fingernails. She held it balanced in her left palm studying the background, and then moved to put her right hand over it as if to savor the moment in time. Catherine closed her eyes.

A warm sensation formed in both her palms radiating from the photo. The feeling swiftly moved up both her arms to extend to the top of her head. Catherine wanted to drop the photo, but felt almost paralyzed. When she opened her eyes, the edges of the photo began to curl up and blacken as if it were spontaneously catching on fire. In a couple of seconds the entire photo went up in flames.

Catherine jumped back trying to get the photo out of her hand, but it had already vanished. The shock made her stumble backward onto Jacob's bed. Almost instantaneously she noticed that instead of a blank space where the photo was, it was there as if she'd never taken it off in the first place.

What the hell? Am I cursed?

Catherine couldn't contain her tears any longer.

I wish it was still back then, and Jacob was here, and everything would be ok. Now Jacob is locked away. And I'm going mad. This is all my fault. I should have checked on him. I was his best friend in the world.

She laid her head on Jacob's pillow, trying to breathe in a piece of her friend and let the fabric wipe away her tears. The pillow helped to muffle the sounds escaping from her lips as she sobbed. She feared Mary overhearing her from downstairs.

"Jacob, what is happening?" Catherine whispered as if she were talking with him now. "Why didn't you live your life?"

Jacob's canvas paper pads flashed in her mind. She rose from the bed to begin rummaging through piles of papers and books in his room but couldn't find any. Then she remembered that he often kept the oversized books she was looking for under his bed.

She knelt down and felt under the bed skirt. At first she didn't feel anything, and then she leaned further under the bed. "Gotcha."

Catherine pulled out a thick book of canvas paper and lifted it to the bed in front of her. The front cover was smudged with charcoal and pencil shavings. Both were favorite tools that Jacob loved to create his drawings with.

She carefully opened the cover with reverence for her friend.

On the first sheet, she saw various dates written and scattered symbols all over. These appeared to be written over a several months. The shocking thing was that the symbols looked very similar to the mysterious symbols that were on the letter left in her apartment, but she wasn't sure because something was a little different.

She flipped to the second page and was blown away.

Oh wow, it's me! This was around the time I left Parsons for good.

The detail was breathtaking. Catherine surveyed every line and stroke Jacob had made from memory. She had never seen something so beautiful. Her heart ached deeply.

How could I have left him when he saw me in such a beautiful way? I abandoned him, just like I felt my parents had abandoned me. How awful...but I didn't have a choice. I had to leave. That's no consolation.

The next page was a drawing of her dorm room at the University of Kansas when she first moved to Lawrence.

How did he? He never visited me at all...

How odd it was to see the room drawn so perfectly as if Jacob had sat there one day and drawn it for her.

Catherine got a cold chill as she was compelled to move to the next drawing and then the next. An image of her roommate was followed by one of the common area where she often studied. Some of the scenes included her in them and others did not.

How could Jacob have seen all this so clearly? Was our connection what made him go crazy? Oh, dear God...

The entire pad was full of images from Catherine's initial experiences at the university during her first few months. After flipping through a dozen or so drawings, the pages were blank.

I wonder if there are more drawing pads...

Catherine reached under the bed again but came up empty handed. She felt defeated and utterly alone. Jacob had seen the world through her eyes. They were more connected than she could have ever known.

19- *Sister Mary Eleanor*

The Sisters of Mercy Convent in Independence, Kansas was about a 30 minute drive from her childhood home. This gave Catherine plenty of time to review the recent whirlwind of events.

First there were those strange dreams, followed by the strange interaction with that homeless guy, then the incident with Olivia, the unusual paper and symbols, the vision or whatever that was at the cathedral, Karen's miraculous recovery, my parents trying to tell me something last night and of course, Jacob's incredible drawings. But what does it all mean?

Catherine sunk lower into the driver's seat. She had nothing to really go on and she felt as though she was losing her grip on reality with each mile marker she passed.

Maybe I should just resign myself to seeking professional help.

Catherine laughed out loud and started shaking her head. "There just has to be a rational explanation." Then she paused and asked, "Who I am I kidding?"

Everything in Catherine's life had been so black or white until now. All things had their proper place, a proper definition. Yet here she was, with a bunch of things that defied explanation, and no one to help her. The time flew by quickly and before she knew it, the convent lay up ahead.

Maybe I should have called first. Or what if they don't have anything for me? What if they can't or won't help me?

Catherine got out of the car and walked toward the office door, rang the bell and looked nervously at the ground. She had already walked through what she would say, during the drive.

The door opened. A younger nun in full habit greeted her. "Yes, may I help you?"

Catherine tried to calm herself. "Yes, my name is Catherine Moore. I am sorry for not calling ahead but I'm hoping you can help me. You see, I was brought as a baby to your convent, and I have some questions. My parents are gone and I have nowhere else to turn."

The sister got a huge smile on her face. "Ah, yes. I see. I've been expecting you all morning. Please come in."

Catherine looked at the nun utterly baffled as she followed her quietly into the room. "Sister Mary Eleanor told me last night to expect a visitor today, a young woman with blue eyes, who would be asking questions. She told me I was to greet you warmly and bring you to see her once you arrived."

"Sister Mary Eleanor?"

"Yes, and if there's anything I've learned during my time here, is that when she says something will occur it simply does. There are those that God grants such gifts to, you know."

Catherine was speechless.

"Please wait here for a moment. I will check to see if she's ready to receive you. I am sorry that I didn't introduce myself, I am Sister Elizabeth."

She cordially shook Catherine's hand and then disappeared. Catherine sat down on the chair provided. Her head was swimming and she felt as though she might faint but she gathered herself as Sister Elizabeth returned.

"She'll see you now. Follow me please."

As Catherine got up to follow, she had to concentrate on each step because she felt like she was floating. Sister Elizabeth led her to a small room that contained only a modest bunk, small altar, kneeler and a sitting chair near a window on the far side of the room. Seated there was an older woman that Catherine couldn't see well without moving in closer.

The young sister left them quickly, closing the door behind her. Catherine just stood there in her tracks. This was not at all what she expected. Instead of looking at adoption records, here she was in a nun's cell.

"Come, come closer child. Let me have a look at you." Her voice was kind and soft.

Catherine complied. Sister Mary Eleanor was a short woman who was at least in her nineties, with deeply etched grooves in her face. She seemed full of joy as she observed Catherine closely for the first time.

"Oh my gracious. There you are beautiful child. I have been waiting to see your face for so long now."

"I'm sorry Sister Mary Eleanor; I really don't know what you mean. Do you know me?"

"Come sit here next to me. I promise I won't bite." She motioned for Catherine to sit beside her on the edge of the nun's tiny bed. As Catherine sat down, her eyes were totally transfixed on the elderly nun.

"You've come with many questions, yes?"

"Yes, sister. But how did you know? Know I was coming?"

Sister Mary Eleanor sighed and said, "Poor dear, so many questions. So difficult for you, I'm certain. Where should I begin? Well my child, I was here the night you were brought to the Sisters of Mercy. I am the only one of us left now." The frail nun's eyes seemed to communicate grief or longing for her deceased sisters as she spoke, "Yet, here I have remained. Waiting for the day you'd return to us. Two days ago, I received a vision from God that the time had finally come." Then the nun's mind seemed to wander and she turned to Catherine, "You are such a beautiful girl, so special, so important to us all."

"Sister, if you were here that night, then please tell about where I came from?"

The nun's wrinkled eyes squinted for a moment as if she were remembering. Catherine could not help but be impatient, waiting for her to speak. "I am so glad I am still here to receive you. I was growing worried because my poor body is not long for this world, I'm afraid."

Catherine felt like she needed to keep her on task and said, "Sister please, the night I came?"

"Oh, yes, yes. I remember that very clearly. We had all come out of our evening prayer vigil. The day had been a dark, gloomy affair, raining all day long. A small group of us were making our way to the dining hall and as we were passing the front doorway, a flash of bright light startled the sisters. We all thought it was lightening. So we continued what we were doing and went along to supper."

Sister Mary Eleanor paused as if she were trying to remember, but after a few minutes Catherine cleared her throat on purpose which seemed to bring her out of her momentary lapse. She looked at Catherine directly and continued her story.

"Then, as I was returning from supper, I saw the light again, but I was by myself. This time the light stayed bright without fading. When I opened the door, I saw a beautiful woman. At first I thought it was the Blessed Virgin Mary like a vision of her divine presence. I gasped and dropped to my knees in the doorway. She was so beautiful, but I didn't want to stare at her. Soon I realized it was not the divine mother at all but an angel. She spoke to me without moving her lips. I could hear her in my mind clearly."

The elderly sister closed her eyes as if to remember each word and recite it perfectly.

"God has chosen you sister, to watch over the Child of Light. She has been brought here to fulfill a powerful destiny. Her life is a key and the key is life. Her earthly parents have been chosen. They will arrive in the future to love her and keep her safe. One day this child will return to you as a woman. She will be confused and fearful, so you must listen well and recall what I am about to say."

Sister Mary Eleanor reached out to hold Catherine's hand. Her grasp was so light, just like a child's touch.

"This is what the angel told me that I must share with you. Please listen carefully, child."

Catherine nodded and waited.

"The world of man will no doubt have harmed the Child of Light and her sorrow may be her greatest enemy. She must open her heart and mind to more than the world around her. Her journey will be a difficult one, but this is the only way. She must make the journey blind. She must see the light of herself in the world again. She must have faith in the days to follow. We are always with her, even when she can see nothing with her human eyes. She must remember that life will always be more than it appears to be, and when she is ready, we shall be permitted to speak to her directly."

Catherine could barely take in the words that were coming out of Sister Mary Eleanor's mouth. It was like a hazy dream now. She felt her head spin and she blinked trying to refocus the room. The nun sat there with her eyes still closed.

"Sister Mary? Are you okay?"

The nun's body jerked as if she had briefly fallen asleep. "Oh, yes child. Please do not worry about me. I am just older than my years and very tired." She smiled at Catherine.

Catherine's head felt like it could explode as thoughts and memories converged in her, but with no definition. She felt the urge to leave the room, despite her many questions, and let the old woman be. She didn't feel as though she could articulate her questions very well either, given her current state of mind.

"Thank you sister. I appreciate what you've told me today. Though I don't know what I think about what you are saying right now." Catherine rose to go, wavered a bit and then got her balance again. Before she could open the door, she heard the sister speak once more.

"You have nothing to fear child, especially from the Infinite One. You posses the most powerful love of all. But, heed this well: not all things in this world are a part of God's love, and there are forces I fear that would wish you harm. Trust your heart to guide you always."

There's no way any of this is true. No way that I was delivered by Angels to the front door. No, no, no!

"Thank you, sister. Thank you." Catherine spoke without turning to look at the woman again and exited quickly through the door.

Sister Mary Eleanor watched Catherine leave. She looked out of the window to the garden where she'd spent countless hours working to grow beautiful things while living her life in prayer and service. After a moment of appreciation for those memories, she unsteadily rose from her heavily worn chair and walked to the kneeler in front of her small altar.

"Heavenly Father. Your Love is my Love. Your Will is my Will. My Life is your Life

20- *Jacob's Window*

Jacob Dean Petersen stood silently, in the dead of night, looking out his bedroom window. Steel bars obscured his view of the grounds below him, but after 8 years, his eyes automatically filtered them out.

The chilly air in his room barely made an impression, as Jacob stood there barefoot gazing two stories below him. When Catherine had left Parsons, he had been devastated, but he thought he could handle it. He thought he could accept that he and she had separate paths to walk: he to New York to study at the Academy of Art and her to the University of Kansas to study psychology.

Within a week, however, things drastically changed. The headaches came on without warning, along with vivid images of places he'd never seen before. He thought he was going crazy, until the day came when he could see Catherine so clearly that he felt he could reach out and touch her. It didn't take long for him to discover that the only relief for him was to sketch whatever he saw in his mind, and that it was her life at the university he may be drawing.

At the beginning of this deluge of unexpected ability, he had wanted to call her, to tell her what was happening to him. He picked up the phone countless times, but found he couldn't dial her number. He didn't know what he would say to her. Plus, he knew if he were in trouble, she'd come back, and ultimately that would cause her sadness to return. So Jacob resolved to deal with whatever it was as best as he could.

No way was I going to be the reason she came back to all her pain.

Jacob had been right there with her after she had heard the news of her parents' death. He held her until his arms ached, and took to the task of cheering her up whenever humanly possible. She was stronger, but not by much, when she left.

She didn't need me calling her reporting impossible events to mess up her new life.

So he coped, or at least he thought so, until the waves of images started to consume him and he felt his grip from reality begin to fade away. He never had any warning of when the episodes would strike him, so he eventually stopped leaving the house, and then his room. As time went on, the darker his mood became, until all he wanted was for this link with her to be severed. He remembered his parents trying to talk to him about isolating himself in his room, and other questions about how he felt vaguely.

Where his memories became more clear was after he was taken to stay at Park Hill. The doctors had started some heavy medications which insured that his visions and drawing attacks stopped. It didn't take long for the long-term care facility to become his sanctuary. Eventually he could function better and the inexplicable voice and face of Catherine which had often appeared in his head like a freight train had all but faded away.

The entire place was silent except for staff walking the halls every 15 minutes or so. A week ago, he had been sitting on the bench as he often did for hours each day allowing his mind to wander on and on, when a flash of intense pain and light came over him, sending him reeling backward, grasping his head tightly in both hands.

The doctors called it a migraine, but he knew better. He knew that familiar pain all too well. He had walked back to his room understanding that the only relief was to draw. As his hands had feverishly drawn with a mind of their own, he had seen Catherine emerge from the blank page for the first time in many years. Recalling this, his face tightened into a grimace.

Why now? For years nothing and now it's as if it had never stopped. It means that she's coming soon, I know it. When I drew her again she was home. I know she's there now. How the hell do I know that?

Jacob's fists slammed down on the window sill out of frustration, sending a loud thud that echoed through the walls. He looked around.

Shit...best not wake the neighbors.

He slowly turned away from the window. He'd been in real trouble for days and he knew it. Five separate episodes now. The doctors had noticed a soar in his anxiety level, and given him something to calm down. It didn't work.

His night medication didn't help him fall asleep either. So night after night he stood watching out the window, half expecting to see an apparition of *her* before him. Anything would be better than the increasing uncertainty that plagued his mind.

Each night he recalled more and more of what he had tried to forget, events from childhood between Catherine and himself. The garden behind her house where they had played hide and seek or the countless forest paths they had explored together. His heart began to ache and he couldn't stop the flood of emotions that came thundering back.

Now he saw the big willow tree in his mind where he had secretly carved his initials with Catherine's inside a big heart. *JD + CJ FOREVER*. He was ten years old at the time.

Sure, sure, forever. I was such a stupid punk kid. Hell, I still believed in Santa Claus back then before the fairy tales in my head crashed and burned into oblivion.

Back then it seemed like Catherine and he would be together, forever. He loved her so much, like nothing he'd ever felt for anyone else. Like something he couldn't even grasp in his young mind. They were inseparable.

But now? What do I say to her when she comes?

Jacob's jaw tightened as he thought of her standing in front of him. Then a familiar ache began, at first in the back of his head and soon spreading to his temples.

Oh God!

Jacob grasped his head tightly to offset the building pressure but it did no good. He desperately searched the various piles of books in his room that had helped him pass the endless hours alone. He was searching for the canvas pad he needed in order to make the pain stop.

He grabbed the pad finally and sat on his bed. As if in a trance, he began to run his pencil back and forth across the sheet of paper. To someone who might be watching, it would appear at first as if he were just scribbling back and forth in the dark, but as if by magic, forms would soon appear and the image would be revealed. In just a few minutes, Jacob sat there, pencil in hand and the pad in his lap, and then just as quickly as it had started, the pencil stopped.

Jacob's head bowed and beads of sweat had formed on his forehead. Something twisted and turned in his stomach.

Why am I supposed to live in this hell...what punishment is this that I am victim now to the very thing I once loved?

He let the pencil in his hand fall to the floor. His eyes focused on the paper that was lit only by a street light that streamed through the window near his bed. Only one image appeared in the center of the shadowy drawing – a single, white cross with a halo of light above it.

What the...now that's unexpected. What does it mean? Catherine's not the religious type either. What does it mean?

Jacob clutched the edges of the canvas pad tightly. He envisioned Catherine now in his mind, her blue eyes dancing as she looked at him and her radiant smile crossing her face like a beam of light. He suddenly longed to see his friend, to go back in time and be with her. Like it was before...

No, I will not. I will not feel this for her. It's gone, over, done. Gone, over, done.

With that thought beginning to repeat over and over like a mantra, Jacob tried to rip up the canvas sheets and pad but the more he tried, the more frustrated and conflicted he became. Finally he threw the entire pad across the room and listened to it sliding across the tile floor.

21- *Safety Net*

When the office phone rang it startled Erica. It was only nine, but she was already daydreaming. To her credit, she picked it up without skipping a beat. After a year as the office receptionist, many of her tasks were now a second reflex.

"Division of Family Services, Erica speaking, how may I help you?"

As the caller went on about their situation, Erica was only semi-listening for key phrases that would allow her to identify who to route the call to. She had a habit of tapping her pen on the desk whenever she was multi-tasking or thinking too hard. Tap, tap, tap, tap, tap.

It's been almost 24 hours since I talked to Catherine. If I haven't heard from her this evening, I'll call her. She's my best friend but I wish she would just let me in more than every once in a while. I wonder how far it is to drive to Parsons?

Erica finally heard the key phrase she was waiting for, so her attention shifted back to the telephone call. "Okay, I am going to transfer you to Dave Carter in the records department. He should be able to help you get the information you need."

Erica hit the transfer button, then Dave's extension, and hung up the telephone. She looked at the clock and saw that it was only ten minutes since the last time she glanced.

This day is going to go so slow.

She stood up for a moment pretending to stretch her legs while looking around for Barb, but she was in her office with the door closed. Erica immediately sat down with purpose. She brought up her browser window and went to Google maps.

Erica didn't have the exact address of Catherine's parent's place but wanted to get a general idea of the location. She typed in the DFS address for starting location and then Parson, KS, for the destination.

In a few seconds, a map and directions were displayed for her. The website showed the trip took 3 hours and 25 minutes for a total of 156 miles. As she hit print, she heard Barb's office door open and her booming voice still in conversation, coming toward her desk. Erica closed the browser, just as Barb got to her cubicle. "Thank you for your time today, I really appreciate it."

"Oh, sure Barb, anytime. I appreciate your input as well."

Erica left the page on her printer and turned her head toward Barb making eye contact. She flashed Barb her usual bright smile, more as a distraction than anything. Barb was a big stickler on the personal use of the work computers.

"Hey Barb!"

"Hello. Have you talked to Catherine? Is there any new information from her doctors?"

Erica knew to cover for Catherine's unexpected trip. "I talked to her yesterday and she didn't have any new information yet. Some of the tests can take awhile I guess." Erica shrugged.

"Well I'm very worried about her. I know she doesn't take very good care of herself sometimes. She'll need a doctor's release you know. Can't take the chance of her getting hurt again here in the office."

"I'll let her know Barb."

Barb abruptly headed back to her office while she was still talking to Erica, which was a normal habit for her. "Tell Catherine to call me next time you speak with her so we can discuss her medical leave."

"Okay, Barb." Erica raised her voice to reach down the hall as Barb disappeared into her office.

Whew that was close. Now what was I doing? Oh yes, directions to Parsons. I think I need to go.

****

Catherine was exhausted. It had taken her nearly an hour to compose herself after meeting with the Sister, before she felt she could safely drive herself back home.

She slipped under the covers even though it was still light outside. She fell asleep moments after her head touched the pillow.

When Catherine's eyes fluttered open again she wasn't in her bed any longer. She was standing in a frozen meadow that stretched as far as she could see. Tall trees of various types encircled the meadow. Everything was covered in ice that sparkled whenever the light caught it.

Confused, she looked down at her bare feet, nearly covered in fresh snow. She was wearing a long white night gown that seemed to hang in the air and flow around her. The air was so frigid that she could easily see her breath linger in the air around her face.

It's so cold.

Catherine noticed that everything around her was vividly clear and crisp. This gave the scene an unearthly quality. A strong gust of wind tossed her hair and nightgown around, causing her to become suddenly aware of how she might freeze to death where she was. She started walking in search of somewhere to get out of the cold.

Up ahead of her she saw a dark cloud forming at the edge of the tree line, like an ominous black cloud of smoke that started to expand to fill the entire horizon. Catherine was suddenly afraid as the darkness moved toward her. She turned to run as the billowing blackness started to extend rapidly toward her.

Catherine stumbled over her own feet and plunged head long into the frozen surface. Her head reeled from the forceful impact of her body hitting the ground. She pushed herself up and got to her feet as quickly as she could.

She looked over her shoulder and the encroaching blackness was nearly on top of her. As she attempted to run again, the cloud engulfed her. Her lungs filled with what felt like fire and she gasped for air. Catherine fell to the ground with a thud. All she could hear was a thunderous roar all around her.

It felt as though her body was being pressed to the frozen ground and it was difficult to breathe, then everything went dark.

22- *Urgency*

Erica called Catherine several times on the way home from work, but it went straight to voicemail every time. She had an increasingly bad feeling about her friend right now that she just couldn't shake.

Normally she would drop by to see her mother on her way home from work, but lately Karen had been doing incredibly well. Now that her mom was settled back at home, she was spending more time with her friends from church. Tonight she was participating in choir practice, so Erica could go straight home and relax.

The entire day had passed very slowly, especially since she had watched the clock all day long. Erica had a hard time concentrating for some reason. Something just didn't feel right to her, even though it had been a typical day like any other.

****

Choir practice had been wonderful for Karen, as always. She was so grateful for being well enough to sing again. Everyone had shown her so much love and appreciation. She felt deeply loved by all her friends who were still in awe, as she was, that her cancer had miraculously disappeared after years of struggle.

Karen had not shared with them just how she'd been healed, mostly because she felt it was a sacred event and she didn't know how to honor it appropriately. The right words just didn't seem to come.

Plus, she didn't want to violate Catherine's privacy. The last thing she needed was people coming to her to be healed! Still they all thought it was a miracle and praised God.

Karen sat her purse down on the entry table as she came through her front door. Despite her new found stamina, she was very tired this evening. She walked into the bathroom to get changed into her night gown. After getting ready for bed, Karen walked into her bedroom and pulled back the covers. She knelt down to say a prayer as she usually did every evening.

"Thank you, God, for the blessings you have given me and the second chance to be a servant to others in your name. Please bless my wonderful daughter, Erica, who has been my strength when I had none of my own. Help her to find someone who loves her deeply and can give her the happiness she deserves."

She thought of Catherine and felt she was struggling. She felt a deep love for her as if she were here own daughter now.

"Please keep Catherine safe and guide her through her struggles. Please bless her with your presence and wisdom. Amen." Karen stood up, slid underneath her covers and turned out her light.

Soon Karen was asleep and already dreaming.

Now she found herself standing in a community park watching lots of children playing games. She looked to her left and saw her husband standing there, smiling. Her heart leapt at the sight of Martin, who had been dead now for over 6 years. He smiled at her as he always had when alive, with a special sparkle in his eyes. She often saw him in her dreams, just as he used to be.

Karen experienced a special moment looking at him for a few moments and then saw Martin's expression suddenly become very anxious, as he looked off to his left. People were yelling and running to the far edge of the park. She couldn't make out what they were saying. Martin began walking briskly toward the commotion. Karen followed close behind him.

She could see people gasping, others were shaking their heads, and others were looking away from the scene with horrified expressions on their faces.

Karen pushed through the crowd, unsure of what she would find. When she got past all the people she saw what appeared to be a large opening in the earth, about six feet in diameter. She looked around but didn't see Martin anywhere as she stepped closer.

Karen screamed when she saw why everyone was so shaken. Three feet down in the hole in a pile of dirt she saw a face which she immediately recognized. The rest of the woman's body was completely covered by earth.

She panicked and jumped into the hole trying help. Catherine's skin was cold to touch, almost frozen. Karen tried to get her out of the ground and began screaming for others to help her. As she uncovered Catherine's lifeless body, Karen held her close to her sobbing over and over again: "No, No, No."

The extreme nature of the trauma knocked Karen right out of the dream with a sudden jolt. She sat straight up in bed. Her cheeks were wet with tears and she was breathing heavily.

Karen sat there for a few moments, before fully waking up. She looked at the clock. It was six o'clock. She grabbed the phone to dial Erica's number. It rang a few times. A sleepy Erica answered.

"Hello? Uh, mom?"

"Erica."

"Mom, is that you?" Erica sat up in bed, turning to see the time. "What's wrong? Are you okay?"

Karen started crying as she thought of Catherine's cold body next to hers in that big hole in the ground. "Yes, yes...I'm fine," she managed to choke out through her flood of tears.

"You don't sound fine, mom. What is wrong?"

"It was a dream. I had a dream, a really bad dream about Catherine."

Erica tried to console her, "It was just a dream, mom. It will be okay. I am sure Catherine will be fine."

"She...she...was dead. All I could see was her face and she was cold, like ice and...and...she was buried in the dirt with only her face showing."

Erica's eyes widened and she understood why her mother was hysterical.

Something was wrong with Catherine! I knew it! I should have gone down there yesterday, damn.

"Mom calm down. I'll be right over, okay?"

"Okay, sweetie."

Erica shot out of bed and grabbed a pair of jeans and a t-shirt from her floor, dressing quickly as she moved through her apartment in a panic. Erica had moved closer to her mom's place about a year ago when she had become ill. This way she could be at Karen's doorstep in minutes if necessary.

Ten minutes later, Erica was ringing her mother's doorbell. Karen hugged her daughter immediately as she came through the door. "It was awful, just awful. It was so real. I have not been able to shake the images from my mind since I woke up."

Erica broke her mom's embrace. "I'm really worried now. Yesterday I couldn't shake the feeling Catherine was in trouble, but I tried to dismiss it. Now let's sit down, mom, so you can tell me all about it."

Karen nodded and they both went into the kitchen to sit at the table. Coffee was already brewing since Karen was trying to occupy herself until Erica arrived.

Erica motioned for her to sit and she grabbed a couple of coffee mugs from the cabinet for them. She poured the coffee, sat a mug in front of Karen and sat down to face her mom. "Okay, now, start from the beginning. Tell me everything and I'll share with you how I've been feeling too."

Karen took a deep breath and began. "Your father was there with me."

Erica nodded. She knew that her mother often dreamt of dad, most of the time doing mundane things around the house or taking her mom somewhere special. It helped her to dream about him occasionally, even if it was just in a dream. They had been together since they were teenagers.

"We were in the community park. I think it was the one that was by our old house when you were little. Kids were playing. Then the dream changed and people were shouting and running. Your father and I went to see what the problem was. There was a big hole and people were staring into it. Well, I went up there…to the edge…and…"

Karen's eyes immediately filled with tears and she grabbed her hand to comfort her. "Oh Erica, it was her. It was Catherine, laying there. She was covered with dirt, except for her face. I just wanted to get her out of there. Her skin was colder than ice. I couldn't get her all the way out. I wanted to save her, but she was already gone."

Karen grabbed a tissue from the box on the table. "Tell me, have you heard from Catherine? Is she okay?"

"No, mom. I haven't been able to reach her since I originally spoke to her, but Catherine's tough. I'm sure she's alright." Erica spoke with certainty, but wasn't feeling so certain now.

"I have a bad feeling in my bones, Erica, that she needs us. Something is terribly wrong. She's more fragile than I'd imagined."

"After everything that has happened, mom, I believe you. I can't understand it all but something big is going on and we are in the middle of it. I will try to call her again and if I can't reach her, I will drive down there myself to check on her. Especially after all she's done for us."

Karen smiled and nodded. "We are her family now, Erica. I know God wants us to look after her."

****

Catherine's head was pounding when she woke up the next morning. She was shivering, literally freezing. Her covers were at her feet. She grabbed them and curled up tight to get warm. She felt as though the life was nearly drained out of her and it hurt to move.

With the shades drawn, the room was mostly dark except for some sunlight that peeked through the slats intermittently and cast pinholes of light across the room. The clock at her bedside read seven thirty.

What...what day is it? Have I been asleep that long?

She was disoriented. After a minute to clear her head, Catherine tried to recall the dream, which actually made her body feel colder. A deep chill ran through her as she began to remember the dark cloud that had consumed her in the dream. A voice in her head kept saying over and over.

This is crazy. This is crazy. This is crazy.

She tried to sit up, but the pain in her head and extremities made her sink back down into her covers.

I wish mom and dad were here.

Tears welled up in her eyes. She still missed them so much.

Did they know? Did Sister Mary Eleanor give them the information? Was I the only one not to know I'm some type of special freak! Maybe they thought they had more time. Surely they wouldn't have kept me in the dark on purpose?

In her search for answers, Catherine had managed to create more confusion than clarity. She wanted to return to her neatly ordered life with everything in its place, but sadly knew that her life was never going to fit into the small box she had confined it to, ever again.

This saddened Catherine and she curled herself up more in the blankets because she was so tired. Once she hit the pillow, she closed her eyes. She didn't sleep but began to think about a moment she had not thought of in a very long time.

It had been a usual day for her, busy getting ready for her day before heading off to school. She showered, got dressed and headed downstairs to find her parents in the kitchen just like they were every day.

"Hey mom, what's for breakfast?"

Her mom was busy preparing this and that and turned to smile at her. "Well, what would you like? I'm making eggs and bacon for your father."

"I'm having what he's having." She motioned to her dad who was busy going through a stack of papers.

Catherine grabbed a glass and poured herself some orange juice before sitting down beside him. "What are you looking for, pop?" She leaned in for a better look.

William stopped what he was doing. "Well, there's an invoice I need but somehow have lost. I need to fax it to our accountant."

"Ah, boring stuff." Catherine smirked.

"Well, pretty soon darling, you will have to concern yourself with all the BORING stuff too." He grabbed her nose as he often did. Even though Catherine was 16, he still did things like stealing her nose like he did when she was much younger.

"Dad, stop that." She smacked his hand away laughing.

"Okay, whatever you say, little one." He went back to riffling through the stack of papers. Catherine shrugged and turned to her mom.

"So, mom, any idea if I can go to the lake this weekend with my friends? I promise that I can stay out of trouble."

Without even turning around her mom responded, "You will have to talk to your father about that." She was always differing to him about such decisions, but it never kept Catherine from trying.

"Come on dad, you know all the friends who are going. It's no big deal."

He stopped what he was doing to comment briefly, "You know I'm not going to give you an answer right now on my way out the door."

Catherine frowned. She had a feeling the answer was already no and didn't understand the way her parents were going about it.

"You're not going to let me, are you? Just like last time. You are both too protective. Everyone else's parents let them go. Why can't you let me?"

Suddenly not hungry anymore, Catherine jumped up and headed into the living room to get her purse and bag. She heard her mom call to her from the kitchen.

"What about your breakfast, young lady?"

Catherine was too upset to care, but answered feebly, "Not hungry mom, see you after school." She headed out the front door to get Jacob, slamming the door behind her.

Catherine was still shivering as she came back to the present moment.

How could I have known? I didn't even tell them goodbye that Sunday morning when I skipped church because I was still upset that they didn't let me go to the lake with my friends.

Tears flowed heavily. She could not stop them even if she tried. Through her tears she began to talk to herself out loud. "Why, were you such a stupid kid? God! How could you have treated them that way? It was so stupid to fight with them that way."

This motivated her to try to get out of bed, but her head was pounding. Standing on her feet was a no-go since the room began to spin as soon as her feet hit the floor. Defeated, Catherine she crawled slowly back into bed and under her covers to hide from the world.

****

"Hey Barb, this is Erica. I can't come into work today. I am sorry about this. It's for personal reasons. Please call me back if you need anything. Thanks."

She hung up her phone and got into her car. She quickly reviewed the directions that she had printed at work and headed out.

She was already nearly an hour into her trip before her mind wandered to recent events and also to what she was going to say to Catherine once she found her. She began to think more about their friendship.

Erica had started at the Division of Family Services nearly one year ago, and during the first couple of months she had spoken to Catherine only a few times. She was so absorbed in getting to know the day to day responsibilities of her new job that she hadn't gotten past the surface yet, which was difficult to do with Catherine anyway.

Erica had always had an almost obsessive drive to do anything as well as possible. Her mom always said when she was a child that she was *10 going on 40* and far too serious for her age. Wanting to be perfect caused her a lot of distress growing up and in school, and friendships were dreadfully few and far between. Most friendships ended badly and were one sided.

Once Erica really noticed Catherine at the office, she instantly admired her for many reasons. The way she carried herself into a room, the way she could instill calm during chaotic times, and then there was something unique about her, though she couldn't put her finger on it at the time.

Catherine was always busy, so even though Erica had worked up the courage to ask her to lunch sometime, it took nearly two weeks for her to actually do it. Catherine was bringing her some old case files to put into storage when Erica finally got the nerve to ask.

"Hey, Catherine. How are you today?"

"I'm doing okay. Can you please file these for me? They're inactive."

"Sure, thing. Umm, hey I was wondering if you'd like to go to lunch sometime this week?"

Catherine looked at her for a moment, with a perplexed look on her face as if she was searching for what to say. Erica wasn't sure what she was going to say next or if she was thinking of a way out of accepting her invitation.

"Oh, thanks. Sure. We'd have to plan a bit just to be sure the office is covered. You know how Barb is."

Erica nodded and smiled. She knew full well what Catherine meant.

Catherine smiled nervously then went back into work mode, "Well, I should get back to work, but I will look at my calendar for a good day and let you know."

Erica remembered on that day how cute it was that Catherine seemed so awkward in social situations, but so very assured when working with her cases.

Will she be mad I came down? Will she be happy to see me or shut the door in my face?

Erica nervously tapped her fingers on the steering wheel. "Geez, Erica. Just calm down and drive. Stop over analyzing everything." This particular tendency of hers was something that Erica had been working on to let go. She often talked herself out of things or got herself so confused that she couldn't make a decision to save her life.

Erica's bottom line reassured her: it's never wrong to care about people.

That's why I'm going to Parsons. I'm going to check on Catherine to make sure she's okay. I won't stay if she doesn't want me to.

"Besides, if she's okay and wants me to go back, I will just get back in my car and drive."

23- *Company*

Catherine's eyes fluttered for a moment and then opened completely to look around the room. For a split second, she swore she saw her mother standing in the bedroom doorway. By the time she propped up with her arms and focused, no one was there.

When did I go back to sleep?

She looked over at the clock. It was almost eleven now so she mustered enough strength to put her feet on the ground and slowly walk to the bathroom. Catherine studied her disheveled appearance in the mirror.

Her face was pale and her eyes had deep, dark circles underneath them. Catherine quickly pulled her hair back with an elastic tie and started washing her face vigorously to get some blood flow going. Still dizzy, she was patting her face dry with a hand towel when the doorbell rang echoing through the rooms.

Shit, who could that be? The last thing I need right now is company.

The bell rang again a few moments later as she stood motionless in the bathroom considering whether to answer.

Just go answer the door for Christ sakes!

Catherine navigated downstairs while steadying herself on the thick wooden banister. Her eyes squinted against the sunlight. There were two narrow panels of glass on either side of the door, but she couldn't tell who was waiting for her. As she hit the doorstop, she quickly peeked out the right side.

Standing there was a guy wearing blue jeans, tucked in polo shirt, and light-brown hiking boots with both hands shoved in his pockets. She sized him up for a moment.

Harmless, whoever he is.

In fact, he looked almost as uncomfortable as she was. Catherine unbolted the door which whooshed as it opened.

"Can I help you?"

For a long time, he stood there just staring at her. As their eyes met, he seemed very familiar. Their gaze locked for several minutes before he spoke at all.

"Hey there, umm, my dad thought you might need some help and he, uh, sent me over to check on you?"

Catherine was puzzled and it must have shown on her face. "Oh, my dad is Bob, by the way."

Catherine's faced changed.

Bob's son? I didn't know he had a son? But how did I not know that?

He looked about her age, maybe a bit older. Then he filled in the blanks for her.

"I'm sorry. I don't think we've met except for a couple of times when we were really young. My name is David."

He stretched out his arm to shake her hand and Catherine willingly accepted. "It's nice to meet you David." Then with an afterthought, "Maybe that's why you seem familiar. I was just trying to place your face."

His face lit up with a huge, yet nervous smile. "I'm sorry to bother you. You know how it goes. Dad was going on and on this morning about being neighborly and all. So, I decided to stop by to see if you needed anything. I've been visiting my folks for the last couple weeks."

David's heart was pounding in his chest, but he tried not to show it. He kept staring into her eyes and felt something so unusual it made him want to leave immediately, yet he couldn't seem to move from where he was standing.

Chill out and, just wait for her to talk. You always say the wrong thing when you are nervous.

"That's so nice of your dad. But really, I'm fine."

David looked at the deep circles under her eyes. "Are you sure? You look a little sick."

Great, David, tell her she's sick. Nice one.

"Well, I have been a little under the weather lately. I know I must look terrible right now, but I just woke up."

David blurted out, "Oh you look fine, great even, maybe just a little pale." He stopped himself and took a deep breath trying to make his next words come out better. "I mean, you are beautiful, even if you are under the weather."

I'm such an idiot.

Catherine was taken aback by his sudden compliment, but there was something very endearing about him. She was still trying recall meeting him before today. "Oh, thanks David. I probably need to hear that today." She feigned a smile.

David just stood there with a cheesy grin on his face and hands were still rooted in his pockets.

Okay, David, now say something not dumb, and get out of here.

Over David's shoulder Catherine saw a car coming down the driveway.

It's Erica! What is she doing here?

"Expecting company?" David turned to look at Catherine.

"Well, I wasn't, but that's my friend Erica from work."

"I guess your morning is just full of surprises."

"I suppose so."

My whole life right now is one big, fat surprise after another. Oh David, you don't even know the half of it and if you did, you'd think I was wacko. And poor Erica, worried about me. I should have called her back.

Catherine stepped outside next to David. She didn't know what to say to him, but she felt relieved to have Erica arriving as a buffer between them. Catherine didn't want to dwell on one specific thing for a single moment.

Erica stepped out of the car to see Catherine's relieved expression.

See, she did need me after all, you worry wort.

"Erica, hi. How did you find me?"

"Umm, by using my super-duper detective skills? Nah, actually I pulled up a map to Parsons and asked around for your family's house. Everyone here is pretty nice. It didn't take long to get pointed in the right direction, and viola`, here I am."

"I wasn't interrupting anything, was I?" Erica nudged her with her elbow. Catherine's eyes got wide.

"NO! I mean no. This is Bob's son. Bob is the family friend who takes care of the property for me. He was nice enough to send David this morning to check and see if I needed anything." Catherine looked at him and smiled.

David's heart started pounding again at the acknowledgment from Catherine.

What is happening to me? But, she's so beautiful...

"Well, I got to run. It was nice to meet you, Erica, and see you again, Catherine."

David finally pulled his hands out of his pockets and hopped off the porch, avoiding the stairs altogether. "Oh, yeah mom wanted me to invite you for dinner tonight around six. She would have killed me if I forgot to ask you."

Catherine didn't feel like being social, but felt like she should accept the invitation.

"Sure, if I can bring Erica along."

David smiled, "You probably know mom, the more the merrier." Then he turned and clumsily ran to his truck. Both, Erica and Catherine walked inside. David watched them as the door closed.

Why am I acting like this? Besides a woman like Catherine would never want to be with someone like me, so forget about it.

Still David could not escape the warmth and feeling moving through him of a deep connection to her. At least he'd see her later at dinner. Hopefully by then, he would have his head straightened out.

Once inside, Catherine was relieved to be out of the awkward situation with David.

Why had it been so strange between David and I?

Catherine turned to Erica with an apologetic look, "I am so sorry I didn't call you. It's been hard since I arrived, and so much has happened already. I'm not sure where to start."

"Well I am sorry for barging in on you without a heads up, but I was worried, and then I got a call from my mom at six o'clock this morning. She was upset because she had a bad dream about you."

Catherine walked into the dining room, pulled the blanket off the table, and sat down. "I'm actually glad you came, my friend. I am starting to not want to be alone."

24- *Monsignor Bartholomew*

Monsignor Bartholomew stared out his large picturesque bay window while he thought with great concern as to how they could help the young woman.

He had been educated as an early initiate into the sacred Order of the Essene to be ready to recognize the time of this important birth, this powerful awakening, this pivotal event that could transform the world into something truly divine.

The ancient Essene were an often misunderstood spiritual group, who for centuries had tracked the cycles of time, communicated with the Angels directly and from daybreak to dusk existed with gratitude for all things living. Initiates learned to communicate with various angelic beings throughout each 24 hour cycle and 7 day cycle. They had patiently watched the sands of the hourglass for centuries now. Rising and falling without fail, again and again. Monsignor sat down at his desk to reflect on his life and the fulfillment of the Great Prophecy.

There had only been one event that had threatened the pivotal secrecy of what was happening now with the Incarnate Angel. His sacred order had been very careful to take possession of the Angel Scroll that had been accidentally discovered in a cave in Jordan, many months after the original discovery of the Dead Sea Scrolls in Qumran. The scroll was the only item in the physical world that recorded the prophecy in detail. Father Mateus had seen to its safety over 30 years ago.

The Monsignor was one of a short list of Essene Brothers and Sisters in the world now. A small group, called The Guardians, was the lasting presence of the Order of the Essene that could be found in the modern world.

Bartholomew nervously arose from his great chair to walk toward a large picturesque bay window. He gazed at everything below him in the courtyard. He had been waiting for the call he received from the convent this week for over a year.

I must be very careful, for I may not break certain spiritual laws and reveal too much to her. First and foremost I am not permitted to alter the blessed one's human path and change the course of her destiny.

He thought now of the sweet Sister Eleanor who was among the dearest to the angels. Very few knew the actual name of this new human angel but Monsignor knew it by heart. She was destined to be the conduit for the holy ONE's grace and beauty to enter the world again.

She was the first of her kind born in human form, but unlike any other angel she was subject to free will. This would make her eventually the most powerful spiritual creature he'd ever seen with his own eyes, even if still she did not yet know who she was.

Before she fully awakens, she will be unusually frail. Her gradual awakening process will eventually expose her whereabouts to the Darkness. She must wake up in time!

Msgr. Bartholomew could feel the darkness coming for her even though the angels and the Essene had taken every precaution to mask her identity. While not interfering with her free will, they must protect her until she awakens to who she really is.

He turned from the window and looked around the room. His own library lay all around him. Portraits of various popes lined the stone walls. Each one of them represented an era of the Catholic Church in Rome all intersecting with this historic moment in time.

Monsignor saw the truth in only following the path to embody ultimate compassion and emulate God's love. The church around him only desired to follow the path of men. It had become a power unto itself over time. Yet, it had provided him the accessibility he needed in order to fulfill his mission and purpose for being in the world.

He knew that the Darkness would use any force it had available to stop her. Those filled with darkness themselves were likely suspects. He had heard rumors lately that somehow the Malum Tutela was actively searching for her and this troubled him beyond words.

Save the Child of Light. That's all that matters.

25- *Dinner*

"Can you please pass the mashed potatoes?"

"Sure, Bob." Catherine grinned and reached to get herself a large portion of potatoes from the ceramic bowl before passing it to him.

"Thanks again, Mrs. Anderson, for inviting Erica and I to dinner. We talked all afternoon, and I feel like I haven't eaten in a week."

"Oh please, dear, call me Helen. We're way beyond formalities like that."

"Of course, Helen, we are." Catherine smiled and went back to eating. She and Erica barely said anything for the next ten minutes or so, because they were too busy eating, although Catherine was quite aware of David sitting to her right.

Catherine felt lighter now than she had for a while. It was wonderful to have someone like Erica to open up to. It had been many years since her parents had died and she had shared much of her inner musings with anyone. Since that tragic event, she had thrust herself into her work, never looking back. As she filled her stomach now, it was as if she took a pause for the first time since her parents died to consider how their deaths had impacted her.

How long have I been like this? I have been so scared and so angry for a long time now. It's like I took a big time-out when I lost them both. I just couldn't bear it. The huge loss hit me like a ton of bricks. I remember not feeling like I could even breathe. How could I deal with that?

"Catherine? Catherine?" Helen's voice repeated.

Catherine felt like she was waking up from a very long dream. She shook her head. "What? Oh, I'm sorry. I was just thinking. You were saying?"

"I was just wondering how long you were staying. It's so nice to have you back. Bob and I have certainly missed you."

"I'm not sure right now. Originally I was coming down just for the weekend, but there's more here to do than I thought."

Helen could see that these years away had taken a toll on Catherine. She felt so sorry for her loss and didn't want to pry. "Well any time with you now is a real treat. We're here if you need anything or get lonely over there."

"Thanks, Helen. I appreciate that."

David turned to face Catherine. "I've heard so much about you from these two, Catherine, for such a long time. I was really looking forward to finally meeting you. Sorry I bothered you earlier. I am glad I didn't wake you."

Catherine looked into his eyes. They were quite striking. He had unusually long eyelashes, too.

Wish I could figure out where I know you from....

"It's nice to meet you too. So why didn't we hang out when we were younger? Or did we? Forgive me, you just seemed so familiar today, like we'd met before, but I can't remember any specifics."

"Well, we moved to Parsons when I was about eight, but mom said we didn't attend the same school. I think our folks became friends when dad went to work at the factory. I guess you had your friends, and I had mine."

"What friends? You spent every waking moment on that darn computer." Helen turned to Catherine. "I could barely get him to go outside anymore after they started selling those THINGS."

"Come on mom, those THINGS make me good money now, so stop complaining. She's been telling the same story since I was ten of course." He shot Helen a stern look and continued.

"Anyway as I was saying, before I was so rudely interrupted, shortly after that I got into computers and pretty much stayed in my room for hours blowing up motherboards and hard drives." He laughed.

Catherine started laughing at the exact moment David did, which caused them both to stop suddenly because they were totally in synch.

That was weird.

"So, well, I guess that explains how our families could be close but we never hung out."

Catherine studied David's face. He was looking at her intently, as if she were the only one in the room. She was self-conscious but could not look away.

"That's probably my fault. They couldn't pull my butt out of the basement to go do much." He shook his head. "I'm such a geek, I know."

Erica joined the conversation as if on cue, "Well I'm a geek too, so I think geeks are great. Of course I know if I started pulling computers apart, I'd blow them up too, but for all the wrong reasons!"

Everyone in the room laughed.

The conversation continued through various light-hearted topics like the weather and Helen's garden plans come spring until everyone had finished eating. Catherine's head started spinning again, for no reason. She felt like her blood was moving way too fast through her veins.

Maybe I am coming down with something.

"So can I get you some dessert, girls? I made my famous blue ribbon apple pie to celebrate your return to us, Catherine."

"Thanks, Helen, but I am suddenly not feeling well at all. Dinner was great, and I know I needed to eat something, but I think I'm going to have Erica take me back."

"Oh, honey, my, my. You do look pale. Why don't you do that and get some rest. My homemade apple pie can wait another day."

Before Catherine could get to her feet, David rose and was helping her up from her chair. "Let me walk you out, Catherine."

Catherine felt too weak to argue with him. Erica came around to take her other arm and they both helped her to the car. David's hand on her arm was unusually warm and sent a tingling sensation up and down her spine which actually helped her balance. She scowled.

I know we've met somewhere. Is he a part of all this too? No, he couldn't be.

Erica got in the driver's seat while David helped Catherine to the other door. "There you go, Catherine, just sit down carefully. I don't want you to fall or anything."

Catherine felt grateful for his kindness and his boyish smile. He shut the door and she rolled down the window. "Thanks, David, for helping me outside." He took two steps back and like an Arthurian Knight he took a deep bow to her. "You are most welcome, my lady."

Catherine grinned at him then laughed. He stepped back toward the car. "I think you're not too broken since you can still laugh. I hope you get to feeling better soon."

Catherine couldn't find the words she wanted to say so instead she muttered, "Laughing is a good thing."

"Well I won't keep you." He leaned down, "It was nice see you again, Erica. Thanks for taking good care of Catherine."

As she pulled the car out of the driveway, both she and Catherine saw David lingering at the end of the driveway watching them. Catherine leaned back against her seat, partly in exhaustion and partly in relief. Erica decided to lighten the mood by teasing her a bit.

"So, what's the deal with you and this David guy?" Erica almost giggled at Catherine's blank expression, but soon realized that she was feeling worse than before.

Catherine stared absently out the window.

"I really have no idea."

26- *Apple Pie*

When the doorbell rang the next morning, Catherine didn't stir from her deep and dreamless sleep. Although the day was well underway, Catherine was oblivious.

Erica scurried quickly to the front door. She had been in the kitchen making some food for Catherine for when she woke up.

As she opened the door, there was a boyish grin there to greet her. "Oh, hey, David. Good morning. "

"Good morning Erica."

"What can I do for you, kind sir?"

"Well, my family was concerned about Catherine of course. Mom sent me over with this." He presented a plate with two pieces of apple pie covered in plastic wrap. "Is she around?"

Erica eyed the piece of pie wondering whose idea it really was to check on Catherine.

There's definitely something tangible between these two.

"Catherine's upstairs asleep. I didn't want to wake her. She's been through a lot recently and hasn't rested much I fear."

"Has she?"

"Yeah, makes me worry about her a little. But Cat's tough and I know she'll get through this. She's the strongest person I know."

"I am sure she is," David agreed quickly.

"When she gets up I will tell her that you came by."

David stood there for quite a while and didn't say anything at all. He wanted to march upstairs and make sure Catherine was still okay, but didn't know why. He felt like he needed to be near her.

What are you thinking David? She's a woman you just met. She barely knows you are alive. Plus she's got more important things going on right now than you.

"David?"

"Oh…uh, yeah, sorry. That would be great if you'd tell her I stopped by, and that I hope she gets better."

"I will, David, no problem."

****

The aroma of eggs and sausage filled Catherine's nose when she finally stirred and rolled onto her back. At first she thought she was back in her apartment, before the recent chain of events had thundered into her life. But soon after she opened her eyes, reality flooded back into her consciousness. She was at home in Parsons.

I've got to get some answers. Sister Mary Eleanor is my only hope and I left too quickly. Maybe if I spend more time with her, she'll explain it all.

Catherine grabbed a robe from the closet and headed down the long staircase toward the kitchen. Her stomach was calling the shots now.

"Hey Erica. Something smells good. Way too good, even."

"There you are sleepy head. Are you feeling any better?"

"I'll let you know after you give me a plate of whatever you are having." Catherine feigned a smile.

"Certainly, Cat. Have a seat, please."

"Wow, it's been a very, long time since I've sat in this kitchen with someone cooking food for me."

Erica's face showed the sympathy she felt for Catherine. There were no words necessary. She dished out scrambled eggs and sausage with a biscuit. "You had a visitor this morning. A certain gentleman we know who delivered a certain piece of homemade apple pie for yours truly."

"David came by?" Catherine felt herself perk up a little, which was strange indeed.

"Yes, he was saying that his mom sent him over with the piece of pie, but I really don't think that is why he came over here."

Erica handed Catherine her plate and a fork.

"What is it with the two of you, Cat? I mean, come on. It's obvious he's quite taken with you. Which might just be reciprocated?" Erica loved to give Catherine a hard time and watch her squirm a little.

"I don't know what you mean. David's a nice guy, the son of my parents' friends, who I met yesterday. End of story."

"Yeah right. Have you seen the way you both look at each other? Plus, he's really cute in a geeky sort of way."

"Erica, don't you think I have bigger issues at hand than some guy I just met? I can't even think about a guy right now."

"Hey missy, don't roll your eyes at me!"

Catherine looked up at her with a piece of sausage in her mouth, "Now, now. You are starting to sound like my mom."

"But the attraction between you and David seems significant to me."

"Not to change the subject so obviously, but I decided I need to go see Sister Mary Eleanor again today. I have to know more."

"Great I'll come with you."

27- *Angelus Aevum*

Catherine shifted her weight nervously from side to side as she rang the bell on the front steps of the convent. After several minutes, they heard the latch turn and a young, novice nun answered.

"Good morning, Sister, I'm here to visit Sister Mary Eleanor. She's not expecting me. I know I should have called first, but I don't mind waiting if I need to."

The nun studied Catherine and Erica intently before asking them to come inside. "Have a seat. I'll get someone to help you." Catherine and Erica sat, and with one sidelong glance, both of them crossed their fingers.

They sat there for almost ten minutes when Catherine recognized Sister Elizabeth coming down the hall.

"It's nice to see you again, Sister."

"Yes, Catherine, you too. I'm glad you came."

"This is my friend, Erica." Sister Elizabeth shook Erica's hand warmly.

"I'm here to see Sister Mary Eleanor again if that's possible. If it's not too much trouble. And only if she's feeling up to a little company."

Sister Elizabeth motioned for them to follow her outside. They came to a beautiful area of flowers and stone benches.

"Ladies, please have a seat. I need to let you know this, shortly after you left that day; God took Sister Mary Eleanor to be with Him in heaven. I am very sorry, we shall all miss her terribly too."

Erica nodded slowly but Catherine's tough exterior façade cracked into a myriad of pieces. Catherine put both hands up to her face to unsuccessfully hide the tears that were now flowing freely.

Catherine was simply unprepared for the wave of desolation that consumed her.

I'm so screwed. She was the only person in this world with any answers. She can't be gone. I just saw her. Why is God punishing me? What did I do to deserve this? Am I cursed because I didn't go with my parent's that day? Should I be dead too?

The sister put her hand on Catherine's left shoulder to comfort her. "I know this is extremely hard for you dear. We all loved her. You must have had a special bond with her. I know she'll still be with you in spirit."

"No offense, Sister." Catherine wiped her tears hastily. "I don't need her to be with me in spirit. I need her with me now. I have no one else to turn to. Everyone I love is dead. This was my shot to get some answers. Now she's gone." Catherine stared off into the garden and shook her head back and forth. Her shoulders sunk lower in defeat.

"Don't give up. I know this feels like the end of the world right now, but it's not. We'll get some answers, I promise."

Catherine looked over at Erica, a little defiant. "How?"

"I don't know yet, but I know I am not giving up and neither are you. We'll figure this out together. You are not alone anymore, remember that?" Erica flashed her that million dollar smile that always calmed Catherine down.

"Alright. Alright. Erica, you win. I am not giving up."

Sister Elizabeth interrupted, "I do have something that may help you. While we were tidying up her cell, we found something that I think you might want to have. I'll take you there now if you'd like me to. We can get it together."

"She left something for me?"

The three walked down a stone path together that wandered around the gardens and eventually led them back to where she had met Sister Mary Eleanor. When they got to the door, Sister Elizabeth took out a set of keys from her apron and unlocked it. As she stepped inside, she quickly made the sign of the cross and leaned down to pull something out from under the tiny bed. It was a box, neatly wrapped in brown paper. She lifted it up and handed it to Catherine.

On the top of the box, in a scrawled handwriting it said:

For Catherine Jane Moore. For her eyes only, to be opened only when I am no longer of this world.

"Sister Eleanor never mentioned anything about this or about you except the day before you arrived. I brought her breakfast that morning, and she told me you'd be here. Then she asked me to make a telephone call once you had gone."

"A phone call?"

"Yes, she gave me a number and a message. I know it may seem strange, but I learned not to question anything she asked of me. Our sweet Sister was so blessed, and very wise, you know. I'm sure she had a number of Angels with her all the time." Sister Elizabeth looked like a young girl speaking of her hero.

"Who did she ask you to call? What was the message?"

"I'm not sure who it went to, but the message was simple: *It has begun.*"

"It has begun? Just three words and that's all?"

"Yes, that's what she told me. She handed me a piece of paper with a number on it and instructed me to call the number, and say this to the man that answered. So I did. He said thank you, and I hung up."

Erica spoke up for Catherine, who was silent now. "Do you still have the number?"

"Perhaps I do. I may have it somewhere." She looked at the watch on her wrist first. "It's almost time for mid-morning prayers. Give me your number. I promise to search for it and call you if I find it."

Catherine and Erica followed Sister Elizabeth back to the main house and gave her a number to reach them.

They had been driving for a few miles before Catherine broke the silence. "Part of me wants to rip open that box and the other part wants nothing to do with whatever is inside. Does that sound crazy?"

"No. Let's wait and open it once we're back to your parents' house? Okay?"

Catherine nodded.

"How creepy is that, though? She died right after I saw her? And what has begun? Who could she have called? I feel like I'm in a movie without the script! Maybe soon the camera crews will just jump out and say, surprise you've been punked."

****

"So, are you ready?"

"As ready as I will ever be."

Erica handed her the scissors and Catherine turned the box so it faced her. She cut open the heavily taped side flaps of thick paper. The tape was discolored and it was clear the box had been wrapped for many, many years.

"Wow, I wonder how long this was under her bed?"

"I love a good mystery." Erica rubbed her hands together in anticipation.

Under the paper was a thick hat-box style container, rectangular rather than round. Catherine lifted the velvet overlapping lid.

Lying in the box was a large book, over four inches thick, with an antique leather binding. On the front of the book were various symbols arranged in a circle around a larger symbol in the center.

"I've seen this symbol before!"

The symbols were arranged like the numbers on a clock face. In the center of the circle of 12 symbols, was a center seal. All of this was part of a more complex symbol. Beneath it was two words embossed in Latin: *Angelus Aevum.*

This is the circle with 12 symbols and a 13th in the center. Just like I saw in my vision after I touched the cathedral window! There's more to this imprint, but it's definitely the same.

Catherine lifted the book out of the box and placed it on the dining room table. She ran her fingers along the raised surface, feeling the heat spread through her body.

"What the...!"

"What's wrong? Are you okay?"

"Yeah, do me a favor. Put your hand on the cover?"

She reached her hand out and touched the cover.

"Do you feel anything?"

Erica shook her head no, and looked at Catherine intently. "What did you feel?"

"It was weird, like a heat coming from the book, but that's impossible. Well, normally not possible anyway." She rubbed both her hands together.

"I don't feel anything, but that doesn't mean you didn't."

Catherine opened it quickly to look inside. It was written in what looked a lot like the Enochian script version of the word "FAITH" that had been written on the paper delivered to her apartment. It looked slightly odd though, a little different somehow, but similar.

"How am I supposed to read this?" She thumbed through more pages and it was all the same.

Erica laughed nervously, "Yeah, blank pages and an empty book don't help much to unravel the mystery of what's happening." She grabbed the pages briefly and fanned through about two inches.

Empty?

"You are kidding. You see this, don't you?"

Again Erica shook her head.

"Great! I see pages and pages full of Enochian script or something like it." Catherine flipped through page after page frantically.

Erica felt helpless as she watched her best friend desperately thumb through the book, and then she did see something: a glowing light was now growing around both the book and Catherine's body.

"Keep touching the book!"

Catherine stopped turning pages. "Why?"

"I do see something but it's not words. I see light!" Erica took two steps back to get more perspective. "It's like the book is glowing and you are too!"

"What? Really?" Catherine looked at both her arms and at first didn't see it. Then she concentrated for a moment, looking at her outstretched arms. A faint aura was visible around her arms and the book. The moment she stopped touching the book, it disappeared.

They both stared at the book, completely amazed.

"That is so cool. I have never seen anything like that before in my life. My best friend actually glows. You and this book are connected. That is why she kept it for you and you only. You can't read it now, but I bet you *will* be able to."

28- *She's Coming Today*

Jacob traced the lines of the cafeteria table with his fingertips. Although the room was filled with various loud noises, he heard nothing at all but the sound of his own voice in his head. He could not stop thinking about her. He'd barely slept at all the night before, sitting in the dark for hours listening to his pencil scratching across the surface of his drawing pad.

When he had opened his eyes this morning to see daylight streaming through the window in his room, he saw only one image when he lifted the paper pad from his chest. A woman's face stared at him. Jacob knew it was Catherine even though her features were somewhat different than he recalled. Those huge blue eyes were his confirmation. Catherine's eyes were unmistakable.

I know she's coming. They don't believe me, but she'll come. She's coming. What will she say to me? Sorry? What will I say to her? I love you. I hate you. I never want to see you again. It's hopeless and don't you know that?

Jacob slammed his right fist to the table hard, catching the attention of one of his psychologists who happened to walk in the main doors in time to hear a loud thud.

"Jacob. Are you having a hard day?"

Jacob didn't look up or answer. Dr. Cartwright sat down across from him. "Come on Jacob, it's me. It's okay to tell me what is bothering you. You know that. So what's with the silent treatment?"

Finally, Jacob looked up at her and softly said, "I'm going to have a visitor today. Someone I haven't seen in a very long time."

"Is a friend of yours coming to visit?"

"She was a good friend before...before I came here." Jacob looked down. He felt like he was under a microscope.

"How do you feel about her coming to see you?"

"I'm not sure. It's been a long time."

Jacob started digging his fingernails into his palms underneath the table.

"Do you want to come to my office to talk? I have some time available. Before she arrives?"

Jacob continued to look down at his lap so the doctor would give up and go way.

"No, I'm fine. I don't need to."

Dr. Clark knew from working with Jacob for years that if he didn't want to talk about something, he dug in, and it was pointless.

"Okay Jacob. If you change your mind, you know where I'll be." She got up from the table and walked away.

Once she was out of ear shot, he got the last word. "You wouldn't understand it, anyway."

29- *Handful of Pictures*

"I just feel like I need to be by myself so I can think on the drive there. But I better run to make visitor's hours."

"Okay. I just want to be there for you if you need me. Drive safe. I'll be here when you get back."

Catherine hugged her. "You are such a great friend. Do you know that?"

Erica quickly responded, "Well you are easy to be a great friend to, you know?"

"Now we both know that's not true." Catherine grabbed her purse to head out the door.

What if he doesn't want to see me? Breathe and calm down. It will be fine. Maybe I should have let Erica come along.

She concentrated on the road ahead, and arrived before she knew it, pulling up the long drive to the main building. She gathered her strength and walked inside.

"Can I help you?" A young woman greeted her as she approached the front desk.

"Yes, I'm here to see Jacob Petersen."

The woman scanned a clip board. "It's free time now, so you'll most likely find him outside in the courtyard. He's usually there sketching something. If you can't find him, just let me know and I will have someone track him down. You just follow the long hallway to your left and it will take you outside."

What do I say to him once I get out there? Don't be angry? I'm sorry, is it my fault you're here? Ugh.

She walked out onto the grounds. Locating him didn't take very long. Jacob was sitting on a bench surrounded by tall trees with his back toward her. She felt a bit dizzy as she approached him. Her thoughts were racing now.

"Jacob?"

He slowly turned to see her standing there and then, without a word, turned back to what he was sketching. Catherine, determined, walked around to the front of the bench.

"Jacob? It's me, Catherine."

Jacob looked up at her intently. When their eyes met, his first impulse was to jump up and hug her, but he stayed seated.

"What are you doing here?"

"I came as soon as I found out where you were. I saw your mother yesterday."

"So you're back?"

Catherine felt a pang of guilt and she sat down to his right.

"Yes, Jake. I'm back finally."

"Why did you come back?"

"Well, I needed to come back. I had some things to figure out and take care of." He looked like the same Jacob she had known, only older, yet he seemed so different. Not at all like the vibrant, happy person that she had known. Now he was brooding and unhappy.

"I didn't know until yesterday that you were in here. If I had, I would have come to visit before now."

"I doubt that." Jacob said under his breath.

"I'm so sorry for being out of touch for so long."

Jacob quickly turned in anger looking directly into Catherine's eyes. "Why do you care? It doesn't matter to me."

His words struck her hard, even though she knew he'd be upset. "It does matter. I shouldn't have run away. I was so messed up after my parents died, and all I could think about was getting out."

He returned to his sketch of a large tree as if he hadn't heard her.

"Jake, please believe me. I am so sorry." She reached out to take his hand.

Jacob pulled his hand back quickly. Not even looking at her, he put the pad down on the bench, got up and walked away.

Catherine's heart was pounding and tears filled her eyes.

Great, just great. That went fabulously.

After a few moments, she gathered herself and realized that his drawing pad was still sitting there. She picked it up lovingly and sat it in her lap. Catherine wanted to take it to him, so she could try to reason with him again, but decided it was best for her to wait.

Jacob had returned to his room and looked out to see if Catherine was still where he had left her. He watched her safely from above, clenching his fists nervously.

Good, she's still there. Now, Catherine, just look at the drawings and you'll see. You'll see how much I...need...want...love...you.

Catherine opened the pad in her lap and started thumbing through it. Pictures of buildings, trees and landscapes were carefully drawn. Then she gasped as she looked at the next page and the next.

Oh my God. It's my apartment in Lawrence. Here's my bedroom, my kitchen and my living room. I don't understand how he could see all this.

Catherine looked around nervously as if she was peeking at something forbidden. The next page caught her even more off guard. It was a portrait of Olivia, her client at the office, with an arm outstretched from somewhere off the page. The details were extraordinary and took her breath away. She was scared to turn the next page.

The next drawing was the old man Joshua from Café Roma. As she flipped the pages it was like a diary of her past couple weeks. She stopped on a page that had the Enochian script that she had seen. These were interwoven with various smaller images of some of her childhood memories. The final picture was just Catherine's face in the present staring right back at her. Her body went numb.

I left him here and all this behind and he couldn't move on at all. He's tied to me in this way. No wonder he's angry with me for deserting him. He was living my life in pieces without really being directly a part of my life. How could I have known? How can he see all this? He must know all about what's been happening to me, right? Maybe not?

Jacob continued to watch her from above, studying her movements more like a predator than a friend. The love and hate were a swirl of feeling that he couldn't contain. He wanted to go to her, welcome her back and hold her tight, but his intense anger stopped him. She had abandoned him and he could not reconcile the pain he felt with the love in his heart. He had dreamt of her return for so long since he had confined himself to the safety of the facility.

Catherine decided it was best to leave for now and come back another time to speak to Jacob about the drawings. She stood up from the bench and carried the pad back to the building. For a brief moment, she felt him watching her, but when she looked up at the row of windows, he was already gone.

30- *Taking Action*

Razoul often paced like a panther when he couldn't get what he wanted. Patience was never a virtue he possessed. Out of frustration, he threw a crystal candlestick across the room and watched it shatter into hundreds of pieces across the velvet red walls.

Razoul had waited for news of the search from the others ever since their last meeting. Each call he received made him more furious that they couldn't locate one single female. He was sure that the Incarnate Angel was unaware they were coming for her. But time was moving fast and their window of opportunity would not remain open forever. He took his cell phone out of his breast pocket and dialed.

"Sirius, I think it's time we went to see the gypsy's daughter."

"Do you think that is wise to reveal our intentions to her?"

"Leave all that to me. I can be very persuasive as you well know."

"Do you really think she can tell us anything new? Any more than we already know?"

Razoul walked over to the ancient bookcase and picked up an ornamental box with a key lock. "Oh yes, I think she will, perhaps with a little persuasion." He carried the box back to his desk and took a small key from the desk drawer.

Sirius knew better than to ask just how Razoul planned to coerce the woman to reveal what they wanted. "Very well then, I will make the arrangements right away. I will meet you at the hanger in an hour."

Razoul hung up the phone and slipped it back into his pocket. He placed the key into the hole of the ornamental box and turned it. As he did, an eerie luminescence spread outward from the box. He removed an ancient amulet that his family had acquired nearly a century before he was even born. It was the Sigil de Ameth, fashioned into an amulet made of pure gold. It was a powerful yet often incorrectly used object that could not only invoke a variety of powers, but also contained the keys to summon the Fallen Ones.

Razoul dangled the amulet closer to him in order to view the various symbols. An evil smile spread across his face. "Yes, I think this will do nicely."

31- *Uncertainty*

Catherine walked in the front door and was greeted by Erica's warm welcome.

"Hey Cat! You're back." Erica studied Catherine's expression and knew the visit with Jacob had not gone well at all.

"Come in here, I want to show you something. A delivery came while you were away. Maybe it will cheer you up."

Catherine followed her into the dining room. On the table were a dozen long stem white roses in a clear crystal vase. She looked curiously at Erica for a moment. "Read the card. They're for you."

"White roses? These are my favorites." Catherine slowly opened the card.

Dear Catherine,

I wanted to express to you how much you've affected me, and send you something to brighten your day.

An Admirer

Erica chimed in with a little tease in her voice, "I bet I know who those are from."

Catherine stared at her blankly. "Who?"

"Well, David, I'm sure."

"Oh yeah, sorry. I'm a bit distracted. Why would he send me flowers?"

"Sometimes you are so clueless. Didn't you notice him at dinner? The way he looks at you like a little puppy dog?"

"I guess I didn't.

"How was your visit with Jacob?"

"Not good."

"Yeah, I figured. Was he surprised to see you?"

"Oh, I don't think he was really that surprised. He was definitely angry with me though. He wanted to know why I came back. Then he walked away from me. I think I told you, he's a brilliant artist. When he got up, he left his drawing pad. I think he wanted me to look at it. I couldn't believe my eyes when I opened it. It was full of drawings of me! In perfect order, he captured all the crazy events leading up to me being back here in Parsons. He saw it all."

"So he can see your life? See whatever happens to you? That's weird. Well, incredible."

"Very. What I can't figure out now is why? Why are he and I connected like that? After talking to his mom and looking at his room, I was so afraid before that my leaving put him in that hospital. Now I'm almost sure of it." Catherine put her face in her hands. "He's there, and it's my fault." She started to cry.

"Don't blame yourself for Jacob's current situation. He's a grown man. They aren't keeping him there against his will, right?"

"No, he's there voluntarily. He could leave if he wanted to."

"See, it's not your fault." Erica reassured her. "Did you try to talk to him again after you saw the drawings?"

"No, I just left his pad with the nurses at the front desk and left. I didn't know what to say and don't think I could take more of his anger today either. I'll go back, once I've had time to think things through."

"Maybe the two together can piece this puzzle together."

Catherine stared out the window, "I sure hope so. I really do." She turned to look at the vase of pristine white roses that David had sent her.

"And what I am going to do about David? A relationship is the last thing I need right now. Besides, if he really knew me he'd be running for the hills screaming."

"Well, I think you should take the compliment at least. You are a wonderful woman you know."

It had been many years since anyone had sent her flowers, let alone an admirer of hers. She'd made sure that no one got close enough for that. "Yeah, maybe you're right. Until then I'm going to go upstairs and take a hot bath."

"I'll be down here if you need anything. Just yell for me."

"I will," Catherine said softly as she slowly climbed the stairs. Her legs felt like 30 pound weights with every step she took.

32- *A Dream*

"I got everything you asked for," David called loudly.

Helen appeared from the basement stairs where she had been down folding loads of laundry.

"Oh, thanks. I appreciate your running for me. I have no idea where your father's off to right now." She shook her head.

"No problem at all, ma, you know that."

"Such a sweet boy," she touched David's left cheek with her hand and gave it a light pat like she had since he was a boy.

"Are you hungry, sweetie? Want me to make you a sandwich?"

As much as she loved to feed people, David loved to eat. "Sure!" David sat down at the kitchen table.

Her back was turned as she gathered the sandwich ingredients. "So, tell me about you and Catherine."

David tried to hide the look of shock on his face. "What do you mean, mom? I mean, she seems nice."

"Come on dear, this is mom you're talking to. I know that look in your eyes. I saw it at dinner the other night. You like her, yes?"

"I can't ever hide anything from you! Yeah, yeah, I do."

"I can see why you like her, honey. She is a beautiful girl, very smart too."

"Yeah, well it probably doesn't matter anyway. There's no way someone like Catherine would give me a chance."

"Why not Davey? You are handsome, sweet and smart. What's not to love?" She handed him a plate.

"Come on, mom, you know I hate to be called that."

"Sorry, sweetie. I remember. Do you want some chips?" David nodded.

"Besides mom, your opinion doesn't count, you are definitely biased."

"Of course I am."

"I don't know much about her though. I know she lost her parents in a car accident which is just stuff everyone else around here knows. She seems really sad, even though I think she likes to pretend she's fine."

"Catherine's parents were a wonderful pair. It was so sudden when they died. Your dad and I tried to help her as much as we could. The longer she stayed here, the more distant she became. Then all the sudden she left and headed for school. She asked us to keep an eye on things. Well that was years ago. Every once in a while we'd hear from her, ask how she was doing, and try to get more details. She said she was just fine every time, but we knew better. Then the contacts from her got longer in between. She's been in Kansas City for over a decade. She's a social worker."

"So has she stayed away all this time?"

"Yes, we were so shocked the other day that she called and was already in town."

"Do you know what brought her back? Is she staying?"

"Well based on the history, it must have been something substantial to get her here. I'm glad she came back. It's not healthy for anyone to deny the past forever. She needs a chance to move on, for her own sake. I know her mother would want that. Honestly, I expected that we'd get a call from her at some point to sell her parent's place. So I guess I don't know answers to either of your questions. Catherine is a very private person. I learned its best not to pry, but to let her tell you what she wants to. Otherwise it seems to push her away."

Helen sat down with her own sandwich. "So, have you asked her out yet?"

"No, no. She seems busy right now. I don't want to bother her. Besides what if she says no?"

"If you like her, you should invite her out so you can get to know her better. Isn't that usually how things are done, even these days?"

"Yes, mom we modern kids still go out for dinner."

"I know! You should take her to that restaurant in Pittsburg, the one your father takes me to on special occasions. What was the name? It's on the tip of my tongue...Gran Sasso! We love to go there. It's Italian and everyone likes Italian. "

"Maybe mom, I'm not sure yet." Then he looked at his mom and decided to tell her what he had done. "I did send her flowers today. One dozen long stem white roses with a card signed, 'An admirer'. How's that for letting her know I'm interested?"

"How did you decide on those?"

"Well it was weird, actually. I had a dream about her last night and woke up thinking about white roses. So I ran to the florist this morning, early." David grinned.

"A dream? That's interesting. What was it about?"

"I was in a big garden and she was running through these wandering stone paths. She was dressed in a long white gown. I kept trying to find her, but every time I caught up to her, she vanished. The biggest thing I remembered was that the garden was full of white roses."

"Have you been around the back of the house over there? Catherine loves white roses because her father grew them, among about a dozen other varieties. When she was little she used to intertwine the stems and flowers to make a crown of them that she wore everywhere until the poor things got droopy."

David could picture Catherine as a small girl running around the garden playing. "I'm so glad I picked the right flowers then. At least I'm not fully hopeless."

"I am sure they will make a good impression. You worry too much." She sighed. "You've been that way since you were a little boy."

"Yeah, I know mom, I know."

33-*Cosima*

The trip to Venice had taken less than an hour on Razoul's private jet. Sirius had barely spoken a word on the way. He was normally a man of few words; however, he had issue with Razoul since his father had abruptly died, and now only spoke when absolutely necessary.

A car had taken them from the airport to the Laguna Nord ferry so that they could reach their final destination of Burano, an old fishing village north of Venice.

Razoul stood at the railing watching the water slap violently against the side of the boat, thinking intently about his approach once they reached Signora Cosima's dwelling.

They had never met and he was unsure how to coax Cosima to doing his bidding to locate the incarnate, without knowledge of what he was doing. He knew Cosima's biggest weakness was that she had been totally blind since birth, which he felt was the key to manipulating her.

Cosima's family had been closely tied to the Bugiardini line for nearly two generations. Her mother Melantha had been very gifted with spiritual sight, and often assisted his father Britius in making strategic decisions to obtain greater power and wealth. This was before Razoul and his brother had been born. Razoul's own brother, Marcello, and Cosima were nearly the same age.

According to the stories he had heard while growing up at the vast Bugiardini Estate in Rome, it had been Melantha who was responsible for the many vast holdings that Razoul now controlled.

Fortunately for Razoul, Melantha had contracted a rare blood infection nearly ten years ago and died leaving her only daughter to carry on her work of advising people by communicating with the other world.

This was a lucky break since he knew that Melantha would never have chosen willingly to participate in what he needed done. She was wise and would have understood the danger to herself and others. The younger Cosima could be more easily controlled.

Razoul looked up to see that the ferry was now closing in on the Burano fishermen docks. He moved away from his vantage point to find Sirius and gather his belongings.

Razoul entered the seating area just in time to overhear Sirius speaking on his phone.

"Sì Sì Signora. Una questione più importante. Vita o morte. Sì Mille Grazie."

As he hung up, he saw Razoul. "I have spoken to Cosima and requested an audience to discuss very important questions, matters of life and death. Your suggestion was good, she is agreeable to meet with us now."

"Of course my suggestion was good. Her mother was a very kind-hearted woman, according to my father. I had confidence her daughter wouldn't turn us away if someone is in dire need of her help. This will factor into my plan perfectly."

"So what is your ruse this time?"

Razoul trusted no one when it came to his particular plans and coercion techniques. He felt too much information offered may inadvertently cause someone to commit a grievous error, so he only shared details when necessary.

"Don't worry yourself, old man. Just play along. I will handle everything."

Sirius' blood boiled every time Razoul tried to put him in his place. His friend Britius had been strong and cunning. He dealt with all matters swiftly and had never been condescending to him or to any member of the Malem Tutela.

Unlike the reckless Razoul, Britius took care of his allies and intelligently surrounded himself with those of great knowledge in order that everyone might benefit. This younger Bugiardini with no sense of honor made him sick to his stomach.

He spat at the ground, pretending to clear his throat. "Very well, Razoul. As you wish."

34-*Cat and Mouse*

"Jacob, your visitor left this for you."

Jacob quickly took it from her and sat back down. She could tell he was in a mood and left without saying another word. He gripped the edges of the pad tightly.

Catherine looked at them. I bet she was impressed and curious about how I could draw that stuff. I know she'll be back. She'll want to know how I can see her and what she's doing. Yeah, she'll be back.

Jacob started remembering their childhood moments together in her parents' garden. They had wandered in the woods for hours and hours, talking about what it must be like to be grown up and do whatever they wanted to instead of what they were told to.

The memory filled Jacob with a brief feeling of happiness, a feeling that he had not felt in a long time. Seeing her today had filled him with many emotions, but most significantly it had filled him with hope again. She was his angel, his everything, and now she was near to him at last.

Now Catherine can't deny me or ignore me. I can't be ignored by her anymore or hid away in the shadows of her life. I love her so much. Maybe she doesn't love me now, but she will. I know she will.

Jacob got up and wandered down to the end of the hall. He picked up the phone and dialed quickly.

"Hello?"

"Mom, its Jacob."

"Is everything alright?"

"Yeah mom, no worries, I'm okay."

"I don't hear much from you, so I thought something was wrong, that's all."

"I had a visitor today."

"Oh? Who was that honey?" Mary didn't want to assume Catherine had made it out there.

"It was Catherine. She came to see me today. You didn't tell me she was back in Parsons. Thanks."

"How was your visit?" Mary ignored Jacob's last comment on purpose.

"Well it could have been better. I was completely surprised." Jacob purposely lied to his mother. "So I didn't act happy to see her, and I feel bad now."

"I am sure Catherine understands, Jacob. Don't worry."

"I sent her away without getting her number. So I don't know how to reach her."

"Oh, I can go over there after a bit and get her number if you want."

No not the phone. I need to see her in person again.

"No! I mean if you could just tell her I'm sorry and that I'd like to see her again when she's not busy. It's been a long time. I guess I was just unprepared to see her today. I don't want her to think I'm angry and stay away."

"Sure, of course I'll tell her for you. I'll go over tonight for sure. Don't worry. I'm sure she'll come and see you again."

"Thanks a lot, mom, I really appreciate it. You still coming out to see me this weekend?"

"Of course I am. Is there anything you want me to bring you? Anything at all?"

"No, I'm fine. Just tell Catherine for me."

"Okay, consider it done. Love you, sweetie."

"Love you too, mom."

Jacob hung up the phone and walked right into another patient standing in the hallway near the door to the stairwell.

"Watch where you are going brat! Can't you see I'm walking here?" Jacob sneered at the boy who was much younger and shorter than he was.

The boy ducked back down the stairs. Jacob smiled with a sense of smug self-satisfaction as he walked back into his room.

Now she has to come back. She'll do it because my mom will ask her to. Hell, my mom is so worried all the time she'll probably beg her to come. Catherine won't say no.

He flopped down onto his bed and laid his head on his pillow, with both hands clasped behind his head. Jacob smiled wide, like he didn't have a care in the world. "Yep, she'll come."

35- *Message*

Catherine's hot bath had relaxed her enough that she felt like laying down. She was in a deep sleep while Erica tidied up in the kitchen downstairs. She was unaware of the doorbell ringing.

Erica hurried to the door.

"Oh, hello there. Is Catherine here?"

Erica studied the older woman. "She is, but she is upstairs resting right now. How can I help you?"

Jacob's mother sized Erica up for a moment and decided she could leave the message with her. "I'm Jacob's mother, Mary. I live next door. I guess Catherine went out to visit my son today, and I've heard that it didn't go very well. Well he called me a bit upset at how he handled things, and wanted me to come speak to her about that."

Erica nodded in agreement. "Yeah. We talked when she came back. I also heard it didn't go very well. Catherine was a little upset, but I think she understood it must have been a bit of a shock for Jacob."

"Yes, I am sure it was. He wanted me to let Catherine know that he would like to see her again if it's not too much trouble for her to go back out?"

"Of course. I'll let her know. I'm sure she'll go again."

"Thanks so much. I'm sorry. I don't know your name?"

Erica reached out her hand. "I'm sorry, I should have introduced myself. I'm Erica, Catherine's best friend."

"It's nice to meet you Erica. Thank you for telling Catherine for me."

"No problem at all."

"Well I better get back. I have some soup on the stove I need to check on." Mary turned and hurried away.

Erica shut the door quietly.

Maybe Catherine will have the chance to get some answers from Jacob now.

The two women didn't realize they were being watched from a distance. Outside the house near the tree line, the unseen visitor, a young man with short dark hair, watched as the door closed.

He resumed his waiting position in the trees, looked at his watch, and noted the time in a small notebook he took from his satchel.

36- *The Visitor*

As Catherine slumbered upstairs, she felt at first like she was floating in nothingness until she found herself in another long hallway, but this time it was filled with doors lining either side.

Catherine tried to open each door one by one, but they were all locked. She had tried several of them with no luck when a flickering light at the far end of the hallway caught her eye.

She slowly walked toward it. At first the light looked more like a firefly than anything in particular. As she got closer the flickering light took shape. It was the beautiful woman from her dreams! Catherine started walking more quickly but her feet felt unusually heavy and it slowed her progress.

Unlike her previous encounters, this time she really took a good look at the apparition in front of her. After everything that had happened to her, she wasn't upset or afraid this time. She calmly approached the figure, watching the way she moved and flowed into a solid form.

"Who are you?"

The apparition smiled. As she did, her light grew into gold but she did not speak.

"Why won't you speak to me? Can you please help me? What is going on?"

Without realizing it, Catherine had asked for help, which meant that this beautiful being had to help her in some way. The vaporous woman soon coalesced into a human form right in front of her eyes. An enchanting woman stood before her in a long white dress with a simple bodice interwoven with gold threads.

"Do I know you?"

The woman nodded no.

"Then why are you here?"

The woman reached her hand out. Catherine took the woman's hand. The woman turned, placed a key into the door behind her and without speaking led Catherine into a room.

Inside the room were shelves that lined the walls up as far as Catherine could see. They were filled with leather books. There was a single candle in the center of the room on a tall pillar. There were four marble columns that stood at four points forming a square. In front of the candle was a tall table with a single book on top.

As Catherine walked forward she saw that a large circle was inlaid in the floor that encompassed the area with the marble columns at four points. Cut deep into this circle were symbols she now recognized from her visions. As she got closer she saw that the book sitting there was identical to the one Sister Mary Eleanor left for her.

The beautiful woman swept her hand in a horizontal motion and the book opened. As it did a light escaped from it. Catherine's eyes grew wide as she walked toward it.

"What is this place, and what is this book for?"

The woman pointed to it but still didn't speak. "Why don't you talk to me? If you are here to help me, why don't you just tell me what is happening to me?"

The woman looked at her deeply, with compassion, but spoke no words.

"I don't know why you want me to look at this book. I can't read anything in it."

The woman pointed again so Catherine stepped up to the table. Instead of not being able to read what was on the page, she saw a single page in front of her with several paragraphs that she could read

When darkness has flooded the world of mankind, a light shall emerge in the darkness that will illuminate the truth and allow the chosen to see the world as it is, not as it appears to be. Ancient words will reveal the path you walk to fulfill your destiny.

You must awaken to your true nature for time is fleeting. You are not what you appear to be and your life is not what you believe. Walk carefully, dear one, for you have allies and enemies.

Simply state your true designation aloud and the answers to your questions will be revealed.

Catherine looked up from the book. She was trying to consider the words carefully, but wasn't sure what it all meant. When she turned to ask a question, she realized that she was alone again.

"Oh, come on. Really? That's just great. You're a big help, all right."

Catherine looked up at the arched ceiling speaking to God or anyone else who might be listening. "What do you want from me?"

As if in response to her question a light appeared above her. It descended downward until it enveloped her. For a brief moment, she experienced a feeling unlike anything she could recall. The light filled her with inexplicable peace and serenity.

37- *Deception*

Drizzle floated thickly from the sky as Razoul and Sirius walked toward Signora Cosima's home. It was a fairly long walk to the outskirts of Burano where they would meet with her. By the time they reached the place, Razoul's long black coat was glistening with rain droplets.

He had allowed Sirius to walk ahead since he knew where to go, but now they had reached their destination, he quickly pushed him aside to grasp the knocker on the door. Sirius stumbled back but didn't fall. Razoul was impatient and knocked a few times before he heard sounds on the other side.

As the door opened, Cosima appeared alone. He was instantly captivated by her youthful beauty. A burning desire stirred inside him. For a brief instant, he wanted to take her right there in front of the old man, but he restrained himself.

Perhaps later, after she's served her purpose.

Her olive skin was perfect and her dark eyes enchanting, but from her blind stare he immediately knew it was Cosima. So instead of using his charming smile he began to speak in a gentle voice.

"Ah, Signora. Grazie per vedere me."

Cosima turned toward the sound of Razoul's voice and smiled. "Sì, Signore. Amici di famiglia. Come, come!"

Cosima opened the door wide and motioned to a wooden table with several chairs.

Razoul studied her curvy form as she walked. Watching her made his pulse quicken. Her dark curly locks bounced when she moved. She was wearing simple dress with an apron.

"Signora Cosima, you speak English?"

"Sì, my mother, she taught me from the time I was very small."

"So you are quite beautiful, and also intelligent." Razoul added, "Just like your mother."

"Thank you, Signore. Please sit with me and tell me of your worries. My madre spoke of your father well."

Cosima took her chair as if she were sighted and waited for both men to take a seat. Razoul turned to look at Sirius whose furrowed brow reflected concern about what was going to happen next.

"Dearest Cosima, my friend and I seek your gifts to help us find a woman who is in grave danger. There are terrible men trying to find her who will surely murder her, and we are trying to stop this from happening."

"With the spirits willing, I will help you. What is the name of this woman you seek?"

"I'd rather not give you her name fair Cosima, in order to protect her privacy you understand." Razoul said smoothly.

"Perhaps you have something of hers to offer me?"

Razoul was ready for this question as well. "Perdonare, Signora, but I have nothing of hers with me. However I have brought an object of special powers to help you find what I seek." Razoul pulled out the wooden box holding the Sigil Amulet. He handed the box to Cosima. She slowly opened the box and pulled the amulet from its resting place.

"What sort of object is this?" She ran her fingers along the imprinted metal but did not recognize the symbols she felt there.

"Ah, this is a very old amulet of the Angels. It will allow you to speak to them about our needs and ask their intervention to save the woman. I have none of your special talents, fair Cosima, but I believe you can make this work. Would you please try?"

Cosima had no reason to distrust Razoul, but she was still intuitively wary about what she was being asked to do. Her mother had often taught her to be very careful wielding her gifts, using objects she had no experience with. Cosima knew well there were many dangers in the spirit world which she did not know.

"I am not sure that I can use this object, Signore, for what you seek."

"Young girl, our families have known each other for many years. I came seeking your mother to use this object but regrettably she has passed from this world leaving you as my only recourse. Of course, she would have more experience than you in this matter. I know she would do this for my dead father, so now what I am asking is if you would do this for me? I cannot bear to see this woman harmed, especially after the tragedy of experiencing the terribly sudden loss of my father." Razoul faked the sound of weeping for Cosima's sake.

"Ah, Signore, do not cry. My mother was a great and powerful woman with sincere compassion. I assure you I am the same. If you know the manner in which to prepare this object, I will pray the spirits allow me to use it well to save your friend. If you would give me a moment in which to prepare myself, I will return."

38- *The Call*

"I had a dream and this time I remember it fully. There was a beautiful woman. I've seen her before in other dreams. This book was there. I could read a page of it before the dream was over. It said something about darkness in the world. It also said I have allies and enemies. The final thing it said was if I called out my true designation all would be revealed. But I am not sure at all what that means."

Catherine opened the book to the first page like in her dream, but everything was still in the language like before and she could not read it. Yet the page had three distinct paragraphs on it, as it had in the dream.

Of course it couldn't be that easy, could it?

Erica watched Catherine's interaction with the book and then the light began to illuminate the air all around her.

"Why can't I read it now? This is too frustrating. Is it too much to ask for a clear sign or something I can really use here?"

"Oh, speaking of some answers. Jacob's mother came by earlier while you were asleep to give you a message." Erica offered.

"Really? What did she say?"

"She said that Jacob called her and felt bad about how he reacted to you earlier today."

"That's unexpected."

Erica nodded in agreement. "He wants you to come back out whenever you can."

Catherine looked out the windows that lined the far wall of the dining room. The sun was setting, causing a soft warm light to cascade across the room. "Well, that's for tomorrow I guess. Not going out there again today. Maybe then I can figure out this connection between us, and just maybe that will help me make some sense of all this."

She started running her hands through the pages of the book looking for anything she could read, when her cell phone rang making both of the ladies jump. She didn't recognize the number.

"Hello, this is Catherine."

"Catherine, this is Sister Elizabeth from the convent."

Catherine's face lit up. "Yes, Sister Elizabeth. Thank you for calling."

"I was able to find the number for you that Sister Mary Eleanor gave to me."

"Awesome. Just one moment, Sister." Catherine fumbled in her purse for a pen and pad, "I'm ready now. Go ahead."

Catherine wrote down the number and repeated it back to her. "Is that right sister?"

"Yes, but I almost forgot. It's an international number; you'll need to dial 39 first."

"An international number? What country is that?"

"It's a number in Italy."

Catherine wasn't sure what to think about that, but thanked the sister and hung up the phone. She held the pad up for Erica to see. "Well I have it; the number Sister Mary Eleanor gave Sister Elizabeth to call when I left the first time. It's in Italy."

"Italy? Really? Wow." Erica leaned in to read it.

"I'm going to call right now, before I lose my nerve. Whoever this is, they must know something. Or else she wouldn't have had her call. He better start talking!"

Catherine dialed the number and waited for it to start ringing. After a few moments it connected and started ringing in a different tone than she was used to. It rang and rang but no voicemail picked up. Just as Catherine was about to disconnect, a message began to play at first in Italian and then in English.

Catherine wrote on her pad: Pontifical Council for Justice and Peace, and then she hung up. She turned to Erica, "Why would Sister Mary Eleanor have her call someone from the Vatican?"

"The Vatican, in Rome?"

"Yes, where else would the Vatican be?"

They both laughed.

"The recording said I had reached the Pontifical Council for Justice and Peace. Sounds like a Vatican office."

"I've never heard of that before. I wonder who could be there that would be interested in your visit?" Erica said curiously. "Maybe tomorrow while you are visiting Jacob, I'll track down an Internet connection so I can do some research?"

Catherine nodded and answered, "That would be great."

But in her head, Catherine was trying to grasp just how far and wide was this story she found herself in the middle of.

I am sure that I don't know the half of it.

39-*Ashes to Ashes*

Cosima entered the room carefully holding a small wooden bowl of various smoldering herbs. The aromatic smoke began to fill the room as she blew very gently downward. She placed the bowl in front of her as she sat down.

Razoul watched her close her eyes for a moment and breathe deeply. She placed one hand out with an open palm. "The amulet, Signore."

Razoul placed it in her hand face up so that the inscribed symbols would be facing her. "Now, Signora, just open your heart and soul to the angels and allow me to say the sacred call."

Cosima nodded and appeared to concentrate.

Razoul stood up and began to speak with an authoritative tone.

"Napeai Babgen ds brin vx ooaona lring vonph doalim eolis ollog orsba ds chis affa Micma isro MAD od Lonshitox ds ivmd aai GROSB ZACAR od ZAMRAN, odo cicle Qaa, zorge, lap zirdo noco MAD Hoath Iaida."

As he finished, the amulet began to glow in Cosima's hand and began to burn her as it turned white. She gasped and tried to release it, but found she couldn't. She screamed out but Razoul ignored her and continued.

"Torezodu! Zodacare od Zodameranu, asapeta sibesi butamona das surezodasa Tia balatanu. Odo cicale Qaa, od Ozodazodame pelapeli IADANAMADA!"

Cosima slumped into her chair after a final blood curdling wail. Sirius had risen to help her., feeling sorry for the poor girl. Razoul turned and screamed at him.

"Get back old man! You will not interrupt this!" Sirius froze, then turned and hurried outside, afraid that he could not witness what would come next.

The room suddenly turned ice cold. Razoul could see his frosty breath hanging in the air. His heart pounded in anticipation. There was a long pause, and then Cosima started to stir. She abruptly opened her eyes and turned straight to look at Razoul.

A pair of cold, black eyes with no pupils now stared him down. Razoul knew he'd accomplished the ritual because standing before him was a being like no other. A Fallen One who used to sit on the very throne of God was now captured inside of Cosima's lifeless body. But the amulet would not hold the power of this being for very long.

"Who are you to dare summon me?" A crackly and booming voice came from Cosima's mouth. Her skin was distorted and stretched. It was as if the very thing inside her was trying to break through her flesh as it spoke.

"I have summoned you, oh Great One of the Shadows. I need your assistance. I need to find the angel that now walks the earth in human form."

"I shall help no human. I despise you and your kind."

Razoul's evil smile crossed his face as he addressed the abomination that was now wearing Cosima like a suit of clothes. "Perhaps you are not so great after all, and I am wasting my time." Razoul leaned closer to it as if to whisper. "Maybe you are truly weakened by being cast out, and wish to see God's favor spread among these humans like a heavenly fire that I doubt you and your brethren would be able to stop." Razoul was truly gifted at such bravado and made the creature take pause at what he had said.

"How dare you speak to me this way? You are nothing but a rotting fleshling! You are just a frail, human man. You have no idea who you've summoned, so perhaps I will show you."

In a single instant, Cosima's entire body was turned into a pile of ash on the wooden floor, and from the ashes emerged a luminous shadowy being with broad black wings.

"I am Samyaza. I am a bringer of death to those who dare to face me. Tell me, son of Britius, why would I spare you?" A long arm stretched across the room to within inches of Razoul's chest.

Razoul did not waiver in his aggressive stance. "I am here to rid the world of heaven's prize—the Incarnate One. This is who I seek and ask that you help me find."

"Why should I care about this Incarnate One? What do I care for the world of mankind?"

"She will end your reign in the shadows, oh great and powerful one. The prophecy states that she is the covenant to bring heaven to earth. I know that you and your brethren once walked among us as Gods doing as you please. Do you think you'll have such freedom once she awakens?" There was a deep moment of silence, before Razoul added, "Or perhaps you feel that this particular favorite angel has the right to be given what you and your brethren were so wrongly denied?"

Samyaza seemed to consider the words that were spoken. "Are you saying you wish to become indebted to me?"

"Perhaps if you'd consider pointing me in the right direction, I can offer you the destruction of this heavenly abomination that is walking the earth." Razoul was hoping for an even trade, and did not desire to make a pact with Samyaza.

As if reading his mind, Samyaza cackled. "All such bargains, silly human, come at a steep price. I wonder if you have the strength to pay me next time I call upon you!" A wave of energy knocked Razoul from his feet and sent him crashing to the floor. "Perhaps you have no strength at all."

Razoul's lungs nearly collapsed when the creature flung him down, but he steadied his nerves and forced himself to stand again, defiantly. Again Samyaza knocked him to his knees crying out, "Bow before me Razoul, son of Britius."

Razoul could barely breathe, but his fierce will gave him the strength to rise to his feet again without fear.

"Oh, you'd like more? Perhaps this little game will serve to amuse me after all. I do not know the exact location of this woman you seek since she's carefully hidden even from the Grigori . . . at least for now. But I can send you closer than you've been. My traitorous brothers and sisters have been concentrating their energies in a particular region to hide her. But you'd better strike while she's most vulnerable, as you said, and I may point you in the right direction."

The fallen angel made the amulet rise up from the pile of ashes. As it floated into the air, it lit up with a peculiar red glow. It flew across the room and Razoul snatched it before it whizzed past him. Instead of it being hot as he expected it was icy cold. He knew the summoning spell was broken.

"Listen well, fleshling. You will find her in the land of grain called the Heart of the Dove, in the United States. The amulet will let you know when you are getting closer to her. But as I take my leave of you, know this pitiful human...you unfortunately WILL see me again."

As the creature disappeared, the ground began to shake all around Razoul and an unholy fire began to consume the table and other objects in the room. In moments the entire house was engulfed in flames. Weakened by Samyaza and the intense smoke filling his lungs, Razoul used his last little bit of strength to move himself toward the door.

He barely made it through the doorway and into the night air before the roof collapsed and the modest dwelling was destroyed.

40- *Storm Coming*

"Wow that was a big one. I hope we don't lose power." A huge storm was brewing which was often typical of springtime in the Midwest. They didn't bother Catherine, but tonight as she looked out and the thunder shook the walls, there was a sense of foreboding.

Then she thought about Erica being here with her and wondered how long she'd be able to stay, especially since Barb wasn't going to tolerate both of their absences very long.

If I didn't have Erica here, what would I do? God, I don't think I've even thanked her yet for coming down to take care of me...great move Catherine.

Erica had been seated on the couch quietly reading a book, when Catherine turned away from watching the storm.

"Hey, Erica?"

"Yeah?"

"I just wanted to thank you for everything you have done lately. I just realized that I didn't thank you when you drove all the way down here to check on me. You've stayed with me, too. Of course, it's a real plus that you don't think I'm a lunatic by now."

Erica put her book down and walked over to where Catherine was standing. She had a serious look on her face. "Catherine, from the moment we met, I knew there was something special about you. There was always something about you that I just couldn't put my finger on. I watched you at work. You were so kind to my mother..." Erica had tears well up in her eyes. "Then you saved her, Catherine. Do you have any idea what that means to me?"

Catherine started to object when Erica interrupted her. "Let me finish, please. I believe that you healed my mother's cancer. You have extraordinary abilities that go beyond anything either of us can understand right now. You mean the world to me and my mother, don't you get that?"

Catherine looked into Erica's eyes and saw something she'd not considered before. Erica loved her unconditionally. This had made her feel uncomfortable, so she had kept her at a distance. But now, it seemed pointless to deny it anymore. Perhaps it was time to let someone into her life. Maybe it was time for Catherine to stop going it alone.

I'm sorry Erica. I know I don't let anyone in. Yes, I know that you and your mom love me. You guys have given me a gift too. I never thought I could have family again after my parents died. It tore out my heart, and maybe even a little bit of my soul."

Catherine sat down on the couch and began to cry like she never had allowed herself to ever before, and Erica sat down to hold onto her. Catherine buried her face in Erica's shoulder. She couldn't have stopped the tears from flowing even if she had tried.

"Catherine, just let it go now. We are your family. We will stand by you no matter what happens. I am going to help you figure this all out. So don't worry, don't worry."

"Thank you. I can't do this by myself. I just can't. I don't even want to try anymore."

Erica held her tight and looked across to the window. The storm had arrived and the rain began to strike the windows violently. Her stomach suddenly was in knots. She couldn't shake the feel that something was coming.

41- *A Watchful Eye*

Brother Artemis sat on his bed at the Super 8 motel in Parsons reading his Bible and praying as he listened to the storm outside. The torrential rain had forced him to leave his post for a brief time but even so, he was only minutes away from Catherine.

The young monk had arrived two days ago per Monsignor Bartholomew's instructions and been there to monitor Catherine's movements and watch for anything of interest. He was not allowed to make contact with her so his days had been shrouded in silence, nestled in a grove of trees near the home. Of course as a monk, spending the day in silence wasn't out of the ordinary.

He glanced at the old clock on the night stand. It was nearly one in the morning and close to his time to report what he'd seen thus far, which wasn't much. He had no idea why he was sent on an errand thousands of miles from Italy to observe this woman, but he knew that it must be very important. Bartholomew was a complicated man but a righteous one who was blessed by God.

He took the phone he had been given and dialed the number. Instead of being greeted by a hello, Monsignor Bartholomew jumped directly into the conversation.

"Brother, I've been anxiously awaiting your call. Is she still there?"

"Yes, yes, Monsignor, she's still residing at the home of her parents. She returned to the convent another time, and left with a package. She has also visited a psychiatric hospital nearby. After she left, I remained there and I was able to find out that she was visiting a young man by the name of Jacob Petersen, though I do not know why."

"I see."

"Also, she is not alone at the home. There's a woman staying with her, perhaps a friend. I have also seen a man visit the home briefly several times."

"So, she's not alone?"

"Si`, Monsignor."

"She had a package with her when she left the convent?"

"Si`, Monsignor."

"Very good, this is a good thing."

She has the Angelus Aevum and everything is in motion. But even so, the books' power in her hands will make her vulnerable to detection.

"This other woman with her, do you know who she is?"

"No, I do not. I believe she is a friend from the city, her license plate matches Catherine's."

"I see. If you can find out her name without detection, please do so. But, you must not be seen. I cannot stress this enough. Also I ask that you find out who this man is as well, we will need to determine if he is a threat to her."

"Monsignor? If I may ask a question?"

"Yes, brother."

"Who is this Catherine Jane Moore? Why is she important to the order?"

"I understand your curiosity, dear Brother. However it is greater wisdom in some circumstances to know less."

"Yes, Monsignor, I understand."

"As a servant of God, I know you realize that this woman is quite important to God, which makes her very important to our order."

"Of course, you know that you can count on my obedience and discretion here."

"Thank you, Brother. Do not hesitate to contact me immediately if something seems out of the ordinary. Your mission is of vital importance. That is why I sent you. Your heart is pure, and I know I may count on you. Do call me with any additional details as you find them."

"Si`, Monsignor. I will."

"May God's grace be with you."

Monsignor Bartholomew hung up the phone, closed his eyes and sighed.

May God's grace be with us all.

42- *It's a Date*

Before they had gone to bed the night before Catherine took the ancient book and decided to put it somewhere safe. There was a panel in her old room that she used to hide things behind as a child. Remembering her dream and the mention of her enemies, it made her feel better to put the book somewhere out of sight.

Bright and early Monday morning, Erica left for the local coffee shop to research the Enochian script and other items of interest from a list they had put together.

Catherine began gathering her things to head back to the hospital to see Jacob and hopefully get some answers. She was nervous, but also excited at the prospect of speaking with him. She was coming down the stairs when the doorbell rang.

Who could that be?

She hurried down the stairs to open the door. "Oh, hello David. I was just on my way out to see a friend."

He grinned. "I'm glad I caught you then. I was just dropping by to see if you might want to grab some dinner while you are in town."

Catherine tried to hide her discomfort about seeing him again. "Oh, that's nice of you. I appreciate the offer. But..."

Sensing what she was about to say, David cut her off before she could decline. "Listen, my parents are really fond of you and loved your parents. I just wanted to do something nice for you. Is there anything wrong with that?"

Catherine didn't want to be rude. "No, David there's nothing wrong with that at all. That's so sweet."

"So, you'll go?"

"Sure."

"Shall I pick you up around six?"

"I think that will work."

"Well I'd better let you get going." David's face was beaming now. As he walked across the porch he turned. "Do you like Italian?"

"I love Italian."

"Great! I know a great place in Pittsburg. It's one of my folks' favorites."

David lingered for just a moment and then took off with a spring in his step. Catherine closed the door, shaking her head, and went to get the rest of her stuff.

Now on top of everything, I have a date tonight. Wait until Erica hears this. Of course she'll say it's a good thing.

Catherine couldn't help smiling just a little.

43- *Through Jacob's Eyes*

Jacob had been anxiously awaiting Catherine's return. He was frustrated because since then, he had not been given a single image of her to draw, which was unusual. At breakfast, he took a full tray of food, but didn't touch it.

Now he obsessively paced his room trying to pass the time, while continuously playing the future encounter over and over in his head. He was about to go for another walk of the grounds when the nurse interrupted his train of thought.

"Jacob, they just called from the information desk. You have a visitor."

Finally, she's here.

Jacob turned to look at the nurse. "Okay, thanks. Is she on her way up?"

"Yes, she is."

Catherine walked up the hallway toward Jacob's room. When she got there, he was staring out his window.

"Jacob?"

"Catherine! I'm so glad you came back." He turned around quickly and came over to hug her.

"I wasn't sure you wanted anything to do with me, Jacob."

"It's not like that, Catherine. You surprised me yesterday. I'm sorry I acted that way after all this time." He pulled back from embracing her and let go.

"It's okay. I understand."

He smiled assuredly. "You always did understand me, didn't you? I was miserable when you left."

Catherine sat down in a chair near Jacob's bed. "I know. I know. I'm so sorry but I had to leave Parsons. Staying was too much for me. Trust me, I tried to."

He sat down on his bed next to her. "I know you had to leave after everything that happened. I'm just glad you are here now. It means so much to me to see you again. So are you back for good? Because if you are, I was thinking maybe it's time to go home myself."

"No, I don't think I am. I'm not sure how long I'll be here. There's just a lot going on right now that I don't know how to explain. In fact, I was hoping you might be able to tell me something."

"Sure. Anything for you."

Catherine looked at him carefully. He was acting more like the old Jacob she knew but something wasn't quite right. She quickly pushed those thoughts out of her mind. "I saw the sketch pad you left on the bench. How do you draw the things you do? Everything you drew was true Jacob. How can that be?"

Jacob looked down at the floor. "I don't know exactly, but it's been that way ever since you left. I see you in my mind and then can draw what I see."

"So you've been doing this for years? It's like you've been with me all along."

He looked at her with a little pout. "Yes, Catherine. I've always been there."

This is happening perfectly. She and I are meant to be together.

"Why didn't you call me?"

"I don't know. I was afraid you didn't want to hear from me. I saw your life, you had friends and you were in college in the big city. How could I compete with that?"

"Jacob, you have to know how much you meant to me!"

Catherine looked around the room. "It's my fault isn't it? I'm why you ended up here." A wave of utter regret passed through her and she put her face in her hands.

Jacob leaned forward and lifted her head. "Everything is going to be okay. You're here now, aren't you?"

She nodded and looked into his familiar brown eyes. "I went into your room Jacob, during my visit to your mom. Ever since I saw the drawing pad under your bed, I have been trying to figure everything out. Not just you and I but everything. All the things you drew in the past few weeks have turned my life upside down. I'm honestly freaking out."

"You know Catherine, sometimes things happen that we can't explain, but they are just meant to be." He paused for a moment, choosing his next words carefully. "Sort of like you and I. Why can I see your life through your eyes? We are joined together for some reason."

It felt good to talk to Jacob, and for a moment Catherine felt like they were younger, two teenagers sitting in her room discussing the meaning of life for hours and hours.

"We were inseparable back then, weren't we? You were my best friend, Jacob. I should have known I could lean on you more. I am sorry we lost touch. I had no idea that anything was wrong after I went away. I just assumed you moved on with your plans after high school, just like I did. I believed in my mind that you had gone to your art school. I did think about you from time to time. I imagined you working as an artist somewhere on the east coast, maybe New York. I can't believe I was so damn wrong."

"Catherine you can't blame yourself. You were going through so much. I only wish I could have been the man you needed. I regret not going after you to tell you how I felt about you. That's what got me here. Not you."

Catherine saw tenderness in his eyes, yet something else was there too, "I don't think it was your job to save me, Jacob. I ran and hid from everyone and everything. I doubt it would have made much of a difference if you had told me how you felt about me. I was discarding everything that reminded me of my parents: the house, the town, and all my friends, including you."

"But I was the closest person to you and should have been there, even if you didn't want me to be."

"Well even if you had followed me to college, I don't think we'd have ended up together, if that's what you are saying. But I wish I could figure out how you could see it all."

"Maybe I have a gift, at least where you are concerned."

"It's a gift for sure. You have so many gifts. The way you draw what you see is breathtaking. You need to get out of here and follow your dreams." Catherine was trying to encourage him as she always had.

"I do think I'm ready to get out of here, anyway."

"Oh, Jacob, that's great! Your mother has missed you so much. It broke my heart when I was talking to her. I was devastated to hear the news of your hospitalization, too."

That's not what I mean, sweet Catherine.

"Well, I said I wanted to leave but I don't want to go home to my parents'. My mom doesn't really need me anymore."

"I don't think that is true, Jacob. I heard about your dad and I am so sorry he passed away. Your mother worries about you every day, and your dad dying a few years ago really affects her still."

Jacob wandered to his window and stood looking outside. "I know she worries about me. I just mean I'm grown, and she doesn't need me around her house to worry about."

"I just want you to have a happy life, Jake. You deserve that. So, are you allowed to leave whenever you want to?"

Jacob turned and smiled. "Yeah, I can leave anytime I want to, and I've decided I want to."

Catherine was happy that Jacob wanted to move on with his life now, and was curious about his plans. "Do you have any specific plans after you get out of here?"

Jacob hesitated. "I have something in mind, yes. I think your coming here is a sign that it's time."

"What are your plans then?"

Jacob crossed the room to Catherine and knelt down in front of her. Catherine was a bit surprised. He looked up at her earnestly. "Catherine, my whole life has always been about you." He took her hands into his that were seated in her lap.

"Jake. Listen, I..."

"Please let me finish. I've thought more you than you can even imagine. I've spent many hours thinking about why you and I are so connected. It was torture for me to be away from you but still be a part of every moment of your life. That's why I ended up here in this lonely place. I was stuck and couldn't figure out what to do about that. But since yesterday, after seeing you again, I am sure I know what this means."

Catherine's gaze never left Jacob's. She saw him as a younger boy at first, and then observed the lines in his face that had been grooved over time. His eyes were beautiful as always. Her feelings for him had always run deep. They had been through a lot together as kids. He was still good old Jacob, just older and more worn. Her heart leapt to him, she felt responsible for leaving him behind and never looking back.

"Jacob, I am so sorry all this happened. If I'd stayed or kept in touch maybe things would be very different for you now."

"That doesn't matter. Don't you see? You're back and I knew you were coming before you arrived. It's a sign! I know it's a sign." He got up and quickly grabbed his pad and showed her.

"See, you saw, right? I knew you were coming. See?"

Catherine's back stiffened in her chair, now suddenly sure of where he was leading the conversation. "Yes, Jacob, I see and that is what I wanted to talk to you about. Do you know how you see what you see? Some other stuff is happening to me too and it could help."

Jacob appeared deflated a bit, but told her anyway. "No, I just see a flash of you or a particular scene in my head and then it's like my hands start moving until the picture is done. It's incredible when it happens, but I can't make it happen, although I have tried many times, believe me."

He sat down and laid the pad on his bed. "It was frustrating when I couldn't see you that way all the time or whenever I wanted to."

Catherine got up and sat on the bed putting her arm around Jacob. "I can imagine, Jake, I really can."

Jacob turned his head sharply, his face filled with a dark expression. "Can you? Can you, really?"

Catherine didn't like the animosity she suddenly felt from him. "Jacob, are you okay?"

"How could you say that? How could I be okay?"

Catherine was now speechless for the first time. Jacob leapt up from the bed, becoming very animated. "I have had no control at all, all these years while you were out having a life for yourself. You went to school, you got out of this damn town and what did I get? NOTHING! Not a damn thing at all. I've sat here for over a decade waiting and waiting for you to return. I knew you would come back. I just knew it. How do you think I feel? Do you think after all that, I am okay?"

Jacob kept pacing and running his right hand through his hair. Catherine was shocked and upset. She had never seen her friend like this before but had dealt with clients who were similarly distraught, so she immediately switched into a different gear.

"Jacob, I can't change the past now and neither can you. I wish I could for your sake. I really do. I hear what you are saying and how you feel. And I'm sorry you feel that way."

Her calm demeanor only made him more agitated and he spat his next words at her. "I wonder sometimes if you really are sorry."

His words wounded Catherine. "What do you mean, Jacob? Of course I am."

"You never called, once. Not once. If you had, maybe things would have been different. Why was I made to see your life but only through a pane of glass, never really being a part of it all?"

Catherine shook her head. "I don't know, but I wish I did."

Play it cool dude, you are gonna push her away.

Jacob flipped his long, brown bangs back and walked over towards her and slumped on the bed. "Me too, Catherine, me too."

She reached over to take his hand and saw his expression change to calm too quickly as he spoke. "I love you so much, Catherine. I wish I would have told you, or called to tell you, but I didn't."

"I love you too, Jacob. You mean the world to me."

She loves me, I knew it. Just tell her. Just tell her what you want now.

Catherine felt torn apart.

"I know I get angry sometimes, Catherine. I just can't help it. It's been torture without you here. I hope you understand that."

"Yes, Jacob, I understand."

Jacob smiled with vague satisfaction. "I knew you would. You always understood me, even when others didn't." Then Jacob's expression changed to that of a small child. "That's why I think that our connection is so important. It's very important even if we don't fully understand what is going on. So..."

Jacob repositioned himself, as if he were working up to saying something. "So, I told you I wanted to leave this place. What I meant was that I wanted to leave here with you. I don't think we were ever meant to be apart. I have thought about this a long time and I believe we are soul mates. Otherwise, how could all of this happen?"

"Soul mates? Jacob, you think we are soul mates?"

"Yes, of course Catherine. I've never even heard of what we have before. What else could it mean?"

Oh, God, no. Jake, we aren't soul mates. He wants to come home with me? I have to fix this now.

"Jacob, our friendship, and everything we shared were a long time ago, but it is still very special to me. You know that."

It was clear that Jacob didn't expect these particular words from her at that point. He stood up, taking her hands and pulled her toward him. He was physically stronger than Catherine expected.

"Catherine, are you saying you don't feel it? The power drawing you and me together? I have dreamt of this moment for so long. I want to be with you forever. Don't you want to be with me?" His voice was soft and sickly sweet.

Catherine looked into Jacob's eyes. She believed he felt this way but had no idea how to tell him she didn't. Letting him down was the last thing she wanted to do.

"Jacob...we just reunited here, can't we just take things a bit slower while we figure this out?"

Jacob began to squeeze her hands harder. "Slower? How can you say slower? Isn't eight years long enough to wait?"

"You are hurting me, Jacob. Let go of my hands." Catherine spoke firmly although she was pleading.

Jacob released his grip and turned away from her to prepare for his next approach. His mind was moving rapidly which made it difficult for him to stay on track. He wandered to the window looking out. His shoulders dropped as if utterly defeated.

"I have spent years watching the world go by. Maybe I'm a fool for waiting for you. When you love someone shouldn't you be willing to do whatever it takes? Am I crazy for wanting that, crazy for wanting to be with you?"

Catherine watched him carefully. She wasn't sure what to expect next or what she could possibly say to get him to let go of his focus on them being together. Her heart was pounding and she wanted to cry. She got up and walked over to the window and began to speak to him softly.

"Jacob, you are not crazy. I am so touched that you want us to be together after all this time. I hate that you have been here so long and have missed so much. Maybe all this means what you think it does. It's just right now I have so much happening in my life. Some incredible and unbelievable things, things I never thought were real or possible. I need to get all this sorted out first, before...before I could think about a relationship with anyone, even you, my friend."

Jacob thought about it for a moment and turned to her. "Catherine, you shouldn't do all this alone. I'm worried about you."

"Don't worry, Jacob. You know I can handle it. I always do. And I'm not alone right now, my friend Erica came down from the city to stay with me at my parents' house."

"I know you are the strongest person I've ever met. But I also know you hate to ask for help. With my artistic gifts, I could help you. Maybe if we spent more time together, then my gift would be to draw other things that you really need."

"I know you want to help me. I appreciate that. I'm just not sure what you can really do at this point."

Jacob's blood started to rush and he fought to contain his desperation. She was slipping right through his fingers and he knew it. "Let me help you! I can, I know I can. Let me prove it to you."

Catherine took a small step back from him instinctively, without even realizing she had. Jacob stepped toward her.

You must listen to me Catherine! You need me, even if you don't see it.

"Just take me out of here now. Let me stay with you in that big house. You can tell me the details. What I haven't seen. It will be just like old times. You'll see."

Just do it, Catherine.

"Jake, sweet Jake, please. Why don't you go home to your mother as a first step? You'll be right next door, and I'm not going anywhere right now. I promise."

Jacob's rage came to the surface and quickly spilled over. "Why are you treating me like a child? Like I am incapable of knowing what I want? Why are you telling me what to do?"

"I'm not trying to tell you what to do, Jacob. I am just asking us to take it slow and for you to be a little more reasonable."

"Just let me come with you for a couple days. Then I promise I'll go home to my mother until I figure out what I'm going to do next."

Catherine's face saddened. "Jake, I just can't do that right now."

Jacob's voice rose suddenly, which made Catherine scared. "God, Catherine! What's the big deal? We're friends, right? What is the harm in a friend staying for a couple days? I need you right now and you need me, even if you don't think you do! How can you say no with everything that has happened?"

Catherine knew now that she could not bring Jacob back down like a patient as she had hoped. "Jacob, I have to say no. I can't have you at the house right now. I need my space. I cannot handle what I have going on right now."

"Then let's handle it together."

"No, Jacob."

Out of desperation Jacob rushed Catherine and grabbed her by the shoulders. "How can you say no to me? Haven't I suffered enough?"

Catherine struggled to break free, but that only made him tighten his grip on her. "Don't do this, Jacob. Let go of me, now!"

"I can't let go of you. How can I let go! Why can't you understand what I'm trying to tell you?"

"Jacob, come on now, please let go of me!"

Now Jacob could see fear in Catherine's eyes, which he had not considered at all.

No, no, no. It's not supposed to be like this.

Their raised voices had drawn a staff member passing down the hallway. "Is there a problem here?" The nurse saw Catherine's mortified expression. "Jacob, what is going on?"

"Nothing! Get the hell out of my room!" Jacob let go of Catherine and pushed the nurse out of his door and slammed it shut.

Catherine was frightened. She had never seen Jacob violent or even a little bit angry. She could hear shouts in the hallway calling a code white and knew staff was about to descend on the room to sedate him.

"Jacob, calm down. You are only going to make things worse." Catherine had taken steps toward him.

She reached out to touch his shoulder.

"Get your damn hands off of me!"

In his fury, he flipped around and shoved her backwards. Catherine fell to the floor. Jacob ran over to her immediately. "Catherine, oh God, baby, I'm sorry. I didn't mean to..."

At that moment, the door flew open and two men and the nurse came rushing in.

"Jacob, come on, let her go."

The men grabbed Jacob by the arms to restrain him and took him gently to the floor.

"Let me go! I am trying to help her."

The nurse helped Catherine up and escorted her into the hallway, then returned to the room pulling what appeared to be syringe from her pocket. Catherine knew what would happen next. They would sedate him, and put him in confinement by himself.

She could hear Jacob screaming from the room for her. Catherine headed quickly down the hall and disappeared into the stairwell. After reaching the bottom of the stairs, she sat down in despair and began to cry.

Jacob no, no, no. It wasn't supposed to happen like this. What have I done?

43- *The Keys*

Catherine drove around the countryside aimlessly for hours replaying the visit with Jacob in her mind over and over again. She was trying to figure out what she could have done to prevent Jacob from losing it, but only ending up feeling more upset about the entire ordeal.

Eventually she found herself driving back home. As her key turned in the door, she could feel her tears welling up again. When Erica greeted her cheerfully, she lost control.

"Oh, Catherine, are you alright? Come inside."

"Erica, I don't know what happened. Everything was fine, and then he got so mad that the staff had to sedate him. It was awful."

Erica just let her cry, holding her in her arms.

Catherine let go of her embrace and walked toward the dining room table to set her purse down. "He wanted to come home here with me. It was like he thought I could save him. How can I do that if I can't even save myself right now? I told him no, and why. But he was insistent on being together. He said he thought we were soul mates. These years have had too much of a strain on him. I feel like it's my fault. I should have been there. I should have stayed in touch." She slumped down in a chair at the table.

"Catherine. You couldn't have known about him, or all this. There's no way you are responsible for a grown man losing his grip. You were both kids doing the best you could."

Catherine looked up through her tears and sighed. "I know Erica. I know. But this is different. He's partly right you know. We are connected in some major way. What am I going to do?"

"I don't know, honey. I wish I knew what to say."

"The visit was going great at first. I just don't understand where it went south. He got angry, grabbed me, then staff got involved and he got sedated."

"Oh my God, Catherine, that's just awful. I am so sorry."

"It's okay Erica. I'll be alright. I'm still shook up. I've been driving for a couple hours. I'll call later to check on him. Oh man, what am I going to tell Mary? She'll be very upset. She's already been through so much."

Erica thought maybe a change in subject might help her get her mind off what had happened. "Well not to change the subject, but I found a few things you might be interested in."

Catherine nodded. "That's good, let's change the subject. Okay, what did you find out?"

"I did a search for Enochian script. Not sure exactly what it means but apparently this language was created by a man named John Dee. He lived in the 1500's and was well-known for communicating with the angels. The script reportedly came from his scrying sessions with another man by the name of Edward Kelley."

"That's right. I remember seeing a site about that. What kind of sessions did you say? Skying?"

"No, scrying. I didn't know what that was either, but it's kind of like looking into a crystal ball only it's a flat, dark surface instead. Scrying is where a person uses a stone to see the future or other spiritual information. They call the flat stone they use a shewing stone. So the words you saw in Kansas City and the writing in the book are related to Enochian script. I printed off a couple examples of it to be sure and compare with the book."

Catherine perked up a little with something else to concentrate on. "So why would the Sister give me a book written in an obscure angelic language?"

"Well there's more. While doing my research I also found the symbol that is on the cover of the book. It's called the Sigil de Ameth. It's also angelic and supposed to be powerful. This also came from the work of Dee and Kelley."

"What is it the symbol for?"

"It was hard for me to understand but there are symbols within the symbols which are angelic calls, plus unspoken names of God and a few other things too."

"Calls?"

"From what I was reading, a call is like a spell or incantation that can summon an angel. There are these passages called Enochian Keys too. It's going to take me a bit to sort through everything I saved on the computer."

"Wow. Thanks, Erica. At least we do know something now. Everything I've been experiencing related to angels."

Erica smiled and nodded.

Catherine glanced over the flowers on the table. They had opened beautifully already. Then she jumped up. "Oh God, what time is it?"

Erica glanced at her watch. "It's almost five. Why?"

"With everything else, I almost forgot. David came by on my way out to see Jacob. He asked me to dinner. He's so nice, I just couldn't say no."

"Really?"

"Yes, and he's going to be here in an hour. I should call and cancel."

Erica looked at her best friend knowingly, "I know you don't feel like it, Cat, but I think you should go. Get away for a few. Enjoy yourself. I'll be fine here."

"I'm sure I look like hell right now. I don't even know what to say to him. Do you realize it's been at least six years since I've been on a date?"

"This is all the more reason you should go! Don't think about it, just go up and take a shower to freshen up and let him take you out for a nice dinner. Besides, it would help you to do something normal right now."

"Ugh, come on really? I'll just make a fool of myself."

"Go, Catherine. Just go."

Catherine started to argue more but realized she wasn't going to do much to sway Erica, and as usual she was probably right. She headed upstairs to get ready.

44- *Sharing a Moment*

The doorbell rang and Erica ran excitedly to get it. When she opened the door she saw David in a pair of khaki slacks and blue button down shirt. "Hey there, David, it's nice to see you again. You look very nice. Come on in."

David smiled and stepped inside, nervously looking around. "Thanks."

"Catherine will be down in a minute. She's still getting ready."

Catherine heard them talking downstairs. She threw her blouse on quickly and went downstairs. She looked much better than before, but her gaze was strained and Erica knew why.

"There you are, Catherine. David just got here."

Catherine noticed David looking at her fondly as she descended to the foyer. A part of her wanted to run back upstairs and tell him to go away, but she didn't.

"Thought I'd better get down here before Erica started telling you all about me."

Erica and David both laughed.

"Well, I better go check my food in the kitchen. You guys have fun!"

Catherine called after her, "Subtle, Erica, real subtle."

David looked at Catherine with admiration which made Catherine feel uncomfortable. "What? Why are you looking at me that way?"

David just smiled coyly. "Can't a guy admire a beautiful woman?"

For a moment she felt silly. "Yeah, sure a guy can."

"Plus you look wonderful, as usual. Not that I've seen you that many times."

"Thanks."

"You're welcome." He motioned to the door. "Shall we go?"

Catherine nodded and walked out the door.

The drive took about thirty minutes and neither of them spoke much on the way. Then David broke the silence. "Are you alright Catherine?"

She answered him candidly. "I think so. It's just been a really hard day. I almost didn't come."

"We could have postponed this if you weren't up to it." Catherine looked at him. His eyes were honest and kind.

"I know. I guess I wanted a change of scenery. Erica thought it might help."

David watched the road but said, "Sometimes it does. I know whenever things get hard for me just doing something new, even if I don't want to, can help a little."

Catherine looked down at her hands in her lap. "Yeah, I guess it can."

As he drove, Catherine studied him. David had a boyish look, but was handsome nonetheless.

If my life weren't totally up heaved, this might be nice. Of course right now I'm just a mess. I am afraid I'm not good for anyone.

This thought made her think of Jacob sedated in a locked room at the hospital. She grimaced.

Knock this off Catherine or you'll have a terrible time and take David down with you.

As they pulled up to the restaurant, Catherine resolved to put everything in the back of her mind and enjoy her dinner as much as possible. She went to open her door to get out but before she could, it opened. David reached out with his hand. "Allow me." Catherine took his hand and let him help her out of the car.

When their eyes met, she felt something strange move through her, from head to toe. It was then she decided that there was much more to him than met the eye.

Who are you?

Both were silent as they walked inside the restaurant. Catherine looked around at the Italian décor. The interior had dark wood furniture and bright white linen table cloths. Each table had a covered candle holder that cast a warm glow on everyone that was seated. The atmosphere was as serene as it was comfortable.

A cheerful hostess in black attire led them to a small table for two in the back, which had a fair amount of privacy. David stepped up to Catherine's chair and pulled it out for her.

He's a gentleman, too.

Catherine looked down at the floor while being seated, but had a smile on her face.

"Thanks for coming out with me tonight, Catherine."

"Thanks for inviting me. It's nice to get out of the house right now. It's nice to take a breather."

David smiled. "I'm happy to help in any way I can."

Catherine chuckled, "You do seem to be a guy who likes to be helpful."

"I suppose I do." Then he looked at Catherine curiously. "Have you ever felt like you've known someone even though you'd never met them before?"

Catherine thought about it for a minute. "You mean like déjà vu or something?"

"Sort of, but stronger than déjà vu, more like seeing them for the first time but feeling as if you already have met them."

"Oh, I don't think so. But I've had a déjà vu experience a few times. Why do you ask?"

David looked down at the table and repositioned his silverware. He grabbed his napkin and put it in his lap to stall. He wasn't sure how to explain to Catherine how he really felt. "Well… it's kind of weird. You might think it's strange."

"I doubt that I would think whatever you have to say is weird or strange, trust me."

"Okay here goes. The very first time I came by your place, it wasn't like I was meeting you for the first time at all. It was like seeing you again after a long time."

"Maybe we did meet when we were kids. Do you think that's it?"

David shook his head no. "I asked my mom about that actually. I asked her if we were ever around each other when we were little. She said that she and dad didn't become close friends with your parents until several years before their accident." David looked at her with regret. "I'm sorry to mention that."

"It's okay David. I think I can handle someone mentioning my folks by now. I still miss them a lot, of course. It was pretty hard on me back then though, because I was entering my senior year of high school when they died. After I graduated, I left town and didn't come back until now. Your dad has been great to manage things for me."

Catherine had averted David's gaze as she was speaking, but eventually stared directly into his eyes. The way he was looking at her was gentle, almost graceful. His large, deep set eyes were brown and seemed to shimmer in the candlelight. His focus on her was so intense that it surprised her.

She felt like David could penetrate into all her inner secrets by simply looking at her. She felt self-conscious, which caused her to switch subjects abruptly. "So what do you do for a living?"

"I'm a computer engineer. Most people think I'm a geek, I guess. I've been into computers since I was a kid. You heard my mom at dinner the other day. Once I discovered my first computer, I never left the house except for school. She's always mentioning that to people for some reason, but it's true. The only person that eventually coaxed me out of that room was Mira."

"Was Mira your girlfriend?"

David looked at her grimly, his expression changed, and Catherine knew she'd triggered a painful subject.

"It's okay if you don't want to talk about her."

David unexpectedly reached out to take her hands in his. "I want you to know something, Catherine. I know what it means to lose the most important person in your life. It can happen so suddenly that it blows a big hole through you. Since we met, I've been trying to imagine what it was like for you to lose your parents, just like I lost Mira. All I could imagine was doubling the pain that I went through. So I know why you left, because I did too, after that happened."

Catherine's heart was filled with empathy for this kind and gentle man. She could see in his eyes what Mira must have meant to him. It touched her so much, that tears began to well up in her eyes. "Did she die in a car accident?"

"Yes. One moment we were planning our wedding, the next thing I knew she was gone."

"I'm so sorry, David."

He smiled sweetly. "Thanks, I appreciate that."

Their intense moment was interrupted by the server returning to take their order, but neither of them had looked at the menu.

"Have you both decided on what you'd like to eat this evening?"

She didn't have a huge appetite, but wanted the server to leave them so she asked, "What would you recommend? We haven't even looked at the menus."

"Ah, allow me." David picked up his menu. "Let's see, do you like lasagna? It's very good here and usually what I order."

Catherine looked at David and then the server. "That sounds good. I'll have that."

David chimed in. "Me too, thanks."

The server left them.

"I moved away several months later and got a job that has been my entire life since then. I try to get home to see the folks every once in awhile. Mom never stops worrying about me even though I ask her to stop. I am a grown man and know what I'm doing. I'm okay, I just found a way to maintain my sanity if you understand what I mean, and that's what I went with. Does that make sense, or am I kidding myself?"

Catherine sat up straighter and spoke with a formal voice. "Well since I'm a counselor and a trained professional who has been essentially doing the same thing for many years, then either you aren't or we both are."

They both started cracking up at the same time.

"Whew, that was close." David was grinning. "Glad to know everything is just fine now that I have a professional's opinion."

It felt good to laugh and be a little light-hearted. It actually made Catherine a little dizzy to let go of her composure even a tiny bit. She felt her body relax completely. "I had no idea that I was going to dinner with such a funny guy." She took a sip of her water and then raised her glass as if doing a toast. "And that's good to know."

It had been a long time since Catherine had spent time with anyone new, and dinner was going much better than she thought it would. It was a welcome break.

The lasagna was as good as any she'd ever tasted. David thankfully kept the conversation moving by asking about her work at the Division of Family Services. She found out that he'd often come downtown to a building near her apartment which was a branch of the company he had worked for in St. Louis. It was indeed a small world.

"I didn't know if I wanted to bring it up or not, but I wanted to tell you about something unusual that happened the day we met. That night I when I went to sleep, I had a dream about you and I."

"You did? A dream about me? What was it about?"

"It's probably silly, but I had a dream that I was chasing after you, well trying to catch up to you. We were in a garden with winding grey stone paths. You were wearing a long white gown. The paths were lined with white roses. Actually that is why I sent you the dozen white roses. I hope you liked them?

Catherine nearly blushed. "Yes, thank you very much. It's been a very long time since anyone sent me flowers. White roses are my favorite because of my dad. Did you ever see the garden out back of my parents' house when you were younger?" Catherine paused for a moment to remember how it once was. "It was the most amazing place for me as a girl. I used to make up all kinds of stories about princesses and princes. To me it was a magical place."

"I've only been allowed inside the front door so far." He grinned. "The reason I brought the dream up is because it was unusual for me to remember a dream, and even though I've never seen the garden, I believe I did in the dream. I usually am figuring out programming problems instead and that can really drive me crazy."

"There's nothing like taking your work home with you. But I've never dreamed about one of my cases, nor would I want to." She immediately thought of Olivia and the ordeal at the office.

If you think that's a wild story, I've got one for you.

"In all seriousness though, it was the most vivid dream I've ever had in my life. I have no idea what the dream meant though, it was an entire dream of me running down the garden paths chasing after you. No matter what I did though, I couldn't quite reach you because whenever I did, you seemed to disappear right in front of me."

Catherine got a perplexed and worried look on her face.

"You okay, Catherine?"

Catherine looked out the window to avoid David's direct gaze. "Yeah, yeah, I'm fine. It's just that there have been so many unbelievable things happening to me lately. For the first time in my usually unremarkable life I have more questions than I have answers. Your dream is interesting, but I have no idea what it means, either."

It suddenly hit Catherine how out of control everything had become and she had a sense it was only going to get much worse. Catherine turned to David protectively.

"Honestly, I have never been this lost in my life. You seem like a really nice guy." She reached out for his hands. "But, you really don't want to get involved with me right now."

"Don't worry about me. I'm a big boy. I think I can handle whatever you are going through, if you let me?"

Catherine pulled her hands back, shaking her head. "You don't even know me, David. So how can you be so sure?"

David took her hands back into his and looked at her softly. "I can tell that you are a very intelligent woman who has a big heart. I can tell that you are very strong but try to take the weight of the world on your shoulders all by yourself. I know your life hasn't been easy and the loss of your parents is still weighing on you heavily."

Catherine was surprised that David knew so much about her from just a couple interactions, but doubted that he would be able to understand everything that had happened in the past couple of weeks. "I don't know if I can even share or explain what's happening to me. I am having a hard time grasping or believing it myself. Most of the time, I feel like I'm the crazy one."

David didn't want to push Catherine too much. He was afraid of chasing her away before they even got a chance to get to know each other. That feeling caused him to develop a huge pit in his stomach. Everything about her spoke to him deeply: her deep blue eyes, the way her dark, wavy locks of hair framed her face, the way she walked into a room, and everything in between.

"What about your friend at the house?"

"Who? Erica?"

"Yes, what about her?"

Catherine looked at him like she was lost for a moment.

"Well, does your friend Erica think you are crazy?"

"Oh...no...I don't think so. She's supportive no matter what and drove all the way to Parsons to check on me. Erica is an amazing friend."

"If Erica can believe you and support you, then maybe a geeky guy like me could, too?"

Catherine just looked at him.

I wish it were that easy David, I really do. I have no idea what to say or do right now. Can you understand that?

"I don't want to push myself into your life. I just want you to know that I don't usually pursue women this way. I never thought after I lost Mira I'd ever feel anything for anyone else again. Then one day my mom asked me to stop by that house and there you were! When you first opened the door, I was startled to see the most beautiful woman I had ever met, standing in front of me. From the first moment I saw you, I wanted to be with you, to know you. Maybe I'm crazy for telling you all this, but I feel like I have to, so you won't dismiss me or run away before I can tell you how I feel. I just want the opportunity to get to know you better.

Would it be so bad to trust him? He has a good heart and means well.

Catherine thought about what he said, and wasn't sure what to say to this man she just met, but after a pause she spoke. "I am so scared right now. I'm so unsure of what I can or should do. I appreciate what you have said, David, and how kind you've been. That does mean a lot to me."

"I'm glad, Catherine. I am here for you and can take anything you want or need to share with me. I know you don't have a lot of reason to trust me, but I would never do anything to hurt you. I hope at least you can understand that."

"Yes, I see that." Catherine smiled to reassure him. "I am not sure why we have such a connection David, but I'm not upset about it either. Even if my life is a mess right now."

45- *Dark Dreaming*

Razoul tossed and turned in his bed. The ordeal with Samyaza and his escape from the burning home had rendered him unconscious. Sirius arranged to have him brought back to the estate where he remained. Now Razoul navigated his dream world in utter restlessness as the others waited for him to awaken.

The boy Razoul found himself on the top of the great staircase looking down at dozens of well-dressed ladies and gentleman. He was only fourteen. He quickly recognized the scene in front of him. It was one of the extravagantly lavish parties his parents threw twice a year. It was truly the only time he saw his mother shine, brought to life by the many visitors who came to share in the festivities.

He watched her below, graciously greeting his father's guests. She was in a full length ball gown made of rich green fabric with embroidered golden threads woven into the bodice. Her beautiful black hair was pulled up with a gold comb that allowed her ringlets to cascade all over the top of her head. He stood now as a young boy, admiring her great beauty and elegance as she exchanged pleasantries with various members of higher society.

His mood in the dream flipped like a switch as his gaze caught sight of his broad shouldered father telling one of his charming stories while surrounded by a group of affluent men. His blood boiled. He despised him completely. The boy Razoul thought often of murdering his father while he slept, but he was still too frightened of his mother's persecutor, to take that final step.

His mother, Chiara Bugiardini, had come from one of the wealthiest families in the province and been practically sold to his father when she was only sixteen. Razoul's father kept her a prisoner in their enormous estate and never allowed her to venture away from the grounds without him. Though she had no control over her life, she remained quiet and never complained about her duties as his wife.

Still, Chiara had a gentle, carefree spirit that longed to be far away with her sons and free of her often cruel husband. From the time he was a small boy, Razoul secretly wished to give his mother everything she wanted and resented his father for caging her the way he did.

Razoul knew he was dreaming and decided to take advantage of the situation. He ran down the staircase toward his mother. The orchestra was about to play.

"Mother, may I have this dance?"

Chiara turned toward Razoul and her face lit up when she saw him standing there. "You, my son, are very handsome this evening. Let me have a look at you."

Razoul made a full circle for his mother, showing off his attire.

She clapped in appreciation for her son who was growing quickly into a man. "Of course, my sweet darling boy let us share this dance together."

Razoul took her hand like a gentleman as they moved towards the dance floor. Once they found their place, he took her right hand into his left and placed his right hand at her waist. As the music played, they began to share a slow, rhythm together. He soaked in the moment with her. How he missed her face, even today.

Perhaps I am dead and this is heaven instead of a dream.

As his mother gazed at him, smiling, he longed for her to be alive. He wanted to pick her up and take her away, to save her. "Mother, how are you?"

"Ah, very well, my son."

"Why do you wish to lie to your oldest son? I know you are truly unhappy here."

"Razoul darling, why do you continue to concern yourself with such things on my behalf?"

"I am your son, madam, of course." His back straightened as he attempted to be taller, more of a man. His head bowed in respect.

"I fear there is nothing you can do about the course of my life. But there is much to be done for yours. Please do not concern yourself for me. I can handle my own affairs."

They continued to move elegantly in unison across the floor, mirroring the paths followed by others dancing near them. "Mother, you could handle your own affairs if my Father allowed you to!"

"You shouldn't worry about me. I only want you to become the man you are destined to be. That will make your mother very happy, and very proud." Chiara's face beamed. "Of course, I am already incredibly proud. Your father says that you are one of the best hunters he's ever seen. You are stronger and faster than any of the other boys."

"I am happy for your pride in me, mother, yet I cannot find happiness in any of it when you are not free. Not when that man refuses to honor you as I do. His continued lack of respect, I find incredibly distasteful."

If he had not been in the presence of his mother, he would have spat on the ground after mentioning his father. As the orchestra ended their piece of music, everyone stopped and clapped.

Razoul kissed his mother's hand and turned to be greeted by Britius who was still much taller than he was. "Don't you have something better to do, boy? There are many eligible ladies waiting for a dance with my eldest son."

Razoul cooled his temper before responding. "Yes, sir, but I was lucky enough to have a dance with my beautiful mother." He bowed to her.

"Well your mother is required elsewhere, boy, off with you." Britius grabbed Chiara's arm and led her in the direction of a group of important dignitaries to show her off.

Razoul was left watching his mother walk away, very upset that the moment with his long dead mother was over. She shot him a smile and a nod before hurrying a-long-side her husband.

The boy Razoul clinched his fist and closed his eyes.

When he opened them again he was in his bed, fully grown, still clenching his fists. His heart filled with sadness and regret.

I failed her. I never saved her from father.

As his eyes adjusted to the light, he saw familiar faces near his bedside, speaking in hushed voices.

Sirius was there of course, as well as Thaddeus Moretti, the only other heir to one of the four original family bloodlines that had originally made up the leadership of the Malem Tutela. There was also another elder member named Dario Lombardi present. None of them had noticed Razoul was awake yet, so he closed his eyes again in order to eavesdrop.

"Thaddeus, you need to be more involved in what has been transpiring. You should have been there. What has happened is not only dangerous for all of us, but arrogant and foolish." Sirius spoke frantically.

Razoul sat up suddenly for dramatic effect. Announcing his lucidity made him wince due to several cracked ribs. He was in tremendous pain, but wouldn't let on to the others see that he was uncomfortable.

"How many times have I told you, old man, that you worry needlessly about far too many things? Have you also told them that what I choose to do will undoubtedly lead us to victory?"

"Sirius has described to us what lengths you've recently gone to in order to locate the Incarnate Angel, Razoul."

Thaddeus looked at the other two gravely. "It nearly cost you your life. I have to ask you, since I still cannot believe what he has said to me. You summoned one of the Fallen?"

"Yes! I, Razoul Bugiardini, have accomplished what not one of you is man enough to do!" He looked fiercely at the others, almost begging them to contradict what he had just said.

Thaddeus fired back quickly, "Well, Razoul, now that you've summoned it, what is your plan for controlling that which cannot be controlled?"

Razoul didn't want to play twenty questions with anyone at the moment. "Leave that to me for whenever the time comes."

"So you have no plan? What do you think this little favor will cost all of us? Or will you damn all of our souls in the end when your new friend expects repayment for the favor?"

Thaddeus paused for a moment and rethought his last question. "No, don't bother answering that question, we all know full well that if necessary you would do just that very thing!"

Razoul smiled like a tiger stalking his prey. "Perhaps you are all forgetting that now we can *know* where to find her. Now we can stop her from becoming the greatest enemy that we have ever seen."

He turned to Sirius, pointing his finger directly at him. "Perhaps you'd like to live your final years of life without all the comforts of your vast wealth and power?" Sirius looked down at the ground in shame. "The energy of this enemy will crumble your vast fortress of wealth to the ground. The prophecy is clear, and the lines of battle are drawn. They were drawn before any of us were born. Our only advantage is that she is weak and unaware of her purpose. I suppose each of you would have been simply content to wander around aimlessly, hoping we'd conveniently bump into her when there's been no way to track her?"

No one said a word.

Razoul stood up for emphasis of his final point but was unprepared for the pain he experienced that nearly took his breath away. It took everything he had, not to stumble and fall. "You may all be cowards, but I am not. I am in charge because I am the only man here in this room, or in the entire organization, willing to do whatever it takes to ensure the success of our formidable interests."

Razoul grabbed for his robe hanging near the bed and miscalculated his ability to do so. The pain was searing and he could not breathe well. It made him reveal his weakened condition fully to the others making him erupt with anger. "All of you, out! Sirius, get me my physician, now!"

46- *The Guardians*

Monsignor Bartholomew took great lengths to reach his destination undetected. As he descended the hidden stairs, the sounds of the tourists and city dwellers of Rome grew fainter and further away. His journey would take him well beneath the city above. The Essene Guardians had used this hidden access to underground chambers beneath the streets for centuries to perform special ceremonies, meet in private, and store valuable documents.

The more modern Essene Brotherhood had originally been started by six families who had carried out their holy work in quiet reverence for God, while still living in the world of mankind. A child of each family had always been chosen to take on the position as a Guardian of the Order and then taught their secret knowledge. When a blood relative child was not available, God had led them to a chosen person who could carry on the holy work and continue the practice.

Every Guardian had a unique contribution to the order itself and the world at large. Right now Monsignor Bartholomew hurried through the tunnel passages because he had grave news for the other five Guardians that he must convey to them in person.

At last he reached the meeting chamber. Seated at a stone circular table were the other five: Aurora, Matthew, Anastasia, Joseph, and Francesca. When he entered, they each removed their cloak hoods and greeted him with warm smiles.

"Brothers and Sisters, thank you for meeting me at short notice. As you know, we are in the midst of very important times."

They all nodded in agreement.

"I have received word from my sources that the Malem Tutela now may possess the means to find the Incarnate Angel. It may only be a matter of time before her whereabouts are revealed to these dangerous men."

The other Guardians, shocked at this news, were in disbelief.

Aurora spoke first. "How is that possible? She is well hidden from everyone right now."

"Razoul has summoned one of the Fallen, Samyaza." Bartholomew looked at her grimly.

Aurora stood up in outrage to what she just heard. "How can that be? Who could be that evil to summon such a beast into the world?"

"I do not completely understand how this happened; however, I am told he used an enchanted gold amulet with the Sigil de Ameth inscribed on it to summon this abomination of the Almighty One."

"But Brother, only someone of purest heart can open the Sigil's gateway. I am sure that there is no one within that group with that ability, especially Razoul!"

"You are right, and that is why Razoul used the amulet by exploiting the help of an innocent gypsy girl. The entire family's home was burned to the ground and the girl has disappeared, presumed dead."

Aurora sat down taking in the graveness of Bartholomew's news. It had been vitally important they not allow the world at large to learn about the coming of the angelic one, let alone discover her current whereabouts. The Order of Essene had communicated with angels daily in order to fulfill their commitment to watch over her until she became self-aware. Now for the first time in her human life, she was in grave danger.

"Whatever can we do?" Francesca spoke quietly.

"There's nothing we can do but pray and ask the angels to guide us." Joseph clasped his hands together symbolically.

"We must do more than pray!" Anastasia offered fervently.

"You all know that they have expressly forbidden our interference with the natural course of her life. There's nothing else to do." Joseph offered with sympathy in his voice.

"If we are unable to warn the girl, then we must find a way to stop the Malem Tutela." Bartholomew placed both his hands down on the table firmly.

Aurora knew that he was pausing for effect only. "By what means do you propose we stop the Malem Tutela, Bartholomew?"

He took his place at the stone table before explaining. "My sources tell me that there is much dissension in the ranks of the Malem Tutela since Britius was murdered by his eldest son. Razoul lacks much of his father's leadership ability and, shall we say, tact and diplomacy. I am certain that if something were to happen to him, the others would not pursue this matter with the same intensity. In fact, they may abandon it altogether."

Aurora frowned, knowing where Bartholomew was leading them when Francesca spoke up first. "Are you proposing murder, Brother? Surely you understand that we are not an order of assassins and above all, the Essene cherish and uphold all life, even a life being wasted by foolish men such as those who call themselves the Malem Tutela."

"I am not proposing murdering Razoul ourselves, dear Sister. I am pointing out that an opportunity now exists to strike at their vulnerability. I am certain that there are current members such as Sirius Rossi or even Thaddeus Moretti, who wish him dead already."

"There may be a way to bolster the opposition into taking action, one they might already take anyway, without any coercion on our part."

Aurora stood up, circled to Bartholomew's chair and placed her hand on his shoulder. Her beautiful face became illuminated directly in the candlelight when she did. Her long grey hair shone like a beautiful window around her face as she addressed the room.

"We must tread carefully now. More than we ever have before. If we give into our greatest fears, we will choose the wrong path, one that can ultimately lead to more death. We cannot decide the fates of others. We cannot stand in the wisdom of our ancestors who lived in peace and acceptance for all things. We must not make rash choices, even in desperate times. Our actions create waves into the world. You all know this too well. "

Bartholomew took Aurora's hand from his shoulder and held it gently. He looked into her eyes. "You have always found the middle way the best, dear Sister. I do not believe myself to be as strong as you are in the old ways, but your concerns are real ones to consider, as always. As usual, you are the calm voice of reason."

Bartholomew and Aurora were both of equal age and often looked up to by the other Guardians for wisdom and strength since the others had less years of experience. The other Guardians often agreed with them when their decisions were united.

Bartholomew looked at the others in the room and knew this was not the time to press forward with what he knew in his heart was the only way to guarantee the angel would be safe. He knew that if the need arose any one of them would offer their life in exchange for Catherine's. Her life was more important than any of them could possibly imagine.

47- *She's Mine*

He had been taken to the quiet, padded room to calm down. Jacob fell in and out of a drug induced sleep. He was still unconscious and his body twitched, showing signs of his tormented dreams.

I must find her. I must go to her.

Jacob found himself standing on the hospital grounds which were shrouded in darkness. An eerie light was cast from the moonlight across the distant rolling hills. He stood staring up at the fortress he had called home for so long. He was used to having dreams like this, where he was free from his body and able to come and go as he pleased. All he could think of now was Catherine and he was lucidly in control of his dream state.

He seized this opportunity to leave his confinement and fly high above the trees. It was exhilarating and he momentarily forgot the focus of his flight away from his drugged body. Once he regained focus, he flew faster than he ever had before, and soon he was close to the city.

Jacob instinctively turned to navigate himself toward Catherine's childhood home. As he came to rest on the ground, just outside her place, he saw two figures get out of a car that he didn't recognize.

It was Catherine and David returning from their dinner. She was smiling and he was helping her out of the car. Jacob's blood boiled on seeing Catherine with another man.

This is why you didn't want me to be with you? You are a liar, aren't you, clever Catherine! I should have known.

He didn't recognize the man but saw there was more than friendship between them. He suddenly wished he was in his body. All he could do now was watch them walk toward the door to her house. His chest hurt and he called out to them both. Then he realized he could not be heard, and so was forced to do nothing.

His new fury caused him to slam back into his physical body lying on the floor in the quiet room. He leapt up from the floor, clutching his chest. His breath was labored for a few moments as he came back to his reality, a 9x9 room in a psychiatric facility. He put his head in his hands and began to cry. Then suddenly a switch flipped, and he turned again to his anger.

Look at me locked up because of her and her lies. She doesn't want to be with me, but she will see. I will make her see how much she needs me. Wait. Calm down. They'll come to release me soon. Put on a good face... breathe... perfect. See you soon, Catherine. Then you'll understand.

48- *Encounter*

Catherine closed the door after thanking David for a lovely dinner and saying goodnight. She had a spring in her step and felt better than she had in quite some time.

Subconsciously she had sensed Jacob's presence for a moment, and it left her with an uneasy feeling. She threw the deadbolt in place before walking into the living room where she found Erica sleeping on the sofa.

Erica hadn't heard her come in. Catherine walked over and took the blanket from the back of the sofa to cover her up before heading upstairs.

"Plenty of time to gossip about boys tomorrow, I suspect." She whispered, smiling.

Catherine knew that Erica couldn't stay for much longer, and keep her job. This made her think of her own job which felt like a lifetime ago. She knew she wasn't going back anytime soon, and decided to get someone out to the house to get the cable hooked up so she could stay connected to civilization and research on the Internet.

There must be some answers out there somewhere.

Catherine changed her clothes and brushed her teeth. As she crawled in her bed, her thoughts drifted to David and their dinner.

He is such a nice guy. I never thought I'd meet someone like him. He seems to get me. Well at least the part of me he knows about. Maybe I'll let him take me out again. Who knows?

Very quickly she fell into a deep sleep where her calm thoughts were interrupted by a torrent of images that leapt from her subconscious to greet her.

Catherine found herself walking down a dark, damp tunnel. Her bare foot steps echoed all around her as she wandered through it. There was barely enough ambient light to guide her. She reached her left hand out to the wall to steady herself. She could see her own breath as it hit the cold air around her.

She was half way toward the light at the end of the tunnel when she realized she was not alone. An ominous presence pressed down upon her, and her nostrils stung from a pungent, acrid odor. It was unlike anything she'd encountered before. There was nothing she could see with her eyes.

"Who's there? What do you want?"

From the darkness, a dark and brooding voice spoke to her. "You will not escape me."

Catherine's heart began to pound in her chest. "Why have you brought me here?"

She picked up the pace as she approached the end of the tunnel so that she could see what was pursuing her. When she reached the end, she stumbled and fell to the ground. As she stood back up, she realized that her hands were covered in a thick, gooey substance.

Oh my God, blood.

Catherine looked, horrified, at the blood dripping off her hands. She tried to wipe them off, to no avail. She turned to see where she was. It looked like a torture chamber. There were five stone slab platforms and long chains with shackles lining the walls.

As she looked back down the tunnel, her eyes caught movement and she strained to see what was there. She stood frozen as the creature manifested at the entrance to the room. At first it appeared as a dark cloud that soon began to take on a hideous shape before her. It was huge, nearly eight feet tall with glowing eyes.

Catherine stood her ground sensing, contrary to the normal compulsion to flee quickly, that she should not run from it.

She shouted at the thing before her. "I demand you let me out of here now!"

The demon cackled, "You demand? Very brave words for such a fragile being that has no way of escape."

"This is a dream, and I know that. I can wake up anytime." She stood up tall and defiant. Catherine was bluffing, she had no idea if she could, but everything in her was telling her to show no fear.

"You are a foolish girl, Catherine." It took steps toward her and stopped a couple of feet away. She did not move, staring the creature down as it towered over her 5' 3" frame.

"Since you brought me here, I have a right to know who and what you are."

"I have many names. I am your worst nightmare."

"I've seen worse." Catherine was stalling, trying to figure out what to do to get this thing out of her way.

"I doubt that, silly human. You are nothing. I am all powerful. You are insignificant." It took an additional step toward her. The smoke stung her eyes and burned her nostrils, but she did not move.

Catherine looked at it fiercely. "If I am insignificant, then why bother bringing me to this place?"

The creature said nothing and grabbed her left arm with a scaled claw that ended in razor sharp points. The touch burned through her shirt and caused her to wince. She didn't run, but looked up at it and spat her words. "You are so fond of hearing yourself speak, yet you have nothing to say?"

This angered the demon and with one more step the force of its power threw Catherine backwards to the ground. When her sight cleared, she was lying in blood, and the creature hovered in the air above her.

"You must be destroyed. You are beyond this world, an abomination to the darkness. Yet your light is so captivating. I shall enjoy the prize of extinguishing it once and for all."

Catherine was pinned to the floor and unable to move. As she watched the creature relish in the moment, something stirred in the center of her chest. It was warm and started to spread through her torso, then to her arms and legs. It felt like the light that had encompassed her before in the previous dream.

Her eyes closed briefly and in her mind she saw she could focus the energy moving through her. Then words flowed through her mind in ancient symbols that she had seen in the book.

Power of God Banish Darkness

Catherine's arms lifted to the ceiling with her index fingers and thumbs touching to form a diamond shape that framed the center of the creature. A bright light shone from her chest and beamed straight up through and out of her hands enveloping the demon.

Then, somehow, she spoke the phrase fluently in Latin. "Vox of deus expello obscurum."

The demon shrieked in a sound that made both her ears ring. The room started to spin. For a moment, Catherine thought she saw several beings of white light near her, and then everything faded out as she abruptly sat up in bed.

She was grateful to be safe back in her bed. She looked at her hands and they were pristine, no blood, but she became aware of a searing pain where the demon had grabbed her by the arm. She lifted the sleeve of her shirt and revealed a ring of deep red burns and blisters. She flinched.

Ouch! That hurts! That was no dream.

49- *Danger*

"You're up early, sweetie." Helen spoke as she entered the kitchen with a stack of clean hand towels and noticed David pouring himself a cup of coffee.

David turned and smiled. "Well, I had a hard time getting to sleep last night, but then woke up early anyway." He sat down at the table and grabbed a muffin from the basket to go with his coffee.

Helen shot her son a knowing look. "So, how was your date?"

"It was wonderful to spend some time with her. We talked about ourselves and laughed a lot, too. Catherine's not only beautiful, but has a great sense of humor."

"Well you look happy, and of course that makes your old ma happy."

"I know, mom."

Helen put the towels in the drawer. "It's good to see you smile. It's been so long since you've been perky."

"Perky? Come on, mom, when have I ever been classified as perky?"

"Oh, you know what I mean. It's been so hard on you since Mira died."

Helen poured herself a cup of coffee and sat down to join her son.

For the first time, the mention of Mira didn't make a deep pit in his stomach. David got a serious look on his face. "It's okay, mom. For the first time since then, I know that everything is going to be okay. I can feel it."

Helen s as her son continued, "After our date last night, I think Catherine feels the same way about me that I do about her, but she's scared. It's obvious that losing her parents took its toll, just like Mira dying did on me. I can tell it's hard for her to open up, but she is trying. I just wish I knew what she's keeping to herself."

"What do you mean?"

"It's like she's afraid to tell me what's been going on in her life lately. I only know it has something to do with why she suddenly showed up in Parsons again after so long."

"Maybe it was just time for her to reconcile things," Helen offered.

"Maybe so, but I just can't shake the feeling that something is really wrong or that she's in danger somehow." He looked at his mom sincerely. "I know that sounds nuts, mom. But I feel it so strongly."

"You should trust yourself, honey. You've had that way about you since you were a child."

He shot her a curious look. "I have?"

"Oh, yes, you used to come up with things here and there that were true, even when you wouldn't have had any way of knowing them. I do hope Catherine isn't in trouble though. I just think you should listen to your inner guidance. I have always believed we have that, and it comes from our soul."

David nodded.

"So, are you going to see her today?"

"Yeah, I've got a few things to do for pop first." David got up to head outside to find his dad. "Besides, I don't want to be a nuisance over there by dropping by too early." He grinned and headed out the kitchen door.

50- *Deception*

"I can make her yours..."

Jacob's eyes fluttered opened and he looked around his room. They had allowed him to come back to his regular room, but the doctor's still had him heavily medicated. He had been drifting in and out of sleep. When he heard the voice, he thought he was dreaming. The room was dimly lit from the overcast skies outside.

"I can make her yours..."

Jacob listened intently without moving. Someone was speaking to him.

He whispered back, so the staff couldn't hear him talking. "Who is that?"

"A friend who wants to help you get whatever you wish."

"Sure, and I bet your friends with Santa Claus and the tooth fairy too."

Great, now the meds have me hearing voices.

"You need to listen to me, Jacob."

"What are you, my mother?"

"No, but I know your pain deep inside and how it's eating you up. Wouldn't you like to never feel that pain again? I can make that happen for you, dear boy."

Playing along, Jacob nodded in agreement.

"You will never be free of your torment unless you take action soon."

"Catherine..."

"How can she reject you after all you've sacrifice for her?"

"She doesn't love me, doesn't want me." Jacob turned over, facing the wall.

"She should be running into your arms."

This comment made Jacob remember his out of body experience and the man he saw with her last night. His body stiffened as jealousy began to consume him again. As if knowing his every thought and feeling, the disembodied voice spoke again.

"You can't allow her to be with him, can you?"

"What can I do?"

"You are smarter than him, better than him."

Jacob smirked.

"Would you like to know why you see all she sees?"

He nodded, listening very carefully and concentrating. He was growing tired again and didn't want to fall asleep.

"You were chosen, Jacob. Chosen by God."

"Yeah, right. Not me. God would never choose me for a damn thing."

"Don't doubt that you are an instrument of God. She's been hiding this from you all along. She didn't want you to know. This is why you have the power to see her and her life. You are more powerful than you think."

"I'm a pathetic mess."

"God sent me to help you fulfill your mission." "Are you an angel?"

"Yes, an angel sent to help you from losing your way, dear boy."

Somehow this didn't make Jacob feel a whole lot better, but some hope was better than none. "I used to think about what it would be like to be visited by an angel. Not what I expected at all."

"Things aren't always how you imagine them. This place is draining you. Once you are out of here, then you'll see."

"I think I'd like to be out of here." Jacob said slowly drifting to sleep again.

"You will be. You will be. But for now, rest."

51- *Friendship*

"I know I shouldn't be surprised right now, but how can something hurt you like this while you are asleep?" Erica carefully secured the sterile dressing around Catherine's arm and fastened it with tape. "I think that will hold, but these things are pretty old, we need to buy some new stuff today."

Catherine looked at her thankfully. "Well at least my mother used to be prepared, and these were still in the medicine cabinet."

Erica looked at her seriously for a moment as they stood in the bathroom. "I pretty much decided what I am about to tell you, last night. I mean I didn't make this decision because of this happening, but it makes me happy I did."

"What are you talking about?"

"I quit my job at the Division of Family Services this morning, before you woke up and came to show me the burn on your arm."

Catherine was shocked. "Why? Oh please don't make my crisis interrupt your life, Erica. You didn't have to do that!"

As they went downstairs, Erica explained. "I called mom last night while you were at dinner. She had another dream about you being attacked by something awful and dark. She obviously knew something was coming for you last night. I have felt more useful being by your side through all this, than at any other time in my life."

Catherine grabbed a mug of coffee and sat down at the small nook in the kitchen.

Erica joined her. Then in her usual bubbly style, "Besides how can I go back to a boring, mundane life in Kansas City when I'm knee deep in the mystical and magical at the moment?"

"I wish I could share your enthusiasm for the mystical, Erica, but I think I understand. I also know that trying to talk you out of this would be useless. We're the same in that regard for sure."

"Also, Catherine," Erica said as she took her hand, "I believe that some things are meant to be. Whatever is happening here is bigger than me, and my gut tells me to stay right here."

Catherine was suddenly moved to tears. She was grateful to have such a wonderful friend, even though she didn't feel like she deserved it. "Thank you so much, Erica. This means the world to me."

Erica got a huge smile on her face.

"Why are you smiling like that?" Catherine asked, wiping the tears from her eyes.

"Ah, I'm just glad we didn't have a smack down over my staying. I'm happy you're letting me be there for you."

"I know I'm a difficult case sometimes." She knew how hard it had been for Erica to get close to her over the past year.

Erica rolled her eyes, "Sometimes?"

They both laughed.

Erica got up and grabbed a notepad from the living room table. "I started making a list of things we probably need to do if we are staying."

Catherine admired Erica's ability to get things moving in the right direction. "And here I thought I was the organized one."

She looked at the list. On the top was getting Internet installed at the house. The rest included a return trip to Kansas City for more of their belongings which Catherine had already thought of yesterday. "Yeah, I'll definitely need some stuff from my apartment very soon." Before she could continue, the doorbell rang. "I'll get it. I have a feeling I know who that is anyway."

"Who is it? David?"

Catherine nodded. As she went towards the front door, she heard Erica, "Shoot, was about to ask about how dinner went last night."

Catherine smiled and retorted, "Sorry we'll have to gossip later, gator."

David waited nervously on the porch as the door opened. "Hello beautiful lady. Sorry to just drop by, I forgot to get your number last night. How are you doing today?"

"I just woke up, so I look terrible right now."

"You look great anytime, Catherine."

"Thanks. I'm glad you think so." Catherine smoothed her hair down nervously.

Catherine stepped aside to allow him in when David noticed her crudely bandaged arm. "What happened to your arm?"

Oh demon attack, nothing big.

"I bumped into a heater in the wee hours of the morning. I'm so clumsy, especially half asleep." Then she changed the subject, "Would you like some coffee?"

"Sure, I'd love some."

"Why don't you head into the kitchen and help yourself. You can chat with Erica while I go change my clothes."

"No problem, I can find my way." David shot an earnest look over his shoulder and smiled as Catherine hurried upstairs.

Erica was rinsing a bowl in the sink with her back to the door when David walked in. "I hear there's some great coffee in here."

Erica jumped a little. "Oh, you startled me."

"Sorry about that. Catherine said to keep you company while she changes her clothes."

"So how was dinner with my best friend last night?"

"Direct and to the point, I like that." David chuckled. "And if you must know, I thought it was wonderful. I really enjoyed myself. It's been a while since I've gotten to treat a special lady to a great dinner."

Erica seized the opportunity to learn more about him. "So, there's been no special lady in your life for a while then?"

"Not since my fiancée Mira, died."

Erica felt bad that she'd pried. "I'm so sorry. I didn't realize."

"It's okay. It's been quite some time and now I think I can finally move on."

"Really? That's great."

David sat down with his coffee and decided to be real with Erica while Catherine was out of the room. "You're her best friend and I know we just met, but I can't get her out of my mind most of the time. She just makes everything all better."

"Well, when it comes to Catherine, I can definitely relate to that."

"You can? I figured you tell me to slow down and not get ahead of myself."

"In fact, I quit my job this morning to stay here with her. So if you are crazy for feeling the way you do about her, so am I."

"Catherine and I have not been best friends for a long time, but with her I feel important, like I belong. She's family." Then she looked at him quite seriously. "She's very, very special. There's really no one like her. She's also very fragile." Erica wasn't sure what had been shared with David so far so she didn't offer any specific details about it.

"I get that. I also know what you are trying to say. Don't hurt Catherine. Don't do all this if I'm just going to jump ship. You can trust me that I'm not like that. In fact, I feel very protective of her."

"You do seem very nice to me, David. You're a nice guy with a big heart."

"Can I ask you a question before she gets back down here? You don't have to answer it if you can't, but maybe you can help me understand better."

"Okay, I'll answer if I can," Erica said sincerely.

"Is Catherine in some type of trouble?"

Erica got up to piddle around the kitchen to avoid looking directly at him. Her eyes couldn't lie if she needed to. "Why do you ask that?"

"I don't know exactly. It seems like she's holding something back that she can't or doesn't feel like she can tell me. I want to help if she'll let me."

"You just need to be patient with her," Erica offered. "If she feels she can open up about other things, she will."

"Is someone after her?" David asked.

Erica thought about it for a minute. "Not exactly, no."

"What do you mean?"

Before Erica could muster a response, she saw Catherine out of the corner of her eye. Grateful, she turned to greet her. "Hey, Cat. You look refreshed."

"Thanks. I do feel better now than when I answered the door. It's amazing what a toothbrush and wash cloth can do for a person." Catherine's arm was aching badly, but she attempted to keep things light especially with David around. She had no idea how to explain her injury in a way that didn't sound like she needed to be institutionalized. That thought punched her in the stomach because it made her think of Jacob. She quickly pushed it away.

"Do you have anything for a headache, Erica?"

"Sure, let me get my purse."

David looked down at the table and saw the "to do" list. He picked it up. "You guys staying awhile then?" Catherine turned and said, "Yeah, we were talking about it this morning."

"Well, if you need anything at all. I'm here to help."

"Thanks, David." Catherine smiled.

Erica returned with a bottle and handed it to her.

"Catherine, I have a great idea."

Catherine refilled her coffee cup. "What's that?"

"Since part of our list is a bunch of errands here in Parsons, why don't you let me tackle that part and maybe David could drive with you back to the city to get some of your things?"

Being alone in the car for that long with David was immediately intimidating. Catherine knew what Erica was trying to do. "But don't you need to get your stuff too? We could all three go.

"Oh, I can just call and tell my mom exactly what I need and she can get it together for me. I don't have to go this time. In the meantime, I can get us some food and supplies and call the cable company so we can get connected to the outside world. I don't want you to go alone either."

"I'm free, Catherine, anytime. It's no trouble at all," David chimed in.

"Okay, you two. I guess that'll work. Why do I feel I'm being ganged up on here?"

Erica and David eyed each other knowingly and then Erica spoke up. "Why, best friend, I have no idea what you're talking about."

52- *Location*

Razoul's physician had tended to him adeptly and he was finally well enough to travel even though he was in a great deal of pain. He refused anything medicinal for pain in order to keep his mind clear. He sat in the library with Sirius and Thaddeus discussing their next move.

"Razoul, even with the Sigil in play, we still don't know her name or where to begin." Thaddeus said realistically. "Scouring four U.S. States will take a great deal of time and resources. She could be anywhere. This will require more men than we have at our disposal, I'm afraid."

Normally Razoul would have risen from his chair to emphasize what he was about to say, but he thought better of it. Movement was difficult with five broken ribs. So he turned to Thaddeus, saying, "I have some ideas on how to narrow down our search. Yes it will take time, but we shall not fail. We cannot fail." He turned toward his butler who had entered the room to clear a tea tray. "Have the boy bring me the map I sent him earlier."

Soon Daniel scurried into the room and unrolled a large map of the Central United States onto the conference table for him. Razoul got up from his chair and motioned for the young boy to get out. He walked over to one of the floor to ceiling bookcases and produced a wooden case that held the amulet with the Sigil de Ameth that Samyaza had enchanted before nearly killing Razoul. He held it up and watched it dangle in the air. "This is will help us to narrow down our search."

Both of the other men got up and walked toward the map to watch.

Razoul held the 2 inch wide amulet over the map over the central states. He drew a larger circle that encompassed six states: Nebraska, Iowa, Kansas, Missouri, Oklahoma and Arkansas.

"The entire area covered by these six states is notably called *The Heart of the Dove*. Samyaza stated the girl could be found there. So this means we can disregard the other states. Watch this."

Razoul removed the amulet from its chain and placed it directly on the map. He slowly moved the amulet from the upper left corner of the marked area to the right and slowly made his way back and forth.

Sirius spoke up. "What are you doing? Do you think this will work?"

"It will work, old man. Quiet your tongue."

Razoul had already covered the upper states of Nebraska and Iowa moving horizontally across the map, and nothing had happened. He almost doubted himself for a moment, but as he moved the amulet to where it was half way across the border of Kansas and Missouri, it began to glow red. Razoul immediately pulled his hand away from it, and the other two gasped. Razoul grabbed his handkerchief to pick it up again.

Underneath it, a perfectly charred edge revealed an area that extended as far north as Kansas City, as far west as Emporia, Kansas, as far east as Sedalia, Missouri and as far south as Miami, Oklahoma.

"There, a much smaller and more manageable area to concentrate on." An evil grin spread across Razoul's face. "I will finalize arrangements today and tomorrow. We will leave in two days. Prepare your teams and contact our favorite mercenaries. I am not taking any chances."

With that, Razoul retired to his bedroom leaving the other two behind him, staring at the map in disbelief.

53- *Road Trip*

"You two have a good time, don't worry about me." Erica called coyly as Catherine and David were getting ready to head to Kansas City.

Catherine looked up from her purse. She was making sure she had everything she needed. "Are you sure you don't mind driving with me on such short notice, David?"

"I told you, Catherine, I'm totally free and don't mind at all." He picked up her small overnight bag and headed out the door to her car.

Catherine followed him. Erica was staring at her with a big grin on her face. "I'm sure you are very proud of yourself, my dear friend, but what am I going to talk about for the hours on the road? I'm nervous."

Erica hugged her tightly. "Trust me. It'll be great. You'll enjoy yourself. Mom thought so, too, and she's usually right."

Catherine nodded hesitantly and headed out the door calling to David, "I'm coming."

David shut the trunk of Catherine's car and hurried to open the driver's side door for her. Soon they were on their way.

They had been on the highway for about ten minutes when David finally spoke. "Thanks for letting me come along."

Catherine smiled.

He continued, "I hope you don't think Erica and I had this all planned out."

"No, I don't think that. I am sure Erica had everything to do with it." She paused and then added, "I'm glad you came with me though. It gives us more time to get to know each other."

"That's exactly what I was thinking, too."

Catherine was curious about David's job.

"So, did you have any trouble taking time off?"

"No, I work for myself pretty much these days. I do a lot of consulting and programming for a number of companies. I just finished a large project that took well over a year, so I'm taking a break right now. That's why I was staying at my folk's house when you came back to Parsons. I love the work and it's really flexible, so pretty much my time is my own."

"That's great." Catherine smiled.

David turned to see her pleasant face. "So, have you missed your job since you've been in Parsons for the past week?"

"Honestly, I haven't had time to even think about it. I fainted at work and my boss was really adamant I take some time off. I tried to go back to work, which was okay for a couple days, and then I just found myself headed for my parent's house. Of course now my boss Barb is probably regretting forcing some down time. I know they are short-handed so I feel bad for her, but right now I need time to straighten my life out."

"Has coming to Parsons helped you do that?" David was trying to gently ask more about what brought her to town.

"Well, I'm not sure how to answer that. I supposed it has in some ways but from what I've figured out, I now have more questions than I did before."

"Maybe I can help you."

Catherine immediately shook her head. "I don't know how you can, but I appreciate your offer."

"Come on Catherine. I know you like me and I like you. I really can be a great person to lean on if you let me. I know you don't know me very well, but I can be trusted with anything you want to share."

Catherine took a deep breath. She did feel in her heart that she could trust him. Finding somewhere to begin telling the story was another thing. "I wouldn't know where to begin."

"How about you tell me what happened when you fainted and go from there?"

He's going to be sorry after I tell him everything and will probably take a bus back to Parsons.

As if he knew what she was thinking, David said, "I know opening up is hard, Catherine, especially after carrying the full load for a long time. I promise whatever you say will not send me screaming for the hills."

She looked over at him and his face made her heart slow down a bit. He made her feel calmer somehow.

"Okay David, you win. I was at work doing a client intake and this woman I was speaking with became very upset over her situation. That happens a lot given the nature of my job. I got up from my desk to go over and touch her arm to console her and let her know I understood how hard it was for her. When I touched her arm, well, it was like I could see into her history. I know that sounds crazy, but I found myself standing in her kitchen. It was so real that I could smell the breakfast she was cooking. What I saw next was her husband chasing her down in a rage."

"I'm sorry. That must've been tough. . Has that ever happened before? Where you could see someone else's experiences?"

"No, this was the first time I'd ever experienced anything like that. It happened really fast and I think the shock of it made me faint. The next thing I remember is all my co-workers standing over me."

"That was embarrassing, I'm sure."

"Yes, very. I had no idea what was happening. I am never sick and certainly didn't want to make a scene in the office either. So my boss sent me home for the day and told me to go to the doctor."

"And you probably didn't do that, did you?"

"How did you know?"

"It doesn't take a brain surgeon to figure out a few things about you, Catherine. You are fiercely independent, you like to be in control of your life, you care about how others see you, and you are also very kind hearted and generous. How am I doing so far?"

Catherine had to admit he had really been paying attention to her in the few days they had known each other. "Well, you are doing very well. You have me basically figured out already." She dropped her shoulders.

"Is that so bad?"

"Well, no. I guess it's a bit unexpected for me. I have always thought I was the most observant person I know and probably haven't given other people much credit for being that way. Anyway, doesn't my story freak you out?"

"Not really."

Catherine looked at him and could tell he was being truthful. "So you believe me?"

"Just because I've never experienced something, doesn't mean that it's not real or true. I have always known the world is much bigger than my little slice of it, which hasn't been that great anyway. So I find the situation you experienced quite intriguing, and hope you will share more with me."

Catherine was relieved to hear this.

Well, what the hell, here goes...

It was then that she made a decision to let it all go and tell him. She spent the rest of their trip to Kansas City trying to bring him up to speed on everything that had happened to her.

54- *Trouble Ahead*

"Monsignor?"

"Yes, Brother Artemis?"

"I want to update you on things in Parsons. Catherine has taken a trip back to the city with a new gentleman. They only took small bags so I believe they plan to return in a day or two."

"Do you know who she's with?"

"His name is David Anderson and from what I can tell, he's the son of the property caretaker. He seems like a family friend, but they don't behave like they know each other well. Her girl friend is still here in Parsons and didn't accompany her on the trip."

"It sounds like Catherine will stay in Parsons, at least for a while longer then. This is good news given some recent developments here. I am grateful she is with friends who can help watch over her."

"What is happening, Monsignor?"

"Trouble is brewing here in Italy, Brother. The Malem Tutela has been able to determine her general location and will be leaving for the United States shortly. It pleases me that she will stay there in Parsons, it's more secure. She would be more exposed in the city."

"Oh dear. Do you think they will find her?"

"No, not for some time brother, thank God. Do not worry. But if you see anything or anyone unusual in Parsons, call me immediately."

"Surely we must warn Catherine of the danger."

Monsignor was silent for a bit.

"Monsignor?"

"We cannot do that, Brother. This is a matter I have already consulted the Council about and our instructions are clear. No interference. Although this current situation with the Malem Tutela makes me fearful for her safety."

"Me too, Monsignor. I will pray for her protection. I will continue my vigil and let you know if anything changes." Monsignor hung up the phone and paced back and forth in his office.

Doing nothing was driving the Monsignor crazy, but if he could do something, he wasn't sure what that would be, or even if Catherine would want his help. It was best to watch the events unfold, although this challenged his ability to remain obedient.

55- *Destination*

"It's so good to see your face Catherine. I hope Erica has told you that I've called to check in frequently."

"Yes, Karen, of course she did, and I appreciate that."

Karen looked at Catherine and David together and smiled. "So where did you two meet?"

Catherine stopped mid bite, unsure how to answer the question when David chimed in. "Oh, our parents knew each other many year ago, and when Catherine came back to Parsons, my mother sent me over to check on her."

"How wonderful for you both. You look great together."

Catherine looked at David and then to Karen. "You sound like my mother, Karen. She was always the matchmaker." Then she laughed nervously.

"Oh you know us mothers, Catherine. I just thought it was nice you had such a gentleman around. You are such a wonderful girl, you know. You should never be alone, especially with all your special gifts."

"I could tell from the first time we met, how special she is. I just hope she'll find it in her heart to keep me around for a while."

Karen seemed to look inside them both. "I do too, David."

Catherine went back to eating her dinner. For a moment she felt out of place, it was hard to hear other people's compliments, since she was so hard on herself most of the time.

David noticed she had become quiet. "We didn't mean to gang up on you, Catherine."

"No, it's not that David, I am fine. It's just been a hard few weeks and the pace is wearing on me. Thank you both for all your support, really. I know it's hard for me to show my appreciation at times."

Karen spoke up quickly. "Just remember honey, you are not alone. I know God has plans for you and that kind of thing can be overwhelming. I am just glad you are okay. My dreams have been really intense lately." Then without skipping a beat, "Who would like some desert?"

Both guests nodded and Karen hurried to the kitchen leaving them alone.

David put his arm around Catherine. "Don't worry, everything will be alright."

Catherine's right hand reached up to grab his hand over her shoulder. "I know, I know, it will be alright. It's like my head is so full of information, I can't see straight." She looked down and felt like crying.

Karen walked in with two pieces of chocolate cake. "This is guaranteed to cure whatever ails you."

Catherine felt a change in her mood. "It looks delicious." The cake disappeared in record time.

"Karen thanks so much for dinner and desert. We'd stay longer but I really have a lot to do at the apartment this evening before heading back tomorrow."

Karen nodded, "Of course sweetie, I understand. Erica's things are in the living room ready to go."

Catherine and David were on their way to her apartment, making conversation about lighter things. Pretty soon they were pulling into the parking garage right next to Catherine's building. Catherine was exhausted and unaware of her surroundings. As she stepped out of the car, she didn't notice a person standing nearby.

David quickly grabbed their bags out of the trunk.

As they walked toward the door to cross over to her building, she saw a man standing there waiting. Catherine quickly recognized him. "Joshua, what are you doing here?"

As the unkempt man came out of the shadows, David moved quickly to intercept him before he reached Catherine. "No, David, it's okay. I know him, sort of."

"Catherine, thank goodness. They said you'd be here. I wasn't sure, but they are always whispering. Whispering all day and all night, whispering..."

"Who is, Joshua? What are you talking about?"

Joshua stopped and looked at her curiously. "Well, the angels of course. They whisper all the time, just whispers in my head. I hear them, but no one believes....but you believe, you know how they are."

Joshua started fidgeting and wringing his hands nervously. "They whispered and I knew I knew I must find you and...."

He looked at David and his eyes grew wide, "Are you are the man? They whisper about you too, you know. They, they said, well, you can protect her." Joshua looked a little relieved as he turned to Catherine.

"You are in danger. That's why I'm here, that's why I came. They whisper and I go. I go where I must go. They are worried, so worried about you now. They said you were in danger. They said you were coming back home and I came, I came here just like I was supposed to." He smiled at her sweetly like a small child wanting to please his parents.

Catherine felt a dark pit in her stomach and her head was swimming. "Danger? Joshua, what do you mean I am in danger?"

David still wasn't sure about how harmless Joshua was, and moved in closer to Catherine as she questioned him. "Did I do good, Catherine?" Joshua looked around nervously.

"Yes Joshua, you have done very well. Please tell me what else the angels whispered."

"I heard them all whispering yesterday. They said a dark one was coming to take you away. I was so worried. They said you could be destroyed by these bad people especially if you didn't know they were coming, so I came to find you."

Catherine thought about the demonic encounter and wondered if that was what he meant. "The angels told you bad people were coming?"

"Yes. They want to hurt you, keep you from fulfilling your mission."

"What is my mission? Who are these people?"

"I...I don't know. I just know it's very important. They do not whisper about other people much, just you."

Oh great, now I have people coming after me.

Catherine felt terrified. She looked at David, trying to communicate this with her eyes. She felt light headed, as if she could black out any moment. She grabbed his arm. "David?"

He caught her as she began to swoon. "Are you alright? We'd better get you inside."

He began to move towards the door, but she told him to wait, and turned to Joshua.

"Thank you, Joshua. Thank you for your trouble."

David quickly moved her through the garage side door leaving Joshua behind.

"Anytime, dear, sweet angel," Joshua said softly to himself.

He walked out of the parking garage. As Joshua stepped out into the night air, he stopped and listened. They were whispering again and from their voices he could tell they were pleased with him.

Peacefully content, Joshua shoved his hands in his pockets and walked down the street.

56- *Fear*

Catherine fumbled for the apartment keys in her purse. Her hands were shaking now. The reality of her current situation had slammed her all at once. Her tough exterior was crumbling and she felt scared and very vulnerable. For the first time in a long time, she was grateful not to be alone.

"It's okay, just take your time. Everything will be okay," David reassured her. He was unsure what to do, but went with remaining calm in order to help her.

"Why can't I ever find what I am looking for? Ah ha! Here they are."

She led him inside and started turning on lights. David sat their bags down in the hallway and followed her to the living room.

She flopped down onto her couch. "What can I do? What if people are after me for some messed up reason? I have no idea what to do now, but why else would Joshua say that stuff? I never used to believe in the possibility of any of this. Several weeks ago, I would have told you that I didn't believe in psychic abilities or even the existence of angels. Now...well, how am I supposed to feel? Oh my God, I just want to rewind my life." Catherine covered her face with her hands.

David sat down on the couch beside her and removed her hands from her face. He held them gently in his. He wanted to show his sincerity for what he was about to say. "For every question I can think of, there's an answer. I will be here to help you figure it out." He paused. "That is, if you will let me?"

Catherine looked at him. This was the closest she had been to him physically. As he held her hands, a wave of calm washed over her. "I don't know why I feel safer when you are with me. I know I'm fighting this connection we have. It scares me, and the last thing I really want right now is to be more uncomfortable than I already am."

She consciously relaxed and drew closer to him, leaning her head into his shoulder. She took a deep breath. His scent was very familiar, comforting, like a childhood memory of sitting in her father's lap.

David put his arms around her, gently. "It's going to be alright. We will find some answers soon. From what you've told me so far, there are some leads to go on. I can help you research. You've got me and Erica both."

Mentioning Erica made Catherine quickly shoot up from the couch. "Oh no, Erica! I have to call her right now. She's by herself now and if I'm in danger, then she could be too! What if they come there looking for me?"

Catherine dialed her phone quickly. "Erica, are you okay?"

"Yes, Cat. I'm just fine. Why?"

"Do you remember that homeless guy I told you about?"

"Yeah, what was his name?"

"Joshua. He showed up in the parking garage here at my apartment. He had a message for me. He said bad people are coming to try and hurt me."

"Wow...did he know anything else? Who are they?"

"He didn't know."

"How did he find this out?"

"Well...he says that he hears angels whispering to him."

"That makes sense."

"It does?"

"Yes, everything we've uncovered so far has to do with the angels. Not too much of a stretch that a guy who hears them would show up with a message for you. Makes sense in a weird sort of way."

"I want you to be careful. Be sure you lock up until I get back. Don't forget the latch on the cellar door in the basement, too."

"I'll be careful, Catherine. Don't worry. I can take care of myself."

"I know, and maybe I'm overreacting, but I want to play it safe. There's too much we don't know."

"I'm glad David is there with you."

Catherine looked over her shoulder. "Actually, I'm glad too." Then Catherine switched topics. "So lock up tight after we get off the phone. We'll head back in the morning. We already went by your mom's. Call me if you need to, any time."

"Don't worry, I'll be fine. You just drive safely getting back tomorrow."

"Goodnight Erica. I'll call you in the morning."

Catherine wanted to drive back tonight, but knew she was too exhausted for that. Filled with anxiety, she walked directly into her bedroom and pulled a suitcase out of the closet to fill with her belongings.

After a few moments of throwing stuff randomly in her bag, David walked in behind her. She was packing frantically as if she were having a manic episode, like one of her social work clients.

"Catherine?"

"Yes?" She didn't look up.

"Catherine, stop for a minute would you?"

Catherine threw several pairs of socks down on the bed, and reluctantly turned to face him.

"Just sit down for a minute." He crossed over to the bed and sat down. He patted the place next to him. "Here, relax."

Catherine sat down facing him. She shrugged her shoulders and let them fall. "I don't know what I'm doing. I think I'm just trying to keep busy."

He placed one hand on her shoulder. "I know. I also know how exhausted you must be. What is the harm in just letting me hold you for a little bit. If you want to pack up tonight, in a bit, I won't stop you."

Catherine nodded. David put his arms around her. She laid her head on his shoulder and closed her eyes. She didn't expect it to feel so good, to rest there. It's as if they were a perfect fit.

This is nice," she whispered.

David chided, "Told you so..."

Catherine lifted her head for a moment. "Now...now...don't rub it in."

David held her tight. "I won't. I won't."

Maybe I'm dreaming. This is heaven. Ah, Catherine what if I never want to let you go?

He put his hand on her head and moved the hair away from her eyes. Catherine unwillingly closed her heavy, tired eyes.

So nice...this feels so good....

"This feels so good." David verbalized Catherine's thoughts.

"I was just thinking that myself." She slid deeper into his chest, placing her right hand on his chest. She listened to his heart beat, which acted like a lullaby putting her to sleep quickly.

David could tell her breathing was slowing and she had fallen asleep. He repositioned, being careful not to wake her, and turned out the lamp next to the bed. He knew she should rest and that he could hold on to her all night, if he had to. He lay awake thinking about all she had shared that day with him. Something incredible was happening to this woman, and it felt right to be a part of it.

I should have trusted my instincts. Someone wants to harm her, but who? I knew she was in danger this whole time... It's time to trust myself more this time around. No one gets a second chance at love, dumb ass, so don't mess this up. I couldn't save Mira...maybe...this time I can make a difference. What was it Joshua said? That I was the one? I hope I am.

It was at that moment, he felt like he belonged there. A sense of purpose filled him through and through. Feeling deeply content with himself for the first time in many years, he closed his eyes and fell asleep holding her.

57- *Dark Whispers*

Jacob finished with morning group therapy. This was his first regular activity since the ordeal with Catherine. He wandered out of the room toward the elevators to go up to his room. Once he stepped inside, he was alone.

As the elevator door slide closed, he heard the angel's voice again. "Jacob...I'm here with you Jacob."

Jacob smiled because he had been waiting all day, hoping the voice would return to him. His mind kept trying to tell him that the angel was imaginary and created from the heavy medications that they had administered during his outburst. He had told no one of his encounter.

"I knew it. You are real."

"Of course I am, dear, special boy."

"I wasn't sure. These drugs have my head all messed up."

"You are gifted, Jacob, exceptionally gifted. You cannot stay here forever. You cannot escape your destiny. You must remain clear and focused. I have come to you because she needs you and you must be ready".

"I'll be ready. What do I have to do?"

"Soon you must go to her, and help her to believe that she's in danger."

"Danger?"

"Yes, it's your destiny to be with her and protect her. There's someone with her and he's not what he appears to be. She trusts him and she shouldn't."

The elevator opened and he stepped out.

"That guy...I saw him the other night!"

"Yes..."

A staff member turned to see him speaking to himself, but disregarding the behavior, she moved on to help another patient. In a few moments, Jacob was back in his room. Feeling validated, Jacob began to talk aloud again.

"I knew it! He's bad for her. I'm supposed to be there with her. I have to go to her now, tell her he's dangerous."

"No, not yet Jacob, be patient. Soon it will be time. Prepare yourself now...you will have to leave this place without anyone knowing or they will warn her you are coming, and then he will know."

"Oh don't worry, I can handle them. I'll be ready."

Jacob walked over to get his sketch pad to draw in as a nurse came in rolling a med cart to give him his afternoon medication. He grabbed the little cup of pills from her. He pretended to swallow them with the small cup of water.

Once the nurse left, Jacob's hand went to his mouth and he spit three pills into his hand immediately. He grabbed a Kleenex to wrap them up and hide them in the trash.

"Yeah, I'll be ready."

Good, Jacob. We knew you could be trusted with such an important mission."

He felt the rush of energy which usually preceded a creative episode where he would be able to draw his visions of Catherine.

His hands moved at record speed around the canvas page. He made long strokes creating the image outline first, and then hundreds of short strokes filled in the picture. He never knew what the image was going to be until it was nearly finished.

As he began to see the entire image emerge on the paper, his face clenched and his forehead wrinkled with a frown. In front of him was Catherine, all curled up, resting in the arms of the other man.

No! She can't do that. I have to stop her...him. What if he hurts her before I can get to her? I cannot fail.

He could not contain his anger. He slammed his fist into the paper and the pressure snapped his sketch pencil in two. He immediately tried to compose himself.

Calm yourself now. The angel said wait. I will wait. No sense in getting locked down again.

He took a deep breath to calm down and got up to pace the floor of his room. After a few moments, he grabbed his jacket to head outside.

58- *Spark*

For a moment after opening her eyes, Catherine had no idea where she was. Once she focused, she found herself lying on David's shoulder. She shot up straight, inadvertently waking him.

"Oh! What happened? I must have fallen asleep. I'm sorry."

She realized that they had both had slept there, exactly where they had initially been. He had been laying on the edge of her bed holding her in his arms all night.

"Do I look like I minded? I haven't slept that well in a long while. Plus, you have been running on fumes and must've been exhausted. The body has a way of making you catch up eventually."

Catherine ran her hand through her long hair. She was a little embarrassed, and jumped up to head to the kitchen. "I'll make coffee."

As she disappeared, David shook his head. He knew she was a lot to handle, but couldn't care less. They were bound by something tangible and incredible that he didn't understand. He got up and followed her to the kitchen. "I like my coffee with lots of sugar, thank you."

Catherine turned, "Oh, no problem, I have to have this to get me going."

He walked over slowly and put his hands on her shoulders. She turned around looking for a way of squirming out of his hold, but a wave of passion suddenly swept through her. David took her face in his hands and gently kissed her on the lips. It was the most incredibly perfect kiss. Catherine felt so weak in her knees that she tipped backward into the counter top and David caught her.

"Easy there now, no accidents in the kitchen this morning on my watch," he whispered in her ear, only letting her go once she had steadied herself.

Catherine didn't say a word. She was intrigued by him. Their connection seemed unreal, more like a novel than something that was really happening. Still, it was comforting for her to have him there, and she couldn't avoid admitting to herself that a part of her really wanted him to be there.

"I've never fallen asleep on anyone's shoulder except for my dad when I was little and that was only when I was sick or running a fever. It startled me that I was still lying there this morning."

David sat down at the small table. "Well, that's good. I was afraid I scared you all the way into the kitchen."

"Oh no, not me, not scared, no way."

"Ah, sarcasm in the morning is so good with a cup of coffee."

They both laughed, and then Catherine spoke seriously. "I have been against anything happening between us because of all I am going through, but I am really grateful you are here. You are just going to have to bear with my fears about opening up. I need time for that."

"You got all the time you need. I'm glad you are happy I'm here, otherwise we'd have to fight it out, cause whether or not you want to be with me romantically, and I feel I am supposed to look after you. So, you have me. Whatever I can do, I will. No one should be all alone, especially if people are after you. I know your folks would at least approve of a friend watching your back."

Catherine reached out to touch his arm. "Yes, they would be very grateful for that. Here let me get you a cup of coffee."

Soon, Catherine was sitting down with two cups of coffee.

"So what do you need to pack up today, before we head out?"

"I have to pack more clothes and grab a few other items, like my laptop." Catherine told him.

"Anything I can do to help?"

Catherine glanced at the clock. It was around nine thirty.

"If you'd call Erica and let her know we'll be headed her way in an hour, I'd appreciate it. Her number's in my phone. I'll start throwing my stuff in a suitcase." Catherine disappeared down the hallway with her cup of coffee.

David took some time to look at all of Catherine's tidy shelves of books. He saw some photo albums and pulled one from the shelf and sat down. As he turned pages, he saw a much younger Catherine with both her parents. They were on vacation somewhere near a river.

She looks on top of the world in these pictures. So happy... she's so beautiful.

As he looked at more of the photos, he realized the most striking thing about her, even back then, were her huge, blue eyes.

Mom always said eyes are the window to the soul...

As he continued to look through the album, a loose photo dropped out. It was a photo of Catherine around four years old. She was sitting at the bottom of a slide wearing a blue dress with a white apron, her legs dangling off the edge.

Who on earth would ever want to hurt such an innocent little girl?

David grimaced as he looked at the photo, thinking about who might be coming for Catherine. He stood up and walked to the window. Looking down to the street, he was half expecting Joshua to be looking up at him, or a black sedan parked outside. There was nothing like that, only a couple people walking down the sidewalk.

You watch too much television, David!

He shook his head at himself and went to make that call.

59- *Immortal One*

Preparations for the trip were well underway. Razoul's men were loading up the car with their bags. He took full use of the solitude to sneak away to visit with his family's most closely guarded secret possession. His trip took him underground, well beneath his family's sprawling estate. Since his father's death, no servants had been allowed in the chambers beneath the main house for any reason.

As he headed down a long stone staircase, he smirked at the thought of the others finding out about her.

What would they think if they knew the key to my father's power and success lay in the hands of an immortal woman he had imprisoned beneath their very feet?

He had considered revealing the truth to them in order to make it easier to track the girl. But there were too many dangers and uncontrollable outcomes if he did. Risks were a part of Razoul's nature, but even he knew it could be disastrous to remove the woman from these chambers. He needed her safe and it was far too risky.

He reached the bottom of the stairs and started down a dimly lit corridor that led to a series of rooms that she occupied. This had essentially been her home for several decades, yet neither had she aged, nor changed a single bit in all these years. As he searched for her, he remembered the first time his father had entrusted him with the secret, and led him here.

"I am about to show you one of the most incredible creatures in the known world. To have her serve this family is quite an honor. No one, not your mother or brother can know of her existence here. I was fortunate to locate and bring her here without anyone being the wiser. Do you understand, boy?"

"Yes, Father."

He was now very different from the young teen he had been back then. Razoul entered the first chamber in which wooden shelves lined the room. Each shelf contained a variety of bottles for tinctures. It felt like an old apothecary shop and smelled of such. He noted a pungent scent that was reminiscent of his childhood.

He called out to the adjoining room, "Madame? May I have a word with you?"

A woman, who appeared to be in her twenties, emerged from a short hallway to his right. She was breathtakingly enchanting. Tall and slender with honey bronze skin. Her eyes were rather unsettling and dark colored. Her tunic dress was ornately adorned with gold embroidered thread and jewels that dangled, making each movement into the room an event worthy of watching.

Her movements spoke even without her saying a word. A stranger would have had no clue that she was completely blind. Her other more sought after senses compensated immensely. She knew more about the world than most people ever would, even from within the confines of her subterranean chambers. Experiencing the world was completely available whether she left her sanctuary or not.

Ashiyah was a rare oracle. She was the rarest that Razoul or any other member of the Malem Tutela would have known. She had the much sought after ability to enter the Akashic Record. The Akashic Record was the depository of all human experiences whether past or present, and even contained potential futures.

There had only been three children born into the world who had Ashiyah's abilities to see and interpret this vast database of the human condition. She was the only one to have survived long enough to eventually become an immortal. She had endured years of conditioning and education in her unique skill. This had allowed her to become ageless in a world that no longer believed in such possibilities.

"You look enchanting, Ashiyah."

"You are most kind Razoul. Your father used to bring me wonderful garments from all over the world. But you are not your father, are you? It's been awhile since you've visited me, boy. I was about to come looking for you." Then she let out several laughs that sent sound cascading all around him.

"My apologizes, dear enchantress. Since my father's passing, many duties have been required of me."

"I suppose so, man child. Yet, here you are now. You need something of me, yes?"

"Yes, I do."

"I knew it from the moment you set foot on the staircase, my pet. The energies of the Akashic Record are very strong here in my domain as you know."

There were things Razoul didn't fully understand about the Akashic Record or how Ashiyah could see all moments in history at the same time, but he respected her amazing abilities. His father had taught him that she was a precious prize that should never be taken for granted.

"Yes, my lady, I do. Then you already know why I've come?"

"Perhaps you should tell me out loud since I receive so few real visitors. Call it a leftover human weakness."

Ashiyah offered Razoul a seat on the high backed couch in the center of the room. She sat beside him effortlessly, despite her useless eyes. "Before you begin with your request, Razoul, I must ask you about something."

Instinctively Razoul knew what she wanted to know.

She felt his energy moving toward deception and spoke again. "So it's true then, you summoned it."

Razoul looked away from her blind gaze before answering. "Yes I did."

"Your father would not be so pleased with you Razoul. Yet, we have already established that you are not Britius despite his bringing you into this world. You are willing to risk everything to achieve your goals. I have lived a long time, dear and I can tell you that your ambition will become your undoing. I have seen it."

Razoul sat up straight and immediately questioned the oracle. "What have you seen about me?"

"Calm yourself now. You know as well as I do that there are many possible futures and not only or always the one reality that you desire."

"Is one of them that I successfully find her?"

"Yes. One shows she dies and you receive all the power you want."

Razoul became super charged at hearing this. "And yet another shows that she will destroy you swiftly. Never underestimate the power of your opponent, silly boy." Her patronizing hit a nerve with Razoul.

"Now you sound like my father!"

"Razoul, there is no reason for you to be angry with me, is there?" This was her subtle way of telling him to find his place quickly.

"That's much better. How about asking me your question now?"

"Yes, my enchantress. I come because I need help finding her swiftly." He pulled a map from his inside jacket pocket and put it in her hands. Ashiyah could see the page even without the use of her physical eyes. She accessed the information as if absorbing it through her fingers.

"Leave me for a while. When you return to me I will tell you the most likely place to begin your search."

As he exited to the main corridor, he heard her voice a final time. "And perhaps bring your enchantress something sweet to eat?"

60- *Quandary*

David offered to drive the full way back to Parsons. Catherine was now thinking that the ancient book held the key to the mystery, and wanted to follow-up on the call the younger nun had made to Italy. Perhaps the man on the other end had information that could help her sort everything out.

"I want to show you the old book I told you about when we get back."

"Sure, Catherine, of course. I was thinking too. I have a friend whose father is an anthropologist at the University of Kansas. Derrick always said that his dad was a real antiquities buff. Maybe he could help us figure it out?"

"Yeah, I think that we're going to have to get some help. This is definitely not my area of expertise."

Catherine looked out the window and her mind drifted far away.

We will find the answers to all this. We just have to. What about these people coming after me? Why come after me? It all has to be connected, but how? I am nobody. Just a woman who lost her parents and has been running ever since...at least that is what I thought. Now I'm not so sure.

As if sensing everything she was mulling over, David reached out and touched her on the arm. Catherine nodded at him that she was okay. As she looked at him, she studied his features. He had a boyish charm which she found attractive.

Life had thrown them together for a reason and now she knew it. Their paths were intertwined like two pieces in a puzzle without a picture to guide them. There was nothing to do but go with it, and see where everything led them.

Catherine started fiddling with the radio.

A couple of hours passed with very little conversation. Soon they found themselves arriving at the house. Catherine was relieved. She felt safer somehow, being there, but vulnerable all the same. She secretly wished they had tracked Joshua down before leaving the city. Maybe he could have told her more than he had in the garage last night. She sighed and opened the door as David met her there.

"I was going to get that for you."

"I know. It's fine. I guess I'm not used to your level of chivalry yet."

"It's quite alright, dear. Just go inside, and I'll take care of the bags."

"Hey you two, how's it going?"

Catherine nodded and stepped inside while David headed back to the car. "Anything happen while we were away?"

"Nope, nothing happened at all. I have been worried though. I'm glad you guys are back safe and sound."

She reached out to hug Catherine. Catherine held on to her for a minute, as David entered behind her with a couple of the bags from the truck. She whispered in Erica's ear, "Thank you for everything. You are a life saver, do you know that?"

"Yeah, I get that, honey. It's all good, you know."

Erica turned to David as he put the bags down in the foyer. "Hey let me help you with all that. Be right back."

Catherine stepped inside and sat on the couch.

While grabbing the bags from the car together, David began talking about the encounter with Joshua. "I'm so glad she wasn't alone when that guy was waiting for her in the parking garage."

"Do we know who is supposedly coming after her?" Erica's voice was concerned.

David shook his head and leaned into the trunk to produce two more bags, handing one to Erica.

"I wish I did. I wish I knew who would want to hurt her, because they would be history."

Erica smiled inwardly. She was pleased that her feeling about David was correct. Now he could help protect Catherine, and her gut told her he was the best news they had right now.

"I'm glad she has both of us. I can tell you really care about Catherine and what happens to her."

"Yes, of course I do. I'm here now and not planning to go anywhere."

They both walked in with the rest of the stuff to find that Catherine wasn't where they had left her. "Catherine?"

They heard her call from upstairs. "Yeah, I'm coming. I'm getting the book to bring it down and show David."

Catherine walked slowly downstairs with the box that she had liberated from her hiding place upstairs.

She placed it on the table and opened it. Before she picked it up, she turned to David.

"You might be a little shocked at what happens when I touch this."

He motioned for her to go ahead.

She grasped the thick binding. As she did, there was a light breeze that moved the curtains as if a window were open. A spray of light began to move out in all directions making David's eyes widen in surprise, "Wow, Catherine you are beautiful! I almost can't believe it."

"I know its freaky, right? You think, how can this be happening, but it is."

"So what do we know about this book so far?" David inquired.

Erica chimed in. "Not a whole lot. It appears to be written in Enochian script or similar language and the center symbol is called the Sigil of Ameth. And you can of course tell that it makes Catherine luminous, for some reason," Erica teased.

"Yeah, I can see that." David gazed fondly at Catherine. "I've never heard of Enochian script or the Sigil, but I was telling Catherine on the way back that I may know someone who could tell us more about the book."

Catherine opened the book to show David what it looked like inside. "Look, just pages and pages I cannot read." She handed it to him.

As Erica was watching, she got really excited. "I can see the words, Catherine!" She turned to David to explain. "The first couple of times I saw the book, the pages looked blank to me and only could be seen by Catherine. This is so cool!"

"Well I can see them too, so that makes three of us. That's probably a good thing if we are going to get some help deciphering it. The book feels warm when I touch it, did you have it sitting on a heater?"

"No. It's just another mystery about this weird thing. If I could read it, that would be awesome, but I can't. The weird thing is I had a dream about the book and in the dream I could. So it's frustrating. I feel like I should be able to read it, but I can't."

"Maybe it will come eventually, like your other abilities." David offered.

Catherine thought about it. "Maybe you are right. Nothing would surprise me at this point."

"Hey Erica, when is the cable guy getting here?"

Just then the doorbell rang. It startled her and Catherine grabbed the book from David and slipped it into the box. "It's probably just the installation guy," Erica said and Catherine quickly held the box protectively against her body.

"Let me get the door, especially with all we've recently found out."

David followed after Catherine as she scooted quickly up the stairs to return the book to its hiding place.

61- *Mission of Mercy*

Jacob tossed and turned. He had been up early for breakfast and skipped morning group. He had returned to his room not wanting to speak to anyone. His head was filled with images of his true love. After discarding his morning meds, he lay down for a bit and fell asleep. The crumpled page of his sketch book was gripped tightly in his right hand.

The angelic voice penetrated his disjointed dreams.

Jacob...Jacob...

"Yes I am here. What do you want?"

Your waiting is over now. Tonight you must go to her and tell her what I told you.

"I'm scared though. What if she won't listen? What if she sends me away?"

You must make her see, Jacob. You are the only one who can save her.

"I will save her."

Yes you will save her and be with her at last. It will be just like I promised.

"I will be with her."

Yes, she's yours and has always been, even if she's turned away from you.

"I will make her see."

Yes, you will.

"I will go to her tonight."

Yes, you must. She will leave soon and you won't get another chance.

Jacob nodded in his sleep. He was mumbling when he woke because a staff member was shaking his arm. He jumped up. "What? What do you want?"

"It's time for therapy, Jacob." A heavy set nurse was standing over him.

"Well get out of my face and I will go."

The nurse backed away and shook her head as she left the room.

"I hate this place. I'm so glad I'm out of here soon," he said under his breath to be sure no one heard him.

He stood up and realized he was still holding the picture in a wad. He unwrinkled it enough to start tearing it into little pieces. He brushed his hands together allowing the fragments to float to the floor.

He made sure to step on the pile and grind it into the ground with his foot, before he headed out the door.

"I'm so out of here. Don't worry, Catherine, I'm coming."

62-Scholar

David hung up his phone and went to find the ladies in the kitchen. He'd kept an eye on the cable guy while calling his friend Derrick

Catherine and Erica were eating some lunch at the table. "You want a sandwich?"

"That would be great."

David sat down across from Catherine as Erica rose to make him a sandwich. "I spoke to Derrick. He said his dad is about to leave on Sabbatical for several months in just a few days, but he'll see if we can meet with him before he goes. We may be cutting it close. He'll call me later to let me know if Henry can see us. If so, then I think we'd better head for Lawrence tomorrow. I already mapped the directions from here on my phone. It should take about two and a half hours to get there."

"I don't think we should tell or show him the glowing mystery. So, I won't handle the book while we are there. Thank you for doing this, David."

"Don't worry. Derrick said he'll make sure he says yes. If I remember correctly, he can be persuasive. I told him I was sure his dad would want to see this."

Catherine's mind wandered. She thought of Jacob briefly, and how she was going to handle that situation. She resolved to handle it after they got back, if they went tomorrow. She took a bite of her sandwich and suddenly a putrid smell filled her nose as a wave of nausea moved through her.

"God, I think I'm going to be sick." She covered her mouth and headed for the bathroom closest to the kitchen.

Both Erica and David ran to her aid.

"Are you alright?" Erica put her hand on the door.

Catherine responded with her head over the toilet bowl. "Did either of you smell that?"

Erica and David exchanged a glance. "Smell what, honey?"

Then they could hear Catherine lose the entire contents of her stomach. Pretty soon they heard the toilet flush as a very pale Catherine opened the door.

"It was absolutely putrid, like rotting meat or like…" Catherine thought of the dream where she had battled the demonic thing attacking her, but realized she had never told either of them the exact details of it.

"Let's go sit down in the living room. I have something to share with you both. It kind of slipped my mind."

"I had this dream before we went back to Kansas City. It was one of those dreams that didn't feel like a dream. This demonic creature came after me, but somehow this wave of white light came out of me and scared it off. I was in this chamber that was damp and smelly and bloody, and there was a point when this thing was only inches from my face. It gave off a stench like nothing I've ever smelled."

David spoke up. "A demon attacked you in your dream? You didn't say anything?" Then as an afterthought he added, "Why didn't you tell me, or at least Erica?"

"I don't know, I was sort of dealing with the immediate issue after I woke up that morning." Catherine touched the dressing under her shirt, as Erica looked at her understanding what she meant.

"What's wrong with your arm?" David questioned her.

"I woke up with a burn where this thing touched me."

David's eyes got wide, but he repressed his initial instinct to get noticeably upset.

"It was really weird, David, and I don't think my brain could hold the thought of a demon taking such an interest in me, or being able to leave a mark on me. I just put it out of my mind. Come on, how would you handle a demon coming to attack you? It was really pissed off, you know? I really didn't want you to worry. So I was in the kitchen just now thinking about Jacob and then out of nowhere that same smell filled my nose and made me puke."

"Maybe that's what this guy Joshua was warning you about?" David offered.

Catherine shook her head. "No, he said bad people are after me. This was definitely not a person. It was dark, demonic and sinister."

"It was just a thought. You can't blame a guy for trying. Don't worry though, I'm on it."

He sat down next to Catherine. Catherine looked at them both on either side of her.

Catherine did something totally out of character. She put her arms around both of them in a group hug. "I'm so glad you guys are here with me."

63- *In the Shadows*

"Tonight is the night. After bed checks, I will wait until the staff is on the far end of the hall. I can slip down the stairs then."

A familiar feeling spread through him as he heard the disembodied voice whisper sweetly to him.

"Yes, it is time my child for you to fulfill your destiny."

Jacob closed his eyes as a small breeze moved his dark brown hair slightly. He took a deep breath and felt a burning strength course though him. It caused him to clinch both fists tightly for a moment.

What a rush! I feel so powerful. I will be victorious.

As if answering his thoughts the voice surrounded him. "Yes, you are powerful, and I have given you all you need to be victorious. You will not fail."

I will not fail.

A crooked smile spread across his face, as if he had a secret burning deep inside him. His growing pleasure was interrupted by a nurse entering behind him.

"It's about time for dinner Jacob, and then group."

Nothing could break his mood. He turned to face the nurse. "Sure, I'm coming."

She looked at him curiously. "You look like you are having a good day."

"Yes, I am having a fantastic day."

He moved to leave the room but suddenly remembered something and turned back.

"Need my jacket. I want to go for a walk after group."

The nurse nodded and left the room.

****

Catherine and Erica were cleaning the kitchen after dinner. David was in the other room poking around on his laptop, doing some research.

"I sure hope this professor can help us tomorrow." Erica chatted away as she dried some dishes.

Catherine smiled as she dried out the sink. "Me too Erica, I hope he can help. It's the most promising lead we've had. I want to try that number in Italy again, too. Maybe I can reach someone there who can help."

Catherine walked into the living room. David looked victorious. "We have an appointment in Professor O'Brien's office at eleven tomorrow. If we leave here by eight in the morning, we'll have plenty of time."

"Okay, David that sounds good."

"You okay?"

"Yeah, I'm okay, just tired. I think I'll go up and take a hot bath."

Soon she disappeared up the stairs and David could hear the water running. He returned to his research, pouring through many websites about angels and the Enochian script. He glanced at the wall clock, and it was around seven thirty now.

"So, what are you up to?" Erica plopped down on the chair next to him.

"Reading and trying to get up to speed on all this stuff happening to Catherine." Erica felt tremendous appreciation that he was with them on the journey.

"You are an incredible guy. Do you know that?"

"I just do my best. That's about all I can do."

"Well, I know she's happy you're here."

"I sure hope so."

"Oh she is. I can tell every time she talks to you."

David looked up and saw Catherine coming down the stairs.

"There she is."

Catherine looked up, seeming in much better spirits. "Ah, talking about me again, I see. Why am I not surprised?"

Erica chimed in. "You shouldn't be. We're your biggest fans, you know."

Catherine shook her head. "I'm not sure what I'm going to do with both of you."

She passed through on her way to the kitchen and poured herself a glass of water.

Erica offered a delayed response to her rhetorical question. "Well I'm not sure what you are doing to do *with* us, but we are here no matter what."

Catherine was at a loss for words.

"Catherine I want to stay here tonight if that's okay with you?"

"Sure, please do. I'll definitely feel better with you here. Then we can leave first thing in the morning for Lawrence."

She turned to Erica. "Could you get him a blanket and pillow from the hall closet upstairs? I think I will try to get some sleep."

"Sure honey, I'll take care of it."

Catherine stood in the living room for a moment, and then made her way upstairs again.

"Sweet dreams, Catherine." Erica called as Catherine was walking up.

Catherine stopped and turned to them both, "I sure hope so." She feigned a smile and slowly made her way up to the top of the stairs.

64- *The Rescue*

Jacob lay fully clothed under his covers. He nestled himself down so that no one would notice he was still dressed. He felt fortunate that the night shift head nurse was Melissa tonight. She often would chat for hours with her boyfriend once everyone was asleep. This was perfect.

He watched the time pass on his clock. The minutes seemed to creep by, but finally, it was nine. He had to get out of there, to have time to reach Catherine and then get back before morning. He quietly rose out of his covers and quickly put extra pillows under the blankets in case anyone did bed checks.

Jacob crept to the door that was cracked slightly. He listened carefully and could hear no one walking the hall. He peeked outside and silently left his room. He gazed down the hallway for signs of staff members. He could faintly hear voices talking down at the nurse's station.

Jacob made his way to the hall door. He inched himself down the hall following along the wall to hide himself. Then, as if he'd practiced it a hundred times, he quietly opened the door and as it shut, put a small piece of paper in the mechanism to silence the door.

Very soon, Jacob emerged into the night air with a big sigh. The moon was full above him and cast the perfect light for him to see his way.

On foot the trip to Catherine's house would take him roughly an hour, but only if he moved quickly.

As he walked, his mind was filled with images of Catherine. Even in his mind, she was as real as if she were standing in front of him.

Soon you will be mine, and we will be together.

The more he thought of her, the quicker he moved, as if he were a cat that could see in the dark. This was his old turf, and he knew the way well. He made his way through thick bushes and branches until he reached the creek. He could follow this to within four or five blocks of Catherine's house, allowing him to enter her property from the back. He couldn't believe he was already at the half way point. He stopped to catch his breath and leaned down to get a drink of water with his hand from the creek.

You are doing wonderfully, my child.

"I wondered when you would show up," Jacob said callously.

Yes, I am here. I will be with you. You must convince her to get this man away from her.

"Yes, I know. I will. I will make her listen. She has to."

She will listen to you, Jacob. You are the chosen one. You are her protector.

"Yes, I am her protector. I will make her listen."

Jacob stood up and wiped his hands on his jeans and then continued his journey. His mind was focused deep in thought for a long time. It jogged him to attention when he saw a familiar fence up the hill. He made his way there, and climbed over it with very little effort.

Across the yard on the other side of the property, Jacob didn't know he was being watched. Brother Artemis was about to return to the hotel for the night, when he saw a figure in the darkness.

Wait, who is this? He watched the man cross the yard to a slanted cellar door attached to the back of the house.

Oh no. He's going inside. What do I do?

Jacob planned to enter through the cellar door that was rarely locked, and even if it was, he knew a trick since childhood that Catherine had shown him to jimmy it.

Brother Artemis shifted nervously for a moment, contemplating his next move as he watched the dark figure disappear inside the house.

Jacob's confidence grew as he found himself inside the basement. He listened for movement upstairs, but didn't hear anything. He ascended the stairs silently and stepped into the kitchen, his breath quickened. Since childhood, he knew the house like the back of his hand. Catherine and he used to play hide and seek as children here, and the memories rushed him. He quickly reached to the butcher block on the counter and pulled a long knife from it for protection.

The moonlight dimly lit up the house as he inched closer to the living room. He stopped when he saw a figure lying there, sleeping, back turned to him. Boldly he walked to stand over David. He watched him for a moment contemplating him great harm.

I could totally wipe this son of a bitch off the earth. But I'll deal with you later.

Then he turned toward the foyer. He took one more glance at David, alert for any movement. When he saw that the man was still sleeping, he moved silently to the staircase.

She'll be in her room at the end of the hallway.

When he reached the top of the stairs, he peeked in the room to his left, to see Erica asleep.

This must be her friend.

He quickly turned, moved down the hall and quietly opened Catherine's door. As he strained to close her door without any sound, he could hear her softly breathing across the room. The moonlight was streaming through a large crack in the bedroom curtains, gently lighting up her face.

Suddenly conscious that he was holding a weapon, he slipped the knife into the waistband of his jeans so that he didn't frighten her.

You are so beautiful, Catherine.

He stood there watching her sleep. He didn't want to wake her, but he had to speak to her.

Shall I wake you, princess, with a kiss?

He leaned closer to her face and then kissed her. Catherine awoke out of her sleep to find herself staring into Jacob's eyes, hovering right over her. She gasped but before she could shout, Jacob covered her mouth and put one finger to his lips.

He whispered, "I must talk to you."

Catherine nodded and he released his hand. She sat up trying to focus on the room and Jacob very close to her.

She spoke softly, "What are you doing here?"

He sat on the bed beside her. "I had to talk to you, Catherine. I'm sorry for coming like this. You are in danger, and I'm here to protect you."

Outside Brother Artemis watched. He could see no movement from the windows and the house was still dark. He grabbed his phone from his pocket, still keeping an eye on the house to see if any lights came on. His heart pounded. He was prohibited from interfering but he was also there to insure Catherine's safety.

Catherine felt more coherent after several moments had passed quietly between them. "What do you mean I am in danger?"

"I am here to tell you that man downstairs is not who you think he is."

"You mean David? You must be mistaken, Jacob. He's become a real friend who's helping me out right now."

"You have to believe me Catherine. I am your friend, and much more."

She reached her hand out to place over Jacob's hand. "I know Jacob, and I'm sorry for the other day and what happened."

He pulled his hand away abruptly. "I don't care about all that now. You have to get away from him, right now. Come with me so you will be safe."

"I can't come with you Jacob. This is crazy. Do they know you are gone from the hospital?"

"Forget the hospital. I don't want to go back there. I want to be here with you to protect you."

"Jacob, I don't need you to be my protector."

"Yes you do. The angel said so."

"What angel?"

"An angel came to me and told me you were in danger."

A wave of nausea passed through Catherine at the same moment he spoke of the angel. She knew from her reaction that he hadn't been speaking to any angel. She remembered the demon in her dream, the reaction after thinking of him, and it dawned on her what may be happening.

"Listen to me, Jacob. You didn't speak to an angel at all. I'm afraid you have been talking to something altogether different, something very bad that wants to hurt me, instead of helps me."

Jacob shook his head vehemently. "No, no, no. I am sure it was an angel. It had to be. I am your protector, and we have to go." He grabbed her by the arm and pulled her out of bed. She nearly stumbled and fell but found her balance again.

Jacob immediately was concerned about the noise, and moved quickly to lock her door. "Be quiet Catherine. I don't want him to hear us."

"Jacob, come on, listen to me. I am fine. I'm just surprised that you showed up in my bedroom in the dead of night."

He went to her. "Don't be scared Catherine. I'm here for you and only you."

Catherine took a step back. "I know Jacob, and it's okay. I know you won't hurt me." Her voice sounded convincing but inside she wasn't sure, and Jacob picked up on it.

"Are you afraid of me, your chosen protector?"

"Please don't call yourself that."

What she said made his voice rise louder. "Why? It's true, and you are the only one that doesn't see it. I am meant to be by your side. Why do you run from that?" He began to pace back and forth.

Catherine knew to remain calm and talk plainly, since Jacob appeared to become more agitated as reality collided with whatever fantasy was consuming him right now.

"Let's just talk this through, Jacob. Come sit down." His shoulders dropped and as he moved near the bed, until there was a knock on the door.

"Catherine? Are you okay?" David's voice came from behind the door. Then he jiggled the doorknob, trying to enter.

Catherine watched Jacob as he reached for the knife in his pants. "Jacob! What are you doing?"

"I have to protect you from him!" He gripped the knife in his hand.

Erica had now joined David in the hallway. Both of them tried to get in the door but couldn't. "He's in there with her!" Erica said frantically.

David tried to ram his shoulder to open the door, but it was too heavy and wouldn't budge. "Go call 911 now!"

Erica ran down the stairs to grab her cell phone from the kitchen.

Jacob started shouting at the door, "You aren't coming in here. You aren't going to harm her!"

"I would never harm Catherine. Just let me in and we can discuss this man to man."

Jacob turned to Catherine and grabbed her arm, pulling her toward the window. "We have to climb down like when we were kids." He was strong and it took all her strength to pull away.

"We are not climbing out the window."

"But you have to come with me. Trust me please. We have to go now."

"Listen to yourself Jacob. None of this is real. You aren't my protector. You are my friend, and I care about you. Please stop this now."

Jacob flung the window up with a whoosh as if he hadn't heard her. He motioned for her to come to him, but she shook her head and stood her ground. Tears began to form in her eyes.

Oh God, why is this happening?

All the while David kept trying to open the door. "Come on, Jacob. I know you care about Catherine. We all do. Let's all talk."

Hearing David's voice again enraged Jacob's fierce anger. In a single motion, he lunged for Catherine, this time with incredible force. She let out a loud groan that David heard through the door. He started pounding his fists on the door harder.

"Jacob you are hurting me! Stop this, stop doing this. Please Jake, please."

"They have already turned you against me. Can't you see that?"

David ran into another bedroom to find something to smash into the door in the hope he could get to Catherine before Jacob hurt her. He couldn't find anything strong enough. Then he had a thought about something he had seen in the basement that would work. He flew down the stairs to find it.

"No one has turned me against you. You are confused and need help."

"No! YOU need MY help!" Jacob lunged again in Catherine's direction, and soon she was backed up against the wall. "I need you, Catherine. I have to have you. We belong together. I can't leave without you."

Catherine's legs were shaking as she watched, out of the corner of her eye, the knife still clenched in his right hand.

Jacob pressed his body against hers and leaned in to kiss her again only this time it was frantic and rough. Her mind raced. He was out of control, and she knew the next couple minutes were going to determine the course of everything. She wanted to protect herself and her friends.

"Okay, Jacob. Let's leave so we can talk. I'll come with you. Just drop the knife and we'll go."

Jacob released her and started to lay down the knife on the bed when the door crashed open. Like an animal, Jacob darted towards David, who was still holding a sledge hammer that he had used to bash the door open.

David raised the hammer sideway to block Jacob, whose arm was coming down to strike him. The knife stuck into the wood handle briefly. David used the opportunity to push forward and knock him off balance.

Jacob fell backwards with the knife still in hand, but leapt up on his feet quickly.

"Jacob! Stop, please stop!" Catherine cried out.

Jacob was distracted for a second, but kept his eye on David. "He has to die! I have to protect you."

Catherine bravely walked toward him trying to calm him down but stopped before reaching him. She could hear police sirens in the distance and they were closing in quickly.

"You don't want to hurt anyone. Please give me the knife. The police are almost here."

"I can't do that, Cat. I can't."

"Yes, you can. Just give me the knife and I will talk to the police."

"It's too late. I'm too late."

"It's not too late. Let me help you."

"You can't help me. I have failed you. I have failed..." He nervously ran his hands through his hair.

"Come on sweetie. It is going to be alright. Everything is going to be alright."

"Don't say that! You fucking bitch!"

Catherine's eyes grew wide.

"You ruined everything!"

Catherine knew Jacob could close the distance between them in a fraction of a second and turn all his rage on her. As she contemplated her next move, they heard police banging on the door downstairs.

Jacob felt the world closing in on him. He was lost.

I failed her. I failed.

He looked at Catherine and for a moment and the old Jacob showed himself to her in his eyes. Then his eyes closed and in a single moment he raised the knife to his own throat and cut his flesh from side to side.

Catherine screamed and ran toward Jacob who crumpled to the ground like a rag doll. "Get an ambulance, quick!"

She tried to put pressure on the wound with her hands but there was too much blood. She held him close to her. "Jacob, no, no, no...."

Soon she was surrounded by police who moved her out of the way to tend to Jacob.

Catherine sat on the floor staring down at her hands stained with Jacob's blood. She was oblivious to the rest of the room, full of activity now. All she could do was sit there on the floor sobbing.

How can this be happening? Oh, God...it's my fault. You didn't fail me. I failed you.

She felt a presence near her and looked up from her position on the floor. It was David looking at her gently with tears in his eyes. He knelt down with a towel and began wiping her hands. He was so sweet and tender that Catherine's heart melted. He hugged her close to his chest and for a few moments the world disappeared, but her relief at feeling safely cocooned in his arms was interrupted by EMTs quickly moving Jacob out on an arm board to the ambulance.

Catherine pulled quickly away from David and started to move after them. "Is he going to okay?"

One of the EMT's turned to her quickly and said, "We don't know but we've got to get him to the hospital. We're doing all we can."

Catherine stood frozen in the hallway, as they carried him down the stairs and out the front door. David came up behind her and held her. They both stood there as the ambulance left with their sirens blaring.

65- *Sighting*

Final preparations were made for Razoul and the other members to leave for the United States. The only thing left was to register the flight plan with his pilot. He made sure no one followed him to the hidden corridor that led to Ashiyah's chambers below them.

Time to check in with my secret weapon.

The anticipation of what she could reveal to him was growing in his chest as he entered her greeting chamber. It was customary not having to announce himself, especially when she knew he was arriving again, so he sat down on the sofa to wait.

A few moments later, Ashiyah emerged into the room. She was dressed in a full length gown made of indigo colored silk that floated in long strands behind her as she walked. Just the sight of her made Razoul's heart leap. He had never desired any woman like he felt desire for the Immortal being in his presence now.

"Ah, Razoul, you have returned at a perfect time." She appeared to float across the room and take a position on the other side of the couch.

"Yes, madam, I am eager to hear of your news for your humble servant." Razoul bowed his head and took her hand, gently kissing it. He was very careful not to linger there.

"I have consulted the Akashic Record and it would appear the angels have altered the energies surrounding the woman you seek."

Razoul's heart sank briefly. Sensing this shift, she moved closer to him and spoke while gently stroking his cheek. "Ah, do not fear, my pet, for your Ashiyah would never let you down." She smiled slyly. "The angels were not shielding their prophet so well."

"A prophet?"

"Yes, they have a prophet of sorts who, from what I can see, has spoken with the Incarnate One."

Razoul's frown turned to a freakish grin.

"There is a man you will find in Kansas City, Missouri. He is a derelict named Joshua Stark. According to the Records, he can hear the angel's communications. I am quite certain if you find him, he can lead you to the one you seek."

"He's a peasant?"

"Yes, but he stays in the city and moves from place to place. I would look for charities that cater to such people."

"You couldn't determine her location from his thoughts?"

"Sadly, no, I am unable to unlock the modifications made by the angels to protect the woman, but I inferred from what I did see that he has laid his eyes upon her at least once."

Razoul reached into his breast pocket for a sleek black box of chocolate from Switzerland that was flaked with edible 24K gold. He offered it cordially to Ashiyah who giggled with glee, as if she were a child.

"Delafee! You are a charmer, my pet! And my favorite! I have not had this since your father's passing."

She stood up to open the box and gazed at the beautiful confection. She twirled around sending fine silk cascading in all directions. Then she stopped, and her face suddenly turned serious for a moment. "Young one, do not underestimate the power of the woman now. When you strike, you must do so swiftly and without mercy."

Razoul nodded and stood up. He took out his phone and called his pilot. "We have our destination. Draw up and register your flight plan. We leave for Kansas City in two hours."

He hung up the phone and walked toward the immortal speaking softly.

"Have no fear madam. I will strike swiftly and without mercy as I always do. I will not fail."

As he turned to leave, she spoke for a final time. "Remember Razoul, I see all possibilities. If you fail, your arrogance will be your shortcoming."

Razoul turned and looked at her without speaking, as she continued. "And if you fail, then everything you worked for, including the murder of your father shall be for naught."

This was the first time that anyone had spoken the truth out loud about Britius' death, even though everyone knew that he had murdered him.

Razoul bowed to her with respect, appearing unfazed, "Thank you for your wonderful counsel, my lady." As he left the room, Ashiyah whispered, "Very soon, boy, you will pay me back for everything."

66- *Shock*

Catherine sat on the couch in a daze. After nearly two hours of interrogation, the police had left. It was almost one in the morning. She was numb now from head to toe, thoroughly exhausted. She laid her head back and closed her eyes.

David and Erica were now in the kitchen discussing the tragedy in hushed tones.

"I can't believe he got into the house without my knowing! He could have killed her just as easily as he tried to take his own life."

"It's not your fault, David. Neither of us knew about the cellar door, or that he'd come here."

"I know, but the man Joshua told her that she was in danger. I should have anticipated this and made sure the house was locked up tight. I feel like I failed her already, before we've even gotten started. Some man I am."

"Don't say that David. She needs you now more than ever. Together, we will keep her safe together."

"I hope you are right."

Erica reassured David, "I am right. There's nothing we can't do here. I am sure of that."

"You are such the eternal optimist."

Erica leaned backward a little in her chair; looking through the kitchen doorway to make sure that Catherine was doing alright. She looked peaceful, her eyes were closed.

"I think she's fallen asleep, and yes, optimism is in my nature."

"I was thinking about tomorrow, maybe we should cancel our appointment with Professor O'Brien. I don't know if Catherine will be up for the trip with Jacob clinging to life."

Erica thought about it. "Yeah, I don't know how she will feel about that. Isn't he leaving for his sabbatical soon?"

David nodded. "Yes, in two days."

"This could be the only chance to see him though." Erica looked strained.

Catherine's voice made both of them jump. "We are going tomorrow guys. Nothing is going to get in the way of that."

"Oh Catherine, I thought you were dozing on the couch."

Catherine pushed the hair away from her ashen colored face. "I can't sleep. Every time I close my eyes I see Jacob." She stood, crossed to the kitchen window, and stared outside.

"How could this happen? How could I let this happen?" She listlessly poured herself a cup of coffee from the pot Erica had made earlier. Catherine took her cup and sat down. For a few moments no one spoke.

Catherine traced the rim of her coffee cup. "I feel like I did on the day I heard the news of my parent's death." Tears welled up in her eyes.

David reached out to touch her arm. Catherine shot him an appreciative glance and then continued speaking, mostly for her own benefit. She stared into her coffee cup.

"The day they died was the worst day of life. It changed me. It made me angry at God for taking them away. I was all alone, orphaned at sixteen. It made me strong but shut off. I fought through my life like a medieval knight on a quest. I wanted to conquer it all, show God that I was worthy of love. Somehow I thought it was my fault that they died, and that I didn't deserve to be happy. I realize now, all that was a child's way of coping with the impossible, and that I had run from everything."

Catherine looked up. "Now I'm done with running. I have to find out my destiny. I need to know why I am here. So we have to go see this professor while we can. Maybe then I can really help Jacob."

Erica met Catherine's eyes for a moment. "I know what you are going to say Erica, but Jacob will be alright. I just know he will be. He can't die."

"I hope so, Cat, I really do, for both your sakes," but Erica wasn't so sure after thinking about the horrific scene upstairs. Jacob was bleeding so badly that if he was alive, he was clinging for life in the emergency room, as they sat here in the kitchen discussing the meeting tomorrow.

"I can't explain it, but I feel I would know if he died. I can't explain our connection at all."

"I just want you to be careful, Catherine. I saw the look in his eyes. He could have killed you."

She recognized David's concern and knew his heart was in the right place. "I'm so sorry he tried to hurt you. He was only trying to protect me."

"Protect you from what, me?" David challenged her.

"When he first got there he said that I was in danger and he came to protect me. He told me that an angel came to him and told him to save me. Only I don't think it was an angel speaking to him."

"Or he just has major mental issues and needs help."

"David, listen. I know how this looks, but you have to trust that I know Jacob's mental condition. I also know my friend. I don't think he was delusional. I believe something was pushing him to grasp on to some fantasy about he and I. I think it was the same demon that attacked me in my dream. In his own mind, I know he believed that he was trying to rescue me." Without warning Catherine began to cry again. "I'm sorry guys. I'm so emotional."

"It is okay honey, tears are good," Erica comforted her. Why don't you try to get some rest and even if you don't sleep, try to close your eyes. You don't have to go upstairs at all. I made up the bed in the downstairs bedroom for you."

Erica looked at David. "You want to get her settled?"

"Sure." David got up and helped Catherine to the bedroom. She was still sobbing and kept a tight grip on his hand.

Once they got into the room, he helped her get under the covers. "Don't leave me. I can't be alone."

Without a word, David gently crawled into bed beside her and put his arms around her while she slept.

67- *The Professor*

The next morning was a mental blur. Catherine had tried to call the hospital to check on Jacob before they left town, but wasn't able to find anything out due to patient privacy laws. She even tried to call Mary next door, but there was no answer.

Now she gazed out the car window as the miles between them and Lawrence, Kansas diminished one by one. As she stared at the ground whizzing past her, she ran through the sequence of events in her bedroom with Jacob. It made her more frustrated when she realized that there wasn't really anything she could have done differently, but that was little consolation to her right now.

Catherine turned away from the window to look at David who was driving, and then at Erica who was riding in the back seat. Both of them smiled at her and Catherine forced herself to reciprocate.

God I am so tired. I don't feel like I slept much at all. I hope this professor can help us determine the origins of the book. Please let him help me.

"We are supposed to meet the professor at his office in Wescoe Hall at eleven. We are getting close to Lawrence now so we will be on time." David informed them.

Erica leaned toward the front seat for conversation. "Have you ever met the professor before, David?"

"Yeah, once at a family party but we didn't speak much."

"What's he like?"

"I guess he looks and acts like a history professor. Elbow patches, you know." David smiled.

Erica chuckled, imagining him. "Yeah, I bet."

She put her hand on Catherine's left shoulder to offer support, and then scooted back into her seat again.

Catherine was mesmerized by the campus itself. Most of the architecture was modern, but everything was surrounded by tall, beautiful trees. There were lots of people rushing about.

Look at all of them...not a care in the world. I wish I was one of them right now.

David circled the parking lot outside Wescoe Hall before finally finding a spot.

"They really need more parking spots. So typical." David hopped out of the car and came around to Catherine's side. Then he backtracked to the trunk lifting out the box with the book in it, placing it into Catherine's waiting hands.

David then motioned in his usual upbeat way, "Come with me, ladies."

They spotted the gold lettering on Professor O'Brien's office door.

"This is the place." David knocked twice and was quickly greeted.

"Ah, David, come in."

"Hello, Professor, this is Erica, and this is Catherine."

"I apologize for the mess. As you know, I'm headed for a three month sabbatical and don't have much time to pack up my most important books and other things I need." His desk was in total disarray. Boxes were scattered around his office.

There were already two chairs in front of his desk, but he grabbed a folding chair from the closet. "Please, all of you have a seat."

"So, Derrick tells me you have a very old book that you'd like me to take a look at?" They all nodded in unison. "It's very lucky you caught me. And please, call me Henry."

"I appreciate your taking the time to see us."

Catherine rose from her chair and placed the box in front of him. She would have taken the book out of the box wasn't quite ready to explain the eerie glow that would have filled the room.

Henry put on his reading glasses and then opened the box. His eyes examined the cover studiously. After a few moments his eyes widened. He looked at Catherine, "May I have a closer look?"

"Of course, that's why we are here."

He ran his fingers across the cover briefly and then lifted the book out of the box. He sat the box on the floor. "Where did you get this?"

"My, uh, aunt left it to me after she died." Catherine said, looking away.

"Do you know where she acquired this? It's rather exquisite, I must say."

"No, I was hoping you could help me with the origins of the book."

"I recognize the symbol on the cover. It's the Sigil de Ameth, I believe. It's a very obscure symbol. I believe its origins date back to around the 13th Century. More recently, I believe it was used in the 15th century by a man named John Dee who wanted to communicate directly with angels."

Then he looked up and smiled. "I am something of an occult buff, I guess. Even though there's not much but fantasy in all that nonsense, yet it is fascinating." He grinned like a little kid.

He's like the absent minded professor from the movies.

He opened the book and quickly thumbed past the first page. He looked amused and surprised. "I assumed this would be written in Latin as most books of this type but it's written in something similar to Enochian script. And the paper used isn't what I would expect either."

Catherine was curious now. "What do you mean, Professor?"

"Well, books with this type of binding typically originate from Europe. Prior to the development of movable type presses, many old books were written in Latin, and the paper was made from vellum which is lamb or calf skin. This book is neither, which is truly intriguing!"

"What language is the book written in Professor, I mean Henry?" Catherine inquired.

"Well, that is another interesting piece of the puzzle here. No books that I am aware of, other than the personal writings of John Dee, were ever written in this script. And like I said, it's similar to Enochian script, but not quite."

Is this a dead end?

"As I look at the pages, this is written with distinct phrases and complete sentences. Also, I see, quite remarkably that there are no visible strokes."

"Pen strokes?" Catherine looked up from the hands in her lap.

"Well the book appears to be hand-written, yet there's no indention from a quill tip or anything in the paper. So it's as if the words were mechanically printed which is virtually impossible since presses weren't widely used. This would have cost a fortune, especially in John Dee's time. The book is certainly an enigma. Very rare."

Professor O'Brien carefully examined the inside front and back covers. On each were four imprinted symbols appearing in a semi-circle.

"These four symbols look familiar, but I cannot place them. They also look burned from inside which is, well…impossible to say the least, very strange indeed."

Suddenly the Professor shot up from his chair mumbling something about finding an envelope.

"Less than a year ago, my dear friend Roger Thornton was exploring some catacombs in Italy when a wall caved in revealing a series of hidden rooms. I remember the event well. It was an exciting and unexpected discovery for him. He snapped a picture of four symbols that were etched into the tomb wall outside the entrance to the rooms that were discovered. He sent me a photo. I am almost certain that is where I have seen these symbols before. Now where did I put that envelope?"

Henry moved around his office frantically. He searched through drawer after drawer with no luck. Then he opened an old metal filing cabinet. "Oh good. Here we go."

He pulled out several pages and an 8 x 10 photo of the symbols. He laid the photo next to the book to compare them.

"Look at that. They match. To my knowledge, these were unique only to that archeological site. The origins are still unknown. But then again, I haven't spoken to Roger much since this happened."

Erica chimed in, "Maybe there's some updated news by now? Could we possibly speak with your friend?"

"Yes, yes, of course. I can get you his information. He's still living in Italy, I'm sure. He always was a lucky bastard. I know he'll want to hear from you, and to see this book."

The Professor opened an old address book from his drawer. "Let's see....Thornton. Okay, here it is." He jotted the name, phone number and email on a pad of paper. He handed it to Catherine.

"Thank you, Henry, I really appreciate this."

"May I snap a picture of the cover and inside? I'd like to email a photo or two to Roger.

"Sure, anything that could help us would be great."

Henry rang his fingers through his hair. "Now where did I put that camera?" He started looking through several boxes for it. "I just saw it earlier. This always happens to me." After riffling through his desk drawers, Henry finally found it. "Okay, here we go!"

Henry aimed the compact digital camera at the cover. He opened the book to get a sample of the text and then took pictures of the symbols from the back cover. He gently put the book back in its box and handed it to Catherine.

"This book of yours is worth a great deal to the right collector or antiquities dealer."

"Well it's not for sale," Catherine quipped.

"Oh, I am sure you don't want to part with it, Catherine; however, due to its value, I would safe guard it against theft."

Catherine felt silly for getting defensive. "Oh yes, you are so right. I will definitely do that. Thank you again, Professor. I will be in touch with your colleague in Italy."

"Here's my card. I'll email Roger with the pictures so he should be expecting to hear from you."

"I will Henry. Thanks."

The three turned and left the office, closing the door.

Henry pushed a button on his camera to review the images he had taken, but couldn't believe what he saw. "What the hell?" He turned off the review mode and took the memory card out to plug it into the slot on his laptop.

In a few moments, the images pulled up on his screen. When he saw them, he immediately grabbed his camera and carefully examined the lens. It was fine. No smudges, nothing. He turned back to the computer and opened the other two images.

Each had a bright light that obscured much of the image itself, plus some other distortion he hadn't seen before. He frowned. After studying them for a few moments, he emailed them to Roger anyway. He picked up his camera for a moment, and looked at it.

"I knew I should have bought the better model."

68- *Crossing*

Razoul gazed out the window of his private jet as it made the last leg of an eleven hour flight from Italy to New York. There the pilot would refuel, and then they'd be on their way to their final destination.

We find the old man prophet fast. Then the woman... I must have the angel's power for myself. No one will stand in my way. Not Sirius, not Thaddeus. No one.

He placed his hand over his left breast pocket as if to double check that the sigil was still safely tucked inside. He smiled.

There's nothing to keep me from being victorious now. Not my father, Sirius or any of these reprobates. Each one of them lacks the necessary vision for the future.

He closed his eyes briefly and his mother instantly came to mind. He remembered his favorite place that he and his mother had shared.

Spring was when all the many varieties of flowers in his mother's garden were blooming. His father had spent countless thousands importing rare and exquisite plants from all over the world. His mother had a special touch with each of them. They seemed to obey her every wish, growing to extraordinary size.

As a boy, he would enter the gate of the garden and if she was not in sight, he always knew where she would be. He would walk the stone path that wandered through the entire place. There were various benches that would allow visitors to rest and enjoy the amazing surroundings.

Mother's favorite spot was the bench that sat on the east side of the duck pond. He tried to envision her there and him coming up behind her to surprise her, as he had often done when she was alive.

Razoul took a deep breath, closing his eyes in order to get lost in the memory of her.

"Madre?"

Chiara turned gracefully, looking from beneath the wide brim of her hat to see her oldest son standing there, behind her.

"My love! You've returned! I had not expected to see you for another week."

Chiara rose from her seat to walk toward him. The breeze caused her long gown to fly behind her as she walked. Razoul was sixteen and it was his gentlemanly custom to bow to her. When she reached him, he took her hand, giving it a sweet kiss. Then Chiara nearly leapt to embrace him. She hugged him as though she'd not seen him in a long, long time.

Without breaking their embrace, "Mother, it's only been a few weeks."

"Ah dearest son, you know that I cannot bear a moment without you nearby. It makes your homecoming so incredibly sweet."

She took his hands in hers. "Come walk with me." Then she pulled him toward the path.

"Yes, of course." He took her arm in his and they began to casually stroll through the grounds.

"So, tell me of your conquests. Did all go well?"

"Yes, very well, madam."

"So what gossip then, from our French allies?"

"Well as you know, the baron has quite the taste for women."

Chiara nodded. She had often heard of the baron's exploits.

"There's a rumor that the baron has sired a bastard child with a young girl that lives in a nearby village. Of course he denies her claims."

"What does the countess have to say?"

"She's quiet, as usual. I believe she's well aware of his actions, yet he has such control over her that she will not fight with him about the matter."

"Yes, I know her. She's not the independent sort of woman."

Then Razoul looked at his mother affectionately. "Well mother, there are very few women like you."

"Yes, I would hate to think of what would happen if your father ever did such a thing."

"True. I believe you could take him if you were angry enough."

They both laughed. Razoul studied her radiant, porcelain face as her head leaned back in laughter. She was like an angel. To this day, he had not met her equal in beauty or inner strength.

They walked in silence for a few moments before Chiara spoke again in a more serious tone. "I do hope you are having the time of your life, my child. I wish for you to be happy. I know how demanding your father can become whenever he's in the midst of an acquisition."

"Do not worry, Mother. Father and I have an understanding these days."

"Oh?"

"Yes, he knows that I am no longer a mere boy who can be pushed around."

"Oh dear, did something happen while you were gone?"

"Well, you know that father can hover incessantly in order to be sure you are doing things correctly. I finally stood my ground with him. I told him that he shouldn't treat me with such disregard, as though I'm his servant."

Chiara looked deeply into Razoul's eyes. "I trust this went well between you and your father?"

Then as if there were a secret joke between them, they both broke out in laughter.

Razoul opened his eyes as he heard the pilot overhead speaking.

"We are due to land at JFK momentarily. Please fasten your seat belts."

Razoul looked around the cabin, surveying his men. With him on the journey were six of his men, plus Sirius, Thaddeus and Daniel who is particularly skillful as an errand boy. He saw that Daniel was fast asleep. He kicked him in the foot.

"Wake up, boy!"

Daniel was so startled that he nearly came out of his seat. Razoul laughed. Daniel nodded groggily and sat up straight while rubbing the sleep from his young eyes.

62- *Prophet's Message*

Joshua had been wandering through Kansas City most of the day, listening to the angels' chatter, finally coming to rest on a heavily worn bench in one of his favorite parks.

A warm breeze surrounded him as he sat there watching various people stroll by. It was one of his favorite pastimes and had been for many years. He found it interesting when angels would comment on particular people and their lives. It didn't happen every time, but often enough he could count on it happening.

The flowers were all blooming every where he looked. Tulips, daffodils, and many more species filled the area around him. He felt something above him and peered upward but the sun was in his eyes. Now Joshua noticed a form that silhouetted against the bright light. The figure slowly approached him now.

A rush of tingly warmth entered his body, making him feel very light. As Joshua looked away from the sky, he saw an angelic figure appear before him. A beautiful, childlike grin stretched across his face, taking 20 years of wear and tear from his expression.

"You honor me, holy messenger."

From anyone else's point of view, he sat there on the bench grinning and talking to thin air.

"We honor you, prophet, with your divine service. I am Arian-naH, and I am here with a message of great importance. Listen carefully."

Joshua nodded.

"Darkness is coming now, and our Angel is in grave danger. But most importantly, you are in great danger as well."

"Me?"

"Just as we have tried to shield the Incarnate One from prying eyes who wish her harm, we've tried to protect you as well. We know now that your identity has been compromised, and there are people trying to find you in order to find her."

Joshua frowned. "What do you wish me to do, great Arian-naH?"

"We want you to leave this place and journey to where she is. You both will be safer the further you are away from this city. We've arranged a path for you to reach your destination. If you walk toward the sun, you will reach a highway to follow. If you are patient, there will be a priest in a blue car that will offer you a ride. You must take it. This person will take you to where you are going."

"Where am I going, exactly? "

"The Incarnate One is now seeking to find her truth. She has returned to Parsons, the town where it all began. When you reach there,

I will return to you with more instructions. Walk in faith, dear brother." Then the angel vanished.

Joshua looked around nervously, to make sure no one had been watching him. When he realized he was safe, he rose from the bench and started walking directly into the mid day sun.

63- *Hospital*

When Catherine awoke in the downstairs bedroom of her parent's home, it took her a few moments to figure out where she was. She had slept much of the trip back from Lawrence and had crashed when they returned. She glanced at the clock. It was almost three in the afternoon.

Her thoughts immediately went to Jacob. She knew she had to check on him. In order to do that, she had to go next door to speak to his mother, or go to the hospital directly. When she thought of facing Mary, her stomach tightened.

She willed herself to get up out of the bed, regardless of how she felt about it.

Catherine walked slowly into the master bathroom to wash her face. When she was done rinsing, she looked closely at herself in the mirror. It was as if a stranger stared back at her. She touched her face in several places. It was as if she was trying to figure out if it was really her. Once she finished drying her face, she went to find David and Erica.

After wandering around the downstairs with no luck, she ventured outside to the backyard. She found them both seated on a stone bench in the garden, talking.

"Hi guys. I finally woke up."

"Did you sleep well?" Erica asked.

"Yes, I did, thank you. At least I think so," she shrugged.

"What are you up to out here?"

"Just enjoying the weather and chatting. We both woke up about a half hour ago."

Catherine got a serious look on her face for a moment. "I have to find out about Jacob this afternoon."

"I'll go with you," David said. As if to offset her immediate objection, he added, "I don't think you should go alone."

"I think I am going to go next door first to see if I can find out anything before I try the hospital. I really think I should go see his mom by myself. I just don't know what to say. What if she's angry at me or blames me?"

"It's not your fault sweetie. I'm sure she will know that."

"But he did that to himself because of me! I can't imagine what Mary thinks of me."

"She's not going to blame you, Catherine. You are his friend, and you have been for a long time. He is a troubled guy."

Catherine looked deeply into Erica's eyes. "I hope you are right."

"Are you hungry?"

"Yes, a little bit."

"Good, let me make you something before you go."

"Okay, Erica that sounds good."

Erica scurried off toward the kitchen door and disappeared.

Catherine was left with David and decided to sit down next to him. He put his arm around her, and she let him. "Don't worry, Catherine. It's going to be alright."

Catherine nervously ran her hand through her long hair. "What move do I make now? Do I wait for the professor's friend to give some insight? I think I am going to try to call that number in Italy again, too. Someone there must know what this is all about. I just don't know David, there's so much happening."

She stood up in frustration and turned to him. "How do I make a good choice when this is all like a bad dream? I am not sure I can keep myself together."

David got up and stood before her with deep compassion in his eyes. "You are strong. Probably stronger than any women I've ever met. You can do this. I don't know why I know that, but I do. Whatever happens, you are not alone. I will not leave your side. My mother used to tell me whenever I got overwhelmed, to take one thing at a time."

"I can't believe you want to be with someone like me. I'd run away screaming if I were you. Whatever is going on, this is just the beginning. I won't blame you if you want out now."

David knew where she was coming from and why she was scared. He also knew that she needed his compassion and protection. "I know you don't know me well yet, but I truly am your friend, Catherine, even if you don't want more than that with me. I will be here. I have to be here. I can't explain it, but walking away from you feels like the worst move I could ever make. Every single part of me knows I'm right where I'm supposed to be. And maybe you don't understand it because you don't see what I feel when I look at you. If you did, you'd understand. So don't worry about me."

He put his arms around her, and Catherine leaned into his arms. A tingling sensation passed between them. She felt safe for a moment, standing there in his embrace.

****

Catherine stood at the front door and didn't see a car in the drive way, but knew that it could be in the garage. She rang the bell twice but there was no answer.

"Mary's not there." Catherine said as she entered the living room. "I'm going to head to the hospital."

Erica spoke up, "I think you should let me or David go with you just in case. I can even wait in the car if you want me to."

"Thanks, Erica, but I'm just going alone until I see what is going on. If I need you, I promise to call. The hospital is only ten minutes away"

Erica looked at David and he nodded as if to say *let her go.*

Catherine grabbed her purse and was quickly out the door.

She could hardly think on the way to the hospital. At a stoplight she leaned forward to notice the sky. Clouds were quickly forming above and it looked like a typical Midwestern spring storm was brewing.

Just perfect, should have grabbed my umbrella.

Catherine parked the car and sat for a moment. Her anxiety made her want to plan out what she'd say to his mother. She finally decided that she was there to check on Jacob and that was all that really mattered.

Come on Catherine; just get out of the damn car already.

It was a small hospital and everything was easy to find, so she bypassed the patient information desk entirely. She found an open elevator and pressed the correct button for the ICU.

As she walked out of the elevator she turned to her left and saw Jacob's mother standing in a room about 15 feet away. She looked very tired. Catherine was walking toward Jacob's room when a heavy set nurse intercepted her, blocking her way.

"May I help you?"

"Yes, I am here to visit Jacob Petersen."

"Are you on the visitor's list?"

Catherine frowned. "I don't have any idea if I am or not."

"What is your name?"

"It's Catherine Moore."

Mary came out of Jacob's room and saw her. "Catherine! She's fine to visit Jacob," she called to the nurse.

Mary crossed to Catherine quickly and embraced her tightly. This made Catherine well up with tears. She whispered softly to Mary, while still embracing her, "I am so glad you aren't mad at me."

Mary looked up at her curiously, surprised at her comment. "Why would I be mad honey? You aren't to blame for Jacob's injuries."

Through her tears, she spoke with a cracked voice. "He came to me that night. I wanted to help him, but I couldn't. I am so sorry."

"There, there, Catherine. Please don't blame yourself. I used to blame myself for Jacob's illness, but even I had to realize that it's not my fault he is this way."

"How is he Mary? Is he going to be alright?"

"Last night was touch and go. At first, he wasn't doing very well. The doctor's said he lost a lot of blood during the incident, so they gave him several transfusions. They told us the next couple days will tell us if he'll recover from his injuries, but he stabilized this morning. I just keep praying he'll pull through all this."

"I'm praying too, Mary."

Mary put her hand on Catherine's shoulder. "You are a dear friend to my Jacob."

"I don't feel like a good friend right now. I was gone too long and Jacob suffered because of that. I can't help feeling like I abandoned him back then."

"Don't blame yourself, honey. You were dealing with your own losses, trying to move forward with your life."

"You are so strong. How are you so strong right now? I am a mess."

Mary looked deeply into Catherine's eyes and said, "I guess I started losing Jacob a long time ago, honey, something I've had to reconcile over the past few years. That doesn't mean I want to lose him now, but it makes it a little easier to deal with this. I hope that doesn't make me a bad mother."

Catherine shook her head. "No, of course it doesn't." Catherine suddenly felt a new determination inside her. "And we're not going to lose him now, not now."

"I hope you are right." Mary smiled wearily.

Me too Mary, me too...

"I was just headed downstairs to the cafeteria to get a soda. Do you mind staying here, just in case he wakes, while I go?"

"Go ahead Mary. I'll be here when you get back." Mary patted her on the arm and left.

Catherine watched her walk away and get onto the elevator. Once the door closed, she took a deep breath and stepped deliberately, one foot at a time, toward the sliding door to Jacob's room.

As soon as Catherine entered, she gasped. Jacob looked terrible. His entire neck was bandaged and he had a breathing tube down his throat. She closed the sliding door and started to move closer when a cloud of black smoke appeared around him. Within seconds the thick fog made Jacob barely distinguishable behind it.

A familiar acrid stench filled her nostrils making her instantly queasy. Her stomach turned. She spat, "Get away from him, you monster!"

A familiar voice encircled her with a hiss. "Why would I want to do that? He's all mine, and you know it."

"Jacob doesn't want you here, and neither do I."

"It doesn't matter either way to me, little girl."

"I know you want to hurt me, so why don't you let him go and take me on instead, if you are so powerful."

The smoky apparition quickly coalesced into a shadowy form standing next to her. It began to whisper in her ear. "Why would I want to do that? When I can hurt you even more if I simply suck the life out of your little friend both slowly and painfully?"

Catherine was angry now. "If you don't leave, I will make you leave."

"Oh sweet Catherine, if you love your pitiful guy here, I wouldn't do that."

"What do you mean by that?"

"If you take me out, I'll take Jacob with me, body and soul."

"You can't do that."

It cackled loudly in her ear and then the apparition possessively leapt to Jacob's bedside. "Oh, you think I can't?"

"You are bluffing." Catherine remembered her dream and the energy that had leapt from her and allowed her to defeat the demon.

"If you think so, then try to make me go."

Catherine closed her eyes and concentrated on what she had done in her dream. Her anger fueled her intense will to make the white light come through her. A light started to faintly glow near her heart. It steadily grew, and now she focused it toward the demon, letting it fly.

As her light struck the beast, all of Jacob's monitors started chiming loud warning alarms. In seconds, several nurses and a doctor rushed into the room. The flurry of people quickly pushed her out of the room. She heard one of the nurse's tell another to call a Code Blue.

"What is happening?"

"Please let us help him. Go to the waiting room. We'll send someone out for you as soon as we can."

Oh my God, what did I do? Shit. Shit. Shit. There has to be a way to get rid of this thing.

Catherine ran both hands through her hair and walked toward the door to the waiting room. Then she heard the dark voice whispering to her again.

"Don't worry; he will be okay this time. But try it again, and he won't be. I promise you that."

"Go to hell."

"Soon, Catherine, soon. Jacob's going to love it there."

64- *Pontifical Office*

Catherine had tossed and turned most of the night, waking up many times. She couldn't calm down her restlessness after visiting Jacob at the hospital. Severe storms rocked through the area all night long as well, making it even harder to rest. It was nearly two in the morning before she fell into a sound sleep.

Now she was opening her eyes in her parent's room where she'd slept to avoid returning to her room. It was only seven. She immediately thought about the ancient book and felt compelled to get it from its hiding place upstairs. She quietly walked through the living room and ascended the stairs. After swiftly gathering the book in her arms, she returned to her parent's bedroom, and closed the door.

She put the book down and sat on the bed with her legs crossed. She softly ran her fingertips along the embossed cover, tracing each line and groove. The area around her body lit up with a faint glow, as it had before when she touched the book.

Suddenly she started seeing brief flashes of images in her mind, but they moved too quickly for her to understand them fully. Still, she thought she could almost access the origins of the book and what it was to be used for.

She opened it hoping she would be able to understand the writing, but it appeared in the same, unintelligible way that it had before. Catherine shut the book abruptly.

"It's time for answers."

Everything inside Catherine made her feel that her answers were in Italy. She resolved to find out who was called after she had visited Sister Mary Eleanor. She quickly dressed and looked through her purse for the number.

Once she found it, she sat back down with the book in her lap and dialed the number. Her heart pounded, but she felt inspired.

A male voice answered, "Ufficio di Monsignor Bartholomew."

"Hello, do you speak English?"

"Sì signora. Yes, I speak English."

"Whose office have I reached?"

"Monsignor Bartholomew's, signora."

"What does he do?"

"Monsignor holds a position here at the Pontifical Council for Justice and Peace of course."

"I see. Well, I am trying to reach him, is he available?"

"The Monsignor has not returned from afternoon Mass at the Vatican yet, he will return soon with the Cardinals. May I take a message?"

Catherine quickly thought about what to say. "Yes, please do. My name is Catherine Moore. Please tell him I am calling about a mutual friend, Sister Mary Eleanor, and need to speak with him very soon. It is urgent."

"May you give me your telephone number signora?"

"Yes of course, it's 1-816-555-1211. It's a number in America."

"I will be sure to give Monsignor your message. May God be with you, signora."

"Thank you."

Catherine hung up the phone, feeling satisfied at having made some progress, and ventured toward the kitchen to get a cup of coffee. David was still asleep on the couch. Before going into the kitchen she paused near him for a moment to look at him lying there.

It startled her when his eyes popped open suddenly.

"Oh, you are awake," Catherine said sheepishly.

David smiled at her so broadly that the corners of his eyes wrinkled up. "Yeah, I'm awake. It was hard to sleep last night with all the thunder."

"I had the same issues, but no nightmares or anything. Well, would you like a cup of coffee, oh protector of mine?"

He laughed. "You seem in better spirits today, which is good to see." He sat up straight wiping the sleep from his eyes.

"I just got off the phone with the Pontifical Office in Italy. Apparently, I called the office of a Monsignor Bartholomew. He was at Mass, but the priest there promised to have him call me when he returns later."

"Well now, that certainly makes me in good spirits too. How about that coffee?"

65- *Journey*

Just as the angel had revealed to him, Joshua had walked for about an hour yesterday when someone stopped to offer him a ride. The very nice person thought it was wonderful serendipity that he was also headed toward Parsons, but Joshua knew all this had been pre-arranged for them.

He had arrived in Parsons yesterday late afternoon. After wandering around to get his bearings and await his next instructions, the storms had hit causing him to stay in an abandoned shed for the night to escape the rain.

He sat silently this morning listening to the angels whispering. This was a private ritual which he had exercised every day for more years than he could count. In the midst of all the many voices in his head, one singled him out saying.

"It's time for you to find her now. Her address is 716 North Central. If you walk down Main Street until you reach St. Patrick's Church. Then turn left and take the next right onto Central. You will find her there.

"Is there any message for her?"

"No message; however, you must stay with her no matter what."

"I will."

Joshua obediently stood up and opened the shed door. Bright sunlight shone on his face. It took a moment for his eyes to adjust. A childlike demeanor peered from behind his rough, wrinkled face. He took a deep breath of air before venturing outside.

The prophet was used to walking everywhere he went and could keep a quick pace. Very soon he stood in front of St. Patrick's Church and knew that he was only a couple blocks away from Catherine's childhood home.

Catherine, Erica and David were finishing up breakfast when the doorbell rang. "I'll get it." Catherine got up to go answer the door. When she opened it, she was surprised to find Joshua standing there in front of her.

"Joshua? What are you doing here?"

"I was told to come here."

"The angels told you to come?"

"Yes of course they did."

"Then come in, Joshua."

"Thank you very much."

They both stepped into the living room where Erica and David were standing.

"Erica, this is Joshua, I told you about him."

"Hello Joshua, nice to meet you."

David wasn't sure about Joshua showing up, and the concern showed on his face.

"It's alright. Joshua is here because the angels told him where to find me."

"You've come a long way, Joshua. You must be starved. Please come into the kitchen and I'll get you something to eat."

Erica chimed in. "Let me."

"Okay, let's go sit at the kitchen table."

Joshua followed her into the kitchen and sat down. David followed close behind and sat next to Catherine.

"Do you know why the angels told you to come find me?"

"Yes, yes I do. The bad people were coming for me. I had to leave before they found me."

"The bad people?"

"Yep, the same ones I told you about before. They can't find you, but they found me, and the angels said the safest place was here with you."

So it wasn't Jacob Joshua had warned me about.

"Do you know who *they* are?"

Joshua shook his head no.

"Why are they trying to find me?"

Joshua looked at her curiously. "You don't know?"

"Not exactly Joshua. I am a bit in the dark with that one."

"Well of course there are those who are very happy you are here, and there are those that wouldn't be too happy you are around."

"That I am around?"

"Yes, being who you are."

"Who am I?"

Joshua laughed out loud as Erica put a sandwich and drink in front of him. Then he pointed a finger at her amused. "Oh I get it, you are testing old Joshua, aren't you?"

"Testing you? No, I'm just asking a question."

Catherine was easily frustrated right now and David knew it, so he interrupted.

"Joshua, Catherine really has no idea why all this is happening to her. So if you are here to help her as you say you are, please answer her questions even if they seem strange."

Joshua's face flushed red. "Sure, sure, I'll tell you what I know. I didn't mean to offend you, Catherine."

"I am not offended. It's okay. I just really need your help right now if you can."

Joshua picked up the glass of tea and nearly drank it to the bottom before speaking. He wiped his face on his sleeve. "I remember the first time I saw you. There was all this light around you which I had never seen before. The angels were happy and excited that we crossed paths. They can really get going sometimes. I knew was looking at a real live angel. And you were right in front of me, drinking a cup of coffee. How lucky could I be?"

It was as if Catherine could not fathom what he was saying to her. Her face showed little reaction. "So that's why you were trying to speak to me the other day at the coffee shop?"

"Yeah I didn't want anything. I just wanted you to know I could see you. I thought it might get lonely being the only one of your kind."

"What do you mean, see me?"

Joshua sat and stared at her for a bit. "Okay, so you are saying you don't remember?"

"Remember what?"

"What you truly are."

Catherine just looked at him. She couldn't bring herself to say what he was suggesting. "Oh wow, you are an angel with an identity crisis? Man, this is heavy." He looked down, shaking his head.

Catherine became a little defiant. "So, you're saying that I am actually an angel?"

"Yes, and you are really one of a kind."

"That's ridiculous. There's no way. Trust me, I am no angel. Really I am not. There's no such thing as a physical angel walking on earth. And if there was, it would not be me."

Joshua corrected her. "Well there used to be no such thing but now there is. The angels have been talking about you for awhile now. I felt so blessed to be near you."

Catherine shook her head, refusing to believe what she was hearing.

66- *Arrival*

Razoul was settling himself into the penthouse suite at the Hyatt Regency Crown Center and mulling over how to find the prophet. The Sigil might also give out a sign when presented near the old man, but he could not be sure.

"Here's the list of places that take care of the poor, as you requested, sir."

Razoul snatched the paper from Daniel's hand, "Perfect. Not so many places for an old homeless man to be hiding from me. This won't take as long as I thought."

"But sir, how will you find out which one he is?"

"That's not for you to understand!" Razoul practically spat in his face. The fear in Daniel eyes reflected over 2 years of his abuse by Razoul's hand. He was so young but already very damaged.

"In fact, I don't care if I have to kill every homeless man fitting his description in this city before I find the one I'm looking for. No one will miss them if they simply disappear one day." Razoul knew this all too well from experience and Daniel knew it. He tried to excuse himself but Razoul stopped him. "I wish you to find the location of this place. I will try there first." He pointed at City Union Mission on the top of the list.

The young boy quickly left the room and was passed in the hallway by both Sirius and Thaddeus. They entered Razoul's room without being announced. Daniel could hear Razoul's fit, as he got onto the elevator.

"How dare you both come into my quarters without any prior announcement?"

Sirius spoke first. "Calm yourself Razoul. The boy was leaving your room as we were coming. I apologize for barging in."

Razoul bit his tongue for once, since Sirius was being conciliatory.

"So what are we doing first?"

Razoul grimaced at them both but then spoke authoritatively, "We locate the old man first, and he will lead us right to the girl."

Thaddeus had been silent since entering but spoke up now. "What do we know about this man? Do we know for sure he will lead us to the girl we seek?"

"My good man, Thaddeus, such worries for a gentleman of your stature and class." Razoul prodded him in the chest to make his point.

Razoul walked to the mini-bar and poured himself a stiff drink. "The old man we seek has lived in this city his whole life and has been homeless for a number of years. He is about 5'6", around 56 years old, has a heavy build, aged beyond his years, and has a long scar on his forearm." He lifted his drink as if making a toast to them. "And yes, I am certain he will lead us to the girl."

Thaddeus replied quickly in a challenging tone. "Do you mind telling us where you get such detailed information? I have seen none of this from our usual sources."

Razoul downed his drink and poured another. "Both of you know that I have my own sources that I don't care to share with you or anyone. Besides you were both leaving, I will call you when it's time to go."

Razoul walked straight into the large bathroom and closed the door. Thaddeus and Sirius just stood there until they heard the shower turn on.

Sirius looked at Thaddeus. "Did you really think he'd tell you about his secret sources?"

"Well there have been many rumors since the ordeal with the young girl and his deadly pact with the dark angel. Even though most of our men have no idea about the pact he made or specifically what happened to the girl."

Sirius turned to go and Thaddeus followed him, speaking softly. "He's playing a dangerous game Sirius. Surely you realize this."

Sirius nodded but didn't speak until they were alone in the elevator. "I agree with you. This is indeed a dangerous game we find ourselves in the middle of, but it is too costly for both of us to hit the bull head on, so to speak. So for now, we bend to Razoul's will. I foresee a future opportunity for us to rid ourselves of the vile murderer of my truest friend, but it must be the right time for us to act. Until then we stay close to him and watch everything that we can to perfect our advantage."

"What advantage?" Thaddeus nearly cried out.

"Be patient boy. I predict that Razoul's greatest weakness will be his complete unwillingness to see his flaws. Yes, his arrogance will get the best of him, eventually."

"I will be patient. I just hope both of us are around to enjoy our life without him when he's gone."

67- *The Prophet Arrives*

Brother Artemis sat in the bushes on his usual stake out of Catherine's place. From his line of sight, he could watch the front of the house and much of the back yard as well.

He had thought originally that the old man he saw ringing the bell at Catherine's home was a derelict asking for money, but she had let him inside as if they knew each other. Since then he had been waiting for the man to emerge so he could follow him for more information, but so far he remained inside. The sun was high in the sky and the air was very humid.

His eyes began to flutter. He had only had a little sleep since he had seen Jacob entering Catherine's house in the dead of night. That night he had to move his position from the house further away because the police had been everywhere.

His phone began to vibrate startling him out of his half-sleep. He fumbled to get it out of his pocket.

"Monsignor?"

"Brother Artemis?"

"Yes, I am here."

"I'd like an update, please. An unexpected phone message was left for me from Catherine today asking me to call her."

"Catherine called you? How is that possible?"

"That is why I am calling you. I'm trying to figure out how she found me. I suspect she found me through the convent."

"Are you going to call her back?"

"I cannot speak to her at this time, though I'd earnestly like to. It's the opinion of the guardians we should not interfere just yet. There is wisdom in that approach. But her recent ordeal with Jacob Petersen was a grave matter indeed. Everything in the Darkness is trying to harm her now that she's on the path. Yet it was her own free will that brought her to me, and I must pray about this for guidance."

"I understand Monsignor."

"Tell me of Jacob now, is he still alive?"

"Yes, he's alive but still in danger as of this morning. Catherine has been to visit him. Also, a strange older man came to her door this morning but she acted as though she knew him. He's been inside ever since."

"A strange, older man?"

"Yes, he was unkempt and in badly in need of bathing."

Bartholomew knew about Joshua and his purpose already, but it was interesting to hear that he was now with her.

"The prophet is there?"

"He's a prophet?"

"Yes, the angels have a prophet by the name of Joshua Stark who lived near Catherine in Kansas City. If she welcomed him into the house, then they have crossed paths already, which I didn't realize they had done so."

"What does this mean Monsignor?"

"If he's with her, then it is because the angels sent him to her. This may be because Razoul and his group have flown to the United States. I found this out today. I am still awaiting information specifically on where they went. Because they fly privately, the information takes me longer to acquire. When I find out I will let you know where they landed. I pray it is not anywhere near you or the girl."

"I will pray too."

"Yes, pray young Brother. Pray for us all."

68- *Rejecting*

"If I am an angel, then why don't I already know that I am?" Catherine paced the kitchen, unable to sit down. "Surely a real angel wouldn't have to stumble around, messing everything up as she goes with no clue whatsoever. Is this some cosmic joke?" She threw her arms up.

"I promise you that you are a real angel. I don't know why you don't remember."

"Joshua, I see that you truly believe what you are saying, but you must be mistaken. I am no angel. There's no way I can be. But you and apparently these bad people too, now think I am. I am so screwed." She dropped her elbows on the table and her head in her hands.

David let her vocalize what she needed to, but knew it was important he spoke. "Catherine?"

Her posture softened a little. Erica put her hands on Catherine's very stiff shoulders and started to gently massage them. "Yes?"

"Since we met, you've shared with me the things that have been happening to you recently, and I think maybe there is something to what he's saying. "

She nodded reluctantly. "I am sure there is a lot to what he's saying right now, but I can't possibly believe this. No offense, Joshua, but..."

"None taken, dear angel, I mean Catherine." He smiled.

"Haven't you ever seen movies where there's a case of mistaken identity and someone gets their whole life turned upside down because people think they're someone else? Well just crank that storyline up a few notches, throw in some cryptic angels, a few demons for good measure and viola here we are in my dead parents' house with people after me."

David turned toward Joshua. "You said people are after both you and her, right?"

"Yes, bad people."

"What do these people want? Do you know?"

"The angel said they knew about me and thought I could find her for them. I know these are dangerous people who want to stop her."

"Stop me from what?"

"They probably don't want you to do what you came to do."

"What is that?"

Joshua gathered his thoughts. He wanted to be careful that he repeated what he had heard perfectly for her. "When the angels speak about you, they say you are here to bring heaven to earth and fulfill an ancient prophecy regarding the Child of Light."

"Like I said, what does that mean? How can I bring heaven to earth? This is ridiculous. I need to take a walk."

Both David and Erica started to follow her, but she turned and said firmly but quietly, "I need to be alone, please." Catherine disappeared out the back door.

David turned to Joshua. "Is Catherine safe here?"

"I think she's safe here. That is why they sent me to be with her, so I would be safe too. I know it is definitely not safe back in Kansas City for either of us now."

"Did the angels say anything else? Anything that could help us figure this out?"

"The only other thing the angel said was that, no matter what, I am not to leave her now."

David got up and looked out the back window to see if he could spot Catherine. She was on the far side of the yard pacing back and forth. He watched her sit down on a large grey stone looking in the opposite direction.

A living, breathing Incarnate Angel...could she really be?

69- *Mom Help Me*

Mom and Dad why aren't you here? I need you. Did you know I was a freak? If you did, why didn't you say anything?"

Maybe mom and dad wanted to wait to tell me about the convent I came from and the sister who found me, but they died before they could explain it all. Or maybe they didn't know anything either. Why is everything a damn paradoxical question with no real answer?

She picked up a flower and began to tear it apart.

I just want my life back. I was fine. I had a decent job that I was really good at and now look at me.

Catherine tried to wrap her head around what Joshua had said, but she couldn't connect with herself being an angel at all. Every part of her was rejecting the notion that she was special at all.

"Hell, even mom said I was a little devil most of the time." This memory made her smile.

"God, I miss you guys."

She got up to walk to a trellis now blooming with just a handful of white roses. As she got closer, their fragrance surrounded her. She closed her eyes. She remembered how the garden had once been, full of life and beauty as far as the eye could see. Now it lay in ruin and neglect with only a scant flower still growing here and there.

In her mind she could see her mother tending to the roses the way she always had, carefully and methodically snipping the expired blooms one by one. She could see herself at the age of six or seven playing nearby.

"They are beautiful, mommy."

"Yes they are, Catherine. They are beautiful just like you are to me." Her mother cupped her rosy cheeks in her hands. "You are the brightest little angel in the world. And don't you ever forget, okay?"

Little Catherine grinned. "I won't mommy."

Catherine opened her eyes, half expecting to see her mother standing there looking down at her. But she wasn't. And all she could do now was cry.

Mother knew?

Through her tears, Catherine stared up at the partially cloudy sky. "What am I supposed to do?"

She held her arms out and inspected them for flaws. "I don't feel very angelic. In fact, I feel like I could punch someone's lights out."

The frustration in her face was apparent now. Suddenly she could feel David watching her from the kitchen window, but when she looked over he had just stepped away.

Why is this happening to me? What could I do to save the world? This is too crazy even for me. I am a pathetic mess these days. I haven't been to work in so long.

That world seemed so far away now to her. She had seen the face of tragedy and lived to tell the tale.

Who am I to be an angel in such a world as this? I cannot imagine being something so wonderful, so beautiful. I am nothing but a bird with broken wings.

A breeze rose up around her and she heard a voice... *"You can fly little bird, if you only try."*

"Mother?"

"There's no reason to be afraid of this my dear. You were born to shine."

"Mother?"

"Yes, it's me honey."

"Why did you leave me?"

"I've never really left your side despite how things might appear."

"I want to see you."

"You can see me anytime you want, if you believe."

"Believe what?"

"If you believe in yourself, you can see a great many things. I promise."

"I want to see things now."

"Be patient Catherine, all you have inside you is now beginning to wake up. Like my beautiful roses, which open one by one, you will open

and become what you were meant to be. You just have to give yourself a chance."

Catherine began to feel a warm sensation in her palms, and rubbed them together nervously.

"Since I have you, what am I to think about Joshua, David and Erica in my life?"

"You are being surrounded by everything and everyone you need for the journey."

"So I can trust them?"

"Trust your heart to guide you. You are capable of anything you can imagine."

"Maybe my imagination is broken."

"It's not broken my stubborn little one."

"Haven't heard you call me that in a long time mom."

"You are so, my sweet, and there's a reason for that terribly stubborn point of view of yours."

"Maybe so. You always said there was meaning in everything right?"

"Yes, definitely."

"How can I be what Joshua says I am?"

"You are that and much more, my child."

"All I want is to kill the pain in my heart. Just tell me how to kill the pain?"

"You must let it go my daughter. I know you are angry that we were taken from you so young. But your anger is like a string of stones around your waist."

"How do I let it go? I still feel like it was yesterday. It killed me inside to lose you both. It wasn't fair!"

"Ah my dear, there are many things in the human world that are not fair at all. But if you can begin to see a grander design within it, then you will understand. Then you will understand its perfect rhythm, its perfect beat."

"What could be perfect about you and dad dying horribly in that car after church? I should have been with you, but I wasn't. We had argued that morning and there was no way to console me. If I wasn't so stubborn then we could have been together that day, and I'd be dead too, but NO, I was left behind, alone and devastated."

"You were meant to live, don't you see that now? There are many who need you."

"If I am so important, why are these people after me?"

"Humans fear what they cannot understand. They are afraid."

"Well I am afraid too, so we have something in common."

"I want to show you something before I leave you for now."

"Don't leave mom, no don't leave."

"Don't worry my dear. I am never far from you."

"Yes, I guess you aren't as far away as I thought."

"Close your eyes."

Catherine obediently closed her eyes.

"Now keep them closed. I want you to think of the garden as it once was."

"Okay I am picturing it..."

"Think of the daisies, the roses climbing the trellis, the green vines all over..."

"It was a sight to see, everything was vibrant and alive. You and dad were amazing back here."

Returning to the garden in her mind made Catherine feel so much lighter. The warmth from her palms spread up her arms and soon filled her entire body to the point that she felt a low vibration start in her chest and pulse through her whole body.

"Remember the days we'd spend here together? Remember the smells in the air?"

"I remember."

"Now make a wish as hard as you can. Wish for this place to be magical again. Feel every living thing that used to be here."

Catherine concentrated on reliving a past moment here in the sacred garden of her childhood.

"It was magical, so very magical..."

The wind picked up and whooshed around her head and she could feel her hair moving in the breeze. There were new fragrances all around her. Then the wind died down just as suddenly as it had arisen.

"Mother? What now, what do I do now? I see it all now just as it used to be."

There was silence in her mind now. Her mother's voice was gone. Catherine willed herself to open her eyes. When she did, she blinked several times as she sat there staring in disbelief.

"How? Oh my God!"

What she saw now made her run to the house and through the door where everyone was sitting.

"Come quick, you guys!"

The three followed Catherine out the door.

David and Erica took two steps out and both let out a collective gasp.

"Isn't it amazing?" Catherine ran now with her arms outstretched down the paths touching various plants as she flew by them. She had the expression of a small child. Her face was glowing in the sunlight.

Erica walked toward Catherine with her eyes wide. "You did this?"

"Yes, I think so. Mother said she wanted to show me something."

"You spoke to your mother?"

"Yes, she just spoke to me."

It took a few moments for David to take in what he was seeing. The extravagance of the garden was breathtaking. He'd never seen anything like it in his life, let alone something so amazing that appeared right out of thin air. He walked toward her. "Catherine, it's so beautiful."

"They are all here, every single plant just like they were when I was a little girl." She clapped her hands.

"I thought I'd have to come out here in a little while and carry you into the house, and look at you now."

"I feel much better, thank you." Catherine took a little bow.

David stood before her now. "Look at what you did! But you are more beautiful than any flower in your garden."

Catherine thought about what her mother had said. She had everyone that she needed now. In her joy, Catherine grabbed David and hugged him tightly. She whispered, "Thank you."

"The pleasure is all mine, beautiful angel." He held her in his embrace.

"Can I get in on all this love?"

Catherine looked over David's shoulder. "Of course you can."

Erica joined the circle.

"Where's Joshua?" Catherine broke the huddle and started to look for him. She found him on one of the benches in tears. She put her hand on his shoulder. "What's wrong Joshua? Are you alright?"

He looked up at her, "Yes, I am wonderful. I am just feeling God's grace all around me and it's a lot to let inside."

Catherine looked around as she sat down beside him. "Yes, Joshua. I am beginning to understand now."

He sighed in relief. "Good, good. That means this old man is doing what he's supposed to, which is all I require."

"I am so grateful you came."

"Oh thank you, sweet angel. That means so much to a man like me."

He was beaming.

70- *My Name is Alice*

Razoul sat outside across the street from the entrance to the City Union Mission. He had talked to a dozen people who were lingering around, but none had knowledge of the man they were looking for. His frustration began to grow. He was deep in thought when a young girl's voice broke the silence.

"This is for you."

Her little hand offered him a single dandelion.

Razoul took the droopy flower from the little girl, annoyed.

"My name is Alice." She looked up as his large form towered over her. Razoul simply stared at her.

She began tapping her little foot on the ground. "You are supposed to tell me your name now."

"My name is Razoul."

"That's better. My mommy always told me that you should be polite."

Razoul looked around but didn't see the young girl's mother anywhere nearby. "Maybe you should find her then. Didn't your mother also tell you not to talk to strange men? Off with you now."

Alice pouted and turned away. "You'll never find him you know."

Razoul grabbed her little shoulder tightly, spinning her around.

"What did you say?"

Instead of being scared of him as he had expected, she just looked at him defiantly.

"I *said* you will *never* find him. The man you are looking for."

"What do you know about the man?"

The little girl shrugged innocently.

"Tell me child! Where is he?"

He shook her by both shoulders, attracting the unwanted attention of onlookers across the street.

Razoul saw this and released her flashing a fake smile for everyone to see.

"He left because the angels told him to. You are the bad man he said was coming here."

Razoul's voice became syrupy sweet. "Well little girl, could you tell me where he went? I just need to ask him something. I'm his friend. I am here to help him."

Her chubby cheeks puffed up. "I can tell you're lying. I wasn't born yesterday you grumpy, mean man."

"And don't you have a quick tongue for such a little thing." It took every bit of his self control to keep from whisking her right off the street with both hands.

"My mommy says that grumpy people just need more love."

"I doubt that will help me," Razoul said smugly.

"Well it was worth a try, I guess." She turned to walk away.

"Please tell me little girl, do you know where he went?"

"You are wasting your time looking for him. He's not here and I miss him."

He started toward her when she turned for a final time to face him. "He did not tell me where he was going, but if he did; I don't think I'd tell you."

Her defiance infuriated him and he turned away for a moment. He calculated the number of steps it would require to scoop her up and then throw her in the car. He committed to that course of action and whipped around.

She was gone.

His eyes scanned across the street and all around.

Nothing. What the...

There was no sign of the little girl anywhere, except for the limp dandelion on the ground where he had dropped it.

He clenched his fists in anger and then pulverized the dandelion with the heel of his black boot.

Damnable angels....just wait until I crush your precious One once and for all.

71- *Roger*

After spending some time in the now enchanted garden, Catherine was sitting on the living room couch, checking her email on her laptop. She scanned the subjects and spotted an email from Roger Thornton already.

Dear Catherine,

I received Henry's email this morning. I was astounded that he said that the symbols in your book matched those that were found marking a series of hidden chambers underneath the catacombs that I discovered last year at San Pancrazio. Though he took pictures, these didn't come out well I'm afraid but I trust Henry's knowledge completely.

We have made little progress in our research to discover the meaning of the symbols themselves or the purpose of the chambers that we have been restoring since then. So far the Vatican has allowed us to preserve the site and have not involved themselves heavily in the project, as one might expect.

I would absolutely love the opportunity to chat with you, and also wish to extend to you an invitation to be my guest here at my current residence in Rome, so that we can review the book together and discover its secrets. Please contact me as soon as possible!

Awaiting your reply,

Roger P. Thornton, Ph.D.

+39 06 557475

"Hey guys? I just got an email from Roger Thornton, Henry's friend. He wants me to fly to Rome to show him the book." Erica came down from upstairs and David, who had been in the kitchen with Joshua, walked into the room.

"That's wonderful. I just knew someone could help us."

Catherine thought of the garden briefly, and then spoke. "Well, it seems that things are starting to look up. I am going to reply to him that we'd love to come."

David chimed in. "We?"

"Of course, I can't go to Italy without my team." At that moment, Joshua sauntered into the room in his usual way.

Catherine turned to Joshua. "What do the angels say about all of us going to Italy?"

For a moment it looked like he was staring blankly, but then Catherine realized he was listening and remained very quiet to give him a chance to answer.

"Oh! The angels think this is a wonderful idea. They are quite happy about this." Then he frowned.

"What's wrong Joshua?"

"The angels say I have to get on an airplane."

72- *Sigil Speaks*

Razoul had been ignoring calls from both Thaddeus and Sirius for about an hour. He'd left for the City Union Mission without waiting for either of them to join him.

If I didn't answer your first call, why on earth would I answer on your second or third? Fools.

Since the taunting by little Alice, Razoul was simply furious. He had been driving around downtown Kansas City in circles for over an hour. He detested being made a fool of and wanted to regain his composure.

Sending a small child to do the work of Angels, how pathetic you all are. Thinking that they can make a fool of me is a big mistake. Surely even you all know how dangerous I can be, and if you don't, then you are fools too.

Razoul chose a new road to turn onto. In his rage he had still been looking for the old man. He was convinced that Alice's appearance was just a ruse to keep him from getting closer to his targets. He pulled to the side of the street and parked to determine his next move before heading back to the hotel. After several moments passed, he turned the sedan off.

As he sat there plotting, the sigil in his pocket began to grow warm for the first time since he had left Italy. He looked around him. Without realizing it, he had parked in front of the ten story apartment building where Catherine lived.

"Perhaps we won't need the old man after all," he said to himself, peering out his window and looking up.

Serendipity and luck are on my side...perfect!

His lips pursed into the most evil scorn.

I have you now.

He sped off toward the hotel to get ready for later in the evening when he would bring back reinforcements to retrieve her.

73- *Quickening*

The Prophet has revealed himself to the girl. That is why I called each of you together again. This is exciting news."

Bartholomew sat in his usual place at the stone table, with Aurora to his right.

In her usual grace, Aurora spoke. "The Quickening has begun, Brothers and Sisters. I expect that things will move rapidly now, so we must be more vigilant than ever. There will be a time soon that she will need each of us. We must be ready. With God's grace, we shall be."

Bartholomew nodded in agreement and then added, "Catherine called my office the other day. I was away at the time. Just when I was seeking guidance about what to do, I learned the angels had revealed the Prophet to her. God be praised."

"We shall do ceremony now both to celebrate this and to honor the angels with whom we are privileged to serve."

Each of the guardians stood, took each other's hands, and bowed their heads as Aurora lit a circle of twelve candles with and a thirteenth in the center. Soon she joined them to close the circle and prayed.

"To the angels and archangels our hearts sing now. Guide us as your vessels on earth to commit to serving God's will in all things. Allow us to be vigilant in our resolve to assist the incarnate treasure who has been sent to bring the heavens to all that inhabit the earth."

Her eyes opened wide and a white light entered the center of their circle, and surrounded them all.

"We call to the angels of the North, bring to us your heavenly wind that permeates all things."

Within the column of light in the center emerged a swirling mass of energy representing wind.

"We call to the angels of the East, bring to us your heavenly fire that renews all things."

From the center emerged a bright flame representing fire.

"We call to the angels of the South, bring to us your heavenly water that cleanses all things."

From the center emerged the sound of waves crashing, representing water.

"We call to the angels of the West, bring to us your heavenly earth that transforms all things."

From the center emerged an undulating mass of clay representing earth.

"We graciously accept these elemental gifts that demonstrate the power of creation during our days in this world in which we seek to serve only you. We now ask for your guidance to enter us and guide our hands in the coming days."

Each of them stood awaiting the information that would soon come to each of them in their own way. The Essene had sought unity with the angels for centuries and did not question whatever task they were given to perform on their behalf.

Different Enochian symbols appeared on each of their foreheads. At first they were dim but gradually they appeared red hot, glowing like fireplace embers. None of the guardians in the circle moved a muscle as they stood there appearing to be branded like cattle.

After just a few moments, the symbols seemed to dissolve. At the same time, each of them opened their eyes and the glow briefly reappeared from inside their eye sockets and then faded away.

Simultaneously they folded their hands together in front of their hearts as if in prayer, and broke the circle.

74- *Connection*

The sun was beginning to set as Catherine gazed down at the garden from an upstairs window. The shadowy fingers of dusk were spreading across it now as she began to believe that she just might be capable of anything. Yet there was still tremendous fear in her.

This was the first time that she had entered her bedroom since Jacob's surprise visit the other night. Erica had put down throw rugs to cover the stained carpet. Catherine was grateful for her friend who always knew how to take care of her.

She was deep in thought when her phone rang.

"Hello?"

"May I please speak to Catherine Moore?"

"Yes, speaking."

"Ms. Moore, this is Roger Thornton calling."

"Wow that was quick. I just replied to your email a few hours ago."

"Well truthfully, I have been sitting on pins and needles since I initially emailed you. The discovery of your book is thrilling, to say the least. It could tell us so much! I'm so sorry for my childlike excitement about this. We academics rarely get this kind of stimulation."

"It's okay. I understand, Roger. Meeting with you is honestly more important to me than I can convey to you right now."

"Oh, good. I didn't want you to think I was a nut."

If you only knew.

"What are your thoughts on the offer I made about coming to Rome? I'd absolutely love to see the book firsthand. And before you answer, I must let you know that it would be my treat. You would be my very important guest."

"Wow. Thank you. The thing is, I need you to extend the invitation to a couple friends of mine. I cannot make the trip without them. They...uh, are related to the book and me in an important way."

"No trouble at all Catherine. Consider them my guests as well. "How soon could you all come?"

"How soon could you get it all arranged?" She laughed.

Catherine was hoping to take the trip right away. Getting out of the country seemed like a very good idea.

"Well there's a flight leaving tomorrow early evening that will bring you to JFK in New York and then on to Rome non-stop. I assume if you know Henry then you'd be leaving from Kansas City International Airport?"

"Yes, that's the nearest airport."

"Excellent. Can you hold a moment? I will make sure there are four seats available for that flight."

I've always wanted to go to Italy. Shit, passports! Mine's back at my apartment. I don't know about David and Erica having one. I doubt Joshua will have one either, if he even has a valid ID.

She took a deep breath and suddenly her worry left. She somehow sensed it would be okay.

"Are you still there?"

"Yes, Roger. I am here."

"Okay, there are four seats available. Could you email me the names of your other travelers and I'll send you the confirmations when I get them?"

"Are you sure this isn't too much, all four of us coming?"

"Not at all Catherine, it's really my pleasure. I am so happy right now I could just kiss Henry, the old dog."

"Okay Roger. Thanks so much!"

"Either I personally or one of my interns will be at the airport in Rome to greet you when your group arrives."

"Thank again, Roger."

Catherine hung up the phone giddy with excitement.

75- *The Search*

Razoul carefully laid out the plans for his systematic search of the apartment building floor by floor.

"I want radio silence when we get there until you hear from me. Check your coms thoroughly. Since we have no idea if she's ready for us or her current capability, we need everyone available and prepared."

Razoul's six henchmen nodded their understanding as they checked their equipment.

"Thaddeus will accompany me. I want all of you on point around the building in case we miss her or she tries to flee. When you hear me give the location, make your way to me quietly as you close your perimeter. Most important, no one touches her but me. I wish to speak with her first."

"That wasn't the plan, Razoul. What could you possibly need to talk to her about? Is this some way for you to play with your prey before you extinguish it? If so, then I am tired of your little games." Thaddeus was seriously impatient with Razoul now. "I am sure I am not the only one." He looked around for support but everyone pretended to be otherwise indisposed.

"Don't worry, Thaddeus. I'll make it quick if you wish...but I speak to her first. Do you understand that?" Razoul's steely gazed looked him up and down awaiting an answer.

Thaddeus caved again due to the lack of support from the others. He nodded for Razoul to move on, but continued to think of a thousand ways he might be able to kill him.

When this is done, you are mine. I am sick to death of this. I'd rather die trying than to be a coward.

"Now let's synchronize our clocks and go over this again. We will head out at one. I will begin my search for her apartment precisely at one fifteen."

As Razoul prepared to review everything a final time, he glanced at the alarm clock in his hotel room. It was only ten forty-five.

76- *Preparations*

"Okay, we need to run by Karen's house to get Erica's passport and then to my place to get mine. So I figure we need to be packed up and out of Parsons by ten in the morning at the very latest. It will take about 4 hours to get to Kansas City, then an hour for stops, and then another hour to the airport. Our flight leaves at 6:40 p.m. according to the itinerary, and we need to be there at least an hour early."

"Boy, we don't have much time to get it together. Luckily there's not much to pack up around here," Erica said. "But this is so exciting! I can't believe we are going on an adventure to *Rome*!"

"Well I am going to run back to my folk's house to get some stuff packed. I hope that my mom has my passport and it's not expired. Will you guys be okay for a little bit?" David looked at them both nervously.

Catherine stood up and walked over to him smiling. "Such a great protector you are."

"I'm serious, Catherine. I am going to worry the whole time I'm there. You know that."

"It's okay. You are only going to be like six blocks away. I'll call you if I need you and promise to lock up while you are gone. Besides, I think Joshua is like our early warning system."

"I just don't want to take any chances." He sweetly kissed her forehead. "Okay, lock this after I go."

"Yes, sir!" Catherine faked a salute and David rolled his eyes.

She locked the door and turned to Erica. That's when she noticed that Joshua wasn't with them.

"Hey, where's Joshua?"

"I don't know where he is. He was just here. Maybe he went outside?" Erica headed for the kitchen and toward the back door.

Catherine stopped her, "Hey let me go. I'll go see where he's at."

"Okay, I'm going to get the rest of my stuff packed up." Erica headed upstairs. "Don't forget to lock up when you come back in or David will kill us both." Catherine heard Erica laugh as she climbed the stairs.

Catherine stepped out into the moonlight and entered the garden. The moon cast an eerie glow on the rows of plants. "Joshua? Are you out here?"

She listened carefully for movement, then called again as she walked into the heart of the converging stone paths.

"Joshua? It's Catherine. Are you out here?"

Catherine jumped as Joshua finally responded from only a foot away from her. Her eyes were still adjusting. "I am here, angel."

"Oh my goodness! You scared me."

"I'm sorry."

"I was looking for you. I just need you to come inside so I can lock up for a while. It's getting late."

"Oh, the other angels say we are safe right now. Don't worry yourself."

"I feel safe right now too, but David worries a lot and I promised to lock up the house while he's gone."

"Well, if you promised, I guess we better go inside then. You must always keep your promises." He raised his index finger into the air and started walking toward the door.

"Yes, I suppose so." Catherine started to follow him. "Hey, Joshua?"

"Yes, angel?"

"Do the angels say anything else you'd like to share with me?"

He thought about it and said, "They told me your real name, but made me swear not to tell you."

"My name?"

"Yes, your angel name, your real name. But don't worry angel, you'll know too I bet once we get to Italy."

His mention of Italy made her realize that she hadn't asked him if he had a passport or even an ID.

"Joshua, in order to go to Italy you'll need a passport and ID."

Joshua kept walking as if he hadn't heard her. After locking up, she found him in the living room sitting on the couch. He made eye contact with her, rifled deep into a long pocket on his military pants and said, "Did you mean these?" He produced a brand new passport and state ID.

"How did you get those?"

"Again you are asking questions you should already know the answer to." He laughed. "I got these six months ago because the angels said I would need them some day. It was a pain in my ass."

Catherine laughed.

"Stay right there Joshua, I'll be right back." A few minutes later, Catherine produced some clothes for Joshua to change into. "These were my father's clothes and might not be the best fit, but I thought you might want me to clean your clothes before we leave tomorrow."

"That's very kind of you. Thank you."

"You are welcome. I also left the box out in the spare room that's ready for you. Feel free to take anything you want. I also found a small suitcase for you to pack some things in."

She could tell that Joshua was surprised at the generosity. "I'm supposed to be here to take care of you, angel."

"Well I am sure the angels wouldn't care if we took care of each other, right?"

"You bet." Joshua grinned.

"Okay you'll find what you need in the bedroom here. Just put your clothes on the kitchen table and I'll be sure to wash them for you. I'm headed upstairs to pack and then try to sleep."

Joshua watched Catherine walk up the stairs and disappear out of sight before he got up to head for the bedroom to pick out some clean clothes. "Why would anyone want to harm an angel?" he said to himself while shaking his head.

77- *Siege*

Shadowy figures moved silently around all sides of Catherine's apartment building. Razoul and Thaddeus forced the security door from the parking garage open and entered the building.

The sigil was tightly gripped in Razoul's right hand as they began to slowly walk the first floor hallway. The sigil was warm, but had not changed since he had arrived. He was counting on it getting hotter, the closer he was to her place.

Razoul was like a pacing panther as he walked each hallway and ascended one floor at a time on the less traveled emergency stairs.

They had reached the sixth floor now and Thaddeus was growing impatient. He whispered, "Are you sure that thing will work?"

Razoul turned quickly, practically growling at him rather than speaking. "Quiet!"

Thaddeus took a step back raising his arms in the air.

As they got to the end of the hallway and near the front windows of the building, the sigil grew slightly hotter in his hand. His heart rate quickened.

We're almost there.

They went up the stairs to the seventh floor. As he stepped into Catherine's hallway, the sigil burned him a bit, which caused him to drop it. It was glowing red hot and practically shot toward her door. Razoul grabbed his handkerchief to pick it up. He ran his fingers over the name plate to the right of her door.

So that's who you are...Catherine Moore.

He nodded to Thaddeus who took position on the other side of the door with his back to the wall.

Razoul broke radio silence with a whisper. "We found her. Apartment #711 on the west end of the building. We're going in. Converge on my position now."

He motioned for Thaddeus to unlock the door. He crouched down with his tools and within a minute the door was open.

Razoul led the way, quietly entering the apartment. He saw a door to his right. He motioned for Thaddeus to take a position behind him. He slowly opened the bedroom door. The moon cast enough light into the room that he immediately saw the bed was empty.

He checked the bathroom and then retreated to the hall walking slowly towards the living room. After a few moments, he realized she wasn't home.

In the next moment, the rest of his team had joined him.

He flipped a light switch, startling everyone, especially Thaddeus.

"Close the door, she's not here. Don't worry, though. We finally know who we are looking for. Turn this place upside down. Let's find out where the little abomination is. Give me anything you think may be a lead to her location."

Within ten minutes every drawer from the kitchen to the bedroom had been emptied. Razoul searched through her trash looking for itineraries or any other clue to her whereabouts.

As he pulled books from her shelf in the living room, he saw a photo of Catherine with her parents. He picked it up. An evil grin spread across face.

"Thaddeus?"

"Yes, Razoul?"

"Take one of the cars back to the hotel, tell Sirius to dig up anything he can on her parents or any siblings. We'll start there."

"Okay, Razoul."

Thaddeus left quickly, grateful to get away from Razoul for awhile.

A man's voice broke the silence. "Razoul, I think I found something."

One of the henchmen handed him a newspaper clipping of Catherine when she was in grade school. The masthead read The Parsons Sun.

"Take this to Sirius. Tell him to find out where this newspaper came from."

"Yes, sir."

Razoul took the photo of Catherine and her parents, practically tearing it from the frame. He looked at her image and spoke to her out loud, "I'm coming for you, Catherine."

Then he looked up. "Let's get out of here, we have everything we need. It doesn't look like she's been here for a while. All her stuff is cleared out of the bathroom and there's no food in the refrigerator."

Everyone filed out the door and disappeared down the stairs. Razoul paused at the doorway and took one more look at the ransacked place.

"I'm glad you weren't here, Catherine. It's much better this way. It prolongs the chase which I enjoy almost more than the kill."

He turned out the light and slammed the door.

78- *Time to Go*

Catherine took a deep breath inhaling the fragrance of a white rose, one of the hundreds now covering the lattice work in the garden.

"I will miss this place so much. I still can't believe it's real."

She looked up at the sky which was illuminated with the light of dawn. "Thanks for your help, mom."

A slight breeze came up around her. She could feel her mother very close. It was a huge discovery for Catherine to realize that she was not alone, in fact that she was never alone.

"I guess it's time for another adventure to begin. I'm not going to be ruled by my fear anymore..."

Catherine slowly walked inside to make sure she had everything she needed.

"Are we about ready?" David met her in the kitchen, and Erica appeared in the living room with her bags

"Yes, I think so. I'll go check on Joshua."

He was seated at the end of the bed with his eyes closed. She placed her hand on his left shoulder. Joshua jumped. "Oh, I didn't hear you, angel."

"Are you about ready to leave?"

Joshua looked a little dazed.

"Is everything okay?"

He rubbed his face a bit. "Yes, I was just listening to them talking and sometimes it makes me a little out of it."

"Well, is there anything new to report from the angelic hierarchy?"

"Yes, it's not great news, but we're leaving and should be fine.

Catherine shot him a concerned look. "The bad people..?"

Joshua nodded. "They didn't know who you were before, but now they do. They are coming here soon."

"I see. Well if they are coming here, it's good we are on our way out."

"The angels are watching them, but this is all they've been chattering about since early this morning."

David poked his head in the door. "Can I take your bags to the car?" He saw the look on Catherine's face and knew something wasn't right. "What's wrong?"

"I guess until early this morning, these people after me and Joshua didn't know for sure who I was. "

"They know now?"

"Yes, and they are coming here."

With decisive authority, David replied, "Well then let's get going. Hop up and get your stuff."

Catherine didn't argue.

79- Closing In

"The public records show the address of her parents in Parsons, Kansas is 716 N. Central. They are both deceased but she still owns the house. I've taken the liberty of mapping directions for us." Sirius handed the papers to Razoul.

"Pity they aren't still alive. They could have proven quite useful. Nevertheless, I can feel that's where she is. We'll be heading out in ten minutes. Tell everyone to be ready."

Sirius nodded compliantly and left.

Razoul looked out the window of his luxurious suite to the street below. His jaw tightened when he saw the same young girl who called herself Alice standing on the sidewalk, looking up at him.

"Keep watch over me all you wish. You know and I know there's nothing you can do to change what is about to happen to your precious little prophecy."

The little girl taunted him with a knowing smile. His blood boiled. He wanted to crush her fragile bones, but knew she would evade him again.

Thaddeus walked in to report their status. "The team is ready."

Razoul appeared not to hear him. He stared down at the unearthly child below, clenching his jaw.

"Did you hear me, Razoul?"

Razoul turned to him angrily, but remained silent.

Timidly, Thaddeus repeated himself. "The team is ready."

"Why didn't you just say so? Let's get the hell out of here."

Razoul grabbed his black, leather trench coat from the back of his chair and charged out of the room.

In just a few minutes, two black sedans were on the highway, disappearing from the city.

80- *Hidden Treasure*

Figures moved through the dim light, more like rats in a sewer tunnel than highly accredited academic professionals.

"Beth? Have you finished the cataloging of Section 4 yet?" Roger looked down at a crudely drawn map of the initial entry chamber and all the adjoining paths and rooms that they had found. The drawing looked like a flower configuration, with a large ceremonial room in the very center.

Beth emerged from one of the rooms to his right. She had a handkerchief over her hair and was rubbing dust from her eyes. "Yeah, I am almost finished there."

Beth was a young graduate student who was obviously enamored with her professor. She walked up to Roger and looked at the map. They were standing in the initial entry chamber that branched down curved hallways in both directions.

"So do you think the room layout itself has any particular meaning?" Beth gazed at Roger with eager eyes.

"I think so. There are exactly twelve rooms that connect to the central ceremonial chamber. Whoever built this designed it deliberately. I think the larger issue is to discover why it was built and what it was used for. Our new American friends should be on their way soon. I am hoping we can crack these questions once they bring the book."

"When do they arrive?"

"Tomorrow, late morning."

"Roger?" Roger was absent as usual and very deep in thought.

"Yeah?" He continued to jot notes in his ledger book.

"What is this woman's name?"

"Her name is Catherine Jane Moore."

Before Beth could speak again, the room started to shake as if they were having an earthquake. They grabbed onto each other and hunched down until the shaking stopped, just a few moments later. A thick cloud of dust hung in the air.

"Are you okay?"

Beth replied, "Yep, fine. What on earth was that?"

"I don't know. We shouldn't be having seismic activity like this in our region. I don't think there are any other structural issues either. Plus, we are not that much below ground. Let's check the rooms for damage?"

Beth nodded, "Of course."

He handed her a lantern. "You start with the first room to the left and I'll start with the last room to my right. We'll meet in the middle."

They both headed in opposite directions. It was hard to see due to the dust still hanging in the air.

Roger moved faster and entered the room he had just been working on first. As he scanned the room, holding the lantern out in front of him, he immediately noticed that a circular section of floor was broken up.

"Oh no!" He knelt down to survey the damage. "What a mess."

He quickly discovered that what initially looked like broken up rock pieces, was something else entirely. He picked up one of the large fragments and moved it to the side of him. Now he could see some detailed carving. "What the..." He quickly moved more fragments of rock to the side. "Beth! Beth! I'm in room 12. Quickly."

"What is it?" Beth carefully stepped into the room.

"The stone cracked here, but it's only a cover stone for something extraordinary underneath."

"Underneath? Hey, this looks just like the first room! There're broken up stones in the middle of the floor there too!"

"What? Are you sure?"

"Of course, the same pile of fragmented stones."

"I wonder..."

"What?" Beth put her hands on her hips.

"Come with me!" Roger grabbed her hand and led the way to Room 11. As they entered, just as he expected, there was a pile of debris just like in the other two rooms.

"Damn, so much to do now. Okay Beth, I am going to finish uncovering whatever is in 12, and I want you to check the other rooms for the same debris."

Beth headed off to the right as instructed, and Roger returned to the room.

"Okay, let's see what lies underneath." He rubbed his hands together.

The circular hole was only about 5 feet in diameter. He had it cleared of the big debris rather quickly. At first he could see the outer edge had a border and there was a circle inside the border with a symbol in the center. He pulled out his notebook and went to a drawing he had made of the large ceremonial circle in the larger central chamber that had twelve equally spaced symbols carved on its outer ring. The one under the rubble in this room was a match for one of the symbols on the larger wheel.

There was a blue type of stone inlaid around the center symbol. He went to wipe the dust off the stones to get a better look. The stones became warm to the touch as he dusted them off. He pulled his hand back quickly. "How is that possible?"

He cautiously placed his hand back on the stones. The stones felt rough, not smooth as he had expected them to be since they were a part of a ceremonial inscription.

Just then Beth returned. "All the other rooms were the same."

"What about the ceremonial chamber?" Roger said not looking up.

"It looked fine, no changes in there that I could see."

"Good. Come here for a minute. I want you to look at these stones."

"They are beautiful. Blue's my favorite color."

"Be serious for a moment, Beth! Now touch the stones."

"Ooh, weird, they're warm. Did you warm up the stones with something?"

"No, of course not."

"The surface is really coarse too."

"Okay, well at least I'm not imagining that the stones are warm."

"No, they definitely are warm."

"Can you tell what kind of stone it is?"

Beth shook her head. "I have no idea. It feels rough and looks fragile."

"Okay, well I want you to head back to the villa and call Bob and Greg because we need to clear away all this debris as soon as possible. If I am right, then each room will reveal one of the symbols from the outer ring of the ceremonial chamber wheel. I also want you to call my friend Andres, he's a gemstone specialist. You'll find his cell number in my Rolodex. Ask him come out to identify what type of stones these are. That may give us a clue about why they were used and why they emit their own heat."

"Done."

81- *Pit Stop*

The group arrived at Erica's mother's house right on schedule. Catherine was grateful to see Karen and visit with her for a little while, although her mind was preoccupied with the strangers who were about to descend upon her beloved parents home. She tried to push those fears out of her head.

"Karen! It's so good to see you." Karen held out her arms to embrace Catherine.

"Come in, everyone."

"Karen, this is a dear friend of mine, Joshua. He's taking the trip with us."

"It's nice to meet you, Joshua."

"Come and sit. I am so glad you are here. I had another one of those dreams about you and was a little worried."

"Don't worry, mom. We are all fine," Erica comforted her mother.

"So, someone is after you right?" Karen looked at Catherine seriously. "That is all I could see in the dream. You were being chased and this dark man was coming after you."

This was the first time that anyone had said anything specific about who was after her. "Yes, Joshua warned me about people coming after us. But you saw a dark man?"

"Yes, I saw him very well."

"Can you describe him to me? I doubt it is someone I know, but it could be."

Karen concentrated for a minute, recalling the dream as well as she could.

"Let's see. He's taller than David. Maybe 6' 1" or 6'2", and he had dark features. Well I mean a different skin tone, like someone from the Mediterranean maybe? There was a younger and older man standing next to him too. But I could tell they feared him."

"Did anyone call him by name?"

"No, at least I don't recall that, sorry."

"It's okay. I just thought maybe we'd get lucky there."

"He had black hair, a beard and mustache, and beady, cruel eyes." Karen shivered. "Are you guys going to be okay? I really don't want you to come face to face with him."

Catherine looked at Karen reassuringly, "Yes, we will. We have a little advantage. Joshua is a Prophet and he can talk to the angels. They warned us about them coming to Parsons just as we were leaving, so they are probably near Parsons by now. And as you can see we aren't there for them to find."

David had been intently listening to the conversation, but broke his silence. "Catherine, I don't think you should go to your apartment, it might not be safe. Let me go get your bag and passport."

"I want to go David. If they have done anything to my apartment, I want to see it."

Karen spoke up. "Catherine, they are probably watching for you there. I agree with David. It's not safe and you shouldn't go."

"If they've been to your apartment then they know what you look like. They will not be watching for me. They don't know me or that we are connected. They will be looking for you. I insist you stay here while I go get your stuff. I'll be very careful." David's eyes pleaded with her to agree.

Catherine didn't like it but she agreed. "Okay David, you're right. Please be careful."

David came over to reassure her, "Don't worry. I'll be right back. Everything is going to be fine." He was smiling at her when he headed for the front door, but that quickly changed as he exited Karen's.

Okay, in and out. No problems....please, no problems.

82- *Apartment*

Karen's house was only 15 minutes from Catherine's apartment. As David arrived, he looked around for anyone who looked suspicious. He saw a black sedan parked on the street and decided to pull into the parking garage where he might be able to get in and out without being seen. His heart was pounding as he got out of the car and locked it.

What am I going to do if someone's there? Don't worry about it. Calm down. Some protector you are. Just go upstairs, get the bag out of her closet and get her passport out of her top drawer and get out.

He entered the downstairs elevator. His finger was shaking as he pushed the button for Catherine's floor. He took a few deep breaths as the elevator jumped into motion and delivered him to the 7th floor. Once the elevator opened, he stepped out and was instantly relieved that there was no one was in the hallway. He slowly and quietly walked to her apartment.

He got her keys out of his jeans pocket, but quickly discovered that the door wasn't locked. He slowly opened it, listening intently. He immediately grabbed an umbrella that was in the entryway in the hope it may serve as a form of protection. He searched the apartment.

When he knew he was alone, he closed the door and threw the dead bolt. The place looked like a disaster area. There were books everywhere and all of Catherine's drawers had been emptied onto the floor.

"I'm so glad Catherine didn't come home to see all this."

He went into the bedroom and started searching through everything that had been dumped on the floor near the drawer where she kept her passport. Within a few minutes of looking under piles of disarray, he finally found it. It had tumbled under her bed. He grabbed it, relieved.

"At least they left her a way to get out of the country."

David went to her closet and grabbed the bags, wanting to get out of there as fast as he could. His heart was pounding after just a few minutes of being in Catherine's ransacked apartment.

He left the apartment and locked the deadbolt behind him to prevent any more unwelcomed visitors.

Once the elevator door closed after him, David let out a sigh of relief.

83- *David Returns*

Catherine had not been able to sit still the entire time David was away. Despite Erica and Karen's assurances that he would return soon, she couldn't do anything until she knew he was safe. She kept looking out the window for him every few minutes.

Her heart leapt with elation when she finally saw David walking up to the door. She preemptively opened the door.

"I am so glad you are okay. I was afraid something might happen to you." She hugged him as if he'd been gone for days.

He enjoyed the feel of Catherine's arms around him. "See, I told you it would be fine."

"So, how was it?"

"I want to tell you it was perfectly fine, but I can't and be truthful. Your apartment was ransacked. But don't worry about it. The three of us can clean up things in no time, right Erica?"

"Yes, of course. Don't you worry about a thing. We'll take care of it when we get back."

"So, they did come looking for me?" Catherine slumped onto Karen's couch. Hearing what David said made the danger to her and her friends all too real.

"The door was unlocked when I got there. It looked like they went through everything, so the place is a real mess."

She got a pit in the middle of her stomach as she imagined strangers rummaging through her belongings. "I am so angry right now. I can't believe they trashed my place."

"It could have been much worse Catherine. You could have been there when they arrived, which is hard for me to even think about. But they made a mistake and didn't even know it." David produced her passport from his pocket. "I have your passport and we are going to be a thousand miles away, very soon."

"That's true." Catherine tried to smile.

"Why don't you all let me make some sandwiches for you?" Karen offered heading to the kitchen. "You need some food before you head to the airport."

"Thanks mom, let me help you."

David casually looked out the living room window.

"What are you doing? Do you think you were followed?" Catherine jumped up to look out too.

He put his arm around her. "No, I don't think I was followed. I guess I am a little jumpy and cautious right now. But you are the most important thing to me, and I am not going to let anyone hurt you. I promise."

She looked into his beautiful eyes. He was the sweetest man she'd ever known. She believed completely that he would protect her or die trying, although the thought that someone might sacrifice themselves to keep her alive didn't sit well.

"I am glad you are here, David. Thank you for everything. It really means a lot to me."

He leaned in for a kiss, but sensing she was uncomfortable, placed it on her forehead instead of her lips. She closed her eyes. "The pleasure is all mine sweet angel."

"Don't call me that."

"Why not? It's true, and you are what you are."

"I can't wrap my head around all that just yet."

"What about the garden, Catherine? You did that! You brought it back from the grave literally within a few minutes. And still you don't believe in yourself?"

"I do think it's extraordinary. And yes, I did bring it back to life. But why couldn't it simply be explained as a rare mind over matter experience? It doesn't mean I am in fact a real live angel."

"Ah, you are such the logical, rational woman. Well, believe what you wish my dear, but I know that Joshua is telling the truth about you even if I don't fully understand it."

Karen called to them from the kitchen to come eat. Catherine was grateful for the interruption. David motioned to her, "After you."

84- *Find Them*

Two black sedans continued to eat away the miles between Kansas City and Parsons. Razoul's eager anticipation was building quickly. They were about 25 miles away. He was imagining the moment he had her in his grasp when the phone rang.

"Yes?"

"This is Grant, sir. I wanted to notify you that the motion detector we put in the woman's place was triggered a half hour ago by a man who came to the apartment with a key. He was only there for ten minutes and then left with a bag. I do not know the contents of the bag. I followed him by car for approximately 15 minutes when he stopped at a residence. He's been inside ever since."

"Her boyfriend perhaps ..."

"That's what I was thinking, sir."

"Good, very good. If we do not find her, we can use him as leverage."

"Do you want me to apprehend him now, sir?"

"No, not yet. If he leaves the residence, follow him and call me back when you have more to report. Otherwise just keep your eye on him."

"Yes, sir."

Razoul hung up the phone and barked at the driver to go faster.

86- *Uncovering*

"Alright, I need Bob to take rooms three and four. Greg you take five and six. Beth you keep working on one and two. I'll finish here and move counterclockwise. We have a lot to do, so let's get to work."

The two young men slowly shuffled toward their assigned rooms with their gear. Both of them would rather be sampling the night life in Rome at this hour, than on the job.

Roger paid no attention to their grumbles. He began to finish clearing the debris, then stopped and turned to Beth, "Hey, first thing in the morning, can you arrange to have our guests picked up from the airport and taken to the villa? They'll be landing around eleven. The flight information is in my laptop. With this latest development, I almost forgot."

"Sure thing, Roger, I'll take care of it. No worries." Beth was her usual bubbly self. It didn't matter that it was after one o'clock in the morning when Roger remembered.

He pulled the last stone from the circle and began to sweep off all the dust. "I can't wait to figure out what you are used for." Roger routinely talked to himself since he spent a lot of time alone in dark places.

A figure stepped into the light and removed his hat. "I came as quickly as I could."

"Ah, Andres! You did get here quickly! Thanks so much for coming at this late hour." He wiped the dust from his hands onto his khaki trousers and shook his friend's hand.

"No problem at all, Roger. You are a dear friend, and I love a good intrigue. Of course, you know I rarely sleep. So, what do we have here?" He leaned down to have a look.

"I'm trying to determine the composition of this light blue stone that is inlaid into the circle around the middle symbol and then the black stone around this outer edge here." He pointed them out as he spoke.

"Let's have a look." Andres pulled out a tool pouch and began to examine the center circle.

87- *Leaving*

Catherine took a deep breath as she returned from the airline ticket counter to join the others. She was relieved to be getting on a plane shortly. All she could really think about was the man who was chasing her.

She remembered how sad Karen was to see them all leaving. Catherine had made Karen promise to be aware of her surroundings at all times, and lock her house up when she returned home each day. Catherine knew that none of them should take chances right now.

"Okay we're set, and in first class too. I haven't ever flown first class before. Guess I will get to see what all the hype is about!" Catherine exclaimed.

"Well, at least you've flown before." Joshua said. "Dang...the things I do for angels."

"It will be okay, Joshua. I promise. Here I bought some magazines. They will help you pass the time." She handed him a couple, and the four of them walked toward the security checkpoint.

As they got closer, Catherine surveyed the other travelers who were around them. There was a man and his wife with a baby girl and another more elderly couple seated on chairs to her left. Then she noticed a little further up the ahead, a man with deeply tanned skin. He was wearing black slacks and a dark turtleneck. He seemed a little out of place, and she thought he looked down at his paper too quickly when she spotted him. It gave her a bad feeling.

She leaned into David. “Hey, don’t stare, but do you see the guy up there reading a paper?”

David nodded. “I think he’s watching us.” The security line was moving forward steadily. They both continued to watch the man without being obvious.

“Well we could both be a little paranoid, but I think you are right. He seems to be looking up at regular intervals. Don’t worry; we’ll be past security soon.” He put his arm around her to calm her down.

In a few minutes, it was their turn. Catherine put her shoes in a bin and then turned to see the man get up and walk through the outside door and cross to the parking garage.

“He just left the minute we stepped in here.”

“I see that.” David put the rest of his stuff in a bin and crossed through the metal detector with Catherine following close behind.

After everyone made it through the security process, the group found a seat to wait for the airline to call for boarding. Joshua couldn’t sit still due to his nerves. The man observing them made Catherine very nervous, and she thought of Karen again.

She turned to Erica. “David and I thought we saw a suspicious man outside the gate a moment ago.”

“No way, really?”

“Yes, and if it was, then he may have followed us from your mom’s house. Is there somewhere your mom could stay for a few days just to be safe?”

Erica thought about it for a moment. “Yes, she has friends in Topeka that are always after her to come see them.”

“Can you call her before we board the plane and explain? Tell her I want her to go to her friends for a few days.”

“I think that’s a great idea.” Erica jumped up and walked to a more private area to call her mom.

Catherine watched her until she could tell that she was actually talking to Karen and everything was okay. She relaxed her tense body, but just a little bit.

88- *Empty Hands*

Razoul’s search party had arrived at Catherine’s parents home with no difficulty. “It appears that no one is here,” Thaddeus offered.

"I can see that. Now get me inside." Razoul bit his accomplice's head off.

"Follow me." Thaddeus motioned for Razoul to follow him to the back of the house. Then he efficiently broke into the cellar door, as if it hadn't been locked at all. Everyone went inside.

They entered the kitchen first. One of Razoul's henchmen checked the fridge. "There's fresh food here. Someone's definitely living here right now."

"So this is the Incarnate One's childhood home. Not much to look at." Razoul's arrogance showed. He reached out to touch the coffee pot. "We just missed them. The pot still feels a little warm."

Then Razoul's phone rang. "Yes?"

"The woman just got on a plane with three other people. The man I saw at her apartment was with her. There was another woman and an older gentleman as well."

"What do you mean they got on a plane?"

"They...they...I followed them to the airport, sir, just like you asked."

"Why didn't you stop them?"

"You told me to do reconnaissance, sir. You also instructed the team not to confront the woman."

"I know what I said, but she was getting on a goddamn plane, you imbecile, and you should have called me."

"I am sorry, sir."

"Where were they going, can you tell me that?"

"Um, the flight was International and headed for Rome, sir."

"Rome?" Razoul practically dropped the phone. "Unbelievable! I go half way across the world to find her and now she's headed for Italy."

"Can you do something now that won't require too much of the brains you obviously don't have?" He didn't wait for a reply. "Contact my pilot and tell him to refuel and be ready to take us back to Rome in a few hours."

"Yes, sir."

Razoul hung up and turned to Sirius and Thaddeus. "Well it appears we will have home field advantage very soon."

They both just looked at him blankly.

"Catherine and some friends are now on a flight for Rome. Help me search the house quickly before we get on the road. I want to see if there's anything here that can tell us why she's going there or where we can find her."

Sirius reacted positively to the news. "Well, this is good to hear, Razoul. We will have her very soon."

Razoul ignored Sirius and turned to the other four henchmen. "We will handle things here. I want you to take one of the cars and head back to Kansas City. I want you to arrange for our bags to be taken to my plane and check us out of the hotel. The three of us will head for the downtown airport once we are finished here."

Razoul heard Thaddeus call for him from the upstairs bedroom. "Razoul! There's a large quantity of blood here on this carpet."

Razoul soon joined him. He was an expert on killing, and knelt down. "There's arterial spray here. Whoever's blood, they lost a lot of it here and not more than a week ago, I'd say. Search the other rooms now, I'll take this one."

He took the sigil out. It was very warm, just like it was in her apartment. He held it close to the blood stain, but there was no discernible change. "Not her blood…too bad, but intriguing."

Razoul went through mostly empty drawers for some clue other but came up with nothing. He joined the other two who were having similar luck.

"She's been staying here, but not for very long. There aren't any recent papers or anything. It appears the house has been vacant for many years, but she returned recently. The blood in the bedroom is not hers either. From the way the sigil is behaving, I don't think she's fully awakened either."

"How can you tell that?" Sirius responded.

"It's just a gut feeling, old man. If this can respond to her energy and she's been staying here instead of her apartment, then it should be glowing hotter that it was in the city, yet it's remained constant so far."

"Perhaps, Razoul, you are right." Sirius conceded.

"Of course I am, and you should know that. I found her, didn't I? Now let's head back and get on the plane. And remind me to kill that man who let her go."

89- *Kyanite*

"I will need to take a sample to be sure, but I believe that both these stones are different varieties of a mineral called Kyanite. The center inlay is blue Kyanite and the outer is black. It's a very fragile substance, so tell your crew to work gently," Andres explained.

Roger was puzzled. "Why would they use Kyanite? I can't think of anyone that would use that for ceremonial purposes."

"Me either."

"How fragile is it?"

"Only a three on the Mohs hardness scale. It's comprised of thin layers like shale. It breaks apart somewhat easily, and anything hard can scratch or chip it."

"Did you touch the stone and feel how warm it is?"

"I did run my fingers on it, but it's not warm." Now Andres looked puzzled.

"It's not?" Roger leaned down and found it was now cool to the touch. "It was warm earlier. Do you know of anything that would cause Kyanite to heat up?"

Andres thought for a moment. "No, I don't. I don't know if this helps, but I do recall Kyanite having a spiritual significance, if not a ceremonial one. But I don't know if you give any weight to New Age thinking."

Roger chuckled. "Not usually, but tell me anyway."

"Kyanite is believed by some to be a conductor of high frequency energy. Many wear it in pendants to raise their spiritual awareness, so to speak."

"Ah, out of the scientific realm. You always were a bit esoteric."

Andres nodded. "Yeah, I told you it was."

"Still, the Kyanite has to have another type of significance for being used here in this context. Otherwise they would have used another gem, one that would have withstood years of use or had more cultural value like jade, lapis or ruby. So, I appreciate even the far-fetched explanation for now."

"No problem at all. What do you think this site was used for?"

"That's just it, Andres. Other ceremonial sites have shown definite signs of use over a period of time, and then were abandoned. This one is different, it appears to be hidden on purpose for some later use, but it's anyone's guess for what exactly. Look at the cover stones we are removing now. The central chamber's wheel or circle was exposed, but why cover these up in all 12 rooms? Until these cracked, we thought these rooms were ancillary, possibly storage sites for ceremonial objects and the like."

"Very interesting, and no doubt the type of puzzle you enjoy Roger."

"That's true, I do. And hopefully soon I will be able to solve this one. Thanks for identifying the stone inlays. I'll have my assistant research Kyanite for both scientific properties and, um, spiritual ones."

"Don't forget to tell your people to go easy on it with their tools."

"Yes of course. Thanks again."

"Let me know if you need me any further." Andres put his cap back on and exited the room.

90- *She's On Her Way*

"Monsignor?"

"Yes, Brother Artemis. Do you have something new to report?"

"Yes, the Malem Tutela was just here and entered Catherine's house. I saw Razoul with my own eyes."

"My goodness! Is the girl okay?"

"Yes, yes. She and the others left this morning, and have not returned."

Bartholomew relaxed and took a deep breath knowing that Catherine was safe for now.

"That is wonderful news. Praised be to God."

"Amen, Monsignor. Amen."

"Do you know where she went?"

"I did not know until a few moments ago. I drew in closer to try and overhear what Razoul was saying as they left. It was tricky, but proved most useful."

"You have a good soul, Artemis. God shall award you for such bravery, my son. What did you hear?"

"Apparently Razoul and his men are flying back to Rome today because that is where she and her friends are going. She is supposedly on a flight to Rome right now."

"She's coming to Rome?" Bartholomew was surprised.

"That's what they said."

"You've done well, Artemis, you may return home now. I must go and consult the Guardians."

"Monsignor, there's one more thing, as they came out of the house, I saw Razoul holding up a gold object, saying something about it leading them to her once they got back to Rome."

"Could you see the object clearly?"

"No, Monsignor, I am sorry. It looked like a gold amulet of some kind. Is it significant?"

"Yes, Brother Artemis, but not to worry. I pray you have safe travels. Please come to me when you are back and well rested."

"Yes, Monsignor. It will be wonderful to see you." Bartholomew hung up the phone with his head swimming.

Is Catherine traveling suddenly to Europe to seek me out?

Bartholomew snapped out of his rambling thoughts. "I must go assemble the Guardians at once!"

91- *Flying*

Catherine looked out the window at the clear, star-filled sky as they sped through the air on their transatlantic overnight flight. She was exhausted, but fought to keep her eyes open. She had only flown once in her life, so she was having a problem sleeping.

She looked over at the others who were deep in thought, except for Joshua who had fallen fast asleep without a care in the world.

Look at Joshua, sleeping like a baby now.

She smiled watching him rest, feeling grateful for him. He was a conduit to the angels and a very valuable person to her now. Catherine decided to try again to get some rest. She repositioned in her seat and laid her head back. In no time, her eyes closed. It seemed only a moment or two before her eyes popped back open again. To her surprise, she was not on the airplane anymore.

"Where am I?"

Instead of seeing the airplane and all the seats filled with passengers, she found herself somewhere else entirely. She looked down and found she was wearing a long white gown similar to the one she remembered seeing the beautiful woman wearing in her earlier dreams. She walked forward and the unearthly fabric seemed to flow around her with a life of its own.

Catherine voiced her displeasure at her current situation. "Can't a girl get some old fashioned rest once and awhile?"

She was in a stone hallway looking down a long corridor. It felt safe to her, so she made her way down the hall. She saw light spilling into the hallway from a room at the far end. As she came closer, she could hear a man's voice. The tone of his voice indicated that he was discussing something of extreme importance.

"She's on her way to Rome. This is extraordinary." Bartholomew was pacing the floor as the others watched him.

When she entered the room, she expected him and the others there to turn toward her, but it soon became apparent that they didn't see her at all.

In the room, Catherine saw a large oval table with both men and women assembled around it. They were wearing monastic robes. One woman stood out to her as a very important member.

"At least she's safe for the moment, but we must guarantee this, Bartholomew, once she arrives." Aurora spoke with her usual confidence then added, "With as little interference as possible."

"Yes, of course." Bartholomew nodded.

Bartholomew? Monsignor Bartholomew? Wow....

At that moment Catherine realized she was seeing Monsignor Bartholomew for the first time. It was he who now stood before her and in this moment she knew that he was definitely connected to everything, just as she had believed. Confirming this, suddenly gave her great confidence that they were meant to be in Rome.

Of all of Catherine's out of body experiences, this realization allowed her to relax and observe what was going on, so that she could absorb every detail for later.

"Regrettably the Malem Tutela also has this information, Aurora, and came very close to finding her today. We were lucky that the prophet found her in time."

Aurora clasped her hands together nervously as soon as Bartholomew spoke these words.

"Malem Tutela? So that's who is after me?"

Catherine felt something pulling her out of the room and she fought hard to remain there listening.

No! Not yet! I am not ready!

In seconds, she found herself in a large library. She was surrounded with tall wooden shelves completed filled with books from floor to ceiling. The architecture looked very ornate and early European with heavy, dark woodwork. There was nobody in the room, so Catherine walked around exploring.

There was a large round table that was covered with papers. The first thing she saw was a map with a small circle burned into it. It was a map of the United States and the area on the map stretched from Kansas City to near Parsons.

"Oh crap...am I in the Malem Tutela's home base?"

Unlike the first place she astrally traveled to, this place made her feel very uneasy, and almost sick. She looked down at herself and noticed that her image began to flicker in and out. As if someone were switching channels on a television, she was propelled to another place that she recognized. She found herself standing in the exact room she had seen before she had passed out in the cathedral garden. There was the exact large circle cut into the floor with 12 symbols in the outer ring. She walked toward the center to have a closer look which she wasn't able to do during her previous vision. The symbol in the center felt familiar to her now, as she stared at it. She leaned down to see if she could touch it.

Instinctively, she began to trace the grooves of the design. As she did this, her finger left a residual glow filling in the symbol with light. Once she finished tracing the outline, she felt a rush of electricity move through her body. It felt as though it might lift her from the ground and she stood back up to stabilize herself.

Her palms grew increasingly warm, so she held them out in front of her. A strange symbol was appearing in the center of both palms right before her eyes.

An exact outline of the symbol seemed to burn itself into each hand, but instead of searing pain, it felt as if she were holding something very cold. She raised her hands above her head and watched what looked like little waves of blue flames cascade down both arms and disappear. Then her body expanded in all directions at once in a sudden burst of energy. Catherine felt herself floating downward for a few moments, and then she awoke again back on the plane.

The sensation in her palms felt itchy now. She looked at them closely, and discovered that the symbol was gone. She quickly rubbed her hands together and turned to her right to speak to David, but he was fast asleep. She looked over at Erica who was asleep as well.

Catherine was drained and in just a few moments, she faded into a very deep sleep.

92- *Puzzle*

Beth's voice came echoing into the chamber. "Roger, is there anything you need before I take off for the airport?" Beth popped her head into exterior chamber four and nearly bumped into the professor who was emerging from the room at same time.

"Yikes, you startled me Beth!"

"Sorry about that."

"You were saying?"

"I am headed to the airport to pick up Catherine and her friends. I could have sent a car, but thought it would be best for one of us to greet them."

Roger was pleased. "Why didn't I think of that?"

"Because I always do, so you don't have to."

"That's true, isn't it? Hey could you help me move these tools to the central chamber? We've almost gotten all the exterior chambers cleared out and I want to work on cataloging the main chamber for a little bit before I head back to the villa."

"Sure." Beth grabbed one of the backpacks and headed toward the room with Roger following close behind. When Roger put the rest of the gear down, he grabbed a lantern in his left hand while holding his notebook in the right.

"I want to compare the symbols in the other chambers with those here for any variances."

The lantern shone across the center of the big circle and the light caught something shiny and reflective. Roger stopped dead in his tracks. Beth was about to leave when she noticed Roger's face.

"What's up, Roger? Everything okay?"

He didn't answer back; it was as if he hadn't heard. He took five steps forward and got down on his knees.

Beth came to look over his shoulder. When she saw what he was looking at, she gasped. "Hey, that wasn't there before was it?"

Roger shook his head and ran his hand through his long hair. Then he ran his fingertip along the symbol. "This is inlaid with gold and it wasn't before. There's no way I wouldn't have noticed this earlier. And it's warm to touch! Feel this." Roger got out of the way so Beth could feel it herself.

She leaned over. "Wow, it's very warm, but how is that possible?"

"I have no idea. I don't know what any of this means at all. There aren't logical answers. First the cover stones break somehow, all on their own, and now this. I know that I have encountered mysteries before, but this project really takes the cake."

"Oh, I have to get going! Don't want to be late." Beth turned to run out the doorway, but Roger stopped her.

"Hey, Beth?"

"Yeah?"

"Let's keep these little anomalies to ourselves for now until we get a better grasp of the situation, our new guests included. I also don't want anyone else but our team in here if we can manage that, too."

"Sure Roger, not a word." Then she left.

"Not that anyone would believe us anyway."

93- *Landing*

"The captain has advised us to fasten our seat belts and prepare for landing." The woman's voice over the loud speaker jarred Catherine awake.

"There you are sunshine." David was smiling sweetly at her.

"We're landing? Why didn't you wake me?"

"I tried, but you were zonked out and wouldn't budge. I'm sorry."

"That's okay I was really tired."

Details of her latest out of body experience flooded back into her mind. She decided to explain to Erica and David after they got settled.

Groggily, Catherine looked out the window as their plane slowly made its descent into Rome. She wiped her eyes.

Even at this height she could see the magnificence of the architecture below them. A childlike excitement spread through her now as she realized that she finally made it to Italy. This had been a life-long dream of hers. In that moment, regardless of the circumstances that brought her there, she was happy and full of hope.

It took them almost two hours to get off the airplane, get their baggage and clear customs. Catherine was worried about their ride and the long delay but as they came around the corner she saw a young blonde haired woman holding a homemade sign that said *Welcome Catherine Moore and Friends.*

Catherine steered her bags toward her and the others followed suit. When she got closer, Beth said, "Are you Catherine Moore?"

"Yes, I am. You must be our ride?"

"Hi, yes, my name is Beth Ricoh. I am Roger's research assistant. Roger sends his regrets that he couldn't be here, but he and the entire team were up all night at the dig site. I got some shut eye, so I could be here. In fact, by the time we get you to the villa he should be in bed sleeping. He will join us for dinner, I'm sure."

"It's a pleasure to meet you, Beth. Thank you so much for picking us up."

Beth reached out to shake Catherine's hand. As their hands met, Catherine felt a sensation in her palm where the symbol had been.

"Wow, your hands are warm!" Beth exclaimed.

Catherine took her hand back and briefly glanced to make sure there wasn't anything etched into it. "Sorry, guess I'm a little warm blooded."

Beth just smiled. "Well that can be an asset here because it can get pretty cold in the evening at this time of year, not at all like New Mexico where I'm from originally."

"Oh, and let me introduce everyone else. This is David."

He took a comedic bow in front of Beth, and Catherine laughed. "As you can tell he's the comic relief of the group. This is my best friend, Erica."

Erica shook Beth's hand. "Thanks for bringing us to Italy, Beth."

"And last but not least, this is Joshua...a dear family friend."

"Well it's a pleasure to meet all of you. Now let's get your stuff to the car and get you settled at the villa."

The group followed Beth in silence to a covered parking area where she eventually stopped at large, white SUV.

"So how long have you been in Italy?" Erica asked Beth as they loaded the bags.

"Oh, let's see, I've been here about a year now."

"Miss home much?"

"Yes, sometimes." Beth admitted. "But working with Roger is incredible."

With the mention of Roger's name, Beth really lit up. Both Catherine and Erica exchanged knowing glances as they all piled into the car. Joshua sat up front like a little kid who wanted to get the best view of a new place.

"It will take us about 45 minutes to reach the villa, especially with traffic at this time of day. There are some extraordinary buildings on the route I'm taking, so you shouldn't be bored."

"That's great Beth, thank you. Are you sure you have enough space for all of us at the villa?" Catherine leaned forward from her spot between David and Erica.

"There's plenty of room, actually. The villa features eight bedrooms total, five bathrooms, and an awesome heated pool."

"Wow, that's big. I had no idea. When Roger said villa I was picturing something much smaller."

"Oh, I understand that. When I first came, I thought the very same thing, but there are all sizes of villas around here. The last place that we were staying at was like a box compared to this place. We're lucky to be where we are right now. Roger's good friend was leaving the country for a year's sabbatical and asked him to watch it. I'd hate to think what this place would cost to rent, definitely too much for a poor, graduate student like me."

Catherine liked Beth whose contagious, bubbly personality reminded her of Erica.

"So who all is staying at the villa, just you and Roger?" Erica chimed in.

Beth looked startled for a moment, almost embarrassed. "Oh, no…no…there are two other graduate students named Bob and Greg there too."

Beth changed the subject pointing out of the car to the right. "If you look over there you can see the Vatican dome."

They all looked to the right and Erica's eyes lit up. "I've always wanted to see it! Hope we can go before we leave."

Catherine thought of Monsignor Bartholomew. "I imagine the Monsignor's office is near there, Erica. So I'm sure we'll get to see it."

"So...how long are you guys staying? Roger didn't tell me."

No one spoke up, then Catherine said, "We're not sure yet. I suppose it will depend on when we get done working with Roger. Our tickets are one way at this point."

Beth smiled in the rear view mirror. "Cool, yeah, Roger told me about your antique book. I can't wait to see it. I can get you to the Vatican at some point, too." She looked at Erica and grinned. "Was there someone you said you needed to see, Catherine?"

"I need to visit the Pontifical Council for Justice and Peace in Vatican City. There's a Monsignor Bartholomew I need to meet with soon." Catherine offered. "Do you know of the place?"

Beth shook her head. "No, but I am sure Roger will. He seems to know everything around here. Just consider me at your service while you are here. If you need anything, I'm your gal."

94- *Intruder*

Razoul hardly spoke to anyone on the long flight back to Rome. He was livid that the girl had slipped through his fingers when he had been so close to finding her. Now that they were back, he behaved like a man on a mission. As his limousine drove up the long driveway to the Bugiardini estate, he bemused the last 24 hours.

How ironic we should be headed for her home while she's headed for mine.

Despite his silence before, Razoul started barking orders at his staff the moment he walked through the front door. "Gerald, get my luggage and take it to my quarters. Tell Margarette that I wish to have food in half an hour. Have her bring it to me in the library. Daniel, come with me, I have need of you!" Everyone scrambled hastily in various directions as he made his way to the library.

Razoul was both tired and frustrated. He immediately strode into the library and poured himself a drink. Then he sank into his father's leather desk chair contemplating his next move.

His phone rang and interrupted his scheming. "Ciao?"

"Mr. Bugiardini?"

"Si, go on."

"The persons you requested we locate were seen at the airport after the flight arrived, however we lost them after they cleared customs."

"You lost them?" Razoul's grip on his phone tightened.

There was a short silence on the other end. "Uh...yes, sir, we lost them. We assumed that they would emerge at the taxi depot to get a ride to their hotel, but they were nowhere to be found." The man swallowed hard waiting for Razoul's response.

"You damn imbeciles! How could you lose four people getting off an airplane!" Razoul was now shouting loud enough for one of the maids on the first floor to hear him.

"We believe someone must have been there to pick them up," the man said sheepishly.

"Obviously, you damn idiot! Just find them now!" He screamed into the phone and slammed it down on the desk. He strode over to the planning table on the other side of the room. As he approached it, the sigil grew white hot in his pocket.

"What's this?" It startled Razoul since it could only mean one thing.

She was here?...but how is that possible?

Razoul went marching down the stairs. "Was anyone else here today?" He confronted Gerard who was coming inside with two of Razoul's suitcases.

"No, signore, no one was here in your absence."

He wanted to question him further, but realized that if the girl's airplane just landed in Rome then it was simply not possible for her to have been there as well.

But why did the sigil respond as if she was?

Razoul looked around suspiciously and then stormed back to the library.

95- *No Man's Land*

"Is this heaven? Or maybe I'm in hell."

Jacob found himself walking through a strange structure made of towering concrete walls. When he tried to focus on the walls around him, he couldn't. It was like they were comprised of a series of movie projection screens. The images were moving so fast that it didn't allow him to catch anything specific.

"Where am I?"

As he kept stepping forward, the length of the hallway seemed to go on forever in front of him. He tried to remember what came before this, but that was also hazy. After walking a while, he stopped. He wasn't going anywhere.

He stepped toward one of the walls and reached out to touch the moving images. Once he made contact, his hand passed through the wall as if it were simply an illusion. Suddenly he flung his body through the wall and found himself tumbling into a familiar place.

What the hell? This is Catherine's old house? I must be dreaming.

Jacob looked around and saw a female figure descending the staircase. The light was dim and for a moment he thought it was Catherine moving toward him, but he didn't trust his judgment.

"Who are you?"

The shadowy figure answered in Catherine's voice. "Who do you think I am, Jacob?"

"I don't know. Why is it so dark? Just show yourself!"

The figure raised her arms in the air which illuminated the entire downstairs. Standing in front of him was Catherine, but he sensed that something was terribly wrong.

"How did I get here?"

"Don't you want to be with me, Jacob?"

"Yes, I want to be with Catherine, but I don't think this is real or that you are her."

The woman moved closer to him. "Do I look like Catherine?"

Jacob nodded yes hesitantly.

"Do I have her voice?"

Again he nodded, trying to figure out what was going on. Then it came back to him. The night he snuck in, the bedroom upstairs, his trying to convince Catherine, and the resulting scene.

"Wait! I should be dead."

"Perhaps, but you, Jacob, are not dead. Not really anyway."

"What does that mean?"

The strange woman approached him and put her arms around his neck. As he took a breath in, he was aware that she even smelled like Catherine, and for a moment he wanted to give in to the fantasy. He closed his eyes.

"I am Catherine, silly boy, and now we can be together right here, forever. Wouldn't that be just like heaven?" She said with a hint of sarcasm in her voice.

Jacob stood there for a moment contemplating if this was his heaven, but he couldn't reconcile his being allowed into heaven, after trying to kill himself. He pulled away from the woman's grasp and took two steps backward.

"I want to know who you are and how I got here."

The woman pouted. "You are really no fun, Jacob. I am offering you everything you ever wanted, yet you are still unhappy? How quintessentially human."

Jacob grew angry at being toyed with like a fly in a spider's web. He grabbed the woman by the shoulders but she disappeared only to reappear behind him.

"Now, now, Jacob. Better watch that awful temper of yours. It gets you into trouble."

He spun around. "Who are you?"

The woman smirked. "I am your long lost love, Catherine."

"No, you aren't her, so quit playing games with me."

"But I could be her and everything else you want if you let me."

"What happened to me after I tried to take my life?"

"As usual, Jacob, if you must know, you failed miserably at the whole dying thing." Her voice was biting in tone now. "You should be very grateful that I saved you from an all out possession by a nasty demon. I thought you'd like it if I brought you here and gave you what you most wanted. Besides, believe me, this is much better than where you really are right now."

"Show me." Jacob demanded.

"Very well, but don't say I didn't warn you."

The room began to spin first slowly and then rapidly. Soon he found himself standing in a hospital room staring at his body lying in bed on a ventilator.

"I look like crap." He turned around and could see his mother sitting nearby. Her face was ashen. Jacob had a wave of guilt rush over him and he tried to talk to her, but she couldn't hear him.

"Mom! I am so sorry for everything I did to you."

"Might as well save your breath, little boy, no one can hear you."

"So I'm in a coma or something?"

"Yes, are you happy now? See you aren't dead, but you are down for the count anyway. Like I said before, you failed, kiddo, and there's nothing you or Catherine can do about it."

"Where is Catherine? Has she been here?"

"What does that matter? You tried to kill yourself to be rid of her."

"I just need to know if she came to see me."

"If you must know, she did come here once. The demon spoke with her and told her you belonged to it now."

"A demon? Catherine was right! I wasn't ever talking to an angel, was I?"

"If you had done what they wanted you to do, you wouldn't have to ask me that."

"If I had done what they wanted?"

"But no, Jacob, you turned the knife on yourself instead. I will say it was funny to watch the demon's reaction there. Your actions were most unexpected."

Jacob's eyes widened as he thought about what she said. "So you weren't the one that was speaking to me about being chosen to protect her?"

"No, but I can be much worse than some lying demon."

"Are you an angel, then, if you saved me from the demon?"

"Majorly wrong again, dear boy. Such a pity because you had such promise. I am neither angel nor demon, but definitely no one you want to mess with. Now you know, and your precious Catherine will find out soon enough. "

"If you harm her, I will…"

"You'll do what? Hurt me? Do you think your impetuous threats meaning anything to me, you pathetic excuse?" She raised her hand and flung him to the ceiling. "I am in control of your fate now, boy, and it's time you recognize it."

Jacob fought hard to breath as his body was pressed against the ceiling.

"So are you ready to come down and behave yourself?"

He stopped struggling and resigned himself. He nodded yes. In a second or two, he was standing in the living room again. He flopped on the couch.

"That's better. Now you be a good boy."

"Not like I have much of a choice."

She laughed. "Very true, you don't. You should be grateful. If it weren't for me, you'd be long gone to hell by now."

His heart sank. He was a prisoner now, and he knew it. "Why didn't you just let me die? I'm a failure, just as you said."

"Oh, you are far too valuable to let something like that happen." She came in closer to touch his cheek. "Catherine has a blind spot for you, and I plan to capitalize on that little weakness of hers very soon."

"Why do you want to hurt her so badly?"

"I cannot let her shove me out of my position in the world. Though I should just let her have it since this world doesn't even deserve me. They certainly have not been grateful for all the gifts I've given them. Nonetheless, I've been here for too many centuries to let her bring heaven here now."

"Can't you answer one simple question? Who are you?"

"Well my, pet, that's a question for another time." She rubbed his head like he was a house cat, and then she vanished.

96- *Casale Valdichiascio*

"Roger's car is here, so he's probably sleeping now. Let's go inside, and I'll show you around. Then we'll bring in the bags and get you settled."

Erica jumped out of the car, excited. "Wow, this is so beautiful Beth."

"You haven't even seen the inside yet. Welcome to Casale Valdichiascio, everyone."

They walked single file into the villa entrance, Beth and Erica leading the way.

Catherine was following in the rear. A wave of nausea hit her, like it had in the kitchen in her parent's house. Her thoughts immediately returned to Jacob. Erica turned around to glance back at her, knowing instantly that something was wrong. She shot a glance of concern at David who was right in front of Catherine.

"You okay?" David took Catherine's arm in his.

She shook her head dismissively, "Yeah...yeah I'm fine. I was just thinking about Jacob and it made me feel a little sick. That's all."

"Don't worry, he'll be okay. You need rest with jet lag and all. Let's go inside and we'll get you settled so you can take a nap."

"Okay, yeah, I'll be okay." She feigned a smile.

They both walked inside, trailing behind the others.

"This is the foyer. To our left is the great room which is followed by the library. In front of us is the spectacular kitchen, let me show you. Not that with our schedules we have a lot of time to cook or anything. The fridge is always stocked, and so is the pantry. Just help yourselves to whatever you want. Upstairs are all the bedrooms." She motioned with her hands. "Follow me."

Beth threw open two large French doors that led out to a large stone patio with stairs that descended to a beautiful area with an Olympic sized swimming pool.

Despite her nervous stomach, Catherine let herself take in the beautiful, sprawling villa, at least for a moment. "It's enchanting, isn't it? It's a truly beautiful place. We are so lucky to be here."

Beth smiled. "I feel that way every day, Catherine. Let's head upstairs and find you all a bedroom."

As they ascended the spiral staircase, Beth filled them in on other features of the property.

"There's a large wine cellar below us, and beyond the pool are amazing gardens if you have the time to explore them while you are here."

At the top of the stairs, the landing branched into three separate hallways. She pointed left, saying "Our team's bedrooms are that way. The other four bedrooms are to the right and this is where you guys will be staying. This other hall has another bathroom, an office, servant quarters and storage closets."

David led Catherine into one of the bedrooms. It had floor to ceiling windows draped with light, multi-colored scarves. There was a massive four poster bed and an adjoining bathroom. "How's this one?"

Catherine looked around wearily. "It's great. This will be fine."

"Okay, you sit down here, and I'll be up shortly with the bags."

"I should make sure Joshua and Erica get settled." Catherine stood up.

"No, just rest, and I'll take care of everything."

Catherine didn't argue with him.

Erica popped her head in. "Hey there, you okay? You should see my room, it's huge! Yours is too, I see." She sat down next to Catherine.

"I'm okay. I just can't stop thinking about Jacob, all of the sudden. I honestly hadn't thought about him at all since we left."

"Well, we were being pursued at the time. I don't think anyone would fault you for him being off your mind for a little bit."

Catherine smiled. "That's true. Maybe I'm a bit jet lagged, too."

"Why don't you take a little nap after David gets your bags up here? I think I'm going to lie down, too, and I'll feel better if I know my best friend is resting too."

"Nice, you are so cute. You always know how to put things in order to get me to agree, don't you?"

Erica grinned, "But of course I do. What are friends for?"

Erica and Catherine stood up. Erica pulled back the covers for her. "Okay then, hop in."

Catherine slipped underneath the covers and felt herself relax. "This bed is so comfortable, oh my god, this is heaven."

Erica kissed her sweetly on the forehead. "See you later on."

David walked in with her bags and sat them down. He smiled when he saw she was in bed.

"I was going to suggest a little rest, but Erica beat me to it."

Catherine was fading fast. She looked up at David's face and started to drift, listening to the sound of his voice. "Sweet dreams, angel..."

97- *Madre*

Razoul had stretched out to rest on the velvet chaise lounge near his father's desk. Though he had no intention of falling asleep, he was out within five minutes. Soon after, he began to toss and turn.

He found himself now in the garden again with his mother. He stared at her beautiful face. This dream was different from many others. He sat by her now as an adult version of himself, no longer a child.

"I'm deeply concerned for you, my son. I know how brave you are and how grown you are too, but in this case I cannot release the concern I have for you. You are walking a slippery slope. You could be lost forever."

"I can take care of myself, mother!"

"Yes, of course you can. But even the strongest of warriors can become vulnerable to injury. This is why I begged for them to let me come to you."

"Begged them? Who did *my* mother have to beg to come visit me in a dream?"

As Chiara looked deeply into Razoul's eyes, he melted, but then fury rose in him.

"The damned angels brought you here? That's who you had to beg for permission to see me?"

"Don't be angry, my son. I came because I love you so much. I knew you needed guidance."

He turned away from her, crossing his arms defiantly. "Well, very soon no one shall have to beg the angels for anything."

"My son, you are in great danger, and I came to warn you. What else is a poor mother to do?"

His face became stony.

"You should trust your son, my lady, to do whatever is required: nothing more, nothing less."

"Oh Razoul, did you not learn anything from your mother's broken heart? How can you become this reckless as to endanger yourself in this way. They showed me everything."

"Lies. They are lying to you, mother. You must trust me, not them."

The tears in Chiara's eyes made his heart ache. "I cannot listen to this, mother. You have been coerced into believing their lies. I do not wish to cause you any pain, but my path is clear."

"Please, Razoul, please stop this for me."

"You cannot ask me to do that! I will not, and cannot."

He walked away. By the time he regretted it and turned back, she was gone.

The winds began to shift and the sky turned from blue to ominous grey. Lightening flickered. Dust flew everywhere, and Razoul became momentarily blinded. He stumbled forward and fell to his knees.

Echoing laughter filled his head. He struggled to look up and noticed a shadowy figure near him.

"Samyaza." He grimaced trying to get to his feet.

"Oh yes, Razoul. It is I. What's the matter? Didn't expect to see me so soon?"

The winds calmed and the dust dropped to the ground as quickly as it had stirred.

"I came to remind you that I'm still watching your pathetic attempt to defeat the earth angel."

"You came for insults? Or do you have another reason to be here? Maybe you could help me if you feel I'm inept at what I'm doing." After Razoul's last encounter with the dark angel, he chose his words carefully.

"Are you trying to get a rise out of me, boy?" The sound of Samyaza's voice boomed and echoed in the air around them as a thick, black smoke stretched out in all directions.

Razoul was silent.

"Besides, you have amused me with this little play of yours."

"What do you want from me?"

"I am here to help you yet again. You should be grateful."

"Then out with it."

"If you face her now, she will be too powerful, and you will fail."

"Ridiculous, she's nothing at all."

"In your pathetic arrogance, you cannot see past your own nose. Your mother was right."

"Leave my mother out of this! She's no concern of yours!"

"Do you really think you are going up against a mere human? You underestimate what she's capable of, especially with her resources. If you threaten her, you'll see her power and lose. You are too late to catch her. Her awakening has begun, and there's nothing that can stop her except one thing..."

"What one thing?"

"There's a way to send her back to where she came from. You will find a scroll hidden in the Vatican archives that bears the Enochian incantation that can send her back. It was hidden long ago so that it would not fall into the hands of someone like you. The pope himself doesn't even know it's there. It's simply an obscure reference that appears to be nothing at all. Unless you know what it's for."

"I have to retrieve something from the Vatican? It's a fortress unto itself."

"Surely someone like you isn't afraid of a little challenge?" Samyaza baited him along.

"No, of course not."

"When you awaken, you will have everything you need."

To prove his power, Samyaza threw a ball of fire directly at Razoul. It struck him in the stomach sending him to the ground with a thud.

In the distance, Razoul could hear his mother screaming.

98- *Adversary*

As Catherine slumbered deeply, she floated gently in a quiet space between the world of the living and the ethers. Her blissful feelings were interrupted by a voice calling her name.

"Catherine, where are you?"

When she opened her eyes, she was standing in her parent's living room. "What the heck? Why am I back here?"

"Catherine? Catherine?" A male voice called out to her from the back yard.

She slowly walked through the kitchen and out the back door to the garden path.

"Jacob? Jacob, where are you?"

"Over here!"

She followed his voice to the back of the garden. She stopped dead in her tracks when she caught sight of Jacob buried up to his shoulders in one of the flower beds.

"Oh my God! Who did this to you?" She tried to scoop up the ground in her hands around, him but the dirt wouldn't budge at all. "What the hell?"

Jacob pleaded, "You have to leave me. It's not safe for you here."

"I'm not leaving you like this. I'll get a shovel."

He shook his head sternly. "You know this is just a dream, or something close to it. You shouldn't have come."

"I didn't exactly bring myself here."

"That figures. She must have brought you here then."

"Who?"

"The woman who trapped me here. She won't let me wake up."

Catherine looked at him, puzzled. "So, you know that you're really in the hospital right now?"

"Yes, she showed me everything. It was awful. And my poor mother too." Jacob started to cry.

"I'll help you. I won't let her keep you long. I promise."

"What can you do? She's out to get you, too."

"I know. She's a demon. I've tangled with her before."

"She's not a demon."

"What do you mean she's not a demon? What is she then?"

A gusty breeze swept through the garden, and the sky began to darken.

"You have to go now, Catherine! She's near. I can tell. Get out of here."

"I'm going to get you out of the ground." Catherine ran to the fence to grab a shovel leaning against it. The wind was stronger enough to knock her off balance. She moved towards Jacob. She looked around the garden and watched all the roses curl up and turn black as the sky seemed to press her downward.

The wind was so fierce that leaves and debris were making it too hard to see Jacob.

"Catherine, get out of here, please!"

Something struck Catherine in the chest. She tumbled to the ground as a woman's voice encircled her head. "He's mine now. You are too late."

Catherine shouted to her unseen foe. "Why did you bring me here? Who are you?"

Jacob wailed. Catherine pleaded, "Stop it. Please stop hurting him."

Then the wind died down as suddenly as it had come. The debris settled to the ground, and she could see Jacob's face again.

Catherine took two steps toward him and the earth began to violently shake. Large cracks opened up in the ground in all directions making it almost impossible to reach him without falling in.

Jacob looked at her pleading, "Please don't come any closer. She's too powerful for either of us. I'm lost now. Forget about me."

"No. I won't. I refuse."

Catherine stared in disbelief as a collection of vines flung themselves toward Jacob. An unseen presence pulled him up right out of the ground with ease. The vines began to wrap themselves around his body. Catherine kept navigating the cracks to get closer to him. By the time she reached him, he was being held seven feet above the ground. Catherine jumped to grab Jacob's feet, but he was just out of her reach.

Her anger erupted and she began to taunt her adversary, "It's me you want, so let him go. Show yourself! Are you a coward? Preying on the weak is the best you can do?"

An amused, arrogant laugh echoed throughout the garden, but Catherine's enemy remained hidden.

"There will be plenty of time for introductions another time. I just wanted you to know that I have something you really want."

"I already knew that, you demon, or whatever you are."

"Can't you tell a demon from something else entirely?"

"I'm not afraid of you!"

"Perhaps not now, but you will be."

"Let him go!" Catherine commanded.

"You insignificant little...you have no power to command me to do anything. The sooner you realize that, the better off you will be."

"I will never let him go. I will never abandon him. *You* should know that."

In the blink of an eye, a fierce woman was standing between Catherine and Jacob. "Of course I do. That's what will make this little game, oh, so much fun!" The woman raised her hands to send a blast of energy into Catherine, knocking her off her feet. "And now, it's time for you to go!"

A wave of intense heat pushed Catherine right back to consciousness. She awoke with a gasp, sitting straight up in her bed. She was back in Italy again.

There was a candle burning in her room and it was dark outside.

99-*Burned*

Razoul's eyes shot open. He was covered in sweat and out of breath. It only took a few moments for him to feel the searing pain in his stomach. It was as if his flesh was on fire. He clutched his belly and lifted his shirt. When he pulled it up, he saw that something was, literally burned into his flesh.

He struggled to get to his feet and stumbled over to a full length mirror so he could get a closer look. Deep frown lines gouged his face once he realized what Samyaza had done to him. There was a knock at the door.

"Go away! I don't wish to be disturbed!" Razoul shouted.

He stumbled toward the adjoining bathroom and turned on the water. He wet a wash cloth to try and sooth his burned skin. Every touch made him wince. He examined his stomach in the mirror for a moment. He could see that there was a layout of some kind imprinted on his stomach, and a series of letters and numbers that made no sense to him.

"A map? It's a map. I am sure this is Samyaza's idea of a damn joke!"

He stormed into the other room and grabbed a staff phone off the desk. "Fetch my physician, and send Sirius to the library immediately." Then he slammed the phone down.

A few moments later, Sirius appeared in front of him. "You called for me? Are you okay? You don't look well."

Sirius' patronizing demeanor infuriated Razoul, even more than usual. "That's why I have you, Sirius, so you can state the obvious. I do hope you were more helpful to my father than that." Razoul spat his words like venom.

"You are behaving like a wounded animal. What on earth is the matter with you?"

Razoul's pain was becoming unbearable. He lifted his shirt and Sirius let out a shocked gasp. "It's a map. I was visited by Samyaza. He told me how to defeat her, at last. We must acquire an Enochian scroll. The map and this information will show us where."

Sirius' jaw tightened. "I told you that Samyaza would be the end of us all."

"Don't cry like a baby, Sirius. If you can't handle this at your age, I am sure I have others who can."

Sirius shook his head. "I made a commitment to your father in the days where loyalty was our greatest currency. I promised that I would stand by you. So regardless of how fool-hearty you are, I am here all the same." Sirius sighed and turned towards the door. "I will get you a salve to sooth your skin while we wait for the physician to arrive."

100- *Meeting*

After Catherine calmed down, she changed into some fresh clothes and wandered downstairs to find the others. She could smell various aromas coming from the kitchen as she descended the staircase.

Everyone jumped a little as Catherine spoke. "Something sure smells good."

"Catherine, I'm glad you are awake. I'm Roger. Welcome to Italy." He crossed the room to shake her hand. Catherine smiled back at him without saying anything. She was still a bit shaky from her dream.

Roger pulled out a chair for her at the heavy wooden dining table, and she sat down. "Thanks so much for everything. You have a beautiful place here."

David brought Catherine a glass of water. When their eyes met, David could tell she was upset. He sat down beside her. "Are you okay?"

"Yes, I'm fine now. I had a bad dream about Jacob. I'll fill you in later."

David nodded.

"Beth and your friend Erica are cooking us up some pasta and bread sticks. I'm starving. She and Erica have been tearing up the kitchen for over an hour now. I tried to help but they kicked me out." Roger held his hands out to everyone. "Ma always said I was all thumbs."

Everyone laughed.

Roger picked up his glass of wine and came over to sit next to Catherine. "After some food, I was hoping we could look at your book?"

"Sure. I'll bring it down after we eat."

Erica and Beth were putting plates down in front of everyone. In no time at all, everyone was happily stuffing their faces.

"So Roger, how is work going at your dig site?" Catherine said.

"It's been quite interesting over the past few days." He shot a look at Beth and then continued. "We are finding out that our original hypothesis regarding the use of the location may be incorrect. But I'm used to that at times, doing this type of work."

"I imagine uncovering history every day as part of your job would be interesting," Erica added.

Catherine noticed that Roger was clearly someone who loved explaining about his work and profession. "Oh, it is. You just never know what will happen next."

"Will we be able to visit the site while we're here?" Erica asked.

"Of course."

Beth chimed in, "Are we not keeping the site closed?"

He waived his hand in the air. "There's no harm in giving our special guests a tour."

"I am excited to see what new revelations will come from our latest discoveries at the site, and of course Catherine's book." He turned to Catherine. "You have no idea how much this may help our efforts."

"Well Roger, I truly appreciate you bringing us here. I hope you can help me understand the purpose of the book."

Roger finished up his plate and got up. "Would anyone care for an espresso?" he asked over his shoulder while rinsing his plate.

Everyone said yes, except for Joshua who had been quiet all through dinner. "Oh, none for me please. That stuff makes me too hyper...nope, no caffeine for this old guy."

Joshua pointed to himself and then headed for the doors leading outside. "I'm just going to take a little after dinner walk."

"Okay, Joshua," Catherine after as he closed the door behind him. She watched him wander off into the distance and out of sight before she announced she was going to get the book.

"I'll be back in just a minute you guys."

As she left the kitchen and headed upstairs, her mind was mulling over the dream and Jacob.

Jacob said she's not a demon. Then what is this thing that's holding him hostage, and how do I beat it?

Catherine brought the book down as Roger was brewing the last two espressos. She had been very careful not to touch the book itself, and had it wrapped in a thick scarf.

"Catherine, why don't you take that to the living room and I'll bring your espresso. It'll be more comfortable."

Erica and David followed Catherine into the living room. The three of them were all alone for a moment. Catherine looked at them both, speaking in lower tones. "I saw Jacob in my dream while I was sleeping earlier. Something has him trapped outside his body. He could talk to me, and he knew he was in the hospital. I thought it was a demon that I encountered while at the hospital, but now I don't know what it is. Or why it hates me so much. It seems to be using Jacob as a way to bring me to a confrontation. I'd rather not do that until I know what I'm dealing with."

"Poor Jacob, don't worry honey. You can beat it, whatever it is, I know you can." Erica said reassuringly to Catherine.

David chimed in, "Of course she can. Nothing can beat you, Catherine."

"I wish I had as much confidence in myself as you two obviously do."

They both hugged Catherine as Roger and Beth entered the room. "Uh, are we interrupting anything?" Beth asked.

They broke the group hug and Catherine spoke up. "Oh no, these two are my best friends, and I am just grateful for all their support. My, uh, life has been, uh, rocky lately, and they've really helped me so much."

Roger handed the espresso to her and sat down on the couch.

Catherine carefully unfolded the scarf that held the book.

Roger stared intently as she did. He was eager, like a kid at Christmas. "May I?"

"Of course." Catherine handed the book to him.

At first he examined the exterior of the book carefully, running his fingers slowly along the embossed leather cover. "Henry said the entire book was written in something similar or close to Enochian script?"

"Yes, we believe so."

"The center symbol on the cover is just like those in the central chamber at the dig site. This is quite intriguing."

Catherine chimed in, "We found out the symbol on the cover is called the Sigil Dei Ameth, which is connected to a man by the name of John Dee."

"Yes, that is what it is called. Though there are a couple variations on the chamber one that we aren't sure about. I'm familiar with John Dee's work. I was always interested in ancient, symbolic writing. What we are struggling with at the moment is that his era was in the 1500's and the catacombs where the hidden chambers were found are much older than that."

"So then where does John Dee come into the picture?" Catherine asked.

"Ah, yes, John Dee. He was an interesting, well-educated man. In fact, during the 1500s he was regarded as one of the most knowledgeable gentleman in England. He kept a vast library of various ancient and rare books. I imagine at one time he had the largest library and private collection in the world. During his research, he became interested in the legendary lost book called the Keys of Enoch."

"So who is Enoch exactly?" requested Erica.

"Enoch was supposed to be the great-grandfather of the biblical Noah. The story goes that Enoch was taken up into heaven as a human and then turned into an angel by God, if you believe in that sort of thing happening. So his family thought he had died and been taken to heaven, never to return. Imagine their surprise when he comes back later to relate that he traveled through the seven levels of heaven and met with God. The Keys of Enoch are reported to be his writings about his experience as God told him to record them. The book itself is a difficult read and most scholars believe that the Keys of Enoch are not Enoch's actual writings but stories of it written by others in more modern times."

"So, John Dee wanted to open up the ability to communicate with angels in order to find the whereabouts of that book. He tried for a long time, but it wasn't until he met a man named Edward Kelley that he reported having success communicating with angels. The Enochian script came out of one of his divining sessions with Kelley, when they claimed they were communicating with unseen angels. John Dee carefully documented the sessions and the information given to them. The information included all kinds of tables and charts which no one has been able to decode or find real meaning in, as far as I know. Of course, there are all kinds of crackpot theories."

Roger stopped talking and looked at the symbols burnt into the front and back covers. "These symbols were etched into the false wall that we discovered in the catacombs. Again, these are similar to Enochian script but not quite."

He started to thumb through the book. "It's at times like these I wish I had become an ancient linguistics major. Maybe then I could make sense of this..." He trailed off all of a sudden as he came to a page that startled him.

"What's the matter?"

Roger hopped up off the couch and ran upstairs. "Just a moment, have to find my notebook!"

He returned out of breath and thumbed through his notebook of findings at the site. He placed Catherine's book on the coffee table and then put his notebook beside it. The pages matched perfectly. Roger's layout of the site and the image on the back cover of Catherine's book were identical.

Roger's boyish pride was endearing. "Now what do you think of that?"

101- *Synchronicity*

Later that evening, Catherine and her crew were in her bedroom discussing some recent developments. "So I think that there's a big reason that we've come to Italy and have met Roger. It cannot be a coincidence that the book Sister Mart Eleanor left for me has those large symbols in common with the center chamber Roger was talking about at the dig site. All this can't be a coincidence. We have to get into that site with Roger so we can see what is going on. Surely the Malem Tutela won't be expecting us to go there."

David's ears perked up. "Malem Tutela?" Erica too, listened intently.

Catherine explained, "Yes, well I sort of had an out of body experience or something on the airplane on the way to Rome. Let's just say that I saw Monsignor Bartholomew and other people in a meeting room. He spoke of an organization called the Malem Tutela. That's who's trying to find me and Joshua. I believe I briefly saw a room in the headquarters of the Malem Tutela during my experience."

"Wow, girly, you are really getting some awesome powers there." Erica teased.

"Yeah, for sure! You are so funny, Erica, I swear." Catherine retorted.

"Well, I do aim to please." They both giggled.

David was serious. "Okay ladies, can we come back to the task at hand? What's our next move?"

Catherine thought for a minute and then decided. "First, I want to go to see Monsignor Bartholomew tomorrow, to find out why he was notified about my visit to the convent. If he's our ally, and I think so based on Sister Mary Eleanor's intentions, then he could fill us in on the Malem Tutela. Who knows, maybe he knows all about the book too."

"Cool. A field trip!"

"Not exactly, Erica. I think we need to try and blend in and be very cautious of what we do. I don't know what resources the Malem Tutela will come up with to find us, or even where they are right now."

"I know. I guess I'm being in Rome has overshadowed the bad guys out there trying to get us. It probably should be the other way around." Erica shivered.

David offered to help. "I'll go ask Beth if she can take us to that office tomorrow. What was it called again?"

"The Pontifical Council for Justice and Peace. She has to ask Roger where it is, though. I remember she wasn't sure about its location earlier today."

"Oh yeah! I got it, boss. I'm on it."

With an exaggerated swagger, David was out of the bedroom and out of sight.

Catherine watched him leave the room. "He can be so darn silly, that boy."

Erica agreed, nodding. "Yes, and that's exactly what you need."

102- *Sedated*

The physician emerged from Razoul's bed chambers to speak to Sirius in private.

"Aside from the burn, I am also treating him for infection. He's suddenly running a very high fever which would not be directly caused from his...well...unusual burns."

Sirius' face looked grim as the doctor continued. "I have him sedated right now. He wasn't happy with me for even suggesting it, but I needed to force him to rest until his fever breaks. He's already run down from his broken ribs, and if he has an infection hiding inside him somewhere, he could get much worse and even potentially die if we don't get a handle on it."

Sirius felt dread as he considered the possibility that the fever was coming from something quite unholy. "Very well, that will be all doctor. Leave the medication schedule with the butler on your way out."

"Very good Sirius, I'll be on my way now. I don't want to be here when he wakes up. He'll be furious with me. I'll be back tomorrow to check on him. He must remain in bed at all costs to ensure his recovery."

Sirius opened Razoul's door and walked in slowly, as if pondering something. He stood over him laying there in a drug-induced sleep. His best friends' son was there, in front of him, completely helpless.

Britius and Sirius had been such good friends for a very long time. They had grown up together, in a sense. He had often envied Britius: his large estate, his clever way of working a room of business men to his advantage, his generosity with those loyal to him, and most of all Chiara, his wife. She was an incredible woman, not only to look at, but also to confide in. There had only been two arguments between the two men while Britius was still alive and both were regarding her.

Of all Britius' wonderful attributes in Sirius' opinion, his antiquated views of marriage were neglectful. Had Sirius been married to such a woman, he would have never viewed her like a piece of furniture.

Now Sirius stood over Razoul, contemplating the fate of his friend's eldest son. He knew full well that Razoul had murdered Britius for his power, but mostly for revenge for imprisoning his mother in such a life. So ultimately Britius died for his own stupidity when it came to Chiara, a rare gem of a woman.

So did he truly blame Razoul for killing his Britius? He often felt the same way about his dear friend when it came to the radiant beauty Chiara, who was also a trusted friend.

He looked at Razoul slumbering, and tried to see either one of his friends in who he was. He didn't. He saw an angry, impetuous, reckless and dangerous man.

But is it my job to stop Razoul? Can I really kill the son of Chiara, knowing how much she loved Razoul? Or how much I loved her myself?

Sirius lifted Razoul's dressings to have another look at the information that was burned there. It looked like the outline of several rooms that were adjoining and underneath there were six letters, a space and then two more. The burned letters were quite big so that nearly covered the lower part of his abdomen.

Perhaps I won't have to kill him after all. At this rate, he may just off himself in the process of his obsession with the angel prophecy. I'd be blameless then, solving this little dilemma nicely.

103- *Sample*

Roger came knocking on Catherine's door early in the morning. Catherine was already awake but she was still lying in bed, mentally reviewing all that had happened since their arrival in Rome, when he interrupted.

"Yes?"

"It's Roger. May I have a moment?"

"Sure, give me a second."

Catherine got up, put her robe on and opened the door. "Sorry if I woke you, but I'm about to head to the site. I understand Beth is driving you to somewhere that you need to go to today."

"Yes, we have plans to visit a friend of mine later, at the Vatican."

"Well, I barely slept last night. It occurred to me that I have a good friend who may be able to determine something about the language your book is written in. His name is Luke Franklin. I was wondering if you'd mind if I send him a sample from the book? I have a scanner in my room and could email it to him before I leave, if you'd allow me?"

Catherine thought about it for a moment. "Do you trust him?"

"I understand the need for discretion here. I plan to simply send him a page of text without letting him in on the other little details unless he can really help us. I just need the book for a few moments, please."

"Sure Roger. One moment, I'll get the book." Catherine crossed to the heavy wood bureau in her room and grabbed the book that was still wrapped in a large scarf. "Here you go."

"Thanks Catherine. I will get this right back to you. My hope is Luke can get back to us later today. I'll return to the house after Beth brings you back here, so we can check in." With that he turned and left, disappearing into his room.

Catherine shut the door.

I hope this Luke can help us. Now, breakfast.

She slipped on a set of clothes and pulled her hair back in a ponytail. Once she went downstairs and into the kitchen, she realized that everyone else in her group was already up.

"Hey guys. I see you are all up early."

Catherine went over to a carafe and poured herself a cup of coffee.

As she sat down at the dining table, Erica started talking. "So did anything eventful happen last night? I figured I better ask now before we get too busy to discuss it."

"No, I slept well. Can't remember dreaming anything. It was nice to get a break. Maybe the angels took pity on me."

Catherine wasn't sure if the angels did or not, but she was happy for a tiny break. She turned to Joshua who was practically studying his bagel, rather than eating it.

"So how are you, Joshua? Are the angels treating you well today?"

Joshua stopped studying his food and looked at her. His demeanor shifted the moment he looked her in the eye. His face softened like that of a small child. Catherine realized just how special he was in that moment. Her fondness for him had certainly grown, and she respected his wonderful gifts.

"Yes, Catherine. The angels always treat me well."

"Of course they do. It was just a figure of speech. Do you have anything new from our friends today?"

"No, Catherine. No messages. But they do seem in very happy spirits today."

"Thank you, Joshua."

"Not a problem, sweet Catherine."

"Joshua, do you always speak in such endearments?"

"Uh, no. Well...at least when I'm addressing an angel, I do." Catherine smiled.

David interrupted the conversation with some details about their excursion. "So Beth will take in a couple of hours. No one arrives at the building I guess until around 9. I hope we can get some answers."

"Well I imagine we have to get something from him. He will help whether he wants to or not."

"I love a forceful woman who knows what she wants."

"You are such a clown, David."

He just grinned at her with his boyish face.

Erica jumped up exclaiming, "How about some breakfast before we go."

104- *Visitor*

Monsignor Bartholomew tossed and turned in his bed chamber. Suddenly he shot straight up in bed. "A nightmare, it was only a nightmare."

In the privacy of his room, he rose to perform the sacred angel calling ritual which he did each and every morning before he began his daily duties at the Vatican.

As he performed the steps of the ritual his mind was distracted by a convergence of thoughts and feelings about the coming days.

How can I help her without interfering? What if the darkness that is after her, comes calling for me? I am an old man. Can I hope to honor God and be courageous too?

A powerful voice interrupted his rambling thoughts. "Do not fear, Brother, for we are with you."

At the sound of the holy voice in his room, Bartholomew ecstatically fell to his knees.

"You honor me with your appearance today, oh holiest of God's servants. I am humbled by your presence."

"Arise dear Brother Bartholomew, I wish to speak with you."

Bartholomew rose to his feet as a bright sphere of light started to emanate from the center of the room growing larger and larger. Soon a form appeared before him. It was rare that an angel would manifest in the physical world, even for those of the Essene Brotherhood.

"Tell me how I might serve the glory of God."

"I am the Seraphim, *Ulian-naH*. I come to prepare you for a visit from the Child of Light who I am bound to serve in this world as her emissary to heaven. She will seek your audience today, and you shall allow her to come to you."

"She comes to see me today?" Bartholomew's heart started to pound now.

"Yes, Brother, she has many questions. Some of which you may answer and others you may not."

Bartholomew allowed doubt to creep in. "But how shall I know?"

"Be courageous. Have faith. You have been given knowledge of what you may share. Other information that must remain secret has not been given to the Essene. Thus there shall be no worry for divulging too much to her. She has the sacred angel book that only she can unlock, once she remembers how. This ability must return to her naturally. Since you have no immediate knowledge of how it works, you can share what you know, without regard for worry about crossing a line or interference with her free will. Even so, be prudent to only answer the questions asked to you directly."

Bartholomew rejoiced out loud. "Praised be to the ONE most high and his emissaries of light for their wisdom in this endeavor."

Bartholomew expected *Ulian-naH* to disappear, but she remained for another matter. "You have a blessed artifact that was given to you many, many years ago for safekeeping. You must have it with you today, and give it to Catherine to give to the Prophet when you see her.

He thought to ask the angel why, but thought better of it. "Yes, I shall do as you instruct me this morning."

"Very well, dear Brother. May peace be with you on this day."

Then in a flash of light, the Seraphim vanished.

105- *Outing*

Beth spoke excitedly as they parked the car on a very narrow street. "It's early yet for where you want to go, but I'll show you around Vatican City in the meantime. There's a whole corridor of wonderful shops a few blocks away. Wandering through some of them should help kill some time. The Pontifical Office of Justice and Peace is also within walking distance from here."

"Excellent!" Erica exclaimed.

Catherine enjoyed her friend's excitement. "Erica, you are so cute when you get excited."

Never skipping a beat, Erica answered her while quickly getting out of the car. "Thank you!"

They all followed Beth down the street. As they turned the corner, the Basilica of St. Peter came into full view. It was breathtaking. Catherine was taken aback.

"It's so beautiful, much more so to see in person. I had no idea."

Catherine felt a strange surge of sensation all over her body, like a rush of confirmation as she stood still taking in the scene with her eyes.

David came up behind Catherine and took her hand while whispering to her, "Yes it is, but not nearly as beautiful as you."

As his breath touched her ear, she blushed. Feeling uncomfortably shy at that moment, Catherine pulled David along to catch up to the others. Beth was in the lead, with Erica close behind followed by Joshua. When they caught up, Beth was discussing the merits of Italian pastry while pointing to a small shop nearby. Joshua seemed in his own world, as usual, and Erica was riveted by Beth's every word.

Everyone but Joshua filed inside the pastry shop. "Oh my, do you smell that?" Erica turned to Catherine.

"It smells wonderful." Catherine agreed.

David was already hungry again. "Do you want anything?"

"No, that's okay. I'm still full from breakfast. Knock yourself out though." Catherine laughed. "I'm just going to step outside for some air, and hang out with Joshua."

She stepped out into the morning light and stood next to Joshua who was watching locals and tourists go by.

"See anything interesting out here, Joshua?"

"No, just watching all the people stroll by and listening in my head. It's kind of one of my hobbies."

"I love watching people too. I find them fascinating. Sometimes you can tell a lot about people just by observing them."

Joshua agreed. "Life is often moving so fast that most people miss a lot of the details. I never want to miss anything important, so I try to just be in a single moment at a time to see what I see."

"That's so true Joshua. You know, you are a very wise man."

Joshua blushed and looked away. "Nah, I'm just a simple man trying to make do with what I've been given. That's all."

"Humble, too, I see."

"Perhaps, Catherine, perhaps. But I am nothing compared to you. I have been blessed to be a part of something bigger than the life I live, yet I am just like everyone else struggling to end their suffering day by day."

Catherine put her arm around Joshua. "The suffering I see is troubling too, Joshua. I just wonder what I could possibly do to end any of that."

Joshua did something unexpected and took her hand while looking deeply into her eyes. "Oh, but you can, sweet pea. Don't be afraid of what you do or do not know right now. Just take a leap of faith and your future will meet you straight away."

Catherine was astonished. Only her father ever called her sweet pea, and for just a tiny a moment he was standing there instead of Joshua. Tears came to her eyes as her heart melted with her feeling closer to her dad than she had in many years.

She whispered, "Dad? Is that you?"

Joshua winked at her, just like her dad used to and then his expression went blank. Joshua shook his head for a moment and saw Catherine had tears in her eyes.

"Are you okay, angel?"

Catherine wiped her eyes realizing that Joshua may not know what had just happened.

"Yes, Joshua, I am fine."

106- *Fury*

Razoul stirred in his bed. His head was pounding and he tried to lift himself up with his arms. As he focused on the room around him, he thought saw his mother Chiara standing there for a brief moment, and then she vanished.

He tried to recall the last thing he remembered.

It was nightfall and the physician was here to tend to me.

He looked at the clock on his bedside table. It was 8:35 a.m. Much of his intense pain had subsided now, but when he tried to rise from his bed, he was far too weak.

"Daniel! Daniel! Get in here!"

A few moments later, the boy entered with his head down.

"Don't just stand there boy, help me get out of this infernal bed."

Daniel nervously did what he was instructed and helped Razoul steady himself, even though he was far too small of a frame for the task. He helped Razoul over to his sitting chair.

"Now fetch me some clothes, boy. After that, go fetch Sirius! I need to speak with him immediately."

Daniel scurried around the room getting Razoul a change of clothes. He put them on the table next to Razoul and hastily left.

Razoul struggled to get himself dressed before Sirius arrived.

When Sirius knocked he was fully dressed except for his shoes.

"What took you so long, old man?" Razoul asked.

"I came as quickly as possible." He was shocked to see Razoul dressed and standing before him.

Razoul just stared at him accusing, "So whose idea was it to drug me last night?"

"The physician felt you must rest. He was very concerned for your well-being. I had no knowledge of this prior to his doing it, but after he explained it to me, I supported his decision. You needed time to mend after your ordeal."

Sirius expected more of a fight from Razoul, but when he simply said, "Very well," Sirius knew that Razoul was more injured than he would allow himself or anyone to see.

"So do you have a plan for securing the document you seek?"

"Yes, of course, Sirius. There is a priest by the name of Father Renaldo Ignatius in Vatican City. I need him found and dispatched here as soon as possible."

"You believe he can get us access?"

"He will have no choice…unless he wants his little secret exposed."

Sirius was very used to using such leverage to get the Malem Tutela whatever they required. "Very well, I will send for him."

"Good, now get my servants to bring me some food. I am starving."

Sirius left quickly. After he crossed the doorway of Razoul's outer chamber, he saw Thaddeus coming down the hallway. "Ah, Thaddeus you look well."

"As well as I can be, Sirius. How is Razoul?"

"Not well. After his last run in with Samyaza, he's been slower to mend. But despite his many injuries, he's as vigilant as ever."

Thaddeus poured on his most exaggerated sarcasm for his next comment. "Nothing can take down the mighty Razoul, not even a fierce Fallen One. But one must hold on to a dream at times, that something could squash him like a little bug!"

"Be that as it may Thaddeus, this is what we have. I am on my way to send a man to find Father Renaldo Ignatius at the Vatican. Razoul wishes to see him immediately."

"Surely you are not entertaining this fantasy of getting into the Vatican?"

"Razoul believes we do not have to. He believes the priest will help us."

Thaddeus resigned himself to the task at hand. "Fine, I will fetch him myself."

"Ah, good to have you on board Thaddeus, this pleases me."

Thaddeus turned to leave, grumbling under his breath. "For now, old man..."

107- *Query*

Luke Franklin was already busy checking things off his to do list. He looked out the window of his chateau at the French countryside for a moment and then decided to check his email.

After deleting a dozen or so advertisements, he saw an unexpected email from Roger Thornton. He and Roger had worked together on an excavation site in Egypt over three years ago. It had been quite some time since they had spoken.

Luke's long term project, a translation for a wealthy client, had consumed much of his time lately. He pulled up Roger's email and took a sip of his coffee. He barely read the email before clicking the attached file. When it finally loaded, he nearly dropped his mug in his lap, spilling hot coffee on his pants.

He shot up out of his chair spastically. "Jesus Christ! Damn, that's hot!" He ran into the kitchen with coffee dripping everywhere and tossed the mug into the sink. He grabbed a hand towel, wet it, and started to wipe his hands and khakis off.

"I'd better just change my pants."

During this flurry of activity, Luke's heart was pounding not from the searing coffee, but from the document Roger had sent.

Could it really be what I thought it was?

Luke fumbled with a new pair of pants and hurried back to the computer. When he sat down in front of it, he was astonished to see several sketched characters of a theoretical language that no one had seen a real living example of in written form in its entirety. It was called the Language of Light. Luke had theorized that this was due to the language being more tonal or vibrationally based than a written one.

Where did the old boy get this? Astonishing...this could be the linguistic find of the century! Could this really be happening? If I can translate this, I'll be famous.

Luke quickly looked up Roger's number and dialed it. It rang and rang. The voicemail eventually picked up. "Roger, I just received your email. You must call me right away!"

Luke hung up the phone disappointed. He emailed him back to cover both bases, in order to connect with him as quickly as possible. Then he printed the sheet Roger sent him and began to translate what he could.

108- *Little One*

"Oh, I'd love to check that out if we have time." Erica exclaimed pointing at another quaint shop across the street.

Beth checked out the watch on her wrist. "Yes, we should have time. What do you think, Catherine?"

She thought about it for a moment and decided not to join them. "Why don't you guys go ahead and we'll meet back here so we can head to see the Monsignor together? Let's say in 30 minutes?"

"Okay crew, let's go." Beth started walking off motioning to Erica and Joshua. Soon she was disappearing out of sight with both following close behind. David stayed back to be with Catherine.

"Where does Beth get that kind of energy?" David remarked.

"Not sure but she's got enough for all of us I think."

"Shall we, madam?" David offered his arm to her like a gentleman.

"Well by all means, kind sir." Catherine took him arm. "So where shall we go?"

"Let's head this way but definitely remember our way. I'd hate to get turned around and get us lost. These narrow streets all look so similar to me, but I think I can handle it."

"I trust you, David."

"I'm glad. Even though wandering around here is a bit like the blind leading the blind."

"Oh yes, it sure is."

Catherine saw an apothecary shop up the street from where they were. "Let's go inside there," she pointed.

The shop was much bigger than it appeared to be from the street. There were many aisles with all kinds of homemade remedies, herbs and other items. The colored bottles on the shelves caught the morning light and Catherine thought they were beautiful. She stopped to admire them as David continued wandering around the shop.

Catherine felt a light tug on her shirt and turned around.

"My name is Alice." The young girl curtsied.

"Well hello, Alice. It's very nice to meet you."

"Did you know that I am very good at guessing people's names?"

Catherine was mesmerized by the young girl. Her eyes spoke volumes, and she was as precious as a little cherub. There was something very familiar about her, and Catherine strained to remember why.

"I'll bet you are very good at that Alice."

"Do you want me to show you?"

"Sure sweetie. Go ahead." Catherine looked around for the girl's parents and spotted David just a couple aisles over from her. He turned and waved to her sweetly.

Alice closed her eyes as if she was thinking really hard and Catherine waited with anticipation.

Then she opened her eyes. Catherine thought they seemed to sparkle more than would be normal.

"I bet that your name is Catherine."

"Wow, Alice, how did you know my name?"

"I told you I was good at this, Ms. Catherine."

"Yes you did, sweetie. I'm just very impressed."

They stood there for the longest time, staring at each other without saying a word. David came up to see who she was talking to. “Hey, who were you talking to just a moment ago?”

Catherine turned toward Alice to introduce them, but she was not there. “Now where did she go? We were just talking.”

“Who?”

“This pretty little girl came up to me, she told me her name was Alice. She said she was good at guessing people’s names. And she did, which blew my mind. I was about to ask her something when you walked up. She has to be around here somewhere. No one came or went.”

Catherine went to the end of the aisle and crossed the store to look down all the other rows. None of them contained the girl. “Alice? Alice, where are you, honey?”

“May I help you, Senora? Are you looking for your child?” The shopkeeper was a heavy set man in dark pants and a frilly long sleeved shirt.

“Oh no, sir, I was just talking to a little girl who was here. Is she perhaps your daughter?”

“I have no children in my life, not for a very long time now.”

David leaned in to talk to Catherine. “Maybe she went out a different way?”

“She was just here, David, how can she just disappear? Yet another mystery in my crazy life.”

”It’s getting close to time to head back. We probably should get moving.”

Catherine was puzzled but nodded to David anyway.

They thanked the shopkeeper for his time and left to meet up with the others.

109- *The Priest*

“Signore, could you please tell me why I was summoned here so hastily? I don’t understand what business Mr. Bugiardini would have with me.” The young priest looked worried. He knew the reputation of the family and wanted no part of their affairs, spiritually or otherwise.

“I am sorry, Father, but I really must allow him to consult with you privately about this matter.”

"Are you certain that he sent for me and not someone else?"

Thaddeus stopped for a moment in the middle of the stairs that ascended to the 3rd floor of the house. "Father, does it truly matter? Are you not a man of God, a devoted servant of his people on earth?"

"Of course, of course, Signore. Please take me to Mr. Bugiardini now. I will cease asking anymore questions. I am here to be of service."

Thaddeus was pleased to have the Father still his tongue. He was tired of averting his questions. It amused him slightly that the priest was so nervous to meet Razoul.

As well he should be…but he doesn't need to know that just now.

They reached the top landing. Thaddeus led him to the library where Razoul would see him. After opening the French doors, he motioned for the priest to enter ahead of him.

"Please be seated. I will let the master know you've arrived."

Thaddeus watched the priest sit down to hesitantly wait for Razoul. He left the room facing the priest as he swung the doors shut. Sirius met him in the hallway.

"Well that was fun. The priest is as nervous as a cat chained to a dog. He's waiting for him now in the library. Shall I notify Razoul?"

"No, I was headed to his chambers to give him the medicinal items the physician left for him. I will inform him myself."

Thaddeus imparted a bow of his head and left.

Sirius hurried down the hallway and arrived at Razoul's private chambers. "Razoul? It's Sirius," he announced as he entered the room. "I have your medicinal items and I am happy to inform you that the priest has arrived. Thaddeus took him to wait for you in the library."

Razoul entered the room impeccably dressed as if he were about to meet the Queen of England or the Pope. Sirius couldn't believe the amount of time Razoul spent on his outer appearance. If his goal was to intimidate the priest upon first look, he would be successful.

"Thank you Sirius. You should sit in on our discussion. I think you'll be most impressed."

Sirius nodded as Razoul took two vials of medicinal preparations. He grimaced on the second vial due to its heavy bitter taste. "Disgusting!" Razoul turned and swiftly left his room heading toward the library with Sirius following closely behind him.

110- *While in Rome*

Catherine's mouth dropped open as the five of them stepped inside the building where Monsignor Bartholomew's office was located. She admired the towering pillars and extravagant features of the main hall.

This was the first time that Catherine had experienced such ornate architecture in person. She could hear Erica behind her clicking images with her camera phone.

On the far side of the main hall was a beautiful marble counter that looked almost like the front desk at a hotel instead of a building that housed a bunch of priests.

Catherine crossed the hall to inquire at the information desk. They were greeted by an older priest who was already standing there. With a very heavy Italian accent, he greeted her as she approached.

"May I help?"

"Yes, Father, I am looking for Monsignor Bartholomew's office?"

There was a slight delay from the priest then he said, "Si' Si', his office is here."

"I'd like to see him, please."

The priest studied her suspiciously. "Your name, please?"

"My name is Catherine Moore."

The priest took out a ledger appointment book. Catherine was disheartened to think she needed an appointment.

"Ah, Signora Moore! Importante! You are expected." He motioned for her to follow him, but Catherine didn't follow.

"Monsignor was expecting me?" She wanted to be sure she heard him right.

"Si' there is an appointment in his book for you, and the instruction to bring you quickly to him once you arrive. We must go this way now."

This surprised everyone but Beth. "Well, I'm going to wait out here until you all are done."

The rest of them followed the priest up the staircase toward Bartholomew's office.

When they arrived outside the office door, the priest allowed Catherine ahead of him, but stopped the others. "Uno, only one may come. The rest of you must wait here."

David nodded to the priest and looked at Catherine who appeared upset about this particular detail. "It's okay, Catherine. Go. If you need us, we'll be right out here waiting for you."

"Okay, David. I'll speak to him and if I need you, I'll come get you."

Catherine's heart was pounding and she had to catch her breath. The priest called to the Monsignor and announced her arrival. In just a few moments, the priest was gone.

When she walked out of the entryway, she saw Monsignor Bartholomew seated at his desk writing something down. Catherine felt that she shouldn't interrupt whatever he was finishing. She studied his appearance for a moment. He had short black hair peppered with silver grey, and was wearing a full length black tunic with a priest collar and a small round cap. Catherine thought he was in his early 60s.

Even though she had seen him before during her out of body experience, she expected herself to be wrong, somehow. In her self-doubt, she expected someone else to be seated there. But here he was looking exactly as he did during her experience on the airplane. The only key difference was what he was wearing. He was clothed in his priestly attire instead of a long brown robe with a hood.

A moment later, he finished writing and looked up at her. As he laid eyes on her for the first time his face lit up. "Oh, Catherine, come in, come in." He rose from his chair to greet her. "Please sit down, my dear."

"I understand that you were expecting me, Monsignor?" She shook his hand, her grip was shaky.

He sat back down in his high backed leather office chair before speaking to her. "Yes, Catherine. I was expecting you today."

"How is that possible Monsignor? I didn't make an appointment with you, and we haven't met before, that I know of?"

"Perhaps how I know is more a waste of time, than the other questions you come to me with today. I know you have been burdened with many of them. I hope I can help you."

"Burdened isn't really the half of it Monsignor, to tell you the truth."

He looked at her empathetically. "I am sure all this has been difficult for you, my child."

"I guess I will start from the beginning then. There was a series of unexplainable events some weeks ago which led me to return to my home town to look for some answers. That journey led me to visit the convent that my parents adopted me from. You see, they died tragically in a car accident when I was a teenager. I didn't know the circumstances of how I came to be at the convent and then adopted by my parents. The day that I arrived at the convent, a Sister Mary Eleanor was expecting me in possibly the same way you were today. I sat with her for a short time and she told me things I didn't fully understand at the time. She was quite frail and I didn't want to press her too much for answers. Then I returned a day or so later to speak with her again, she was already gone." Tears started to well up in Catherine's eyes but she held them back.

Bartholomew made the sign of the cross at the mention of the sister's death.

"Even though she was gone, I didn't leave that second visit empty handed. At the convent, Sister Elizabeth gave me a box with a very unusual book inside. It was found under Sister Mary Eleanor's bed with instructions to give it to me."

"Ah, yes, the Angelus Aevum," Bartholomew added.

"I did learn that Angelus Aevum essentially means *Angel Incarnate or Incarnate Angel*"

"Yes, it does."

"Well what else can you tell me about this strange book? Or can you tell me why it literally glows when I touch it? I know it sounds weird." Catherine stood up and walked over to a window looking down at crowds of people moving through the city below them. Monsignor Bartholomew didn't answer her right away and appeared to be thinking carefully about how to respond when Catherine turned from the window to add, "Besides, what good is this book if I can't read it?"

He looked at her seriously, yet sincerely. "First, I can tell you that you are the only one who can use the book for its intended purpose."

"And what would that be?" Catherine's head was spinning and she tried to compose herself.

"Let's start with other matters first, if I may. Just remember that you must keep the book safe. No one can be allowed to take it because it's the only one of its kind."

"Of course. Can you please tell me about the Malem Tutela?"

He looked startled at her mentioning them directly. "How do you know of them?"

"Maybe it's less important how I know of them than why they're after me."

Her quick response upped the ante. "The Malem Tutela is a clandestine group who seek to use the powers of darkness for their own gain. These men have been around for a very long time. The organization is now run by a dangerous young man by the name of Razoul Bugiardini. His father was murdered recently, and so Razoul is now in power."

"Why do they want me?"

"There's no other delicate way to say this, Catherine, they mean to kill you before...." Then he stopped himself.

"Before what? Monsignor, please tell me what is happening to me!"

"You are rapidly changing. Once the change is complete, they will not be able to harm you."

"Are you saying I will be invincible?" Her eyes were now wide.

"You will be powerful and able to protect yourself if necessary from extreme harm. Perhaps I should start elsewhere, allow me to tell you a little story." Catherine settled down to listen to him.

"In ancient times, before the time of Christ, a powerful prophecy was given to a holy man by an angelic messenger who appeared to him during his daily prayer session. The angels instructed him to record the information that he was to receive and to conceal it from others who live against God. This holy man was a part of a spiritual community called the Essene. Since that day, the various generations of Essene people throughout the ages, have safeguarded this prophecy. And we were successful until recently. Somehow the Malem Tutela discovered the secret, which we thought would not happen. Razoul's father tried to steal the angel scroll before it was hidden from this world and he failed. Razoul is trying to stop the prophecy before it becomes fulfilled. I am unsure how, but I suspect that he acquired some of this information from the estate of John Dee after his death."

"Yes I know about John Dee. He keeps coming up in my research."

"Yes. He was successful and received a great deal of information from the angels. He was not an evil man as he only sought knowledge for its own sake. He died nearly destitute, and his estate was auctioned. Perhaps he learned that some information is simply not meant to be known."

Catherine added. "While trying to figure all this out, I learned about John Dee because we thought the language in the book was Enochian script."

"Yes, but the book itself is not written in Enochian script. It is written in another language that only an angel can decipher."

"So tell me about the prophecy, Monsignor, and why I'm in the middle of it."

He folded his hands thinking for a moment. "I will tell you the prophecy, Catherine, but it is up to you to decide how it applies to you. All human beings are given free will by God leaving us to determine our own path toward righteousness. The prophecy was first revealed to an ancient Essene holy man and was regarding the first angel to be born into the world as a human being."

"I was always taught in Catholic school that angels never come to this world as human beings."

"That has been historically true. But the messenger angel foretold a time when the world would change greatly, and need the angel's to serve them in a direct manner."

"I see. Please go on."

How can I be this angel? I am just an ordinary woman.

"So the prophecy said that a chosen angel or specifically a *Child of Light* would come down from the rank of Seraphim in heaven. Not an ordinary angel, but one that could be born of flesh and blood. This angel would journey into the human world in order to open a door to heaven for those suffering on the Earth. The prophecy also said that it would be a difficult journey because becoming human creates an illusion that we are separate from God. In essence, this angel would forget who she was by becoming human, and then have to remember who she truly is, all over again."

Catherine wrapped her head around the specifics of the prophecy. It wasn't as if what he said surprised her with everything that had been happening lately, especially after sweet Joshua's convinced she was a real live angel.

"So everyone apparently believes that I'm the angel of the prophecy? Wow, no pressure. What if I'm not? What if everyone is wrong?" Catherine stood up in exasperation.

"What truly matters is what you believe in your heart, my dear. Unless you believe, it doesn't matter what the prophet or myself or even the Malem Tutela think about you."

"So I guess if the angel fulfills this mission, it would be very bad for people like them?"

"Of course it would. They seek to destroy light, and we seek to protect it."

"I see. So was Sister Mary Eleanor an Essene?"

"Yes, through a very long line in her family."

"And you too?"

"Yes, Catherine."

"So Sister Mary Eleanor gave the book to me because she believed I am the angel in the Essene prophecy? Where did this book that I am safeguarding come from?"

"I don't know exactly, but I know that it was given to Sister Mary Eleanor's grandmother and then passed on to her so that it could be used during this important time."

"Did she know what it was to be used for?"

"To my knowledge specific information on the book's use was not given to her or her grandmother by the angels. What I do know about the book, which I can share, is about the language it's written in. There is no other book that exists in the world that has been written in this lost language. The book contains specific codes and instructions for the Incarnate Angel to bring down the barriers between heaven and Earth. It also contains energies that will help awaken the angel to her true purpose. If the Malem Tutela were to learn of its existence, they would want it. That's why I would trust only those who have proven themselves worthy. Be very careful."

Catherine thought of the page that Roger had sent to his friend, but pushed it out of her mind in order to ask another question.

"We came to Italy at the request of an archaeologist named Roger Thornton. He wanted to see the book. It was a fluke that a professor we originally consulted with about the book is a friend of Roger's. We became connected because the professor knew of an archaeological discovery of Roger's last year. Roger says that a hidden series of chambers was accidentally discovered at the catacombs of San Pancrazio, and that he had found markings in these chambers that also appeared in the book."

Bartholomew's face showed a small amount of surprise. "I doubt this was a fluke, as you say, but these chambers bear angelic markings?"

"Yes, we are supposed to go there later today to see the site."

"Interesting. I will consult with my brothers and sisters later regarding this information and let you know if I discover anything helpful to you. Where can I find you?"

"Here, let me give you my cell number. I think its best that few people know where we are staying at the moment."

"Yes, child, you are right. Please tell no one of the Essene presence in Italy and remember that even if you do not see us, we are still there watching over you your entire life. Because of our faith, we believe in you, even if you do not."

Bartholomew reached into the pocket of his robe and held out a small box for her to take. "Please give this to the Angel's Prophet. I am doing this as instructed by the Seraphim. He will understand."

She slipped the box into her purse. "Of course. Thank you, Monsignor." Catherine left to return to her friends who were anxiously awaiting her arrival.

111- *Dark Bargain*

Razoul entered the library with his usual vibrato and force. Sirius was close in step behind him, following silently. The priest looked like a deer caught in the headlights.

"Hello, Father Ignatius. I hope I haven't kept you waiting too long?"

Razoul poured himself a glass of brandy. "Would you like a drink, Father?"

"No thank you."

"Alright then, we'll get to business." He sat in a chair across from him.

Razoul enjoyed watching the priest become uncomfortable. "You look a little pale. Are you okay?" He enjoyed playing with his prey.

"Yes, I am fine, Mr. Bugiardini. I would, however, appreciate it if you'd let me know why I've been summoned here."

"A direct priest. I like that. Very well, I've asked you here because I have a serious problem that I believe you can help me with."

The priest assumed he understood what Razoul was leading into. "If you have anything you'd like to confess, my son, of course I am here to help you."

Razoul let out a burst of laughter that hurt his ribs terribly, an oddly satisfying feeling.

"Oh no, Father, I have nothing at all to confess to you of all people. I just have a photograph I'd like you to take a look at."

"I don't understand, sir."

"You will shortly, I promise." Razoul went to his desk and produced a drawing of the map layout and letters that were hidden underneath his shirt and jacket.

"What can you tell me about this?" He handed the paper to Father Ignatius and went to pour himself another drink.

The priest studied it. "This design looks familiar somehow, but I can't place it."

"Give it a little time, Father. I imagine that you have a shred of intelligence underneath that cloak of God that you wear."

Father Ignatius' face glowed with fear, fueling Razoul's prowess. "What does this have to do with me?"

"I heard about your new appointment. You recently obtained a position working for Cardinal Vespucci, the chancellor in charge of managing access to the Vatican archives."

"If there's a document copy you require sir, you need only put your request in writing to our office."

"Ah, see, that is my quite serious problem, Father. I require this document right now, not three weeks from now, which is customary."

The priest stood up foolishly to try to leave. "I am sorry sir, I cannot put you at the top of the list, but I can request your request be expedited if you wish."

Razoul rose and stepped towards the priest, towering over him. The priest immediately sat back down, while an arrogant smirk spread across Razoul's face.

"I believe, Father, that you *will* bring me the document that is designated on that piece of paper you hold."

The priest stammered. "Why would I do something like that? Signore, the official documents must never be removed from the Vatican, under any circumstances. As an Italian, surely you know this. You must know that what you are asking me to do is...is...impossibilità!" Father Ignatius feverishly shook his head.

Razoul pointed his finger at him. "You *will* do this for me, priest."

"No, No, I cannot. I am not even permitted to enter the new secured archive personally. How can you expect me to make you a copy of it? How do you expect me to do this unspeakable offense against the Church?"

Razoul ignored the priest pleading for him to be sensible. "I learned a long time ago that priests can be very resourceful when they want to bend the rules to suit their own needs. And believe me; this matter serves your needs, as well as mine."

Mustering the last of his will, Father Ignatius rose. "I cannot do this for you Signore, and I will not. If that will be all, I must go!"

Razoul erupted at the priest, who was only a foot away from him. "SIT DOWN PRIEST! I am not finished with you yet." The priest cowered quickly and sat as commanded.

Razoul turned to Sirius who had been standing there watching the whole play developing before him without saying a word. "Sirius, there is a woman downstairs waiting for me. She believes that she is here to secure employment; however, I'd just love for Father Ignatius to meet her. Please go get her and bring her up."

Sirius left the room.

"Please Signore, I beg you to reconsider what you are asking of me. I cannot steal from the holy church. It is impossible."

"Well, for your sake I hope you are mistaken about that, but I believe you will change your mind in just a few minutes." There was a short knock at the door. "Yes, Sirius, please bring her in. I have someone I'd like you to meet priest."

When Father Ignatius saw the woman, he turned white. There was a similar reaction on her part. She was terribly confused as well.

"I believe you two know each other."

The woman shook her head no, and so did the priest.

"Now, priest, isn't it a sin before God to lie? Of course, you are guilty of much, much more than a simple lie."

The priest finally understood Razoul's game, and he hung his head.

"Sirius, you may show the woman out."

The woman was so shocked that she didn't say a single word. She shot a sorrowful look at Father Ignatius as she turned to go.

"So are you ready to discuss this matter with me Father?"

Father Ignatius was defeated. He nodded yes.

"Good, because I know all there is to know about your forbidden love for that woman and your bastard son that you've been hiding in Palermo as well. I would hate for anything to happen to either of them."

"Don't harm them, it is my sin. They are innocent. I will do what you ask."

"Do you have a plan then, Father?"

"It will be difficult and require me to forge official documents from the Cardinal himself. The Cardinal leaves on official business tomorrow morning. I think I can forge the paperwork and process it as soon as he leaves. As long as no one questions the paperwork, the document will be securely delivered to his office within 24 hours."

"And when does the Cardinal return?"

"Not until three days after that."

Razoul came over and patted him on the back a little too roughly. "Very good, priest. I knew you were a very smart man. Bring the document to me as soon as you get your hands on it."

"I will do my best." The priest got up to leave, taking the paper with him. He slipped it shakily into his pocket.

Razoul grabbed him by the shoulders and kissed him forcibly on one cheek and then another. As Razoul pulled away, he whispered to him. "Pray you don't fail me, priest. Otherwise I'll make you wish you were burning in hell, with your sweet, precious family."

112-*Discovery*

"Luke? Can you hear me, Luke?"

"Yes, Roger, I do. I'm so glad you called back. I have been studying your sketches all day waiting for you."

"Sorry, I've been out of cell range, several feet underground. Just got signal back and it's still choppy."

"Still slumming around Italian catacombs?"

"You know me, Luke, if it's not subterranean then count me out!"

"Yes, I remember all too well. Glad I got out while I could."

"So I'm dying to know, what do you think about the images I sent this morning?"

"It's extraordinary to say the least. Where did you get this? Please tell me you have more."

"How would you like the chance to see a leather-bound book of at least 600 pages, just like the few sketches I sent? Sorry I couldn't scan a whole page... my scanner was on the fritz. Couldn't get any of the pages to scan." Roger taunted.

"Are you kidding me?"

"It's at my house along with the owner of the book and her friends."

"This is quite possibly one of the most amazing discoveries ever made. One I never thought I'd see in my lifetime. The Language of Light was thought to be lost forever, kind of like the white whale of linguistics or Shangri-La. This could prove my original thesis!"

"How quickly can you get to Rome?"

113-*Debrief*

"This goes without saying, but nothing I share with you all can leave our little group. I don't think at this point we should chance, it or trust anyone but ourselves." Catherine was finally back at the villa with her confidants.

"My book is more than rare. It's one of a kind. We must protect it at all costs. One of us must have the book close to them at all times. And we need to find a hiding place somewhere on the grounds for when we are away. It's too risky to take it wherever we go."

"The book has been handed down from the Essene community. They were a group of spiritual practitioners in ancient times before Jesus was born. They communicated with and honored the angels every day. "

Erica interrupted, "The Essenes were thought to be the creators of the Dead Sea Scrolls that were found in the 1950's, right?"

"That's right." Catherine continued, "There was holy man who received a prophecy one day. He was told that an angel that the prophecy calls the Child of Light would be born. The angel would appear to be just like any other human, and then there was something about the angel bringing heaven to Earth, whatever that means."

"Wow, that's deep," Erica exclaimed.

"Everyone thinks I am the prophesized angel in human form. That's why they're after me."

"So how did Monsignor Bartholomew become a part of all this?" David asked.

"He's a modern counterpart of the Essene ancestry that is secretly active in the world today. So was Sister Mary Eleanor. They swore an oath to protect the Angel Scroll containing the prophecy, ever since it was given to them. He also said the Malem Tutela somehow discovered the prophecy and want to stop it."

"Oh this is bad, Catherine. We need to get some help protecting you." David proposed, concerned.

"We do have help. He said that the Essene Brotherhood has been and will continue to watch over me."

"Do they have machine guns?" David blurted out.

"Alright, calm down. He didn't think the Malem Tutela could find us at the moment, so we're okay for now. We do need to keep a low profile. I know we need to go to Roger's dig site this afternoon. I don't know why, but it's very important that we do. Bartholomew said that he didn't know about the chambers and would consult the others. And Joshua, he gave me this for you." Catherine handed him the small box as Roger came into view.

Roger greeted them. "Hey, everyone, how was your morning?"

"Delightful!" Catherine answered for the group.

"That's great. Did you get your business taken care of?"

"Yes I did, thanks to Beth."

"Speaking of? Where is she?" Roger looked back toward the kitchen windows.

"She went upstairs to clean up before we all chip in to make lunch."

"I better get cleaned up too. I'll see you inside." Roger rushed inside to go upstairs.

Erica spoke up after he disappeared. "He's awfully chipper today. I mean he's a very agreeable guy anyway, but he looks like he's got ants in his pants the way he's buzzing around."

Catherine wondered about how much she could trust Roger. Monsignor's words weighed heavily on her, and she was weary to trust anyone.

Joshua broke his usual silence as if he knew her struggle. "Well it's a very good day because you know more than you did when we got up this morning."

Catherine smiled and put her hand on his arm. "You are so right, Joshua. It really is. Thank you for reminding me."

It was then that Catherine fully realized how much she could learn from looking at the world through Joshua's eyes.

114- *Face Off*

Ashiyah stood in her marble kitchen and poured a cup of jasmine tea for herself. She had been monitoring the current conflict as fully as she could, while annoyed with the angel's little distortion tricks.

She was so deeply inside the Akashic Record as she stirred her tea, that she didn't realize someone was in the room with her until she returned to the present moment.

Without even turning around to look she calmly stated, "Hello, sweet sister. I've been expecting you for a while now."

"So sorry to keep you waiting."

"Would you like some tea?"

"Well it is the civilized thing to do." Her sister pulled up a chair at the far end of the table and sat down.

Ashiyah grabbed another porcelain mug and poured the tea for her.

For a while they sat there drinking their cups of tea, each seated on the furthest ends of her rectangular dining table, staring at each other.

It was Ashiyah that spoke first. "Even though I don't need to ask, what have you been up to?"

"Small talk? Really, sister? Come on."

"Then what is it? Why have you come?"

"I have come in peace to ask you to join me."

"Join you? That's a new one."

"You are quite literally the queen of neutrality, as we well know. But given the current situation that seems to be unfolding in your own backyard, I decided it was worth it to try."

Ashiyah studied her immortal sister carefully, intent on revealing her intentions.

"And of course I knew where to find you, in this fortress hidden from the world, just a dull reflection of who you once were. Oh yeah, where is the man pet you serve? Such a shame about the father, though..." Her lips exaggerated a pout to feign sadness over Britius' death."

Her sarcastic prodding proved too much for Ashiyah. "Pandora, enough! You come into my sanctuary and dare insult his name?"

"Insult who? That pathetic human man who convinced you that the world should just forget the old ways? Then to top it off, you let him imprison you? The ancient humans consulted you about every important move they made. You had legions of seers connecting to your domain and paying homage to you to enter! You could have used this powerful arena as your playground, yet instead you cower in the shadows like a fool."

"You are still a spoiled little child, Pandora. How can you have so little wisdom after the centuries that have passed in this world?"

"You will see how wise I truly am, soon enough."

"Oh? I thought it was beneath even you to meddle in the petty affairs of humans."

"Generally true, unless I'm bored and decide to incite a riot or two just for fun of it. But in this case, how can I stand idly by while an angel descends to Earth and threatens my domain?"

"How is the Incarnate Angel a threat to you? I can see why Razoul feels threatened. He stands on the shadow side of the Akasha and she stands firmly on the opposite. But why do you care?"

"Are you always so short-sighted? What do you think will happen to my little toy sand box if she succeeds in connecting heaven and Earth?"

Ashiyah looked at her with compassionate eyes. "How sad for you that you feel the entire human race exists simply for you and you alone. You seriously need to get a handle on your ego."

Pandora glared at her fiercely and stood up.

"I gave them everything they ever wanted and then they conveniently turned their backs on me. They blamed me for unleashing the horrors of the world. Me! You know as well as I do, that all the horrors humans of this world experience are self-created. They are nothing but these ungrateful, pathetic creatures. Therefore, I plan to take their special little prize away from them. Let them see how it feels to be cast into the shadows."

"This is about revenge? Can't you find something better to do with your time? Go create something useful for once." Ashiyah pleaded with Pandora to use reason.

"You are one to talk, Ashiyah. You sit in your convenient mode of neutrality, using it as an excuse for hiding out, fading into a distant memory. You are an immortal like me. You should act like one."

"Should I act like an angry little girl then, just like you?"

"I am no child!" Pandora's created a ball of white fire and hurled it at Ashiyah.

Ashiyah caught it in her hands with little effort. She rubbed her hands together and put it out. "Now, now, Pandora, you know you can't hurt me." Then she added. "Although you'd probably really like to."

Pandora knew it would turn out this way. "Support me sister, this is all I am asking you for."

"Why do you need my approval now?"

"You are so predictable Ashiyah. You always answer a simple question with another question."

"Perhaps I am as predictable as the passage of time. But would I be any other way? I do not exist to serve mankind. I exist to hold in balance the recording of each human moment that has passed or will ever pass. How could I take sides when I have that kind of responsibility?"

An evil grin spread across Pandora's face. "Well, we shall see if you take sides soon."

"What do you mean?"

"Your little pet is after the same prize I am, and I guarantee I will not allow him to impede my endeavor in any way. Either Razoul stands down or I will crush him. Then what will poor Ashiyah do? You'll be cast out of your sanctuary forever."

"You wouldn't dare." Ashiyah whispered.

"Oh, I would dare? Once I get done dangling the angel's pathetic friend as bait to draw her into my little web, I'll be back for your benefactor. I would warn him to stay away from her if I were you!"

Before Ashiyah could raise an objection, Pandora vanished.

115- *Sword of God*

The whole crew at Casale Valdichiascio was running around gathering up gear. They were almost ready to leave for the dig site. Catherine was upstairs brushing her hair, when someone knocked on her door.

"Hi Joshua. What's up?"

"You wanted to see my gift from the Monsignor, and I need to tell you something."

"Yes, come in. Come in." Catherine shut the door. "What did you need to tell me?"

"You were saying we needed a good hiding place for the book while we are away. Well I guess I'm kind of an expert at that. I think I found the perfect place. It's outside the house, hidden, and it won't get wet either!"

"That's wonderful. Sounds absolutely perfect!"

He bowed to her. "It is a pleasure to serve you, angel."

Catherine played along and curtseyed in her pair of khaki shorts. "It is indeed a pleasure to help you as well, my friend." Then she stopped kidding around.

"And now, the gift."

He handed her the box. She opened it. Inside was the most beautiful round Christian amulet with a symbol she didn't recognize. "What is this image? Do you know?"

"I don't know, but the angels told me the necklace is the Sigil of Archangel Michael. He's the Sword of God! I guess they wanted me to have it." He was like beaming child.

"Well, something this important shouldn't be hidden away in a box you know. Please turn around." She fastened the amulet around his neck. "There, that's better." She pulled him over to the mirror. "Well, what do you think?"

"Oh, it is better! I feel so strong now. I don't know why I didn't put it on right away. Only one thing though."

Catherine watched him as he put it underneath his shirt. "I need it by my heart so I will be fearless like Michael."

"Oh, Joshua, you are so wonderful." Catherine threw her arms around his neck and held him tight. When she pulled away finally, his face was flushed red. "Are you okay?"

He looked at her sheepishly, and then said, "Well it's not every day I get an angel hug. Warn me next time, would you please?"

"Sure, honey."

Catherine heard the others heading downstairs. David called to her to let her know it was time. "Be right there!"

She turned to Joshua. "How long will it take you to hide the book?"

"Oh, it will take me just a few minutes."

"Okay, I'll go down and make sure the rooms are clear. When you hear me slam the door, come down and go out the back door with the book. I'll tell the others you'll join us in a few minutes."

"Okay, Catherine, no problem."

Catherine hurried downstairs and looked around. She slammed the door behind her and joined everyone in the car.

Catherine slid in next to Erica who was seated in the back.

"Where's Joshua?"

"Oh, he said he needed to use the restroom before we go."

"I can't wait for you to see the chambers, Catherine. You'll find the similarities uncanny," Roger boasted. "Oh yes, speaking of your book. My friend Luke is very excited about it and is on his way to Italy in the next day or two."

Catherine felt weary about involving someone else, but realized that the damage was done. She decided to make the best of it. Thankfully Joshua had found a great spot to hide it from now on.

"That's great. Did he know the language?"

"Yes, that's the unbelievable part. He said it's the lost Language of Light."

"Really?"

"Yes, he never expected to see a full passage of it written anywhere. He nearly flipped when I said you have a full 600 page book."

David and Erica shared a glance of concern.

"I'm sure he'll be a big help."

"If I know him, he'll be virtually obsessed."

"Uh, Roger, Luke won't mention this to anyone will he? I mean, for now I'd like to keep the book between us and not involve anyone else."

"I understand. I assure you that Luke will exercise the utmost discretion."

116- *Leak*

Luke Franklin packed quickly after speaking to Roger. He didn't want to waste any time arriving in Rome. There was one more flight leaving in a few hours that would get him to Italy by evening. If he hurried, he should just make it.

While riding to the airport he dialed Ms. Natalie Fischer. In graduate school, Roger was a class ahead of Luke and Natalie was one class behind Luke.

Luke and Natalie had dated off and on in graduate school, but ultimately they went their separate ways. Their work pulled them in different directions.

He looked out the window as it rang several times. Just when he thought he'd have to leave a message, she answered. "Hello, Luke. What's up?"

"You are never going to guess where I'm headed now."

She played along, "Let's see, the President of Israel invited you to dinner?"

"Very funny, Natalie. I'm headed to Rome. You remember Roger Thornton. This morning he sent a few sketches from a book he has."

"And you are already headed to Rome? Wow, must be good for you to drop everything."

"It's definitely good. In fact it's much better than good."

"Okay, spill it Luke, for Christ's sake."

"You don't want to venture a guess? Just think totally lost languages for a moment... Are you thinking yet?"

"Of course I am, but drawing a blank."

"Roger has complete sample of the Language of Light in written form."

"No way, Luke! That's incredible. So you have a real sample? That will set you so far ahead of everyone out there."

"Not just a full page sample, Natalie, try a whole book! His scanner wasn't working so I just have some hand sketches, but if it's legit, it's going to change the world."

"How on Earth? Where did it come from?"

"I don't know yet. Roger said a woman named Catherine Moore contacted him and has ownership of the book. I'll know more once I meet her."

"Oh, you just have to send me the page, Luke. I have to see it with my own eyes. How thrilling!"

"Okay, sweets, I'll send it along."

"Cool, can't wait."

"Okay, I gotta run. I'm at the airport."

"Okay, Luke, so glad you called. Don't forget that email or I'll have to come to Rome to see it for myself."

"Promises, promises."

He hung up before she could say anything. He got out of the taxi with a big smile on his face, paid the driver a huge tip, and hurried to catch his flight.

117- *Puzzle Piece*

They arrived 30 minutes later at the dig site. The closer they got, the more nervous Catherine was. She had a pit in her stomach about it, for some reason.

After reaching a place to park, they all followed Roger into an old building, walking in single file. "First we'll have to go through the main catacombs, and from there we can reach our excavation site. I brought an extra bag of gear."

Roger passed out yellow hard hats to everyone. Catherine helped Joshua with his, whispering to him as she snapped the fastener in place, "It'll be okay. Just stay close."

A bright beam from Roger's flashlight circled the group. "Most of all, watch your step and your head. These ceilings are low, and there is loose dirt and rocks everywhere. Once we get to our destination, you will find that the ceilings are vaulted, which is fortunate for us taller folks. At least we have service lights, otherwise we'd all be moving like little moles with flashlights."

"Such colorful phrasing, Professor!" Beth teased.

"Well it's true, not sure we could have done this without the lights for obvious safety reasons. Okay, let's go. Follow me. Your group is the only outside group I've allowed in here. We've had an outside consultant or two. Other than that, no one has really been here besides my team."

"I thought these particular catacombs were open to the public?" Erica asked Roger.

"Yes, they are. The semi-public entrance is on the other side. This is a secondary entrance that is private."

One by one, they followed Roger into the dimly lit tunnel. "It takes a few minutes for your eyes to adjust to the low lighting. Then you'll be able to see a lot better. Hope none of you are claustrophobic. Guess I should have asked that before now." Roger laughed.

Catherine heard Joshua let out a groan behind her and she reached back to take his hand. "I'm okay, angel," he whispered.

"Good, Joshua. Be brave, okay?"

After following several long corridors they came to what essentially looked like a square cut out in the wall. Roger shone his flashlight on a stone crypt nearby. "See this here? You see the four symbols burned into your inside book covers. Plus, this is the only crypt like this in the whole area."

"We still don't know how this more modern crypt got here or why. It could have simply been a marker of this place for anyone who knew what they were looking for. As you saw when we were coming in, the people of this particular time period were buried in cut-out type shelves created in the stone walls".

"We discovered the false wall completely by accident. Greg was taking some photos and samples of the mysterious crypt when he stumbled over a stone and smacked right into the wall. The force of him hitting it cracked open a two foot wide hole. I still remember when he came running up to tell me about his little accident, and the large chamber on the other side. Before we go in, notice the seal on the floor. It's engraved with unusual symbols as well."

They all filed inside, one by one. When Catherine crossed through the doorway, something made her feel queasy and she felt a familiar burning sensation in both her palms. She tried hard to hide what was happening from Roger or Beth. She slowed her walking way down and asked Joshua to go ahead of her. David looked back in time to notice her retreat and slowed down as well.

"You okay?"

She whispered, "When I first walked in, I felt a wave of nausea and my palms started to burn. The last time I felt this sensation, a glowing symbol appeared in both hands. I thought I should hang back since it would be hard to explain magical glowing symbols in my palms."

"I'll walk with you, and if anything gets weird, I will get you out, okay?" Catherine motioned to him that they should catch up to the others.

They followed the sounds of voices until they reached the central chamber where Roger was showing the others a massive circle cut into the floor. "Catherine? See, this is like the imprint on your book."

Catherine shot a glance of fear at David. As she walked further toward Roger, her whole body seemed to be shaking on the inside.

"Also in the middle of the room is this stone pedestal. We don't know what this is. I had a wild thought just now that it could be to place your book on perhaps."

Catherine didn't feel well at all, but something drove her to walk to the center circle and stand directly in front of the pedestal. Sweat started pouring off her forehead and for a moment she thought she would fall down. She was about to step out and have David take her outside when the heat suddenly subsided and changed rapidly to extreme cold.

Catherine's hands were tingling again. She put them flat on the pedestal to hide her palms from Roger and Beth, just in case. As she pressed the pedestal with both hands, one of small outer rings of the circle lit in an eerie glow. It startled everyone including Catherine.

Roger turned quickly, "What the hell? What did you do, Catherine?"

"Nothing, Roger. I just touched the pedestal to steady myself."

"Don't move from that spot, Catherine. In fact no one else move either." Roger knelt down. "My God, how is this glowing? He reached his index finger down to touch the glowing blue Kyanite to see if it was warm, like before. It wasn't warm, it was now ice cold. "I have no idea what light source could possibly be in this floor. Somehow you must have triggered it, Catherine."

Playing dumb, she said, "How could I do that?" The vibration in her body intensified so much that her teeth started chattering. She kept both her palms flat, following Roger's instruction not to move.

David suddenly felt they were in danger. He wanted to get Catherine out of there and fast.

"Is this room safe, Roger? Especially now that it's mysteriously glowing?" David asked.

"No one has been hurt so far on this site." Roger tried to reassure everyone.

"No offense, Roger, but you don't sound very sure of yourself right now."

"I am okay, David. I am sure Roger's got this under control. Do you mind if I move my hands but not move from this spot?"

"Sure, Catherine."

Catherine looked at the flat stone underneath her palms.

Okay, here goes. 1, 2 and 3!

Catherine lifted both hands at once. The entire room lit up in a brilliant, bright light just like a strobe firing once and staying on. When she looked around her, everyone was still there, but no one was moving. It was like they were frozen in time. Catherine started to panic when she felt a familiar tug on her shirt. She whipped around quickly.

"Alice?"

"Hello, Catherine. It's nice to see you again."

As Catherine looked closely at Alice, she finally recognized her from before when she was unconscious.

"I know you from before we even came to Italy. You showed me the convent and spoke to me. I didn't recognize you in the apothecary shop, but I should have. In fact, you are the only nice spirit that I've encountered that will actually talk to me. Why is that?"

Alice got a huge smile on her face. "That's kind of complicated. But the easiest way to explain it is to say that I am assigned to guide you. So I can interact with you more than the others can."

"Are you an angel, then?"

"Why, yes, I am."

Catherine looked at everyone standing there still frozen. "Are they okay? I mean will they unfreeze?"

Alice giggled. "Yes, Catherine, they will be fine. Doing this made it much less complicated to speak with you. No one else can see me, and you would have looked strange standing there talking to yourself."

"I suppose that would look strange," Catherine conceded.

"I am here because there's not much time. I couldn't help you directly until it was appropriate for me to do so, and now you've awakened enough to realize the importance of your mission, even if you aren't ready to accept your destiny just yet."

"Why haven't you made yourself known until now? I sure could have used you a long time ago, especially to understand why God took my parents from me. Didn't anyone realize I needed some help?"

Alice took her hand. "You were so upset that I couldn't even get through to you to manifest. You thought was God punishing you, and that took you further away from me and my help. But trust me; you've seen me many times over the years. I can take any form I choose."

"So why a six-year-old girl named Alice?"

"I figured this form would be less threatening or less overwhelming for you for our first encounters."

"Well, now that you are here, and I know you are here, will the real angel please show herself?"

"Of course." In a single moment, Alice grew to over 9 feet tall and was no longer a child.

"Oh my God, it was you from the beginning! I thought you were the most beautiful woman I had ever seen." The memory brought tears to Catherine's eyes. "Of course, I had no idea you were an angel. Where are your wings?"

"My wings? Would you like to see?"

Three sets of magnificent wings 10 feet in diameter came out of her back. They weren't like bird wings at all, but like ribbons of energy that constantly changed shape in a fluid motion.

"Not quite what I was expecting."

"Well artists have a stylized way of envisioning us. And often shape their experiences with elements of nature."

"Is your name really Alice?"

"No, but the Alice you saw was once a real girl that I was happy to watch over a long, long time ago.

My true name is *Ulian-naH*. Angel names are more tonal in nature and don't conform well to human speech, so this is as close as we can get in this world. You also have a different name."

"Any chance you are going to tell me?"

"I cannot tell you your real name but I can give you a hint. Your parents were influenced to name you Catherine Jane so that your initials were the same as your angel name, thus hopefully prompting you to remember, eventually."

Catherine remembered Monsignor's words about the angel having to remember. "I see. Okay, I guess I can live with that."

"I am also here to discuss the matter with Jacob."

"Oh no, is everything okay?"

"Things are not worse yet, but they are currently no better, I am afraid."

"That damned demon!"

"That is where you are mistaken Catherine. It is not a demon you are dealing with there."

"No? Then who is she?"

"She's an immortal being."

"There are immortals living on Earth?"

"There are only a handful of immortals left now on Earth, but the only one you must concern yourself with where Jacob is involved is Pandora."

"THE Mythical Pandora?"

"The myth of Pandora is based on an ancient story. Essentially she is a real being, and the stories are based on a fair amount of truth, like most of your myths."

"I remember the story. Pandora was responsible for unleashing all the evils of the world, right? It's where we get the phrase like 'opening Pandora's box.'"

"Well, that is one story, but not the truth of the matter. Pandora didn't unleash all the evil, mankind did. Mankind's limited thinking ruined the many gifts that Pandora had bestowed upon them out of kindness. Originally she wanted to make the world better. But the world was not ready for what she gave them, and that's when things went bad. Mankind became self-righteous and needed a scapegoat. This is something that she's very upset about. She feels like all human beings owe her. Your bringing heaven to Earth would definitely mess up her petty plans to make all humans suffer."

"Is that why she has Jacob?"

"Yes, she saw this as an opportunity to gain leverage over you by using him. So she destroyed the demon that was originally attached and took him herself. She's trying to lure you in."

"Why would she do that?"

"So she can find your weakness and kill you before you can protect yourself astrally."

Catherine threw up her hands. "This is just great! You are telling me that not only do I have the Malem Tutela after me but I have an immortal being, wait, not just any immortal, but Pandora herself, after me? How can I do this?"

"We never anticipated her involvement, Catherine. We thought we foresaw everything we needed to in order to assist you. She's taken great exception to you being an angel in human form and wants to stop you from completing your mission."

"She's basically jealous of me? That's got to be the screwiest thing I've ever heard. It's just ridiculous, an immortal being jealous of a weak and fragile woman like me? Now I think I have truly heard everything."

"One more thing though before I leave you. Once you believe the truth of your identity, you will become more powerful than the Malem Tutela or even an immortal like Pandora. Just know that fear is your greatest enemy. It makes you see yourself as insignificant and small when you are anything *but* that. You must go back to your childlike wonder again to find the path you seek. I must go now. I will turn back the clock a little bit and no one will remember the flash of light or you touching the pedestal."

"You can do that?" Catherine asked.

"Only for short periods of time, otherwise it would be far too disruptive to the continuum of time."

"So no one will remember this?"

"Right. Now, go back and stand by David as you were before you stepped into the circle. This special place is for another time in the future. You must not allow the book to be placed on the pedestal until you remember everything."

Then *Ulian-naH* vanished.

The world rewound the few minutes before she had been compelled to step into the circle. This time she decided to succumb to the urgency to get out of the chamber fast.

She looked up at David. "Get me out of here, please," she pleaded.

"Absolutely, sweet pea." He picked her up cradled her in his arms. Catherine held onto him tightly and gazed into his eyes.

"Hey guys, Catherine's dizzy. I'm going to take her out for some air."

"Do you need any help?" Erica called out to David.

"No, I have her."

David looked down at Catherine once they were headed down the first of three corridors. She had a huge smile on her face. "You must not be too sick, lady, you are smiling too much. Did you just want a free ride out of there?"

Catherine shook her head no. "You just called me sweet pea back there."

David smiled back at her. "Yes, I guess I did. Weird though. I never have called anyone that before."

Catherine held her head close to his chest and whispered. "My daddy used to call me that."

David felt tremendously strong and filled with purpose. He carried her all the way to the car to wait for the others.

118- *Rest*

Erica and the others started walking out of the chambers about 20 minutes after David had taken Catherine to the car. Everyone was talking excitedly as they got to the car, until they saw that she was asleep in David's arms.

Erica was concerned. "Is she okay?" David nodded.

"I think out of everything, the past few days finally caught up to her. She's been through so much. Let's try not to wake her," David whispered. The car ride back was almost completely silent.

It was nightfall before Catherine awoke nestled snuggly in bed. There was a candle lit on her night stand. As her eyes adjusted to the light, she saw a familiar figure come in. It was Erica.

"Hey there sleeping beauty, I thought I'd come bring you some food. You've been asleep for hours now, but I figured you need to eat." The aromas from the plate smelled wonderful.

"Joshua got the book for you and brought it up. I put it in the drawer where you've been keeping it."

Catherine propped herself up, but it was difficult. "How did you get to be such a darn good cook? It smells delicious."

Erica shrugged. "Mom cooks well, but for some reason when I get in a kitchen, I am in heaven."

"Erica, I have to ask you, what do you remember about the site when I first entered the central chamber?"

Erica thought about it as if she needed to remember something specific based on the way Catherine had asked the question.

"Don't worry, it's not a test."

Erica laughed. "Okay, okay, I guess you know me pretty well don't you? I remember you walking in behind us and David was with you. Then a short time later he announced he was taking you outside."

"I thought so."

"Why do you ask?"

"The most extraordinary thing happened to me, Erica...then the angel took it all away and reversed time so no one would remember it!"

Her friend looked confused so Catherine relayed everything to her. Erica listened wide eyed while reminding her to pause to take bites of food.

Downstairs the rest of the crew, including Bob and Greg who had been working at the site non-stop for two days, were all seated at the big table, enjoying the dinner that Erica had prepared.

"I do hope Catherine is feeling better. I am sorry she got ill just as I was about to show her everything connected to her book," Roger shared.

"She's just got to be exhausted, and probably still jet lagged too. I think she just needs her rest right now." David protected Catherine.

Roger continued, "Well good news is my friend Luke will be here this evening. He's the linguistics expert who understood the language in the book. I'm sure that will pique Catherine's interest. I'd say we all get a good night's sleep and perhaps we can go to the site again I the morning. I know Luke will want to see it too."

"I imagine Catherine will go if she's feeling better," David offered.

Then unexpectedly, the often silent Joshua added, "I think Catherine should slow down and get her rest. I don't want her to get sick."

Upstairs, Erica and Catherine were continuing their heart to heart. "Catherine, I have to tell you something. I've never said anything to you like this." Erica put her hand on Catherine's arm. Catherine sat her fork down.

"I believe you are the angel that everyone thinks you are. I have complete faith in you that you can and will complete your mission. It's not that far-fetched that God would send an angel to get things squared away in the world. The world's in chaos right now and I can't think of a better time for a sign of God's love to become something tangible in the world. Many have lost their faith, not only in God, the force that binds all things in harmony, but mostly in themselves. I know that even if you don't admit it to yourself, your beautiful garden was only the beginning of the miraculous things you can do. I am not trying to pressure you or put the weight of the world on your shoulders either, but wouldn't it be a shame to waste the grace you obviously were given?"

Catherine got teary-eyed whispered, "I'm so afraid, Erica."

"My mother used to say that everyone is afraid and has fear, but it is what you choose to do when faced with fear that matters. So it's perfectly natural, I think, especially in this case, for you to be afraid. Who wouldn't be? It's not every day that someone comes along and says, 'Hey guess what, and you're an angel'."

Catherine moved her tray to the side. Without speaking, she grabbed Erica and hugged her as hard as she could. Erica inserted humor with ease, "How did I get a best friend that's really a living angel? How cool is that?"

Okay, fear is a normal thing. I think I can accept that. Relax, for once. Maybe everything will be alright.

"I should get up and go downstairs. There's a lot I need to tell David and Joshua."

Erica shook her head. "Oh no, you're going to lie back down and go to sleep. Don't you worry about anything. I'll fill the guys in later."

Catherine did what she was told.

"What, no argument?"

Catherine just smiled and snuggled in under her covers. "Maybe I'm turning over a new leaf."

Erica beamed. "Alright now, sweet dreams, my friend."

As Erica closed the bedroom door, she heard a muffled voice behind her say.

"Sweet dreams."

119- *Shed a Tear*

The full moon outside cast its glow through the arched cathedral windows of his bedroom illuminating Razoul's pained expression. He awoke from the nightmare tormenting him at two in the morning. As usual, he could remember every little detail. His memory was uncanny like that of a calculated hunter or killer.

In his dream, he had pursued the woman relentlessly until he found her. He recalled pausing in front of her to savor the moment just before the kill. He now felt the same power of triumph fill him, as in the dream, like the barbaric victor of some ancient war.

He wielded a long knife and brought it close to her beautiful eyes. She calmly stared at him without flinching or blinking, even one time.

Why does she show no fear of me?

He lifted the knife high above them both. When he came down for the killing blow, he met resistance instead of piercing straight through her heart. As the knife struck her, he was picked up from the ground and flung backwards by a searing white light.

Razoul slowly got out of bed and walked to the window looking out over his domain. He could see for miles with the full moon's assistance.

I must go see Ashiyah about this. Everyone should be asleep. I'll be undetected.

Razoul turned to get some decent clothes from the wardrobe and literally felt his ribs cracking. He grabbed his side to catch his breath. In a few minutes, he had dressed himself and was stealthily leaving his bedroom. He checked the outer hallway which was clear. Then he decided to use the back service stairs in lieu of the main staircase.

He reached the bottom floor and cautiously scanned for anyone who might be there. The kitchen was dark and quiet. He found the cellar stairs and quietly descended them. He was so intent on reaching Ashiyah that he had no idea he was being trailed by Thaddeus who had caught sight of him sneaking around suspiciously near the kitchen. Thaddeus had been well trained by his father in stealthy pursuits and easily followed Razoul.

He could not tell what Razoul was up to until he saw him walk up to a wall and pull something secretly attached to the wall lantern. To Thaddeus' surprise, a section of the wall moved away completely, revealing a narrow stone staircase. Thaddeus tried to follow, but the wall closed behind Razoul before he could get there. He thought it was unwise to attempt to reopen the door in case he was heard.

Thaddeus went immediately to Sirius' bed chamber and burst in, startling the old man who rubbed his eyes to focus. "What are you doing here in the wee hours of the morning, boy? Surely whatever you need to tell me can wait until morning."

"No, it can't. I followed Razoul down into the cellar area. I saw him open a false wall and go inside."

Upon hearing this, Sirius' face visibly relaxed and his demeanor shifted. He started shaking his head. Thaddeus could tell Sirius knew something about the hidden place below. "Do you already know what is hidden down there?"

"Yes, my boy, I do. I have now for many, many years. Yet Razoul's father didn't know I knew."

"He didn't?" Thaddeus' reflected his young age of 23, a child about to learn the biggest secret in the world.

"No, he thought he kept it secret from everyone in the Malem Tutela. Like you, one day I followed him down there. Only I went further than you did tonight. I reopened the door after a few minutes and went down the narrow staircase. I followed the corridor and down at the end there was a dim light spilling into the hallway. I went up very quietly and could peek into a crack in the doorway. There was an entire furnished dwelling down there! I could hear Britius talking to someone, but couldn't make out any detail." Sirius paused, took a deep breath and said. "Then I saw her, the most enchanting woman in the world."

"A woman? There's a woman living underneath the estate?"

"Yes, and you must not tell a single soul. She's no ordinary woman."

"What do you mean?"

"As I sat there crouched and spying on them, I heard Britius call her Ashiyah. Several moments later, she looked directly to where I was hiding and actually smiled at me. I was terrified at first because I instantly assumed she would reveal me to Britius, but that was not why I ran away. "

Thaddeus had been hanging on every word and grew impatient as Sirius paused, working up to telling him the rest.

"Out with it, man. I must know more."

"When she looked at me, it was in her eyes, and I felt like I was already dead." The color drained from Sirius' face. "Perhaps here was Eve herself standing before me, but I felt as though she could hold up her smallest finger and erase my very existence if she willed it. She knew I was there, but didn't reveal my presence to Britius. I still have no idea why. I got out of there as fast as I could."

"Who is this Ashiyah?"

"She's an immortal."

"An immortal oracle...she cannot die?"

"I believe Ashiyah is centuries old, and was the key to Britius' swift rise to power. I never dared to reveal his secret."

"Why not, Sirius? This knowledge would have proved useful."

"I had no reason to expose him or their arrangement. Britius was wickedly cunning and ruthless beyond all measure. But he was not at all this way with those he considered to be family. He was quite generous and good to me for all the years that he was alive. I am sure that Razoul has continued to consult with her after Britius' death. It is imperative that Razoul not find out that we know this information. He would certainly kill both of us to keep his secret."

Thaddeus agreed, but he was reeling from Sirius' story. He began contemplating how they could play the information to their advantage.

At that same moment, down in the bowels of the Bugiardini estate, Razoul sat impatiently on the ornate couch in Ashiyah's receiving room. Britius had warned him long ago that one never goes to get Ashiyah, but she comes to you. His growing disregard for rules nearly got the better of him when she finally appeared.

"Hello Razoul. I am very sorry to have kept you waiting for so long. I was engaged in some important private business." She flowed into the room wearing the color of red crimson, ornamented in shiny gold jewelry. This color was a rare choice for the immortal. In fact, that last time he saw her in red crimson she had learned of Britius' death. This led him to conjecture that something had upset her.

Razoul rose to greet her and took her honey colored hand into his. "That is quite alright, my goddess." He kissed her hand. "Will you please sit with me?" She circled the couch to seat herself on the other end as Razoul took his place. He studied her. She seemed different. "Are you alright, my lady? You seem out of sorts."

For the first time, Ashiyah was truly divided inside. Pandora's words had cut her deeply, she was now unsure of the correct course. Ashiyah was furious that her immortal sister had her in such an alarming state of consciousness. She turned to him directly, her magnetic, penetrating eyes boldly commanding his attention and responded, "I am rarely out of sorts, Razoul. You know this. So what can I do for you this early in the morning?"

"I awoke from a dream that troubled me, and I thought you could let me know if it has some deeper meaning."

"Of course, I am here to help you. Tell me about this dream."

"My men and I were pursuing the woman and at last I had her right where I wanted. I reveled in my victory over her then moved in to strike her down with my dagger. Using all my force I struck her heart, but instead of her falling to the ground, a blinding light burned me to oblivion."

"Perhaps the dream is a bad omen for you Razoul or a warning not to be overly confident. Both of these are things we've discussed before. Issues that I fear will be your undoing."

Moving past her warning, Razoul asked, "Please tell me, my lady, that you've been able to find her?"

She rose and produced a map of Rome and the surrounding areas. "I have not located her specifically, but can tell you to concentrate your search in this broad area." She pointed to the southeastern corner of the map. "The angels are concentrating over ten times the amount of energy there. That must be where she is hidden."

"Is there no way to narrow this down? That area is roughly 10 kilometers in diameter."

"Sadly no, even I cannot see clearly past their light. In fact I have never encountered such a collective effort before to protect anything. I did, however, see something else that you may find useful. A powerful book is now in the arena of play. It's called the Angelus Aevum. It's unlike any magical book that has ever been allowed into your human world. It's an object that has highly unique, creative and destructive capabilities. The angel has it in her possession. If you succeed in reaching her in time, you must find the book before others do."

Razoul looked at her, slightly wounded. "*If* I succeed. Have you so little faith in my abilities?"

Ashiyah felt she needed to tread carefully now. A small part of her desperately wanted to warn Razoul about Pandora's plan right here, right now.

"There are always dual possibilities in the Records, as you know. Even though I advise you on your best course, just as I advised your father, I am as neutral as the enduring memory of the universe. I may not take sides." As the words flowed out of her mouth, she became nearly consumed with the paradox she found herself in.

"I attempt to heed well all your counsel. Soon I will have the means to send the angel back where she came from. The Fallen One has assured me of this. I will fatally wound her and toss her directly back to God."

"I have seen your interactions with Samyaza and must tell you that he intends to destroy you eventually. His kind always does. They play games in the world for their own amusement and soon grow tired of them. Whoever is involved in such dangerous games with these creatures eventually lose his life."

"Is there a way to destroy Samyaza?"

Ashiyah nodded yes. "It is very dangerous magic that could hold him in the shadows forever. If you obtain the Angelus Aevum and use it properly, it would have enough power to thwart his attacks."

"If I bring you this book, you will show me how to unlock its secrets. Am I right?"

"The only one who can use the power of the book is the very one you seek to destroy." Ashiyah was suddenly aware that asking Razoul to do something wasn't the same as interfering. This justified pleading with him.

"Razoul, I can make you the most powerful man in the world. If you abandon this course, I will stay by your side and ensure you want for nothing ever again." She moved in very close to seduce him with her energy.

Razoul looked at her keenly. He sensed something he had not felt before. "You shock me with your words, Ashiyah, and offer me little that I don't already have now." He backed away from him slowly and deliberately, continuing to study her. "Why are you telling me to drop everything I've worked so hard for?" Before letting her answer, he continued, "I will be like a God to those that pursue the darker arts. I, Razoul, will have stopped the conduit for goodness sent by the Almighty himself. I will ensure the war between good and evil from which we all benefit, even YOU. In a bold move, he strode across the room, enfolded Ashiyah into his arms and put his forehead directly onto hers. "I smell fear in you. What are you not telling me?"

For the first time in centuries, Ashiyah responded with a human impulse. In seconds she was across the room from him, without even moving Razoul.

"You misunderstand my motivation. I only wish to protect you in accordance with the covenant I made with your father long ago. My only fear is that you will recklessly end your life far too soon, something that would dishonor his memory." Ashiyah offered a believable cover for what she was hiding.

Razoul spat at the ground upon her mention of his father. "How you can still care about such a pathetic man is beyond me. No wonder you have so little expectation of me. But you will soon see just what I am capable of. Good day, my lady. I bid you farewell." He bowed quickly and left.

Ashiyah's eyes became pure white and shifted rapidly from side to side. A low light illuminated the air around her as clear images began to float in front of her. The images switched rapidly, one after another, then no image at all. She altered and reviewed the path of choices and outcomes, exploring faster than even the quickest computer.

When she came out of her trance-like state, a single tear rolled down her cheek. It was so foreign to Ashiyah that she slowly lifted her hand to catch it on the tip of her index finger.

Such a small human thing that simply should not be...

120- *A New Day Dawns*

Catherine awoke with tremendous energy. She was feeling more rested that she could ever remember in her entire life. She bounced out of bed and jumped in the shower to get ready for her day. She felt so light and hopeful she thought that she must be still dreaming. She pinched herself just to be sure.

OUCH! Okay not a dream. Maybe this is how other people feel. I could sure get used to feeling this good.

Catherine warmed up the water and stepped in. "Oh God, this feels awesome."

As she got herself washed up she made a mental inventory of everything she had learned so far about her various experiences and then thought about what Erica had said to her so sweetly last night.

Okay, I know I'm afraid, but maybe Erica is right. I don't know the first thing about being an angel, but it is right up my alley. I do like helping people after all. Perhaps it's time to get with the program instead of worrying so much. Maybe I can do this...

Catherine finished rinsing her long hair and turned the water off. Within ten minutes, she was dressed. She got to her bedroom door and paused for a moment.

Okay Catherine, this is it. A new day is here with a new outlook, right? Ready?

She took an enormous deep breath and closed her eyes.

Here we go!

Catherine threw open the door and was immediately blasted by the smell of bacon wafting up from the kitchen downstairs.

Perfect! Breakfast!

She came bouncing down the stairs like a little kid coming down on Christmas morning and practically slid into kitchen. When Catherine stepped into full view, everyone in the room stopped what they were doing to stare. She didn't look the same as yesterday.

"Good morning, everyone!"

Completely ignoring that she had commanded the attention of the room, she walked over to the stove and remarked to Erica and Beth, "This smells so good. I'm starving."

Catherine was radiant. The dark circles underneath her eyes had disappeared. The transformation that occurred while she had been sleeping was tangibly apparent to everyone.

David was the first to speak as she came around to sit at the table. He pulled out her chair for her. "Catherine, you look simply radiant today. Some good sleep must have been just what you needed."

"Yep, just what the doctor ordered." She looked up at him and grinned.

"You do look amazing this morning, my friend," Erica put a glass of orange juice in front of her.

"Thank you."

"I could swear she's really glowing!" Joshua admired his angel from across the table.

Roger chimed in too, "Good morning Catherine, I'd like you to meet Luke. He came in last night while you were resting up."

"It's great to meet you, Luke."

"I have been anxious to meet you, Catherine. I heard you were a bit under the weather. I'm happy you're feeling better today."

"Thanks."

"Roger didn't tell me you were as enchanting as your book is intriguing."

"Oh you! Behave man for once!" Roger smacked him away and said, "Let's eat."

Everyone was busy eating. The only audible sound was the clinking of their forks. Catherine broke the silence first. "This is quite possibly the best breakfast I've ever eaten. I don't know what it is this morning, but I feel better than I ever have. I mean everything is better.

Colors are more vibrant. The sky outside is intensely blue. I took the best shower ever, and now the food unbelievable."

Catherine's three companions were beaming too. Each one of them was overjoyed to see Catherine so carefree. Any subconscious doubt her friends may have had about the truth of who she really was evaporated at the breakfast table that morning.

Luke ventured, "I'd love to take a look at your book this morning, Catherine, if you don't mind."

Catherine looked up. "Sure. Once we're finished, I'll go get it for you."

"I must admit, I'm very keen to look through it."

"My pleasure." Then without skipping a beat, Catherine turned to Erica. "How would you like to go site seeing today? Maybe see some places you showed me in your pictorial book on Rome?"

Erica happily answered, "Sure, I'd love to."

"What about you guys? David, Joshua? Are you up for it too?"

David replied, "I'm following you."

"Me too," Joshua almost whispered, still staring at Catherine in adoration.

"I think these two guys are practically speechless, Erica. Maybe it's because I'm the one who thinks we should go play for a change."

"Oh, I imagine so!" Erica chuckled.

Roger jumped into the conversation. "I was hoping to show you the site again now that you are feeling better, Catherine. Luke, Beth and I are headed out there around ten."

"Well Roger, if you don't mind and I hope this isn't an imposition, but I would love to spend some time today exploring a few historical sites with my friends. There's plenty of time for me to revisit the site later, right?"

"Um, well of course there is Catherine. I often forget the pull of such a beautiful city if you've never been here. I don't want to keep you away from one of the most enchanting cities in the world. I'll get Luke caught up on everything while you all have a little fun."

"Oh I knew you'd understand." Catherine was being unusually charming. She turned to ask, "Beth, do you have a metro map?"

"Sure Catherine. I have several in my room."

"Great, I think between us four we can figure it out from there."

Her friends nodded.

"Okay Luke, I'll run up to my room and get the book for you so you can look it over before you guys head out."

Then Luke had a thought, "Oh Roger, can I get my laptop connected to the wireless. I totally forgot to send an important email."

"Sure buddy, boot it up and I'll get you the pass key for the router."

While Catherine ran upstairs to bring the book down, Luke took his laptop off of standby mode. Roger came back from the living room with a piece of paper and handed it to him. Luke entered it quickly. "Great I'm online, thanks!"

Catherine returned with the box as Beth and Erica cleared the table for them.

"Here you go, Luke."

He set his laptop aside and hungrily put the box in front of him.

121- *Drag Net*

An ornate table commanded attention in the former ballroom of the Bugiardini estate. Razoul sat comfortably at the head. He sat there taking reports from his teams that were actively trying to determine Catherine Moore's whereabouts. He stood to begin his inquiry, mostly for effect. "So tell me how our efforts are progressing."

Thaddeus spoke first. "We are on schedule for delivery of the document tomorrow, as you requested. For a moment, Father Ignatius was actually considering abandoning the mission. You'll be happy to know that I redirected his panic by merely explaining the gruesome details of what happened to the last person who refused you."

"Very good, Thaddeus, that pleases me greatly. I'm happy you've learned the power of persuasion for yourself." Thaddeus calmly nodded in acknowledgement, but his fist was tightly clinched under the table after Razoul's patronizing remarks.

A rarely seen member of the Malem Tutela was also seated at the conference table, Nathan Cicero. Nathan used to be employed by the Italian National Police. He was a computer genius who could hack nearly any system if given enough resources. He was extremely useful when trying to collect protected information, forge official documents, or in this case, find any trace of Catherine in Italy.

Razoul turned to him next. "Nathan, how's my little computer worm?" Razoul began to pace.

"Um, good, Razoul. Thanks."

"Just wonderful you're doing so well. And Nathan, how do you think I'm doing on this fine day?"

"Um, I don't know?"

"Very well then, let me tell you how I am. I am very upset today despite the beautiful weather, all the wealth I ever wanted, and hundreds of men at my disposal at a moment's notice." Razoul gestured in a grandiose manner as he spoke. "I am deeply upset because here I am with one of the most brilliant technical minds in the world, but yet he has somehow been unable to find a digital crumb to lead us to one little woman."

"I'm doing everything I possibly can, Razoul. I have packet sniffers phishing and sorting millions of pieces of data moving back and forth for any mention of her. The issue is how broad the parameters for the search are. It could take some time. I guarantee if there's any new information floating about her on the net, I will find it eventually."

"Well Nathan, tomorrow is your deadline."

"That's impossible. There's no way."

Razoul placed his hands on Nathan's shoulders from behind. "Nathan. How long have you known me?"

"Five years."

"Very good. And in these five years have you learned how I feel about the word 'impossible'?"

"Yes sir, I have. Nothing is impossible."

"Correct. Now if I narrow your search a bit, do you think you could POSSIBLY FIND THIS BITCH FOR ME EXPEDITIOUSLY?"

"Yes sir. A narrowed search would be great, sir."

Razoul took his seat again at the head of the table. Nathan practically crawled back into his chair like a whipped puppy.

Razoul took his seat again at the head of the table. "Concentrate only on the southeastern quarter of Rome. Add these two words to your search."

He quickly wrote down "Angelus Aevum" on a small piece of paper, crumpled it up, and threw it at him. While Nathan was fumbling for the ball of paper that had bounced off his chest, Razoul turned to the other men and roared: "REPORT!"

122-*Essene Influence*

"I apologize for taking so long to call this meeting and reach you. I have been unusually tied up with my official duties, I'm afraid," Monsignor Bartholomew spoke breathlessly to the other Guardians as he entered the room. He'd been in a rush to arrive.

"All is well dear Brother. Please come and rest a while. We are anxious to hear your news." Aurora got up and led him to the table. She poured him a glass of water.

"Thank you, Sister." Bartholomew drank the entire glass of water before speaking.

"As Aurora has probably already told you, Catherine came to my office yesterday morning. Beforehand I was visited by her watcher; she instructed me what to do. I discovered that she came to Italy at the request of an archeologist named Roger Thornton. After researching Mr. Thornton, I found out that he has permission from the Vatican to work on preservation within the catacombs at San Pancrazio, but I seriously doubt anyone is truly aware of the significance of the chambers they discovered. Catherine was given the Angelus Aevum as expected by our dear Sister Mary Eleanor. In trying to determine what the book was for, she decided to share the information with a professor of antiquities. That is how Mr. Thornton became connected to all of this. Catherine told me that that the hidden chambers they found at San Pancrazio feature symbols matching those that are embossed into the book cover. She asked if I knew what the chambers were for, but I told her that I didn't. We here all know of the existence of the sacred angelic chambers, but the book and the chambers are useless if she doesn't embrace her true nature. ."

"Does she believe?" Joseph asked.

"When I saw her, there was much fear in her, but we must pray for her liberation."

"Yes, of course," Joseph agreed.

"I did explain to her how important it is to safeguard the book."

"What of the Malum Tutela? Is she safe?"

"Yes, Aurora, for now she is safe. They have not found her. Brother Artemis came back from the US and since then has been assigned to follow her."

"Do we know what Razoul is planning?"

"I'm about to find out. My sources say the Malem Tutela took an interest in a Father Ignatius who works at the Secret Archives office. They summoned the priest to the Bugiardini Estate two days ago. Because of this, I believe Razoul is after something that is stored in the archive. I'll be going to meet with the priest after we conclude our meeting. I'll make a plea to the priest to confess to me what is happening. I can't imagine what Razoul would use as leverage against him. It's not worth his risk."

Anastasia spoke up. "Do you think he's discovered something that can harm our angel?"

"I know of no nothing in the Secret Archives office that could be used to bring harm to her," Bartholomew said, offering them reassurance.

"Just because we do not have this knowledge, doesn't mean it is does not exist," Aurora added.

"Yes, Sister, agreed. I will find out what I can from the priest."

"As you complete your tasks today, be well and at peace." Aurora then turned to Matthew and asked, "In the meantime, Brother Matthew, would you please consult with the angels about this knowledge that Razoul is attempting to acquire?"

"As you wish, Sister. It will be so."

"The rest of you, please continue the sacred vigil for our angelic sister that she become filled with faith and embrace her destiny on this very day."

One by one, the guardians went their separate ways.

123- *The Book*

"Absolutely enchanting...you *are* the rarest little book in the world, aren't you?" Luke made cutesy faces at the book, which Joshua found extremely funny for a grown man, and he couldn't contain his giggle.

Luke carefully lifted the book from its resting place and unfolded the scarf on the table.

Roger walked past Luke and pointed at him with his thumb. "Don't mind this guy; he's taken to speaking to inanimate objects this way. That's why he doesn't have a suitable girlfriend."

"Come on, Roger. Low blow."

Luke was examining the front cover. "Very interesting with this embossed sigil and the title too. *Angelus Aevum*."

Catherine sat down. "It means Angel Incarnate, I am told."

"Yes, it does." Luke was wide-eyed as he began to thumb through the pages. "This book could take several lifetimes to translate."

Or longer, Luke, much longer.

"I imagine so." Catherine played dumb.

"I still cannot believe my eyes. I'm really looking at a book right now that not only contains pages written in a lost language, but written in THE lost language. Do you know what I mean?"

"Actually I do, Luke. Lately I've also been confronted with some unbelievable things that even though I see them with my eyes." Well. I'll leave this to you to peruse for now. I'm going to head upstairs to plan our excursions with Erica. I'm sure the boys can keep you company." She shot a look at David and Joshua who were watching him intently.

"Yes, you bet we will." David said squeezing her hand as she walked by him.

Catherine bounded upstairs the same way she had come down. Erica was seated on her bed with a metro map and a list of tourist spots. As she studied the list she remarked, "There are too many options. How do we choose?"

Catherine flopped down on the bed. "Well maybe we thumb through your book and see if anything jumps out at us."

"That's an excellent idea!"

"I think St. Peter's is a must."

"That sounds great, Erica. Let's go there. I do love a good cathedral, for sure."

Catherine turned the next page and as soon as her eyes hit it, she felt an immediate connection to it. "Ooh, I want to go here." Erica leaned over and read the page aloud. "Ah, St. Maria Maggiore. Sounds perfect."

"So, did anything happen while you were asleep?" Erica turned to Catherine in seriousness. "I'm very happy you feel so much better, don't get me wrong. But I was wondering if something else happened?"

Catherine thought for a minute then said, "Yes, I do have something to share with you, but it's a secret." She leaned over like a child and whispered in Erica's ear. "It was you. You are responsible for this change you see."

Erica pulled back, shocked. "Me? How could I be responsible for such a transformation?"

"Because you are an amazing woman, my friend. And I'm honored to know you. You've helped me see that I can't run from all this. When you said it would be a huge waste, you were right. So I decided that I should accept it, at least as much as I can, and I'm going to try to open up to whatever is happening right now. You believe in me, and it's time I started to."

Erica started crying.

"Oh honey why are you crying?"

"I feel like my heart is bursting. No one has ever said such a wonderful thing to me before. Well except my mom, but she's definitely biased."

"Well then, it's about time someone did. I'm glad to be that person."

"Me too, Catherine." Erica grinned through her tears.

"Okay, girlfriend today is not a day of tears. Today is a day of play. I think we are good with two places to start, and we can figure out the rest as we go."

"Sounds like a plan. Let's see if the boys are ready, and if we can pry the book away from Luke."

Catherine put on her shoes and then joined them all in the kitchen where Luke was scratching notes to himself. "I think we're going to head out shortly, boys," Catherine said as Roger came around the corner.

"That goes for us too, Luke. We need to head out. Beth, are you ready?"

"In a couple of minutes, Roger. I still need to load my gear."

"Are the other guys coherent?"

"Nope, haven't seen the whites of their eyes yet," Beth said exiting the front door with a burlap backpack.

"Well, I wasn't expecting them, just thought I'd ask."

Luke stopped pouring over the book for a moment and grabbed his phone noticing that he had several text messages from Natalie: *Well? Where are you? Did you forget about me?*

He texted Natalie back real quick: *Sorry been totally engrossed, sending in a few.*

"Okay, Roger, I'll be ready in a moment. I just need to send one email before I space it off again."

"Okay, Luke, I'll meet you outside in five."

Roger left through the front door as Beth was returning to grab her purse.

Erica approached Beth with the metro map. "Beth, can you get us pointed in the right direction? What way do we walk to get to the nearest station?"

"We're closest to the Anagnina station on the orange line. It is very close, only three blocks from here. You will go to the end of the drive and turn left. Just walk straight and you cannot miss it. Where're you going first?"

"The Piazza San Pietro is first."

"Ah, St. Peter's Cathedral is a must see. Okay, that means you just stay on the orange and get off at Ottaviano-San Pietro Station. Let me write down my cell number just in case you need me. "

Beth noticed Luke at his computer. "Are you coming, Luke?"

"Yes, just sending an email real quick."

Catherine wrapped up the book carefully. As she put it in the box, she playfully teased him. "Don't worry Luke. You'll see her soon."

Luke opened Outlook and addressed a new message to Natalie. He attached the document received from Roger and then typed:

Natalie,

Sorry for the delay. I am headed out to Roger's site to explore right now so in a rush. Attached is from Catherine Moore's book which is called the Angelus Aevum or loosely translated: Angel Incarnate.

Ciao,

Luke

Luke hit send and closed the cover. He grabbed his phone quickly and said. "Enjoy yourself today. Rome's an incredible city, one of my personal favorites. See you later on tonight.

124- *Saving a Soul*

It had been fairly easy for Monsignor Bartholomew to suggest a meeting with Father Ignatius, especially with his particular position, but Bartholomew seldom pulled rank with other priests as he had today. It was absolutely necessary to bring Ignatius to his office today, without delay.

Bartholomew had been waiting impatiently for his arrival and tried to fill his head with Vatican duties in the meantime. Around eleven, Father Ignatius arrived looking disheveled and distraught. The priest at the front desk escorted him to the Monsignor's office. Bartholomew greeted him warmly. "Father Ignatius, I truly appreciate your taking time to see me today. I know that Cardinal Vespucci only left this morning. I'm sure you've been quite busy handling his affairs in his absence."

"It's no problem at all, Monsignor. I come here joyfully of course, even with my very full schedule." His face was visibly strained.

"How do you like working for the cardinal? I know your appointment is fairly new."

"I enjoy it very much." He looked down as he said this.

"Good, good. It is always such a pleasure to be doing God's work. Yes?"

"Yes, yes, a pleasure."

"You seem upset, Father. Is there anything I can do?"

"Upset? Why would I be upset?"

"You seem distressed. I sense that something is troubling you."

"Yes, I am somewhat troubled today," Father Ignatius admitted.

"You know you can speak to me in absolute confidence, about anything at all."

"Yes, Monsignor, and I appreciate your offer. I truly do. But this is a situation I must work out for myself."

Monsignor looked at him kindly. "Perhaps, then, if I cannot help directly, I will lead us in a prayer for a satisfactory solution for your troubles?"

"Si' Si', that would be wonderful."

They bowed their heads and Bartholomew began to pray.

"Heavenly Father, please grant your kindness and mercy to Father Ignatius. Send your Holy Spirit as an inspiration to his heart. Allow him to always follow the righteous path and uphold your commandments faithfully."

He paused for effect and then continued.

"We are but fallible men that live in a world filled with evil and temptation. Do not allow us to willingly commit sin as other men do. Keep us as your servants free from torment of sin and regret. Show us the holy path and give us the courage of St. John and your other martyrs who died for their faith, to walk your path without reproach. Bless your humble servant.

Father Ignatius erupted into sobs. He covered his face and continued to cry deeply into his palms. Bartholomew came quickly to his aid. "There now, Father. I am here as a servant of the Lord to walk you out of the darkness."

"There is no absolution for me. I am truly damned."

"We are open to God's forgiveness at any time as long as we ask and are penitent."

"I cannot bear this burden any longer. I may be killed for this, but I wish to meet the angels and enter God's kingdom. I do not wish to be damned for all eternity."

"Trust that your confession is only between us and God."

Bartholomew locked his office door and asked not to be disturbed under any circumstances. He then took a seat next to Father Ignatius.

"Now please, tell me your troubles."

Father could not look him in the eye, but after taking a deep breath and gaining his composure, he started to speak. "I was summoned to the Bugiardini estate, which was very strange. I thought perhaps someone in the family was ill or there was a child to be baptized. At least something related to my priestly duties in this world. But it wasn't. It was Razoul Bugiardini who sent for me. Do you know of him?"

"Yes, and I doubt very much he would summon you for something holy."

"Yes, Monsignor, this is definitely a truth. He wants me to do something unspeakable. I refused him but....but he has ways of making people do whatever he wants. I cannot refuse him without causing pain or death to myself and two people I care very much about."

"I see. What did Razoul request of you?"

"He handed me a paper with a catalog designation on it. He wants me to steal a document from the Secret Archives while the Cardinal is away on business."

"Surely you offered him a copy?"

"At first, yes. I don't wish to steal a holy document from the archives. But he refused and said I must bring him the original parchment. He threatened me in a very specific manner. What should I do?"

"Well my son, if I knew what he was threatening, I could assist you better. Do not carry such a heavy burden on your heart."

"I have sinned before God, Monsignor. I have carnal knowledge of a woman and...and...I have a son who lives with her in Palermo. Razoul discovered this somehow and now he not only threatens to share my sins with the world, but to kill them both. They are innocent in this."

"This is quite serious."

"I must have absolution before God, Monsignor! You must help me to save my soul."

Bartholomew thought quickly and then asked, "When are you to deliver the document to Razoul?

"Tomorrow evening I am to contact his man, I believe he's called Thaddeus, to meet him and surrender the document."

"Do you know what document he is after?"

"When I filled out the document request, I looked up the document title by the designation he gave me. It's called Treasure of the Enochian Key. It is an obscure single page parchment that was filed away and registered from a source unknown. There's not even a translation in our computer system which would make sense if the document was considered unimportant. It would not have a priority to be translated."

"Yet it is so important to Razoul that he'd destroy you, and this woman and your son to get it?"

"Yes! What am I to do? If I give it to him, I protect my position at the Vatican, but know I'm damned as a thief and a liar who broke his priestly vows yet again. If I do not deliver then I am not only damned for breaking my vows, but I will have the blood of my offspring and his mother on my hands. Razoul does not make empty threats."

"Father Ignatius, it is clear to me you wish to absolved from your sins."

"Yes, of course I do."

"I have a solution to your problem that will not require you to make a private confession to the world about your discretions, nor steal a valuable artifact for very evil man who undoubtedly will commit more evil in the world."

"You do? And will you absolve me of my sins? I cannot bear it."

"Yes, Father. Let us tend to the pressing matters for tomorrow first. Then I shall perform your absolution for your sins."

Father Ignatius grabbed the Monsignor's hand and began to kiss it repeatedly. "Oh, thank you, thank you. I owe my life to you."

"Father, listen carefully. There's not much time."

125- *Tour of Rome*

After everyone in Roger's entourage left, Joshua secured the book in his special spot. Soon they were on their way to sight see. They successfully found the Metro station and were headed toward St. Peter's Basilica.

"I think this was the best plan yet," David spoke excitedly. "We all just need to have some fun and relax. I just hope we aren't going to be exposing you to the bad elements out there, though."

Catherine responded, "Well I'm trying to trust my intuition more, and I think we'll be fine with our little outing today. At least it *feels* safe enough."

David looked at her with loving eyes, "I trust you." Catherine blushed.

As they sat next to each other, Catherine couldn't deny how she felt about David. He was kind, sweet and loyal to her. He was like the man she wanted to marry when she was a little girl.

Maybe meeting him was just meant to be...but can we really be together? One day at a time, I suppose.

"I trust you, too." She leaned her head on his shoulder.

Erica turned around, "We have one more stop to go and then it's ours."

"I'm glad someone is navigating because I'm not paying any attention."

"No problem, I've got this. I just want you to enjoy yourself today."

"That's a great idea, Erica. I'm actively practicing the art of going with the flow. It's a new thing for me, but I'm managing." Catherine rolled her eyes.

Erica cracked up, along with David who seemed to enjoy Catherine's lighter side too. In a few minutes, they were stepping off at the station and making their way up to the street through thick crowds of people walking in both directions.

"It's very crowded here," Joshua remarked. Catherine put her arm around him and said, "Don't worry, friend. We'll be somewhere more open soon."

Once they reached the open air, they could see St. Peter's Basilica in the distance. It was about a ten minute walk to reach the entrance. As they walked, Catherine was scanning the crowd watching the different kinds of people that were all around them, as well as looking for trouble. Out of the corner of her eye, she noticed David vigilantly doing the same.

To her surprise, she saw her guide appearing as Alice across the street. At first, Catherine started to point Alice out to the others and realized that they wouldn't be able to see her, even if she did. So Catherine quickly waved and Alice waved back to her.

So nice to know she's always around.

Then a thought, that was not Catherine's own, popped into her head so clearly, that it startled her.

Well, it's so nice to have such a beautiful angel for me to watch over.

Ulian-naH is that you? Can I just call you Uli?

Uli...hmm...I think I like that.

Your name is long so I thought Uli was nice. So we can talk like this in my head?

Now that you've relaxed, yes we can. I am never further away from you than a single thought.

That is so cool.

Have fun at the Basilica with your friends.

I will.

David's voice snapped her out of her angel conversation, "Catherine? Catherine?"

"Oh! Yeah? Sorry, I was just thinking."

"You'd better pay attention because we're crossing the street."

"No problem. I will."

They crossed the street and continued toward the entrance to St. Peter's on the far end of the public square.

126- *Monster*

Jacob had no concept of days, hours or minutes. Even though everything around him appeared to be Catherine's parent's house, it wasn't real. While the creature that had him captive was away, he would try to leave the house, but the doors were sealed. When he tried to look outside from the windows, there was simply nothing at all. He often thought of Catherine and what she must think of him now, or his poor mother languishing every day at the hospital with his empty body.

Maybe this is hell...

Jacob picked up what appeared to be Catherine's pillow and hugged it for comfort. He had a huge pit in the bottom of his stomach.

As time went by, he thought more and more that maybe all this was some drug-induced dream, or that he had finally lost his mind. Then she would return to startle him with her shrieking voice. A cold fear snaked up his spine as he heard her calling to him.

"Oh, Jacob? Jacob, darling? Where are you hiding? Don't hide from me. I'll certainly find you."

Jacob came out of the bedroom to see Pandora again, revealing herself as Catherine's human form. "I'm not hiding. I was just lying down for a while. There's nothing to do in this little illusion of yours, anyway."

"So very sweet. Were you all snuggled up on your girlfriend's bed reminiscing about the good old days?"

"You are such a bitch!"

"Yes, so I've been told repeatedly." Pandora pretended to buff her nails on her shirt and blow on them.

She appeared within inches of his face for effect, "Or maybe you weren't doing that at all. Maybe you were checking out the mess you made on the floor when you tried to off yourself."

Jacob tried to push her back, but she disappeared too quickly, he almost fell forward.

"Nice try, tough guy. Getting a bit testy, are we?"

"When can I get out of here? What is this place?"

Pandora looked at him curiously and spoke, "So, do you think your girlfriend will give me what I want in order to set you free?"

Jacob's expression changed to shame, "No, I don't think so, and I don't want her to."

"Well, you'd better hope so. I can keep you here as long as, well, eternity."

Jacob was defeated. "What do you want from me? And do you really have to appear as Catherine every time?"

"Well I thought that you'd prefer this, to this." Pandora changed her form into a hideous monster. Her entire body expanded to where she now towered over him. Her skin was covered in luminescent blue scales, her eyes were a deep yellow, and her hair was made of flames. The flames coming from her head quickly started to char the ceiling above them, and a thick, acrid smoke spilled across the hallway.

She bellowed when she spoke. "Do you like me now, leeetle booooyyyy?" She reached out her hand to touch him with a long, curved, talon-like finger.

Jacob started to uncontrollably cough because of the thick smoke that began to burn his lungs. "Okay, Okay, I get it. Please stop. Demonic monsters can take any form they want."

In an instant, she looked like Catherine again. The smoke was gone, and the ceiling restored to normal. "I keep trying to tell you and that little bitch of yours that I am not, and will never be a demon, how insulting! I'm an immortal you wretch."

"Immortal? I don't get it."

"Of course not, because you are just not very bright, are ya?" She flicked him hard in the forehead.

"Ouch! You must love to hear yourself talk." Jacob rubbed his forehead with a grimace.

"Okay, let's have a little history lesson and then, as they say show time! So, think of a being with infinite power."

"Oh, so you are going to make me guess?"

"Yep, just for my amusement. So, think Greek mythology and the phrase 'let the cat out of the bag'. That should get you somewhere."

"I don't know."

"Or think of a box that was opened that should never have been opened, even though these pitiful human's begged me for it."

Jacob thought about it hard as if it would help him get away from her. The answer was on the tip of his tongue but he couldn't get to it. "I can't, I can't remember."

"Oh wow, you are stupider than I thought. Didn't you pay attention in school?"

Jacob was tired of her game and shrugged.

"You are taking too damn long. I am the legendary Pandora you stupid worm!" For dramatic effect, Pandora lifted him up above her with one hand.

"Hey, that's what I was going to say!"

"Sure little monkey, now come on, we have to go now!!" Pandora grabbed him by the arm and whisked him away.

127- *Basilica*

The foursome was awestruck when they entered St. Peter's for the first time. "It's so big. I feel like a little bug," Erica said in awe.

Catherine stood there for a moment trying to take in the magnitude of the architecture towering above her. It felt familiar to her, even though she hadn't even seen pictures of it until she was looking through Erica's tourism book.

The arched ceiling above her was hundreds of feet in the air and she strained her neck to look straight up. There were hallways and open arches everywhere. For a brief moment, she forgot that there was an organization trying to find her and an immortal holding her childhood friend captive.

"Now this is a church! I have never seen anything like it in my life!" David exclaimed.

"I think that's an understatement. I had no idea it was so huge. It's so beautiful!" Catherine began to walk down the main hall toward the huge center dome and the altar that she could barely see on the far end.

The group scattered to explore different places as they admired the beautiful architecture in the cathedral. Catherine was particularly drawn to a statue of Mother Mary in the Chapel of Pieta. There was an exact duplicate of the original inside her childhood church in Parsons. She studied it and looked above at the ceiling to see an angel depicted there.

"Did I ever look like this? Well I know now the wings are wrong, but still." She closed her eyes and tried to envision herself with wings and all glowing like Uli was. Suddenly something smacked her hard and she went flying backwards. When Catherine struck the ground she wasn't in the Chapel of Pieta within St. Peter's anymore. She felt disoriented and started to call for help in her mind.

Uli? Uli? Where are you?

"No sense calling for *her* right now. We need to have ourselves a little chat."

Catherine instinctively knew who was there. "Aren't you going to face me finally? Wasn't a fair fight last time because, as I recall, you were invisible...*Pandora*."

"Well, what do ya know? The precious human angel has a brain after all."

"Why are you here, Pandora? What do you want?"

"Straight to business I guess. I'm here to make you a generous offer."

"I can't imagine what you'd have to offer me."

"Oh, that's what you think!" Pandora raised one hand over her head and pulled it back down in a yanking motion that magically delivered Jacob to the stone floor.

"Jacob!" Catherine knelt down to see if he was okay. "Did she hurt you?"

He looked up at Catherine. "Why do you want to help me? You should hate my guts right about now."

"Jacob, I love you. I would never turn my back on you." For the first time in what seemed like an eternity, he smiled as Catherine touched his cheek.

"Alright, that's enough you two."

Pandora tossed Jacob with a flip of her wrist, and he hit the wall hard. He fell down onto the floor unconscious. With her hands on her hips, she stepped closer to Catherine. "Okay, angel, here's the deal."

"I'm listening." Catherine wanted to check on Jacob, but Pandora had a field of energy around him. She glared at Pandora

"You walk away now. Forget you are an angel and you can have your little loser back. And to sweeten the pot, I'll take care of your little Malem Tutela problem."

"And if I say no?"

"Then I will have to torture your little buddy here for a really long time, hmmm....how's *for all eternity* suit you?"

Jacob began to stir and his voice was strained. “Catherine, don’t do this. Don’t say yes, not for me, not for anyone.”

“Shut up, you little worm.” Pandora spat at Jacob.

“And then, when I get bored with my little play thing here, which shouldn’t take too long, be ready, because I’m going to come for you.” Pandora took a cheap shot at Catherine, knocking her backwards onto the ground.

God, Uli, where are you?

“You have 24 hours, and I’ll be back.” Pandora grabbed Jacob by the neck, lifted him up like he weighed nothing, and they disappeared through a wall.

There was a loud pop in the air and in moments, Catherine found herself on the floor near the statue of Mary again. The lighting was different, and when she checked her phone, the clock read four.

“That’s crazy, it can’t be that late. We’ve been here since 11.” Catherine rushed to get on her feet and find the others. “They are probably sick with worry.” She stepped outside to get a signal and dialed Erica’s number. She picked it up on the first ring.

“Catherine, oh my God! Are you okay? We’ve been searching everywhere for you.”

“I’m okay. My ego’s bruised a bit, but anyway, long story. Can someone come and get me?”

“Where are you?”

“I’m outside St. Peter’s.”

“No way. We waited for hours for you to show up. We scoured the church from top to bottom. David even went around looking for hidden doors or something in the area where you were. I think the priest thought he was mentally ill. About an hour ago, we decided the only option was to return to the house to see if you were here.”

“I’m so sorry, but definitely not my fault. Is Beth there?”

“I called her when you went missing and they all came back. We’re on our way. Stay right there. ”

“Thanks, I’ll be out on the steps waiting. Come get me.”

Catherine walked to the bottom of the steps and sat down. A moment later, little Alice was seated to her right.

“I am so sorry, Catherine. I tried very hard to reach you.”

“What happened to you, Uli?”

"I didn't know that Pandora was shadowing my movements in order to find you. I am not used to dealing with kind. Are you hurt?"

"No, not really."

"Thank the heavens you are alright."

"That's just it, Uli. I am not alright. She has Jacob and won't let him go."

"What does Pandora want?"

"Oh, she basically told me to walk away from being an angel and then she'll give him back, or at least put him back in his body. She said she'd take care of the Malem Tutela problem for me as well. I have 24 hours to decide."

"I see."

"As if I trust her to do what she says," Catherine mused.

"What are you going to do?"

"I can't walk away now, can I? Many, many people need me to become what I am, right?"

"Yes, they do."

"I don't believe she'll give Jacob back either, no matter what I do."

"She will not."

Catherine pleaded with Uli, "What would you do?"

Alice touched her cheek with her small hand, "You know I can't tell you that. This is your life. This is your choice, whether to become who you truly are. That is true of all human beings."

"The whole human free will thing?"

"Yes."

"What I really want to do is kick Pandora's ass."

Alice giggled. "Me too, trust me, and about a billion other Seraphim."

"I know that I can no longer turn away from my true self even if I am afraid. It is who I am, and anything else would be a waste."

"You are very wise."

Catherine was exhausted. She felt Alice's small hand resting on her shoulder as she said, "We'll speak later. Your friends are coming. If you walk up to the street, they'll be here in a minute or two."

"Okay, Uli."

Just as she said, Catherine walked the distance from the stairs, through the square and up to the road, and she saw Beth's car. Catherine waved to them. Everyone but Beth hopped out of the car immediately. In 5 seconds, she was surrounded by her friends.

"Oh man. Am I glad to see you guys!"

They all stood in a big group hug until Beth honked. "Hey, let's get home, I can't park here."

David's face reflected his hours of desperate worry. He picked her up and put her in the back seat. Joshua took shot gun and Erica got in on Catherine's other side.

Beth turned to Catherine, "Are you okay? We've been worried sick that you got mugged or something."

Catherine established her cover right then and there. "I am so sorry to worry you guys. I guess I was so awestruck by the architecture that I wandered out a different door and before I knew it I was in some place I didn't recognize. I couldn't even see the church anymore. I swear the city is a big maze. My phone was acting stupid and couldn't get a signal. I was famished so I finally stopped to eat somewhere. I thought honestly I'd find my way back to the Metro at least, but I didn't. Then my phone decided to work again, damn thing, and I called."

Sounds like I'm basically an airhead but much better that than explaining what really happened.

"Oh my God, that same kind of thing happened to me about a year ago. Were you scared?" Beth asked. Catherine nodded but it was hard to keep from laughing. "Okay let's get you back to the house."

Catherine laid her head back on the seat to relax. "I can't believe this is what happened with our play day. It really started out so well."

Both David and Erica looked at her sympathetically. "I know, sweetie, but we'll have more time to play." Erica whispered.

David put his arm around Catherine and pulled her close. He kissed her on the forehead and whispered. "I'm never going to let you out of my sight again. I have never been that scared in my whole life."

Catherine closed her eyes and held on to him tightly as they ventured back to the villa.

128- *Search Query*

Nathan chugged the last of his energy drink and tossed it on top of his already piled high trash can. He wiped his eyes which were blurry due to his lack of sleep over the past several days. He was accustomed to being a night owl and operating on little sleep, but the repeated lack of sleep was starting to catch-up with him.

Nathan was seated at the desk in his elaborate room of very expensive toys. He was looking up at three flat screen wall-mounted 25 inch monitors that split his desktop.

When Razoul first approached him with work, Nathan had made a list of every piece of premium equipment he had ever wanted. This was the exchange they had made for certain duties whenever Razoul needed him. Nathan now lived in a grown boy's paradise that was only interrupted when he actually had to deal Razoul in person.

It was after nightfall when Nathan got his first possible hit on Catherine's whereabouts. A prompt popped up on his screen, "MATCH FOUND". Nathan clicked on the search query match with his mouse.

"Let's see what we have here. Drum roll please! I gotcha, oh yeah...you cannot escape the master of disaster."

After his brief moment of self satisfied glory, he decided to inform someone about his find. Then he'd get back to work again. He knew it would still take time to locate exactly where the email physically came from, but now it was only a matter of time.

He pushed his chair back with a big shove, and it rolled him across the wooden floor like a little kid. He got up with a bounce and walked out of the room in triumph. Still displayed on one of Nathan's monitors was the email that Luke had sent to Natalie earlier that morning.

Nathan's room was placed on the far end of the estate on purpose. This was to keep him out of the daily affairs and inner workings of the Malem Tutela's affairs. He started toward Razoul's quarters. He had hoped that he'd run into someone who he could give the message to Razoul instead of delivering it himself. But no luck, the hallways were deserted.

He knocked on the door with apprehension and flinched when Razoul voice came booming from the other side of the door.

"Come!"

"It's Nathan. I have some important news for you," he said, opening the door and closing it behind him. He stood there waiting to be acknowledged, but instead received Razoul's caustic impatience.

"Will you spit it out already so I can back to what I was doing?"

"I found her. It'll only be only a few hours before I can give you the exact address where she is and ahead of the deadline."

129- *The Call*

Hunger gripped Catherine when they returned to the villa. Erica had put some noodles and bread together for her. "God, I feel like I haven't eaten in a week!" Catherine exclaimed between bites.

"Well, I was going to ask you Cat if you even tasted the food before you swallowed it."

They both laughed.

Luke walked in the kitchen and before he could speak, Catherine answered him. "Sure, Luke, I'll get the book for you."

He looked at her a bit surprised, but simply said, "Thank you."

She retrieved the book for Luke and then excused herself to go up and take a hot bath. She needed time to think after her ordeal at St. Peter's earlier. Hot baths had always helped her chill out. She was about to slide down into the hot water when her phone rang. It was an unknown number, but she answered it anyway.

"Hello?"

"Yes, Catherine, this is Monsignor Bartholomew. I wanted to check on you to see if you needed anything?"

"Monsignor Bartholomew. So nice of you to call. I think that I am set. I seem to have everything I need."

"How are you doing? I know you were dealing with a great deal of confusion when we met."

"Well I'm sure you'll be happy to know that things are much clearer now. Though I can't say I know what I am doing at all, I am trying to accept who I am."

"This is very good news. Just open your heart to the process and you will have everything you require."

"I appreciate the time you were able to spend with me, explaining things. I just wanted to be sure to thank you."

"It's my pleasure. The other Essene Guardians wish me to convey to you their love and devotion for all you do."

"Wow. Okay. Please give them my thanks and my blessing?"

"Yes, I think that would be an appropriate response."

"Oh, good that makes me happy,"

"I don't wish to keep you my child, it is getting late."

Catherine had an idea come out of nowhere, which meant either she had a sudden epiphany or Uli was coaching her. Either way it made perfect sense.

"Monsignor?"

"Yes?"

"There is something that you and the Guardians can do to help me. May I come to your office tomorrow morning?"

Bartholomew thought of his morning meeting with Father Ignatius "I have some important business at the Vatican around 9.but I should return to the office by 10:30 for certain. Shall we set an appointment for then?"

"Yes, that would be perfect."

"Very good. I will see you tomorrow."

Catherine hung up the phone and slipped her body slowly into the tub. "Ahhhh…that's so nice."

About an hour later Catherine was startled by a steady tap on the bathroom door.

"Yeah?"

"It's David, are you okay in there?"

"Yep, I'm okay, why?"

"It's been over an hour since you came up here. I just wanted to be sure."

"Really? Geez, I must have gotten so relaxed I dozed off."

"Beth is already in bed and Roger is going up shortly. I pried the book from Luke's fingers and put it in the box in your drawer. I imagine he'll head to bed soon, too."

"Okay. I'll get out of the tub and be down shortly."

"We'll be out back waiting for you."

Catherine dried off and went into the bedroom to get something wear. She pulled the drawer open so she could see the book. "I'll be back to see *you* later." Then she rolled her eyes.

Now I sound like Luke.

She threw on her pajama pants and a t-shirt and came down the stairs. Luke passed her going up the stairs on his way to bed.

Speak of the devil…

"How are you feeling, Catherine?"

"Oh much better, thanks."

"I'm glad to hear it. I understand that you've had a rough couple of days."

"You don't know the half of it," Catherine whispered as she reached the bottom of the stairs.

Luke turned to speak once he reached the top. "Did you say something else?"

Catherine smiled sweetly at him. "Nope, was just agreeing with you. Good night."

"Good night, Catherine."

Catherine opened the fridge and poured herself a glass of cranberry juice. She walked outside, "Okay it's time for a long debrief. You guys ready?"

"I was born ready," David said.

"I'm sure you were." She shot him a flirty glance.

Catherine sat down. "Okay…this is what happened."

130- *Possibilities*

Catherine should have been in a deep slumber the moment her head hit the pillow, but all she could do was toss and turn. She felt like there was something she forgot to do. She tried another position, but it didn't last long. Eventually she decided it was best to try and figure out why she couldn't sleep instead of fighting it.

Catherine turned over and closed her eyes to focus.

Okay, maybe this will work. What do I need to do next?

Nothing came to her.

Concentrate, Catherine, just relax and concentrate.

Still nothing came.

Why didn't I spend my time learning to meditate properly?

She followed her breath in and out for a few minutes.

What do I need to do?

Much to her surprise, she saw the book appear clearly in her mind's eye.

Yes, that's it! Awesome.

She hopped out of bed and got the box. She sat herself in the middle of the bed and placed the book in her lap. Immediately the glow spread all around her, just like before.

"Let's see what happens if I try to make it glow brighter instead of being freaked out."

She concentrated, closing her eyes. Catherine tried to visualize the light growing brighter and brighter around her until it filled the room. She started feeling warmer and warmer, so she opened her eyes.

Oh my God, I did it!

A brilliant light had filled the room around her just like she had visualized. She stretched out her arms to both sides. Then she watched her hands closely as she moved them. The light seemed to stream out of her skin and flow with her gentle movements back and forth.

This is so cool. I imagine this is what people describe after doing LSD. Let's try something else.

As she shifted her focus toward minimizing the light, faded like a dimmer switch. Catherine opened the book and flipped through the pages. She tried turning the pages a certain way. She moved her index finger back and forth on the words. Nothing happened no matter what she did or how she turned pages. Then she suddenly remembered her experience while at the catacombs.

Hmmm...what about this?

Catherine consciously focused her attention on the book. Then with the book open in her lap, she placed both palms face down just like she had on the pedestal in the chamber.

To her surprise, the book lifted up and hovered there about 8 inches above her lap. She tried to move the book to look at it. It kept floating there. The twelve symbols in the outer ring that was embossed on the book cover began to glow orange and pulsate. The circle or ring holding those 12 symbols began to glow an electric blue, just as they had in the chamber that night. It was like the whole book was waking up.

Whoa, this is incredible!

She focused her intention much harder and the symbol began to appear in both her palms, just as they had during her flight to Rome. Something filtered into her mind, like a really distant memory. At first it was fuzzy. She tried to relax and let it come. Slowly it came through. She saw herself in the chamber but not with Roger. She was standing in the center, but she wasn't alone. Standing on each of the 12 other positions were a mixture of men and women. They had their palms face up. She could see their palms glowing as well, but with their own symbols.

She wanted to see more, but she was finally getting tired. "Okay that's enough for now." The book floated down onto the bed as if following her command. The symbols slowly faded out on the cover and then from her hands.

Catherine now believed that she could learn to use the book. It would just take time. She placed the book back in her drawer. After turning out the light, she curled up under the covers.

Hopefully I did good, Uli.

Wonderful, Catherine, simply wonderful.

There you are my angel, good night.

131- *Gotcha*

Nathan was rudely awakened by a swift kick on his shoe. He was sitting at his desk, fast asleep. "Wake up, Nathan. Razoul sent me to get the address from you since you didn't call.

Nathan noticed it was daylight outside. "Sorry must have fallen asleep at some point."

"Do you have it?"

"Have what?" Nathan was still groggy and disoriented.

"The woman's address, stupid!"

"Oh yeah, okay. I have it written down here somewhere. Just let me find it." Nathan fumbled through various scraps of paper strewn across his desk. "Here it is." He handed it to Thaddeus.

Thaddeus snatched it out of his hand and left the room.

"You're welcome," Nathan called behind him.

"You're an imbecile," Thaddeus replied from half way down the hall. He was headed to get Sirius and take him to the ballroom to see Razoul. Thaddeus reached his room and knocked. "Sirius, it's time."

132- *Watch*

Catherine woke early faced the day with a surplus of energy just like the day before. She knocked quietly on David's door first. He answered in his boxers. "Oh, Catherine, good morning. I thought you were Joshua. He seems to always need something in the morning."

Catherine's expression was endearing. "Nope, not a Mr. Joshua, just a Ms. Angel here to see you."

"Oh, I see that. What can I do for you, Ms. Angel?"

"Can you come to my room before you go downstairs?"

"Sure."

"Bring the others too, but quietly please. I don't want to wake anyone else."

"Okay, will do."

Catherine went back to her room to wait. She was brushing her hair when the group entered the room in single file.

"Lock the door. I want to show you all something that I discovered last night."

Catherine sat on the bed with the book in her lap. She focused her mind on expanding the glow again. Everyone gasped as light flooded the room.

"That's not all. I figured out something important too about the chamber and everything. Watch this."

As Catherine repeated her actions from the night before, the book lifted up. Joshua was so baffled that he came over and ran his hand underneath it and over it, as if checking for hidden wires.

"Don't you believe, Joshua?"

"Of course, angel. I just wasn't really prepared for this. I had to check." He shoved his hands nervously in his pockets.

"Watch the 12 symbols on the cover and the circle."

Just as the night before, they began to glow and pulse.

"That's incredible!" David exclaimed.

"Catherine, YOU are so incredible." Erica clapped her hands.

"And last but not least...I know why my hands were burning those couple of times. It first happened on the plane and also in the chamber before I even touched the pedestal." Catherine raised her palms to show everyone.

"Does it hurt you?" Joshua was visibly concerned.

"It doesn't hurt. Do you want to feel them? They aren't hot"

"That's okay. I'll take your word for it.

Erica could not contain her excitement. "So you can work the book! You are definitely the Angel Incarnate." Then after a pause, she added, "See, I told you."

"Yes, Erica, you were right. But I still have a lot to learn. I am supposed to be able to read it and also to do the incantations in here. But so far, I think I can only turn it on. But it's a start, right?"

"A good start, I'd say," David said with admiration.

"Also I need to see Monsignor Bartholomew today at 10:30. I forgot to mention it last night. He called just before my bath. After passing out in the bathtub, I spaced it. I have a new plan that I need to discuss with him."

"What's your plan, Ms. Angel?" David sat down on the bed next to her.

"The Essene have been safeguarding this prophecy and communicating with the angels for a very long time. They were also given the task of protecting me, without interfering. But that has changed now. I know who I am. I just don't know how to be who I am very well yet. I need them to help me become more of the real me fast, if I have any hope of standing against Pandora or anybody else that's coming my way."

"It is a perfect plan. But it is a plan that none of us can follow through on an empty stomach and mine is growling. See you downstairs."

133- *Execute*

Thaddeus and Sirius arrived in the ballroom to find Razoul seated at the conference table, as if he had been waiting for their arrival. He handed the paper to Razoul. Razoul looked at the address and said, "It's not that far from here. This is excellent." Then he looked up at Thaddeus.

"Has the priest secured the document?"

"Yes, the priest assures me that he has taken possession of it."

"When are you to meet him then?"

"Originally I had arranged with him to meet at one of our secured locations near the Vatican at eleven; however, this morning he said that he must attend a meeting on behalf of the Cardinal. He felt it would draw too much attention if were absent. I agreed and now we are meeting at two when he can get away." Thaddeus braced for Razoul's usual snide comment, but none came.

"The delay is fine. We will not go after the angel until nightfall. We must be precise and perfect in our execution of the attack. You will take the lead, Thaddeus. Once you have her and the book is secured, I will make my presence known."

Thaddeus bit his tongue.

"Is there something you wish to say to me Thaddeus?" Razoul was always trying to bait him into a conflict.

"No, nothing. You can count on my precision in this matter, of course."

"Very good then, you both may go, I need to make preparations. We'll meet here to go over details at two thirty once you've retrieved the document from the priest."

"As you wish," Thaddeus bowed and ushered himself and Sirius out. Once they were fully clear of the ballroom, he practically threw a fit.

Sirius stopped him. "Let's go up to my chambers and speak privately."

Once they entered the old man's room and closed the door, Thaddeus exploded, "Can't you see what that snake is doing? He is sending me in first, that way if she's more powerful than he thought or something goes wrong, I can take the hit for him!"

Sirius knew that what Thaddeus said was true. It was likely part of Razoul's strategy to let him assume any necessary risks. "Thaddeus, I certainly think you can handle a mere woman and her companions. If things get out of hand, then kill her yourself."

"That would make Razoul's blood boil, wouldn't it?" Thaddeus reveled in the thought of that happening. "Ahhhh…what fun it would be to rob him of his elusive prize! It would indeed be an easily justified and secret revenge on him for all he's done to humiliate us."

"Tread carefully, Thaddeus. I am certain Razoul will be watching your every move and will know if you cross him deliberately."

"Perhaps, but if it's between me and her, I shall save my own life and deal with the consequences later."

134- *Her Plan*

They arrived at Monsignor Bartholomew's office by taxi about 15 minutes early. Catherine checked in with the clerk, but the Monsignor had not returned yet. So the group of them found a small table to sit at and wait in the main hall.

Erica started the conversation. "I think Roger is beginning to get some strange idea about us. I expect him to start pressing with questions soon. I've tried to placate him as much as I can."

"I know Erica. I've been concerned about that too. He's paid our way and so far I haven't been able to do any of the work with him, as I am sure he was expecting. Of course, that is what I was expecting at first, too." She paused. "Then Luke was added to the mix. I am not sure if it was the best thing to do, but I let him copy pages out by hand yesterday after I explained to him that I just didn't feel comfortable leaving it behind. So I hope those few pages will keep Luke fairly occupied for awhile. We just have to stall Roger for a couple more days."

"I've thought about that too," David added. "I've even considered suggesting we move to a hotel. That way you can do what you need to without worrying so much about an academic and a linguist pulling on you right now. Plus, the longer we stay, the more nervous I feel." David looked as though he was thinking about whether to share something else, then he decided to spit it out. "I can't shake the feeling that the Malem Tutela might find us there."

Catherine put her elbows on the table and leaned her chin on her hands. "I'm not sure who to be more concerned about, the Malem Tutela or Pandora. I guess I figure an immortal being like her outweighs some group of Italian thugs. So many details right now, it's overwhelming. Maybe we should move locations tomorrow, just to play it safe? Erica, can you take care of finding us a new place to stay? Not far from the main part of Rome, but obscure enough they wouldn't think to look there?"

"Sure. I'll make some calls today and get our reservations made."

"Great." Catherine sighed. "I guess we'll find out soon enough if I have the mojo to save Jacob. If I can't, at least I tried, right?"

"Of course. No matter what happens, I am here by your side, whether your plan succeeds or not. No one here at this table is expecting a miracle from you right now either. Just believe in yourself and do the best you can."

"Let's go." They followed Catherine to the front desk. When the clerk saw her coming toward him, he motioned for her come with him.

"The Monsignor just returned and will see you now, please follow me."

Once they reached the office, the others knew to stay behind in the receiving area. David hugged her before she went in, whispering into her ear, "Knock'em dead, slugger."

"Okay, I will."

The Monsignor was seated on a beautiful antique couch in the back of the room waiting for her.

"Catherine it's so good to see you again." He rose to greet her, taking her hand. "Please have a seat. The couch is much more comfortable than the other chairs. I hope you weren't waiting long. My business took just a little longer than I expected."

"No, not at all."

"Now dear, please tell me what can we do to serve you?"

"I need you to train me to use my gifts."

"Those will develop over time, my angel." He bowed slightly.

"I realize that but, I have a pressing need to know everything that the Guardians know. I believe that my time to learn everything is running out." Catherine pointed at her watch for effect. "In fact, I suspect that the immortal who threatened me yesterday will be back by tomorrow to keep her promise."

Bartholomew was visibly shocked, which Catherine didn't expect.

"An immortal?"

"Yes, Monsignor an immortal. Apparently the prophecy and the fact that an angel has been born into the human world has angered Pandora. She has threatened to astrally torture one of my best friends since childhood if I don't abandon my path. His name is Jacob and he's currently in a coma back in my hometown. In fact, she dangled him in front of me in the middle of St. Peter's Basilica to prove her point. Then she offered me a deal and disappeared."

"This is indeed a grave circumstance Catherine. I had no idea. What deal did she offer?"

"Just walk away and forget you ever learned that you were an angel. I'll give you your friend back and throw in taking care of your Malem Tutela problem for good measure. That was the deal she offered me."

"And if you refuse her?"

"She'll torture Jacob endlessly and when she grows bored of that, she will come and destroy me too."

Bartholomew began to pace. "This cannot be. We were not prepared for this threat."

Catherine looked at him sincerely. "I believe you. I know that you were not prepared because even the angels didn't anticipate Pandora's interference."

"You are indeed a wise angel to come to me with this. In light of this new threat, the game has changed tremendously. The Essene Guardians will do whatever we can to assist you."

"I had hoped that you would say that."

Bartholomew came over and hugged her tightly. "Catherine, you are the most precious gift that God has ever given to mankind. We will protect and serve you even if we must sacrifice our lives in doing so. This has been our sacred pledge for centuries." As if to solidify the pledge to her, he placed his hands in prayer and bowed.

Catherine reached out to put her hand on his shoulder gently. "Well I do hope that there will be no reason for that, Monsignor." Catherine was extremely uncomfortable with people throwing themselves on a bomb for her.

"There is a matter I must see through to its conclusion at one today, but I will be finished with that quickly. I will call the Guardians together. I can send a car for you at your address around three if that is alright."

"Yes, of course, Monsignor. I will bring the box with the Angelus Aevum with me. I have been slightly successful with turning it on, or however you would say it. May I bring my friends with me?"

"I will be taking you to the most secret place of the Essene. Out of respect for the other Guardians who will be quite surprised, even startled, to meet you this afternoon, it might be best for you to come alone this time. This way we can also focus more powerfully on your training without any distraction. We have quite a lot to accomplish this evening." As if to answer Catherine's questions before she asked them, he continued, "I can guarantee your safety. Your driver is also part of the Essene Brotherhood, of course. I can also guarantee that once inside our meeting chamber that even Pandora cannot find you there."

"I understand. If that is how we must proceed, then I will do it. I have my address for you also. I'll leave you to your work now.

"I will see you soon, Catherine. Be well and travel in peace."

Once the door was closed, he finally let his true feelings show. "Heaven help us."

135- *The News*

"It's a go! I was right. They're sworn to protect me. He said they would teach me as much as they knew. He also said their secret meeting place was safe from Pandora's prying eyes."

David hugged her to congratulate her. "That's wonderful news. That makes me the happiest man alive right now."

"Good, keep those happy thoughts going because there's a catch too that I know you won't be happy about. Apparently there have been no outsiders in their sanctuary, ever. Out of respect for the other Guardians, he didn't feel that we should overwhelm them with all of us at once."

"We're not going?"

"No David, not this time, but I will do my best to rectify that once I meet the others."

David was visibly upset. "I told you that I wouldn't leave your side Catherine. I don't want to. If they are sworn to protect you, then they should do what you say. Just tell them I have to be there."

"Monsignor assured me of his ability to keep me safe. The driver of the car he'll send is also one of his trusted brothers in the Essene order."

"I don't trust anyone right now Catherine, especially where you are concerned."

Catherine touched David on his arm gently. "Do you trust me?"

"Of course I do."

"Then I need you to trust me that this is the path I must walk right now. I can't explain why or how I know that, but I do. I need you to protect Joshua and Erica while I'm gone in case something happens. Can you do that for me?"

His face softened. "Of course I will Catherine. You know I will."

"Okay then, let's head back to the house for some lunch. I need to rest. I imagine it will be a very long night cramming my head with angel stuff."

David followed behind the others as they left and soon he became consumed in thought. Every instinct told him to resist her going alone, but something in his heart told him that Catherine was right.

I do trust you Catherine but I really don't trust anyone else. I am hopelessly in love with you, too...wish I could tell you how much...Maybe I'm just being paranoid, but what is the terrible feeling I have?

136- *The Hand Off*

Thaddeus anxiously awaited the priest's arrival. It was now five minutes past two. He paced nervously back and forth outside the entrance to the warehouse. Just then he saw a figure out of the corner of his eye and spoke without looking at him, "You're late."

"My apologies, sir. It could not be avoided. Someone entered my office as I was leaving, and I had to assist them."

"Whatever the excuse, at least you are here now. Where is the document?"

Father Ignatius reluctantly handed him a slender tube with rubber caps on each end. Thaddeus had been instructed to inspect the document before allowing the priest to leave.

"Wait right there. I need to have a look at this." Thaddeus popped off one of the ends and slid the parchment out. When he did, it fell on the ground.

"Be careful, Thaddeus. The document is extremely fragile."

"I'm not an idiot priest!"

Thaddeus picked it up and unrolled it to examine the paper's age and consistency. Then he pulled a slip of paper out of his pocket and held it up to the document to check that the designation numbers matched.

"Alright priest, you may go. If the document turns up missing, you will take the fall for it. Otherwise you know what will happen."

Father Ignatius nodded that he understood.

"Off with you now."

Thaddeus quickly got into his car and sped off. He dialed Daniel's phone. "I have it. It's legitimate. Tell Razoul I will be there in 20." He hung up and checked his watch. It was now 2:30. "Six hours until we move out."

137- *Getting Ready*

When they arrived back at the house, everyone else was gone. Catherine was relieved since she didn't want to face Roger just yet.

After lunch, they all decided to take a relaxing swim in the beautiful pool. Joshua was in absolute heaven the whole time. He hadn't gone swimming since he was little boy.

It was almost three.

"I am so nervous. You'd think I was going on stage tonight performing for 20,000 people or something," Catherine shared with David.

"You will do fine. Remember, you were born to do this. I wish I was going with you, but I promise to hold down the fort while you are gone."

"You are so sweet. Thank you for being you."

"I am what I am, and that's all that I am, Ms. Angel." He bowed.

"Alright, funny man." Catherine reached up to hug him as the doorbell rang.

"I think that's your cue. I'll get the door."

Catherine came down the stairs and hugged both Erica and Joshua who had come down ahead of her and were waiting to say goodbye.

"Alright, guys. Please do wait up for me."

Catherine glanced looked outside through the open front door and saw that the driver was standing by the open back door of the sedan. "I guess I'd better scoot."

"One minute there, Ms. Angel. There's something I forgot to do."

Catherine stopped and stood there expectantly.

David put his arms around Catherine and leaned in for a kiss good-bye that quickly made Catherine melt into his arms. A wave of energy passed through them both as they shared a long, enduring kiss. Catherine felt dizzy all of the sudden and stepped back. There was only one word she could manage to say once he released her, "Wow."

"Okay that's it, you can go learn now." David had a huge grin on his face and then added, "See you soon."

Catherine just stood there speechless for a few moments. Erica and Joshua were standing there now as well with their mouths wide open.

"Okay then...see you all soon." Then she turned around slowly as she attempted to steady her legs that now felt like Jell-O.

Oh my...that was the most incredible kiss I've ever had.

Still reeling from the energy of David's unexpected kiss, Catherine walked slowly down the sidewalk toward the open door.

138- *Delivery*

"Read this for me, Sirius, and see if you believe this is a real incantation, as Samyaza said." Razoul had carefully removed the scroll from the tube and placed four small paperweights on each edge to keep it flattened.

Sirius put on his glasses and sat down. He read the scroll carefully spotting several key phrases that commanded an angel return to heaven, forever.

He peered at Razoul over his glasses and nodded. "It appears this is meant to send an angel back to heaven for good and most likely will kill her body in the process, once you successfully recite this in her presence."

"Yes, this is what I need to get rid of her. I will have my victory tonight, at last."

"There are also several warnings at the beginning of the scroll that you should be aware of which make this is one of the riskiest incantations imaginable."

"Don't be dramatic, Sirius. What warnings? Out with it."

"If you make a mistake while reciting this, you will be wounded gravely. Also, if you are interrupted, and do not finish in sufficient time, you will be wounded gravely. This is foolishness Razoul. Surely even you can see it. Don't you think the Fallen One knew this when he sent you on this little mission? Might it be possible that he is setting you up to perish for his own amusement?"

"I must not and will not fail, Sirius."

"How do you know?"

"Because I have the most supremely gifted Latin teacher sitting right in front of me right now, and you are going to teach me to recite it perfectly."

"Razoul, you expect me to teach you correct pronunciation of this and flow of this incantation in less than six hours?"

"Yes, old man. Get started."

139- *Training*

The activity of Rome drifted past her line of sight in a blur of colors and expressions. Catherine touched her lips still feeling David's kiss.

I can't believe he did that. I can't believe it made me feel the way it did. Shut up, Catherine, you are sounding like a little girl. It's not like you've never been kissed. Well, it's definitely been awhile...

The driver hadn't said a word.

What will the meeting place be like? I wonder what the other guardians will say? Maybe they see right through me? Maybe they will just tell me I'm not ready...

She tried to push the doubts from her mind, but it was difficult for her. The longer they drove the more her anxiety started to climb.

"Um, driver?"

"Yes, Senora?"

"How much longer until we get where we are going?"

"Not much further. We will arrive shortly."

"Is Monsignor Bartholomew meeting us?"

The driver nodded, "Yes, he will meet us." Then he turned his eyes back to the road in front of him.

Catherine took a deep breath and tried to relax.

Uli? Are you still there?

Yes Catherine. I am here.

What should I do? I mean what should I say to them?

Just be yourself Catherine. That's all you need to do.

Be myself? How am I supposed to do that when I'm really not sure who I am?

Just try to have faith in yourself and the rest will follow.

Catherine's inner dialog with Uli was interrupted by a jerk of the sedan coming to a stop. They had stopped in front of a stone apartment building with tiny windows. The driver got out and came around to open the door. He took Catherine's hand to help her out.

"Here you are. Please go inside and follow the staircase down one floor. Knock on Room 111 and Monsignor will be waiting for you."

"Okay, thank you."

The driver bowed as Catherine went inside.

"Okay, Room 111, piece of cake."

Catherine opened the front door. It was extremely weathered and the green paint that had once been clean and crisp was now cracked heavily and there were grooves all across its surface. Once she was inside she found that the entire building was silent, except for the sound of her own breath which was heavy with anticipation.

Oh man...You call these stairs?

The staircase leading downstairs was very narrow and steep. The steps were wooden and heavily pitted and in a way didn't look stable, but she started down them anyway.

Once she reached the bottom, the hallway was very dim and it took a moment to adjust to the lighting. She focused on the first door numbers that were barely visible, *101.* The next door read *103.*

Okay, four more to go.

When she reached the door that should have been 111, there were no numbers on it at all. "This better be it." She said under her breath.

Should I knock? I can't remember if the driver said knock or just go in?

When she was about to trying knocking, the door opened swiftly. Standing in front of her was Monsignor Bartholomew in the long, brown robe that he was wearing the first time she had seen him during her out of body experience on the plane.

"Come, come, Catherine. Come inside."

Bartholomew ushered her into the room, checked the hallway briefly and then closed the door behind them.

"Follow me."

She followed him down the narrow hallway of the flat to the final room at the end. It was a small bedroom no more than 8 foot square, with a small window and closet. Bartholomew opened the closet door revealing a vertical, iron spiral staircase going down. He stepped aside and motioned for her to go first.

"Please, watch your step."

Catherine put the box under her left arm and started down the stairs. The steps were tightly packed and went down farther than her eyes could see in the scant light. The smell of damp Earth was all around her. She wondered how they had cut the long vertical shaft necessary to put in the stairs in without anyone knowing.

Once she had descended 30 or more stairs, a welcome dim light started to spill up the stairs from below. She had started to feel like a cork screw going down, down, down and it made her dizzy.

Eventually she reached the very bottom and moved out of the way for Bartholomew to exit the stairs as well. To her surprise she saw man-made tunnels lit by recessed modern lighting, each extending in the four directions from the area they were standing in. Bartholomew chose one of the tunnels and started to head down it. Catherine followed him, trying to make small talk in order to calm her anxiety.

"Who made these tunnels down here?"

Without turning back Bartholomew answered, "These tunnels were originally hollowed out for a burial crypt below the city. The original entrance to them caved in over 100 years ago, and the site was abandoned. Since that time, the city and people have forgotten about them. The Essene Guardians decided to reclaim the space by gaining access through the apartment above, so that we would be able to meet in safety without detection. Very few know about them. We own the apartment building that you passed through as well."

The thought of how long it took to dig these tunnels by handmade Catherine shudder. The further they walked, she began to hear voices. Eventually they emerged into a large room that was lit with at least a dozen tall pillar candles on iron platforms. There was a large table in the center where she could see the source of the echoing voices. Bartholomew cleared his throat when they entered.

"Ah, Brother Bartholomew is here." Aurora rose and greeted them. Catherine reluctantly stepped forward from his left side into full view of the other Guardians.

"And this must be the beautiful Catherine!" Aurora was an older woman, but immensely radiant. Aurora leaned forward to hug her, and Catherine hugged her back. There was something immediately calming about Aurora's touch, and Catherine's disintegrated.

Now that she was calmer, she looked at the features in the room. She noticed immediately that someone had carved the angelic symbols from her book into the wall and inlayed them with gold. Catherine couldn't resist placing her hand over the 13th Symbol even though it was twice as big as her outstretched fingers.

"I see that you chose your own symbol from the wall, Catherine," Aurora praised.

"The symbol has appeared in my palms a couple times. At the time I didn't know why any of this was happening."

"The 13th Symbol is an image that is embedded with your unique energy. Some part of you already knows about this and what we are about to help teach you."

"I think I have a lot to learn."

Aurora immediately corrected her. "You have a lot to remember, my dear. Everything you need is already inside of you just waiting for your permission to let it out. Come over here. I'll introduce you to the other Guardians."

Catherine came over to the table and placed the box on it. "This is getting really heavy."

Bartholomew took his place to Aurora's right.

"You have been meeting with Brother Bartholomew. I am Sister Aurora. To my left is Brother Matthew."

Brother Matthew stood up and placed his hands in prayer, bowed and said, "It is my esteem honor to meet you, angel. I shall serve you to the best of my human ability." He looked much younger than Aurora, maybe in his thirties, with very short hair, small facial features and dark eyes.

"It's nice to meet you, Matthew."

Aurora continued around the table one by one.

"To his left is Sister Anastasia." Sister Anastasia could not contain her excitement and leapt up before Aurora could get her name out. She bowed, putting her hands quickly into prayer. "I have yearned to reach this moment my whole life. My goodness, I am grateful for my many blessings! I will serve you always."

Anastasia had the enthusiasm of a teenager, but was actually middle aged. Her sweet round face and small, short frame seemed ready to explode with joy at any moment.

"Thank you, Sister Anastasia, for such a very warm welcome."

"To Anastasia's left is Brother Joseph." He was more solemn than the others. His demeanor was very formal and a huge contrast to Anastasia's warmer welcome. "I am humbled to meet you and will do my best to serve you." After bowing in prayer to her, he sat down.

"I am pleased to meet you, Brother Joseph."

"To Joseph's left is the final Guardian, Sister Francesca. "She is a master of meditation and opening the mind's eye." Francesca looked a lot like an angel to Catherine. She was radiant and confident, but completely approachable. Francesca stood up and said while bowing, "I very much look forward to helping you with your mission as much as I possibly can."

"I truly appreciate your assistance, Sister Francesca."

Aurora sat down and began to guide the work they would be doing while Catherine was with them. "Brother Bartholomew has advised us of the unexpected threat. We are saddened of course to hear of Pandora's involvement and have empathy for your friend as well. We now feel the priority in your training is to awaken the knowledge you possess that has been forgotten. By using the Angelus Aevum and Francesca's abilities to open your mind, we hope this will be the push you need to recover this knowledge."

"I have already been trying to work with the book. May I show you what I learned?" Catherine was eager to demonstrate.

Aurora motioned for her to do so.

Catherine took a very deep breath. She opened the box, took it out of the scarf and placed it on the table in front of her. She placed her hands palms down on the cover and closed her eyes.

She heard Francesca's voice speaking softly to her. "Let go of any expectation, Catherine. Clear your mind and focus on balancing your energy with the book's energy. They are meant to work in harmony."

The book, as Catherine expected, activated itself underneath her hands as light filled the room. She could feel the symbol pulsating in her palms and naturally lifted them up in front of her about ten inches from where the book was floating. "Okay, Catherine, that's very good. I want you to try something else."

Catherine kept her eyes closed. "Okay."

"Think about the knowledge contained inside the book and the knowledge deep inside you. They are from the same source. Think of yourself and the book as communicating with each other. Visualize energy moving from your hands to the book and move this energy back and forth consciously."

Come on, book, wake up. Come on, Catherine, wake up.

"I keep thinking of other things. Nothing is happening."

"When your other thoughts intrude on what you are doing, just acknowledge the thoughts and release them. Then bring yourself back to the task at hand."

"Okay, I'll try."

Catherine focused again and found the suggestion helpful. Her body became warm and tingly. "Something is happening. I can feel it."

"Good Catherine, just stay with the process. I know you can do this."

The darkness behind her closed eyes suddenly illuminated into an infinite array of colors like a kaleidoscope. She began to see images in her head, but when she would try to focus on what they were, the images would fade. She kept trying over and over but became more frustrated as she failed.

Her eyes flew open. "I can't do this." As a result, the book slammed into the table with a huge thud. "Every time I tried to see the images that came through, they dissolved. I am not good at this kind of stuff."

She looked at Francesca who was gazing at her with loving, understanding eyes. "The best way to open up this communication is to relax. Don't try to see anything specific as it begins to appear. Just open yourself to receive and allow it to become whatever it is. You can do this. Now let's try again."

"Okay, I can do this. I just need to let go. Just let go." She took another deep breath and closed her eyes. This time it was easier to make the connection. In a few minutes, she started to see the colors again, and then prompted herself to relax more deeply.

Just breathe and allow, relax....

Images started to flow one by one. She first saw images of herself from her childhood that progressed in sequence to images of her as an adult. Then everything began to stream in more quickly. She could see places in the world she had never been before from overhead as if she was hovering above the Earth. Then she could see many angels, in groups of three or four, but she didn't recognize any of them.

Catherine took a huge deep breath. Then she was in a place with more angels. It wasn't a concrete place like the room she was in, but a gathering place for them. Suddenly she found herself in the center of the group. They were all speaking to her without moving what would have been their mouths. Catherine felt herself fill with a peace like she had never experienced before.

What are they saying to me? This is familiar, somehow. I can feel that they love me deeply, but there are speaking? There are no words...

The love spread all through Catherine's body, her heart and soul, and she felt an old emptiness leave her slowly. Light spread all through her now. The feelings in Catherine became overwhelming. This time, however, she surrendered to the wave of emotions and felt them carry her away. There was nothing else she could do but let go. She came out of her experience and began to wail, sobbing as if she had never been able to really cry in her whole life before. She couldn't think anymore, only feel.

"Oh God. Oh my God! It hurts!" She grasped her chest while trying to catch her breath, but the enormity of it made her back away from the table. The room got even dimmer.

Bartholomew moved quickly to catch Catherine as she collapsed. Aurora brought over a blanket and spread it out. He gently laid her down.

The guardians encircled them. As she lay there unconscious, the group began to offer healing prayers for Catherine's liberation from the pain of this world.

140- *Assault*

A disgruntled Thaddeus was busy making preparations for the assault on Catherine's location. His team was assembled to review the tactical plan.

"Demetrius, I'd like a report on today's surveillance of the property."

"At 0800 hours we identified several viable entrances to the property. One located in the front, another straight across in the rear and one service entrance on the west side. The property in question appears to be occupied by a total of 8 individuals. Five of the individuals were seen leaving together early this morning; Roger Thornton, Beth Ricoh, Luke Franklin, Bob Kelly and Greg Parker. The other four were seen leaving the property at 1000 hours, which included the rest of the occupants: Catherine Moore, David Anderson, Erica Baylor and Joshua Stark. The location was quiet until Catherine Moore and her associates returned to the property around 1300 hours. I have prepared a map of the house's interior layout."

Demetrius placed the map in front of Thaddeus. "This is the first floor. There is a kitchen here in the rear with an open dining room and living room. There are no walls separating the rooms so our entrance through the rear and front here and here will allow us to gain control once we get inside. Team 1 will enter through the front and Team 2 will enter through the rear. Team 3 will come in through the west service entrance in case there is anyone to secure in that area of the house."

Demetrius then referred to the upper level map. "Once the downstairs is secured, Team 1 will secure the prisoners while Team 2 will make a room by room sweep upstairs. As you can see there are eight bedrooms on the upper floor, four on each side."

Thaddeus studied the maps and listened to his plan. "Very good then, you and I will be Team 1, and I want you to you select your best men for the other two teams. I want you to have two additional groups, Teams 4 and 5, standing ready for anything unexpected."

"And last but not least, you have all heard this instruction before, but I wish to make this detail absolutely clear. No one is to lay a single finger on Catherine Moore. I will take care of her for Razoul, and give him the all clear once everything is secured."

Demetrius gave him a quick nod, and then turned to the other men. "Is everyone fully briefed about your mission and equally clear about Thaddeus' instruction?"

The room erupted in a coordinated, "Yes, sir!" from every man assembled there.

The roar of the men bolstered Thaddeus' confidence in their mission. "Alright Demetrius, you have your orders. Have your teams ready to move out at 1900 hours. We will setup our perimeter by 1930. We will make our assault of the house after sun down at precisely 2035."

"Yes, sir! Men, move out!"

141- *Waiting*

"I wonder what time Roger and the others will be here." Erica said, sipping on her tea. "Or more importantly, when Catherine will get back?"

It had been hard for David to pass the time since Catherine had been taken to see the Guardians. "I just wish we could have gone with her. It makes me so frustrated just sitting here. I have to do something!" He paced over to the front windows and glanced outside at the sunset as if willing Catherine to appear. "I won't feel better until she's back safe and sound."

"The angels are very happy about her training. I guess if they are happy, we should be happy, too," Joshua spoke with certainty.

David returned to the table and sat back down. "I'll try to be patient, Joshua. Right now I have a bad feeling that I can't shake. Like something is very wrong, but I have no idea what or why."

Joshua suggested, "Well, whenever I get like that, I take a long walk to clear my head."

"I think *more* when I walk, so I am not sure that will work for me," David offered.

Joshua stood up. "Well suit yourself. I'm going to get one more cup of coffee and then take a walk myself."

"There are cups with lids on the top shelf to the left of the stove if you want to take it with you." Erica knew her way well around the kitchen.

Joshua poured his coffee, popped the lid on and then proceeded toward the back door. He stopped dead in his tracks for a moment before opening the door. David and Erica watched him slowly walk outside, abruptly turn to his right, and disappear from sight.

Trying to stay positive for both of them, Erica turned to David. "I bet she'll have more cool stuff to show us when she gets back. What she showed us with the angel book was amazing. Seeing her do that made me want to rub my eyes and blink a few times to see if I was imagining it though." Then she chuckled lightly.

"Catherine never ceases to amaze me. I feel so fortunate to spend time with her. I wish she knew how incredible she is."

"She will soon, David, I'm sure. It just takes time to adjust. At the rate she's going, though, she'll be all lit up in no time."

"Do you think she knows how much I love her?"

"Of course she knows, David. We all know." Erica's reassurance eased his anxiety a bit.

"It's just hard for me to see why she'd want to be with someone like me. I mean's she's an angel, and I'm just a loner geek. That hardly seems enough to me."

"Listen, who we are or what we do doesn't have anything to do with true love. Just be yourself, and everything will be fine."

"Well, I'll do my best. Hey, what time do we check in to our hotel?"

"As early as eleven. I'm going to go upstairs and pack. That will kill some time. I want to have it done before Catherine comes back."

"Yeah, I will figure out something to do with my time to keep from going crazy. You know, I think I'll go for another swim."

Just outside and away from view, Joshua was crouched down on the east side of the house. He ducked into a group of bushes just as the angels had instructed him. They had warned him not to walk his usual path. He was awaiting more instructions.

In a few moments, Arian-naH appeared to him. "You must leave this place now, Joshua."

"What's happening?"

"They are coming, and we need to get you to safety."

"The…the…the…bad people?"

"Yes."

"I must go tell the others!"

"No, Joshua, you can't. They saw you come outside and we need to move you now. Close your eyes and let me take you somewhere safe. You'll stay there until we tell you to move."

Joshua obediently closed his eyes. He felt very warm and filled with peace. In a few minutes, he opened his eyes. He was somewhere in a forest surrounded by trees, away from the Malem Tutela's perimeter of men that were surrounding the villa.

142- *Waking*

Catherine awoke on the floor. She was startled and for a moment and didn't remember where she was. She found herself lying on a pallet made up of soft bedding and blankets. Aurora was holding her hand and began to speak, "Here, Catherine, take a drink of water." She held it up to her dry mouth. She drank it all.

"What happened?" Catherine propped herself up on her elbows, beginning to remember. Her head hurt, but the pain was already fading.

"You lost consciousness after the exercise, dear. A large part of the pain that you previously experienced in this world came out of you to be healed. The connection you have with the book allowed this deep healing to happen."

"I remember now. It was a flood of anguish that I could not hold back anymore. It was like experiencing all the pain in my whole life in one single moment."

"You must let go of your buried emotions. This world has been especially difficult for you to live in, especially being who you are."

"That's true. I haven't thought about my early life in such a long time. I remember being very frustrated as a little girl. No one around me seemed to see the world the way that I did. I felt alone and afraid of everything. Especially after my parents died."

For the first time, Catherine didn't feel the familiar knot in the pit of her stomach. "This is the first time that I've felt okay mentioning their death too."

Aurora smiled brightly. "It feels good for you to not feel so wounded now?"

Catherine took a deep breath. "Yes, it really does. I feel much lighter."

"Are you well enough to begin again?" Aurora stood up.

"Oh yes, let's get started again. I feel much better!"

Catherine returned to the table in silence and sat down before she spoke. "I have a burning question before we start again."

"Of course, Catherine, we will answer your questions to the best of our ability." Bartholomew spoke to her more like a daughter than like a woman he just met.

"What is the deal with my angel name?"

It was clear that the group didn't expect the question she asked. Aurora spoke. "No doubt, you understand that you have an angelic name, in addition to your human one?"

"Yes, that's why I asked. It seems very important and I wanted to know why?"

"The world may call angels by a variety of human names, so that they can identify them, but these are not their true angel names. In fact, angel names are more tonal than language based. An angel's true name conveys a specific frequency of energy that is associated with them. When you came into this chamber, you placed your hand over what you called the 13th symbol. The frequency of your name and the symbol are one and the same.

"So the symbol that appeared on my palms before is like being branded with my own name?"

"In a way it is. You must realize that you are also a physical being and can express your angelic self within the limits or confines of your human self. The more wounded you are, the more it blocks your angelic power. Your symbol allows you to embody more of your light.

Catherine looked down at her hands thinking about her symbol that had appeared there.

I wonder if...

For a few moments, she concentrated on her symbol intensely. The symbols appeared, just like before.

"Always remember that your mind can either limit your power or enhance it. It's one or the other. You need only to think of something to turn it into a reality in this world. Humans have this ability too, but often are not consciously aware of this power. Because your divine essence is much more awake now, you can consciously use it to help yourself and others."

"So what is my angel name?" Before anyone could answer her question, "But, you aren't going to give that to me are you?"

"Only you can remember your true name. Once you remember and speak it aloud, you will be able to access all of your power. Only then will you be able to become the Angel Incarnate. When you speak your name out loud while energizing your symbol too, your full energy will move into the world. That is what we are here to help you do."

"Okay, I understand. I'm ready to try again now." With renewed purpose, Catherine turned toward the book to begin again.

143- *Captured*

"I wonder where Joshua is. He should be back by now," David said as he opened the refrigerator.

Thaddeus and Demetrius knocked in the front door, sending it sliding across the mosaic tile in the foyer. The sound was deafening. David reacted quickly and grabbed Erica by the arm trying to run out the back door. At that moment, the other assault team was coming in the kitchen door. In a matter of seconds, they were surrounded by men in full tactical gear with guns pointed right at them.

"Get down!" one of the men shouted.

David and Erica immediately dropped to the ground with their heads down.

Thaddeus rushed into foyer as a man from the other team shouted. "CLEAR!" He motioned for Demetrius to follow him upstairs. One by one they knocked open bedroom doors and each time found the rooms completely empty. Thaddeus's fist tightened when he figured out that Catherine was not there.

He stormed downstairs as the third team entered the dining room from the west entrance. "The west area is clear, sir."

"Where are the other two? You said there were four people! Did your top notch surveillance miss that she left the premise?" Thaddeus grabbed Demetrius by the shirt and knocked his gun out of his hands. Thaddeus pushed him backwards into the wall. "You incompetent fool!"

"Where is she?" Thaddeus shouted at David.

"She's not here," David replied into the floor without moving a muscle.

"I can see that! I want you to tell me where she went."

"I don't know where she is. She didn't tell us where she was going."

Thaddeus pointed his gun at David and moved closer. "Let's see if that's really true." He grabbed David's shirt and hoisted him up in one motion. "Demetrius, secure these two now and put them in the car. We're taking them with us."

144- *Gloating*

Razoul felt that he was now assured of victory over the angel. To him it no longer mattered if Catherine was too powerful or if his recitation of the incantation was flawed. He had survived Samyaza's attacks before, so he doubted a minor slipup in pronunciation would cause him death as the scroll had warned.

"Now that, old man, is what I would call destiny. We have two of her companions. Surely this proves that the fates are moving in my direction now. I will win, and nothing will stop me. It's my purpose to kill her."

Sirius looked at Razoul, but remained silent. He feared giving his opinion and knew that nothing could dissuade Razoul once he had made up his mind. Luckily Razoul was on his way elsewhere.

"Call me when the team arrives. I want to be notified immediately."

"Where are you going?" Sirius asked him.

"I will not be gone long."

Razoul would seek Ashiyah's counsel before the angel finds out about Razoul capturing her friends.

He arrived quickly in her chambers.

"Ashiyah?"

She appeared quickly this time. "Yes Razoul? I am here."

"Ah, my lady, you look very well today as always." Razoul kissed her hand. They both sat down.

"I came as soon as I could to see you. I have been preparing for the battle. We have captured the angel's friends. Now I will bring her right to me. She will surrender to save her friends, and I will be victorious."

"You are very assured, which is good to see, just before your big moment, Razoul."

"The fates are turning in my direction. I can feel it."

"I have seen that as well."

An evil smile of satisfaction spread across his face. He took both of her hands in his. "After this is done, my lady, we shall celebrate with all your favorite foods and treats. And perhaps dance the night away?"

Ashiyah looked him in the eyes with her charismatic demeanor and said, "When this is done we shall dance, but who shall lead?"

Razoul's phone rang. It was Sirius.

"Perhaps a subject for another time, my lady, for now I must take my leave."

145- *Discovery*

"Still no name, but this is getting easier for me to control." Catherine opened her eyes. "This last round I felt as if the book was becoming clearer in my mind, the more that I opened to it. The visions were clearer too. I felt like I could fly."

"Well you can fly, but that is a lesson for much later my dear," Aurora answered.

Suddenly, the entire room began to shake. A brilliant flash of light illuminated the room. Sitting cross-legged in the middle of the room was a familiar face.

Catherine jumped up. "Joshua! What are you doing here?"

Catherine heard somewhere behind her, a whisper. "It's the prophet."

Joshua didn't answer Catherine and she put her arms around him. He started to tip over and appeared dazed. Now she was holding him. Joshua's eyes flashed open. He smiled wide when he saw Catherine's face above him. "Angel..."

"Why are you here, Joshua? What happened? Did Pandora find you?" Catherine was desperate to learn what was going on.

Joshua shook his head and sat up.

"I never will get used to angel travel." He brushed himself off and stood up. "It wasn't Pandora. It was the bad people. The angels saved me but...but...the others..."

"The Malem Tutela? What did they do?"

"They came looking for you, but you weren't there. The angels say they took David and Erica away."

"No! That cannot be. It's my fault. David was right! I should have insisted that they come with me. How could I be so stupid?"

"The angels say that they are okay. Unharmed," Joshua tried to console her.

"But, why didn't the angels save all three of you? I mean, why get you to safety and not the others?"

"They said there was no time, and that they had to protect me first. I didn't agree with them, though. I wanted to go back to warn the others, but I was afraid. I'm sorry."

"It's not your fault, Joshua. This is my fault, honey, not yours. I shouldn't have separated myself from you guys."

How could I not have realized that you were all in danger because of me?

Bartholomew came up behind Catherine and placed his right hand on her shoulder. "Catherine, if you had been there, you would have been totally unprepared and helpless to save your friends. It is not your fault. You would not have had the power to change it, and you'd probably already be dead."

Aurora spoke up. "Razoul obviously has taken your friends in order to trade their lives for yours. Now we must discuss what to do."

Uli? Are you there? Where are you? I must find out what is going on.

"I have an idea before we do that. I want to speak to *Ulian-naH* right now. Uli, come out, wherever you are!" The guardians looked around them for a sign, after hearing Catherine command Uli to appear.

"Uli, I mean it. I want someone to explain a few things. Come here right now."

Uli's visage as little Alice slowly began to materialize before them.

"I am here, Catherine." Alice smiled sweeter than ever.

"What on Earth is going on? And don't think appearing as a little girl will make me any less angry at you."

Don't be angry Catherine. Your friends are safe." Alice spoke softly to sooth her.

"But for how long? This is terrible, Uli. Why didn't you save them too?" Catherine started pacing the floor.

"Please don't be angry that we were only able to retrieve the prophet. His life was in true danger. They would have tortured and killed him because of his role as a helper to us. We knew that, even if the others were taken, you would be able to save them because Razoul would not want to kill them, but use them instead to lure you out to face him."

Catherine sat down in her chair and put her face in her hands. "What am I going to do? How can I save them? I still cannot remember my name. Without it, I have little power."

Alice walked over and took her hand, "You will remember, dear. Remembering now is less about physically remembering something and more about experiencing a full feeling of who you really are. If you try too hard, it will not come."

"How am supposed to not try hard, when everything is now on the line?

Aurora interjected at that moment. "We need a plan. Perhaps we could somehow persuade Razoul to release them?"

Bartholomew simply shook his head. "Razoul Bugiardini is not a man that you can persuade to do anything. He has a cunning and cruel mind. He will not stop pursuing a particular course once he sets his mind. Even the Polizia stand clear of him, I am told."

"So there's no way the police will come in and save the day," Catherine mumbled.

Sister Anastasia couldn't contain herself any longer. "Catherine my dearest angel, I know things look dire right now, but there will be a good outcome. I can feel it. Never let go of hope. Hope is what allows us to rise to any occasion."

Catherine wanted to utter a sarcastic comment to her, but had too much reverence for Anastasia. She nodded in agreement.

"You are right. I must keep hope alive, Anastasia. If I don't keep my faith, then my friends won't have any hope of making it out of this alive. But having faith in me is the hardest thing to do right now. Funny, it used to be faith in others that I had a problem with. That's why I cut off people for so long. For years I mourned the loss of my parent and my inner guilt practically killed me. I always felt in my heart that I was to blame for their death. That if I had been with them that day, I could have stopped the accident somehow. The only way I compensated for this fact was to push myself hard and pour all my energy into my work."

Catherine began to cry. What she had done to herself over this guilt, for so many years, finally hit her. She could see clearly now. The intense anger that she felt after they died, became like a sword that she had repeatedly stabbed herself with.

"Joshua, David and Erica are my new family. Now that I have a new family, I cannot let anything happen to them. I just can't. Razoul is trying to take them from me. I cannot let him win the game he's playing. There's no other choice for me to make. I must face him and demand that he release them. I could do nothing to save my parents, I accept that now. But in this case, I *can* save them."

"I'll help you prepare, Catherine," Francesca said. "Follow me." Catherine got up to follow her and spoke to Uli as they went into another room. "Please go check on my friends so that I know they are still okay."

Uli nodded and disappeared.

146- *Vanity*

Razoul returned to his chambers to freshen up before interrogating the prisoners. He paused for a moment to admire his reflection in the mirror, as if he were about to go on stage. He saw a flash of light a behind him and he spun around to see Alice standing there behind him.

"Do you really think you can win against a living, breathing angel?"

"Get out of here you damn little rat!" He swung his arm around to hit her, but punched the air instead. Alice reappeared on the other side of the room.

"Hey, that's not nice!" she cried.

"If anyone gave you the impression that I am nice, then you are sadly mistaken. Now get out of my hair, you annoying little bug "I bet your daddy was mean to you. That's why you are so grumpy all the time," Alice retorted with a syrupy sweet voice.

"GET OUT!" Even though Razoul knew he wouldn't land a single blow on her, he picked up a small statue from a shelf nearby and threw it at her in his fury. It did nothing of course. As soon as it reached her, she disappeared and then reappeared elsewhere.

"I knew it!" Alice exclaimed excitedly.

"He was mean to my mother. That is why I murdered him, just like I will murder your angel freak whenever she gets here to try to save her friends."

"Why? What did she ever do to you?" Alice put her hands on her hips in defiance.

"She's an abomination, and it is my destiny to remove her from the planet."

"That's what you think? You so are funny Razoul." Alice said taunting him again.

Razoul tried to come back at Alice with another calculated remark, when she disappeared from his room, for good, this time.

A moment later, Alice appeared in the basement cell where David and Erica were being held. They could not see her, but Alice could make them aware of her presence at least, before returning to Catherine. Alice put both her hands on Erica's shoulders. Then she put her hands on David's shoulders.

"Did you feel that David?" Erica asked.

He looked at her. "You mean just now, that light breeze. I felt it on my neck."

"I did too. I feel a lot calmer now. Do you?" Erica smiled.

David relaxed a bit for the first time since they had been shackled and delivered to the holding cell. "Yes, I do. It felt like someone was letting us know that everything will be okay."

"Catherine's coming for us. I just know it."

147- *Status*

When Uli returned to Catherine, she appeared before them in her angel form this time.

Catherine looked up at her, "Well? Are they okay?"

"Of course, they are just fine. He's holding them in a cell in the basement of the property. They were all alone down there, except for a guard at the door. I helped them feel that everything would be okay, so they are feeling much better now."

"What else can you tell me Uli? Did you see how many men Razoul has? Did you see what Razoul was doing now?"

"I saw Razoul. For an evil man, he's much more open than most to seeing unusual things." In Uli's usual style, she added, "Boy was he was not happy to see me. I got him all off balance for you. He has about three dozen men all over the estate right now. They are definitely preparing for your arrival. You don't have to worry about them, though, because Razoul told them he'd kill them if they touched you. It will be between Razoul and you, only."

"Okay Uli, thank you for checking on them. Francesca and I have been working on my technique and I'm getting better now. It's time to try the book again." Everyone gathered around her for support.

Catherine placed her hands over the book. She breathed slowly and visualized the light coming out of her and connecting with the book. This activated a tangible glow around her body and the book sprung to life. It hovered in the air in front her.

"Open and reveal to me that which I must know." Responding to her command, the book opened and a page of words projected several inches into the air and hung there. The characters began to shift and change, until the words came into full view and she could read them.

She read the words aloud. As she did, she recognized the passage from her previous dream, but the ending this time was slightly different:

When darkness has flooded the world of mankind. A light emerges outside the darkness that shall illuminate the truth and allow the chosen to see the world as it is, not as it appears to be. Ancient words will reveal the path you shall walk to fulfill your destiny.

You must awaken to your true nature, for time is fleeting. You are not what you appear to be. Your life is not what you believe. Walk carefully, dear One, for you have allies and enemies.

Simply state your true designation aloud and the power of heaven will be yours to command.

Catherine closed her eyes and relaxed. "I must know my real name." She spoke softly.

Francesca was behind her and said, "Relax and open, Catherine. Let your name simply come to your tongue."

For a moment Catherine looked as though she was about to speak, but then she threw her arms up in the air. "Damn it. I almost had it. It was right there on the tip of my tongue and I couldn't hold on to it long enough to speak it."

"It may take time, Catherine, but it will come," Aurora reassured her.

"We don't have a lot of time. If Razoul is half the man that you've described, then I cannot afford to lose a second before I face him. He could take out his frustration on my friends if I take too long!"

Bartholomew added, "You must calm yourself and think clearly. Until you remember, you will not be able to face Razoul safely. The world cannot afford to lose you. You are too precious to all people to have something unnecessary happen to you.

Catherine turned to Joshua, who had not made a peep since just after his arrival.

"What do you think, Joshua?"

"Who, me?"

"Yes, you, Joshua."

"The angels are confident in you, and so am I."

"If the angels weren't as confident, would you still be?"

Joshua was choosing his words carefully. "I have always had faith in you. From the very moment I met you. You are an angel, Catherine. That means that you can do anything."

"I hope you're right."

Then, suddenly, Catherine took command of the room. "Uli I want you to go there and report back anything you think I should know. Brother Bartholomew, do you know where this place is?"

"Yes, I know the place, but I think we should discuss this first."

"Just what should we discuss Brother Bartholomew?" Catherine said almost defiantly.

"I would like you to reconsider leaving right now. You need more time. You need rest, and it's very late."

"I appreciate your concern for my wellbeing, but the way I see it, when it comes to that crucial moment, either I will remember my name or I won't. I can see that there's nothing I can do to control that. I have to have faith. I must choose to walk in faith and save my friends."

Bartholomew could see that he could not dissuade her, so he conceded.

Then Francesca said, “One more session, Catherine, and then it will be time?”

“That’s a great idea.”

After Catherine and Francesca left the room, the other Guardians were completely silent, and one by one they knelt to pray.

148- *Impatience*

Two fully-armed sentries paced the long stone wall across the back of the Bugiardini Estate, keeping watch for any movement from the far away tree line on the edge of the estate and through the courtyard below them.

Razoul emerged into the night air and walked to the edge of the balcony. He nearly knocked one of the sentries down in the process, but barely noticed. His gaze was far away as he looked out over the acres of land before him. He was deep in thought.

A memory from his childhood surfaced, as Razoul stood there looking beyond the open area at the vast acreage of forest where he had hunted as a small boy. During the hunt he and his father had little conflict between them. Razoul could put his hatred aside in order to pummel his prey which often was a fox, rabbit or other small woodland creature.

He had barely heard the briefing that he had received from Thaddeus a moment ago. Razoul had been so consumed by replaying a hypothetical future scene between himself and Catherine, over and over in his mind. He was on the balcony now to clear his head. The longer he waited, the more impatient he became. He disliked prolonging the inevitable and just wanted to get it done. He screamed into the night.

“SHOW YOURSELF, CATHERINE! IF YOU DON’T, YOUR FRIENDS WILL SUFFER!”

He momentarily felt better, having bellowed at the top of his lungs, until a shiver went up his spine, causing the hairs on the back of his neck to rise.

Like a cat, Razoul spun around quickly to attack his unseen foe, but found nothing. His dark eyes scanned the huge balcony surface, but he didn’t see anyone at all, except for the two sentries.

“Where are you? Here to taunt me some more? It won’t save your angel, you know!” Razoul raised his fist into the air. He waited for a few moments, but the little girl didn’t appear as he had expected. Yet, his instincts communicated to him loudly that he was not alone. Someone was watching him.

Razoul ducked back inside, into the ballroom. "Thaddeus! I want you to go downstairs now and bring the prisoners up here. I wish to speak with them now."

"But Razoul, the prisoners will be far more secure if we leave them downstairs. Bringing them up here poses an unnecessary risk for all of us." Thaddeus attempted to reason with him.

"I don't care about the risk. We are being watched, and thus the angel knows our every move. Perhaps the angel doesn't believe that her friends are in enough danger, and that delays her arrival. I want her to feel my growing impatience."

149- *Time to Go*

Good Catherine, your energy and focus are much more stable now. Just relax into it, and open up." Francesca spoke to her with a soft, quiet voice.

A glow began to spread around Catherine's body, without the book activating it. "Excellent, truly divine. You are making such great progress."

Catherine breathed deeply and continued to open her mind to other possibilities. In the midst of her mental exploration, she saw Uli's face clearly in her mind. Her eyes popped open as Uli fully materialized near where she and Francesca were working.

"Catherine!"

"Yes, Uli what do you have for me?"

"Razoul is very impatient now. He just ordered his man Thaddeus to bring David and Erica up from their cell. He thinks you don't believe that he's serious! He said he'd prove to you they were in great danger."

"Thank you for your help, Francesca. I think it's time for me to go."

Catherine got up and entered the other room. The Guardians were still assembled in prayer, but stopped once she entered.

"I must go to my friends now. I am out of time. I have to try and help them."

The Guardians rose from the floor and came over as a group to surround Catherine. They linked their hands together, forming a circle.

They began to chant in low tones. It was a language Catherine couldn't understand.

They are giving you an Essene empowerment.

What does it do, Uli?

It's like a spiritual transmission of energies to help you.

Ahhhh....

Catherine closed her eyes, imagining that with each breath she drew in the energy from the guardians around her. Her body became much warmer and tingly as the chanting continued.

150- *Rivalry*

Ashiyah sat motionless in her receiving room on her velvet couch, just as she had many times before while awaiting her visitors. This time it wasn't Razoul she expected, though. She could feel Pandora was very near, and sat down to wait for her.

Moments later, Pandora appeared in the room with a loud bang and smoke billowing in all directions.

"I see you're making a grand entrance as usual, my sister." Ashiyah gazed at her coldly.

"That is because I have style, and you, my dear, do not," Pandora replied flippantly.

"Why are you here now, Pandora? I tire of your games."

"Your monkey upstairs is preparing for the angel's arrival. He still intends to kill her. Was he unaffected by my previous warning?"

Ashiyah sat there in silence, which told Pandora everything.

"You little devil! You didn't even warn him, did you?"

"No, not exactly. I told him to stop pursuing the angel, that I would give him all he desires and more."

"Not even going to give him a sporting chance? And you call me the heartless one!"

"Pandora, you must stop all this, please. There is no reason for all this bloodshed and chaos. Immortals are above such games. Think wisely for once."

Pandora looked upon Ashiyah with disdain. "If you want me to stop, then make me stop!"

Ashiyah knew what Pandora was doing now. She was trying to provoke her into taking one side or the other. But before Ashiyah could speak, Pandora continued. "Oh wait, that's right. You are as neutral as the Akasha itself and won't lift a compassionate finger to intervene. That sounds like everyone's loss and my gain if you ask me."

Ashiyah stood up and walked closer to Pandora. With great authority in her voice and posturing she said, "I would reconsider your position, if I were you."

Pandora was undaunted. "I would reconsider yours." Then, in a flash of light, she was gone.

"Very well. As you wish..."

Ashiyah took a deep breath and held her face up toward the ceiling. She put her hands to her sides, with her palms front. Soon, the air around her started to ripple like a shimmering liquid.

Seconds later, a powerful blast of light filled the room for several seconds and when it disappeared, so had Ashiyah.

151- *Halo*

The chanting finally stopped and the room was perfectly silent. When Catherine opened her eyes again, the entire room and the people in it looked different to her. It was as if the empowerment she had received had granted her a whole new set of eyes. As she looked to her right, she could see energy emanating from the angelic symbols carved in the wall. The very brightest was her symbol.

Catherine looked at each of the guardians with affection. She could see their auras giving off a multi-colored glow that surrounded each of them. The colors that she could see were so brilliant that it was almost overwhelming. It took Catherine a little bit to adjust.

"I don't know what you did, but everything looks amazing!"

"We wanted to give you a spiritual transmission for clarity, one that helps to lift the veil of life's illusions, before you confront Razoul," Aurora spoke first.

"Thank you. I am so humbled. I feel very calm yet wide awake. Those are the only words I can find to describe how I feel right now."

The guardians reverently bowed to Catherine. Then they assembled in a new circle, as she watched. Bartholomew began to speak.

"We call to the Seraphim now. Please be with us, powerful angels of mercy and light. Guide us to know your wisdom. Guide us to embody your grace. Guide us to embrace your light. Reveal to us now the proper path..."

In several moments, a glowing orb formed in the center of their circle. The orb started to shift and soon an angel was standing among them. The guardians broke the circle to create a path towards Catherine.

"I am Arian-naH. I am here to do the bidding of the ONE divine source that flows through all things."

"Thank you, Arian-naH," Catherine said.

"I am here to move you from this place to where you are going."

"Are you the angel that moved Joshua to safety?"

"Yes, all the angels have different powers in the human world. Mine is to move objects and even human beings across long distances."

"I see. So you will take me to Razoul, then?"

"Yes. Are you ready?"

"Just one moment, and I will be."

Catherine grabbed Joshua and hugged him. He held her tightly and whispered, "Come back to us, angel."

Catherine broke the embrace and promised, "I will come back, Joshua with David and Erica." But tears welled up in Catherine's eyes as if she wasn't too sure that she was telling him the truth.

She composed herself then turned to Bartholomew and the others. "Please watch over Joshua, and keep him safe."

"Of course, we will," Bartholomew answered solemnly.

"I am also leaving the book with you. It must be kept safe at all costs." Then she turned to her new teacher. "Thank you so much for helping me, Francesca."

"The honor is all mine dearest Catherine."

"Now, I am ready."

The angel took her hand and in an instant they were moving very fast. Catherine saw energy flow by her in beautiful hues of pink and lavender. It gave the illusion that she was standing still. It was like being propelled down a multi-colored swirling tunnel. After several moments, the energy dissipated and spread out. Catherine wasn't sure what she expected to see, but she knew she was not at Razoul's estate.

"Where are we?"

Arian-naH turned to her and took her hand. "There is one thing we need to do, before I take you to Razoul." She led her forward. Even though Catherine could see no floor or ceiling, it felt like she was standing on solid ground. When they stopped, Arian-naH stood back and disappeared. Catherine was now surrounded by twelve other angels. She could see various but unique colors emanating from each of them. They were all beyond beautiful. The sight took Catherine's breath away.

In front of her was Uli, looking like her angel self. Uli's eyes were filled with mesmerizing blue light as she spoke. "Catherine, please kneel."

Catherine was transfixed on Uli's eyes as she knelt.

"Dearest Catherine, you are honored among the Seraphim in heaven. We commune with you in humility as the sacred vessel of the Infinite ONE's divine love, now fully present in the human world. We wish to present this gift to you and welcome you back to us, little sister."

As Catherine watched, Uli put her hands together in front of her. A glow emerged from her clasped hands, and then dissipated to reveal a perfect halo of twelve stars.

Catherine took a deep breath and bowed her head as if in prayer. Uli placed the halo just above Catherine's head where it appeared to float. As Uli let go of the halo, a blinding light shot through Catherine's entire body. Her awareness of her surroundings expanded and Catherine could feel a deep connection to everything in the entire world, all at once. At the same time, she felt divine peace and love spread through her.

The entire experience brought tears to her eyes and she began an even deeper release of the emotional weight she had been carrying. Through her tears, she spoke to Uli. "Thank you so much. I feel what you have told me is true. For the first time in many years, I feel that I am home."

"You are home. Now you can make your journey. Remember who you are. Do not doubt the power you have within you. Release your fear and go now, in faith."

Arian-naH appeared to Catherine's right and she rose to take the angel's hand.

"I am going to take you to the Bugiardini Estate now."

With a renewed confidence, Catherine replied, "I am ready."

A flurry of light erupted around them and in a few moments, Catherine found herself standing in thick grass.

In front of her, she could see a large stone castle about 200 feet away. For a few moments she stood there watching. Then she closed her eyes in order to contemplate the moment. A light breeze blew around her which reminded her of the day her garden had come back to life, just because she had wanted it to.

Please be with me now, Momma...

152- *Show Down*

"Where is your angel now?" Razoul stood face to face with David and Erica, who had been brought to him by Thaddeus.

"I don't know where she is," David spoke defiantly. Razoul grabbed him by the throat. As he did, an alarm sounded.

Demetrius came in swiftly, "Sir! We've spotted her. She's on the south lawn!"

Razoul released his grip from David's throat and shoved him down to the floor.

"Watch the prisoners! Thaddeus come! I shall see her myself."

Another sentry stayed to guard them. Erica immediately tended to David, "Are you okay?"

"Yes, I'm fine, but I hate being helpless! Catherine is going to face that beast and I want to do something!"

"I know David, me too. Right now we have to have faith in Catherine. We have to believe and have faith that she can do this."

"I know, I know. I am just so afraid for her right now."

Erica started to cry, "Me too."

David took her hand and said, with an authority that seemed to come out of nowhere, "Hold my hand and close your eyes. Now let's see Catherine win over evil. Just focus on our faith in her, right here and right now."

Razoul and Thaddeus had made their entrance on the south balcony. When they emerged outside, Razoul barked at another sentry, "Report!"

The sentry was looking through his binoculars. "She's standing out there on the edge of the forest. So far, she has not moved." He handed his binoculars to Razoul so he could spy on Catherine, as she stood there getting her bearings.

"She looks pretty pathetic for an angel. I could break her in two with my fists. This will be easier than I thought."

Razoul shoved the binoculars at Thaddeus. Thaddeus scanned the forest edge for anyone else who may be there to assist her, but saw no one.

"She's alone, Razoul."

"Even better. Let's bring her friends outside so she can see them. Fetch Sirius, too. I don't want him to miss any of this."

From the distance, Catherine could see movement on the upper tier balcony. There was a lot of commotion.

"I guess they know I'm here. Are you there, Uli?"

A soft voice answered her, "Yes, Catherine, of course."

Catherine looked ahead at her destination with renewed determination and started moving forward, one step at a time. Quickly she closed the gap half the way between herself and the castle.

That's when she saw both David and Erica being brought out onto the balcony. She stopped walking for a moment. A strange mixture of fear, anger and other emotions flooded through her as her heart began to race. Then she saw Razoul. Though they had never met, she could tell it was him. Everything from his stance and posture communicated that he was in charge.

Razoul walked up to the edge of the balcony and casually leaned his hands on the stone rail. He stood there arrogantly, staring down at her. She stared back at him, keeping direct eye contact.

"I am here to retrieve my friends, Razoul. Release them to me, now." Catherine raised her voice so she would be heard.

"Why should I release your friends to you?"

"Because I have asked you to do so."

Razoul laughed. "You come to my home and start making demands? Who are you to challenge me?"

Catherine chose her words carefully, having decided that even if she didn't know her name yet, she would act as if she did.

"You know who I am. I am the angel you've been looking for. I am the angel that will be your undoing, and I am the angel that demands her friends back!" Catherine's posture was assertive and direct now.

"Well, angel," Razoul spat his words, "my deal to you is that I will let your friends go, as long as you surrender yourself to me!"

"If I surrender myself to you, then what do you plan to do with me?" Catherine said innocently, like a child.

Razoul stood up proudly. "I will send you back to where you came from, and the world will be rid of you!"

Catherine focused her mind for a moment and a glow started to emanate all around her. She heard many of Razoul's men gasp. Even Razoul took a slight step back, revealing his surprise.

"As you can see Razoul, I am wide awake. *My* deal to you is that you release them now."

Razoul stood looking down at her with rage brewing behind his eyes. Without a thought, he vaulted himself over the stone wall and dropped to the ground almost twelve feet below. He landed with a thud. His men ran to the edge to see that he was alright.

Now Razoul stood directly in front of Catherine, only 80 feet away.

"I don't think that there will be any new deals tonight. My deal is the only deal. Surrender yourself now, or I will kill your friends. Thaddeus!"

Thaddeus moved into position beside David and Erica, cocking his gun for effect.

"You see, angel, I have all the power, and you have nothing." He took several long strides towards her.

Catherine stood her ground. Her psychology background helped her to know that she couldn't back down, not one little bit. Razoul's threat had caused the light around Catherine to grow larger in response. She was unsure what do next, though her inclination to run was overwhelming.

"You will not harm my friends, and I will not surrender myself!" After speaking the words, Catherine's body began to shake and she felt the energy around her turn into a cyclone made of fire and then faded.

Razoul was threatened by Catherine's defiance and took another step toward her as a surging wave of energy and light appeared, blocking his path. Suddenly a furious Pandora materialized.

"Who are you?" he demanded.

"Pandora, of course." She bowed with her usual flair.

"What are you doing here?"

"I am the immortal who is here to rob you of your pathetic life!"

Catherine's voice rang out now, "Pandora! Why do you come here? This isn't your fight."

Pandora nonchalantly turned to her, "I'll deal with you later!" She threw a ball of light toward Catherine and it knocked her off her feet. The impact sent her to the ground. Uli's voice in her head told her to be still.

As she turned back toward Razoul, he drew his gun and fired it at Pandora. He hit her directly in the chest, but she did not waiver. She waved her index finger at him.

"Now, now, pathetic monkey, don't you know that bullets cannot harm me?" She increased her size to nearly ten feet and moved to overcome him. Even though she never touched him, Razoul was thrown violently backwards into the stone wall. He dropped to the ground. Pandora towered over him now, savoring the moment.

Ashiyah appeared, blocking her path, "Sister, this will end now!"

Pandora was clearly shocked to see her and took two steps backward. Catherine stood up now, watching the two immortals face off.

"Ashiyah, now you wish defy me? Step aside. As you said before, quite clearly, this is not your fight."

"Neither is it yours!" Ashiyah pushed her sister back and onto the ground. Pandora's agility was on her side. "How dare you strike me?" Pandora sent a fire ball at Ashiyah, but she easily avoided being struck. It hit the stone wall with a crash.

"Leave now, Pandora, or I cannot be held responsible for what will happen to you," Ashiyah warned.

Catherine could see Razoul on the ground, and that he was moving now. He didn't get up and just lay there watching the conflict unfold in front of him.

"What could you possibly do to me, Ashiyah? I am an immortal. I am powerful. You are out of shape"

Ashiyah's eyes were ablaze now, as energy began to pull into and collect around her.

"I am sorry for this, sister..."

Then Ashiyah began to recite.

"Crossing the span of space and time.

To the place where the ancestors roam.

To the land where there is all time.

To the Akasha, you shall go."

Pandora let out a shriek and fell to the ground writhing. She began to shrink until her form completely disappeared.

Ashiyah took a long look at the ground, and then approached Razoul.

"My lady…I thank you."

Ashiyah looked at him with sorrowful eyes, "What is done is done. The balance of light and dark is restored." Then she faded away.

Razoul felt bolstered by the events that he witnessed. To his knowledge, she had never directly involved herself in any of his family's matters. He fully believed that her actions meant that fate was on his side. He leapt up arrogantly.

"You see angel? I have an immortal at my command. How do you stand a chance against me?"

Without thinking, Catherine replied, "I am the divine vessel of the Infinite ONE. My light is more powerful than your darkness. I bring hope, where you do not. I bring love, where you do not. I bring life, where you only bring destruction. You are the one without any real power."

Something clicked inside of Catherine as these words flowed effortlessly out of her mouth. Something simply needed to come out. One by one, the dominoes of her illusions began to fall. She felt like she was in two places at once.

In her mind, she could see the vision of a single truth. It was like a familiar voice calling her by name. This profound insight distracted Catherine so much that she didn't see Razoul charge toward her, until it was too late. Razoul literally lifted his boot to less than waist high and kicked Catherine to the ground. She flew backwards and struck the ground with a force knocking the wind out of her.

Razoul smirked and put his boot on her midsection. Catherine tried to break free, but he was too strong for her. She starred up at Razoul's dark, evil eyes. He took great pleasure in towering over her while she was pinned down underneath his boot.

Catherine sensed she had arrived at her moment of truth, and knew that she was either about to die, or rise in triumph. It was one or the other, and nothing in between.

She looked deeply inside Razoul now, as he spoke callously, "Now you see, angel. All your love doesn't matter in this world filled with many men like me. You are no match for the great Razoul Bugiardini. You don't belong in this world. This is my domain, not yours."

Images began to swirl around in her mind. All her human memories flew by one by one, as if her entire life were flashing before her eyes.

Is this what happens when we are about to die?

Catherine braced herself. She stopped struggling to get up from underneath the weight of Razoul's boot. S he could feel her heart beating and the echo of her breathing. Time seemed to slow down dramatically. She took herself deep within as Francesca had taught her.

Razoul reached into his pocket producing a piece of paper. In flawless Latin, he spoke to her:

Permissum obscurum sceptrum ago hominum

Let darkness rule the lives of men

Permissum angelus oraculum adveho laxo

Let the angel prophecy come undone

Ostendo sum vicis ut brought vos hic

Reversing time that brought you here

Reverto ut locus of Seraphim

Return to the place of Seraphim

Nunquam ut reverto hic iterum

Never to return here again

But, instead of panicking, Catherine surrendered to the moment. Her thoughts drifted into the great expanse, which at first was blurry and then became clearer. She was floating toward a pure bright light now that didn't hurt her eyes. A beautiful, angelic music floated through her and she could hear the voice of the ONE again calling her by name...

It's true. Oh my...it's true...I am, and my name, I have a name.

Razoul felt Catherine's body go limp under his foot. "Yes, angel, that's right, back now to where you came from."

He lifted his boot from her body and stomped it on the ground in victory. He turned to his men and lifted his fist in the air. "That is how it is done! Victory is ours!"

All the men began to cheer, the sound of which briefly downed out her friends' screams, as they both struggled to break free and help her. All they could see was her body lying lifeless on the ground next to where Razoul gloated.

Catherine could hear nothing of Razoul's triumph or her friends crying as she came to a stop in the place between worlds. Uli and the others stood nearby in silence.

I can remember now. I wanted to be born. I volunteered. But before I couldn't see it, believe it. I am not afraid. I am not only human. I am...

Both the cheering and screaming abruptly stopped as a bright light flashed behind Razoul. He quickly turned around to see Catherine standing before him.

"What!"?

Catherine's eyes were now an icy blue and she was glowing. Her physical form grew quickly. This startled Razoul, not only because she was still alive, but that she was now physically as tall as him. Now she stood there eye to eye with him, her palms glowing with fire.

"How are you still alive?" Razoul demanded clutching his stomach suddenly, as a searing pain shot through him.

Catherine's blue eyes began to glow even brighter and the aura around her body grew ten-fold. She had no fear. To her it felt as though she had stepped into her body for the very first time.

"What...What...What are you doing to me?" he screeched at her, stumbling backwards. He looked more like a scared boy now than a formidable foe.

"I am doing nothing to you, Razoul. But what you have done to yourself is an entirely different matter." The voice coming from her mouth was powerful and different from anything he had heard before. Razoul fell to the ground grabbing his stomach.

"The...the incantation was flawless...you should not be here."

"I suppose you could say that, because until now, I was not fully here. But now I am, and your game is over."

Razoul let out a wail, as his stomach pains increased. When he looked into Catherine's eyes he didn't see the same woman as before. She came closer to him now and gazed down at him with compassion instead of hatred, which infuriated him.

"I don't want your pity, angel, regardless of what you are doing to me!"

"You are in pain, Razoul, because you are dying. But, I promise that I did not kill you."

Razoul's anger erupted like a beast and he leapt to his feet pointing his gun at Catherine's head. "You, damnable angel. You will not win."

He tried to aim at her, but then his eyes began to play tricks on him. Catherine's form first turned into his mother. He could swear Chiara was standing right in front of him. Catherine could see the illusion that was created from Razoul's own mind, and let him be.

"Madre?" he whispered, his voice was barely audible. He could see Chiara's beautiful brown eyes and her soft smile. She was wearing his favorite of her many dresses. He began to cry as the pain consumed him and he collapsed for a final time.

He looked up at his mother, who was calling to him softly, "Razoul, my dear son..." He could even smell her perfume in the air. Then Razoul's eyes closed.

Catherine could hear David and Erica calling for her. She started walking toward the huge staircase to reach them. She ascended the stone stairs, and as she took each new step the fiery light around her grew. By the time she reached the top, a sentry waiting for her screamed, "Halt!" But he was so stunned by her appearance, that it made him take several steps back.

She looked at him with a serene expression. Without saying a word, she grasped the end of his machine gun and pointed the muzzle toward the ground. The man immediately dropped the gun and ran away.

Catherine surveyed the situation calmly. The rest of the Malem Tutela's men stood on alert on the other side of the balcony. There were more than a dozen guns pointed at her, but she was unaffected.

She gazed now at her friends with love, and they stood there in awe. Catherine calmly walked over to them. She placed a finger on each of their shackles and as she did, they immediately dropped to the ground.

Catherine took one of David's and one of Erica's hands and said, "I promise that we will never be separated again. I love you both. You are my family. Now I just have one more thing to attend to. Please come with me."

It appeared as though her body was being consumed by fire now. The unearthly flames billowed around her with each step. She led them across the balcony, David on her left and Erica on her right. All three stood there in front of Thaddeus and Sirius. No one moved.

Demetrius broke the silence, "Orders, sir?"

Catherine reached up to the sky with both arms and then motioned backwards. As she did, every gun leapt out of the hand that was holding it, flew up into the air and simply evaporated. There was a moment of chaos as Demetrius and the other hired men scattered in all directions, leaving only Sirius and Thaddeus standing there.

"Now gentleman, does anyone else in the Malem Tutela have further business with me?"

Neither of them answered right away, but then Sirius spoke, "Who…who are you?"

With an all-knowing expression on her face, she raised her arms up to either side. When she did this, a forceful wind came in from all directions, the power of which caused the two men to drop to their knees.

She placed her hands in prayer and bowed humbly for a moment. Then she looked up at the sky and called out in an unearthly voice that echoed through the air like thunder.

I AM *Chirolae Jonais.*

ABOUT THE AUTHOR

A powerful spiritual mystic and innovative thinker, CJ Martes has spent the past twenty-five years touching the lives of thousands of people in over 50 different countries with her amazing insights.

Known for her ability to openly communicate with angels in order to support and guide others through difficult times, she's lovingly known as an *Angel on Earth* to many who know her.

CJ's life was changed forever in 1997 when she received an unexpected visit from a group of 13 Seraphim Angels. They not only helped her to heal during a very difficult time in her life, but made some startling predictions about CJ's path and her purpose.

During their initial visits with her, they spoke often about a book that she was destined to write which they called Angel Incarnate. This book Angel Incarnate: *One Birth* is the fulfillment of their predictions and is inspired by a True Story.

Since that fateful day, the Seraphim have continued their daily communication with CJ in order to assist her work to inspire others to believe that they are truly powerful beyond measure.

She and her wonderful husband David have raised four children and enjoy living in the Midwest.

There are four books planned in the Angel Incarnate Saga.

Book 1: Angel Incarnate: *One Birth*
Released 2012

Book 2: Angel Incarnate: *Two Worlds*

Book 3: Angel Incarnate: *Twelve Stars*

Book 4: Angel Incarnate: *Phoenix Thirteen*

Visit the official book website for more information: www.angelincarnate.com. Or CJ's website: www.cjmartes.com.